Like a bird on the wire

Like a bird on the wire

CHHAVI BHARDWAJ

AMARYLLIS

AMARYLLIS
An imprint of Manjul Publishing House Pvt. Ltd.
• 7/32, Ansari Road, Daryaganj, New Delhi 110 002
Website: www.manjulindia.com
Registered Office:
10, Nishat Colony, Bhopal 462 003 – India

ISBN 978-93-87383-67-8

This edition first published in 2018
Second impression 2018

Cover Design by Aquarius Inc.

Printed and bound in India by Replika Press Pvt. Ltd.

For my parents

Contents

PART ONE

Nethra Kaul

Seven Years!

Palampur, 2015

'Congratulations! Hard work paying off,' read the text message. It had been seven years since he had last heard from her. Seven years! And though a part of him was relieved, even happy; the other part was already ruminating on the pun—the subliminal implications of that terse 'hard work paying off.'

Was it relief?

Nostalgia?

Anxiety?

He couldn't put a finger on it and that flustered him all the more…because even today, seven bloody years down, nothing, *nothing* could affect him the way she did. Not in as many ways. Not as *intensely*. He knew this and hated himself for it.

That morning's herald had been no better for Nethra Kaul. The newspaper at her doorstep carried a coloured photograph of Avinash Rathore on the front page. More precisely, it carried the news of Avinash Rathore receiving the 'PM's Excellence Award' on Civil Services Day. Bad start to a bad day.

Ten minutes later, her head throbbing hard and her chest burning inexplicably, Nethra stood leaning against the kitchen cabinet. Her lemon tea tasted particularly atrocious this morning. She realized she was holding the *Morning Herald* still, and gazing intently at Avinash Rathore in his black *bandhgala*. She knew the black *bandhgala* all too well. Did she know, as in *really* know the man inside it?

His appearance didn't seem to have changed much really—he didn't seem to have gained weight, or lost that self-assured mien of a show-stopper, the same quiet elegance, the gravitas....

'L'uomo perfetto,' she said to herself, and smiled wistfully. It had been seven years!

It was 8 o'clock in the morning. Avinash Rathore had returned from New Delhi after receiving the PM's Excellence Award—the IAS' Oscars—as it were, the previous evening. He looked at his watch—ninety minutes before he left for office.

For several years now, Avinash Rathore had followed an unwavering morning routine. His day would start at five in the morning, with a ten kilometre, sixty minute-long sprint along Palampur bypass—something that had greatly swelled the ranks of young, female joggers along the otherwise geriatrically infested road of the torpid, little town that Palampur was.

Next came his daily fix of office files and *dak*—stuff that always lay stacked officiously inside four monstrous red boxes that everyone in the Rathore household had now come to dread. It was a reverential sort of dread, obviously, the kind which the sheer drudgery of such description so rightfully deserves. But Avinash Rathore was not one to get trapped in the labyrinthine ordinariness of red boxes. Oh no people, not him. The real stuff followed soon after—books, case studies, reports, and journals on subjects ranging from project finance to data analytics to urban management—along with editorials and op-eds of five different e-papers. Hard-core policy. For solid ninety minutes. At seven-thirty sharp every day, he set the day's agenda—a short, bulleted note on his iPad.

Today had been no different. He sat sipping *nimbu paani* as Malavika, his Ralph Lauren-clad wife, walked across the living room answering congratulatory calls and occasionally shooting fretful looks in the general direction of *ardalis*[1] who laid the table for breakfast.

'Did your batchmates call?' Malavika asked her husband.

'No.'

'Even *Nethra* didn't?'

'No.'

'*Tch...*' she clicked her tongue and sighed as she slumped on the couch, '...they are all *batchmates*, after all!'

Malavika liked invoking the 'batchmates' concept often, mostly to their collective convenience, and almost always in context of her husband's one particular batchmate, Nethra Kaul.

'Anyway...I have planned a party at the Officers' Club tonight and I expect you early, only for today...' she leaned in now, rubbing her hand gently across her husband's thighs. The 'I expect you early' part had the coquettish intonation Malavika had often been told she ought to obtain a patent for.

'Sure,' his fingers closed on hers and he smiled his warm, reassuring smile, looking into her eyes. This was a happy space, their seventh 'itch-free' year together.

The hottest thing about Palampur these days was its Collector, Avinash Rathore. More precisely, Avinash Rathore was what the Palampur public had *got the hots for* these days. Aunties, uncles, and girls of all ages were cooing about their collective crush—oh, that natural confidence...oh that rare pith of raw courage wrapped firmly in suave sophistication, oh that coconut like quality—hard on the outside, soft on the inside, oh that voice, and that remarkable, *remarkable* charisma...but most of all, people, most of all, oh those looks, those damn good looks!

---

[1]An umbrella term for peons, helpers, cooks of all description.

But at the Palampur Collectorate today, Collector Saab's inexplicable tartness had his staff in a stomach-churning tizzy. *Something* was clearly different today. Something was *amiss*. Collector Sahab wasn't his usual collected self.

The staffers had been hoping to detect some semblance of exuberance—a smile here, a bounce there—some deviance, just a hint, from his I-am-a-man-on-a-mission manner today. After all he had landed the *sarkari* Oscar! And even the ultra-confident Jennifer Lawrence had tripped on her way up and blabbered tipsy nothings to the press after she landed hers…but not *their* Collector Saab. No way. Clumsiness, friskiness, uncontrolled exuberance—these things and their Collector Saab just did not go together.

As the object of everyone's affection and attention stormed out of the weekly review meeting after tongue lashing two of his subordinates for what would ordinarily pass off as routine administrative ineptitude, the perky tongues in Palampur Collectorate were set wagging.

'*Bade Saahab kaafi pis aaf hain aaj*…,' Mishraji, the Joint Collector, spoke while rolling some tobacco in his palm, '…*phood wale Srivastavaji waj sweating bhai…in that air condeesun haal.*'

At which Gupta, the diplomatic Deputy Collector smiled and *tch*-ed meaningfully, and two clerks sipping chai elbowed each other, and Sinha, the Tehsildar, ever so keen to put his signature *tadka* into any gossip brewing anywhere in Palampur, chipped in with '*Arrey* Sir…did you see *todayj* Dainik, Sir? HCM *haj prayjed bade saahab* like anything, Sir…' (It was Sinhaji's USP—to rub people up the wrong way, the way it hurt the most) '…and one more thing Sir you *notished?*', he paused and then continued in a voice more hushed, more scandalized, 'HCM's hand is on Saahab's *solder* Sir, *SOLDER…us* Dainik *wali photo me…Project 21 to ab pakka….*'

'*Arrey pucca, bullsit…*', Mishraji glowered back, '*aal this* photo *bizness ij* total *showbaaji bhai*. And let me tell you *thi real newj* which *Dainik doejn't* tell you…,' and here Mishraji assumed that necessary saturnine, been-there-done-that expression, 'inside *newj,* straight out of *thi* mouth of *haarse aj* they say...*saahab's patta* is cut from *Project 21...conphirm,'* he said with an overall air of authority that, other than him, only the Chief Secretary could probably carry, and then looked around to add, *'jack toh bahut lagaaye thay Saahab... par* nothing doing *bhai...wahan to aise aise...,'* and a malicious wave of the palm here, *'...bahut istaalwhaart log hain...*that *ij* why he is *pis aaf, bas.'*

Now, everyone in Palampur Collectorate knew Mishraji had a problem. No, problems. With *Bade Saahab* Avinash Rathore, who was Mishraji's nemesis. And in front of whom, Mishraji would always go, 'Yes Sir, ji Sir, right Sir, Sir, Sir Sir,'—impressed smiles and meaningful nods and *ye-to aapne-bilkul-theek-kaha-Sir...*sugary *sarkari sirsiraahat*, as it is called, thinly veiling one hundred percent, authentic, unadulterated animosity.

Animosity, spawned by problems such as the ones that follow

Problem 1: The Online File Tracking System—a Rathore Saahab initiative that had truly and greatly jeopardized Mishraji's bread and butter. With every single file in the office (even *'chillar'* tree-felling-permission-seeking, 50 grand-for-a-signature type) on this system, Avinash 'Orwell' Rathore had designed elaborate algorithms to track 'defaulters', a term Mishraji singularly disliked, more so when applied to him, just as much as he hated the hilariously inadequate time limits Rathore had assigned for clearance of files by officers.

Problem 2: The biometric attendance, access control and CCTVs which had kind of made life at office, pure hell. Where was the leisure? Where was the *'itminaan'* of having *chai samosa*, six times a day, at Guptaji *ki* canteen? What was the point of a *sarkari naukri*, by the way?

Problem 3: The new, 'improved', open hall seating arrangement where everyone could see everything—just like his son's office at

Bangalore—where deals that went behind closed doors and also under the tables, could no longer be.

Problem 4 (This was probably the biggest of them all): Avinash Rathore's sheer...well, his bloody unbelievable ability to get things done. Bloody done! Things Mishraji had variously dismissed, rubbished, ridiculed as impossible, impractical, 'un'-implementable. IT things, process reforms, things Mishraji knew the 'system' could not, and will never accept, became things that eventually *happened* and got accepted and worked well, before his own bloody eyes. Just like that!

And this was the real problem, people. A problem that had hurt Mishraji's bloated *sarkari* ego the most.

So gone were the golden days of good-old *nazranas, shukranas* and *jabranas* in Palampur Collectorate. Gone baby, like really GONE. And the worst part was that Rathore had managed it all alone—in the face of Karmchari Sangathan's several memorandums, representations and apprehensions about old bureaucracy's 'intrinsic inability' to change—as cogently pointed out by the only *angrezi* speaking journalist in Palampur.

And all this while, as stuff happened, Mishraji who hailed from the illustrious Patwari family of Unnao, UP had only wondered disbelievingly, 'What has bureaucracy really come to these days? Where is the *iqbaal* it used to possess? *Ab kya humse angootha bhi lagwaenge Bade Saahab*?'

Now, Project 21[2]—the next big breakthrough in governance. One

[2]'Project 21' was an ambitious, technology driven convergence project that the incumbent government had embarked upon as a flagship mission. It sought to harness technological advancements in networking, mobile communications and computer science to create synergies across government departments and organizations in the delivery of public services. If implemented well, it would make 90% of official correspondence redundant, integrate departments and their programs over a single

could say it was about application of big data analytics in government. All in all, hot stuff! The case of six blind men and the elephant, for you and me. The HCM was determined to push this dream project of his—steering it through the Department of Finance's paranoia and the skepticism of his colleagues in the Cabinet—he was determined to get it going by the end of the following year, a year and a half before the state went into elections.

While the idea of lateral entry for the top job did creep into the HCM's mind at the outset, it was expeditiously nipped in the bud by senior hawks at his office.

'The project needs an administrator, Sir, not *just* an engineer, or *merely* a manager,' concluded a senior aide to the HCM. 'True Sir,' other senior aides averred. 'Must be true, then,' the HCM relented.

Hectic parleys ensued soon after word got out that the HCMO[3] was looking for a 'young, dynamic IAS officer' to lead the project. This was the HCMO throwing its weight around, standard fare. Throwing its weight around, and kickstarting *inadvertently*, one would suspect, several rounds of intense lobbying, of kissing of the necessary backsides, of pulling out of influences that lay way beyond and far beneath the straitjacket of service code.... Oh, the HCMO enjoyed every last bit of it, they enjoyed watching real people stepping out of their saintly garbs, and doing things utterly 'un'saintly—to get into power, to stay in it. It was great fun.

So after three months of endless scuttlebutt that fed the eternal rumour churning mills at State Secretariat, three probables were listed for the job. The one who came out the cleanest, as also, the 'junior-most' was Avinash Rathore.

That Avinash Rathore was worried about his '*patta*' having been '*cut*' by some other *ishtaalwart* was obviously far from the truth.

---

platform, cut sub-optimality in resource allocation and more importantly, eliminate irrelevant offices, schemes, functions and processes that in absence of a systematic and holistic review had continued to tax government's resources.

[3]HCMO, naturally, would be HCM's Office.

On the contrary, the HCM's body language had been very positive. What actually upset Mr Rathore, what actually was amiss, what kept coming back to him all through the day, like an annoying refrain, were the four words in that message, 'Hard work paying off…!'

Those four words and everything about them kept pounding in his head as he pored over files, walked into and emerged out of four meetings in quick succession and grimly thanked two MLAs along with several 'significant others' who had turned up with gladiolus bouquets and marigold garlands to congratulate him. Those four words were all he could think of as he finally reclined on his sofa, all sharp and dapper, amidst a jubilant gathering that pranced around to musical chairs at the party that evening.

How he wished he could vanish, sublimate, tune out that clutter, shut the doors. How he wished to be *only* with himself—for that was the only way she would ever come to him, pursing her lips in a smile, in silence. He threw his head back on the sofa, and closed his eyes.

'Oh! It's work…,' Malavika explained to one of the guests, rolling her eyes, shrugging, being her vivacious self.

He could see her now—she was standing at the edge of that wooden bridge, breathing in and out, the wild strands of her unruly hair gamboling with the winds, sweeping across her face—pure joy!

He felt his breath moving in the same rhythm as hers…in and out…they were thus locked together, in a way.

Thank you, these two words had constituted his reply to her message, a typically taciturn, Avinash Rathore-sort-of-reply—just these two words, no how-have-you-beens, no endearments, nothing else. It had taken him a full three hours to write those two words—mighty efficient!

All this while, even as Malavika lived up to her reputation of being a perfect hostess and graciously engaged with everyone at the party, she could see that her husband was distracted. For the first time in seven years, he *seemed* distracted. Instinctively, she knew they had communicated. Nethra Kaul and Avinash Rathore had finally gotten in touch.

'Keep your nerve…,' she told herself, 'it shall pass…keep your nerve.'

So, here it was…one more of those rare, terrible evenings when Avinash Rathore would, if only for a few hours, excuse himself from the colourful canvas that his life was, on the pretext of some unavoidable work in his Bungalow Office and write a really long letter—a four or five page outpouring addressed to Nethra Kaul. Only when he woke up the next day, in the dawn of his here and now, with all his controls right back in place and the gooey stuff swept cleanly aside, he would re-read and regret the maudlin mess those pages were, feel foolish and burn them black, flushing the ashes of a long estranged heart down his office toilet.

Not so SISSY

Kisalpur, 2015

So Nethra Kaul had read the news, and she had looked at the picture. Wholeheartedly. She had even braved a thirty-minute 'how-to-stop-sulking-and-start-living' tele-lecture from her agony-aunt, best friend and batchmate Madhavi, who in keeping with the great tradition of all agony aunts, had for the nth time, explained how 'it was only passing through pain that one could hope to reach anywhere.'

Nethra had had a strong urge to ask her where this was, this elusive *anywhere* she was supposed to be reaching since the past seven years, but of course she didn't. She knew Madhavi loved delivering these lectures. They gave Madhavi a sense of greater control over her own life. Only upon seeing the suffering of others do we realize how *little* our suffering is…something like that.

So Nethra had heard her friend out and promised that more pain indeed was what she was prepared to embrace, with arms wide open. Her friend deserved this little bit of assurance, after all. After all these years, and a distance of twelve-hundred kilometres that now lay between them, Madhavi could still sniff heartburn like she always had, and she could still find time to deliver lectures that they both knew meant nothing, amounted to nothing, now.

And that morning, Madhavi had only *picked up* on her friend's heartburn. In their batch's 'IAS @ LBSNAA Rocks!' WhatsApp group where the same *Morning Herald* picture had just been posted[4], it was heartburn, heartburn, heartburn, ad infinitum. Unadulterated peer envy, simmering deep down inside perfectly bona fide messages as given below:

- So proud of you, Avi (blush, blush)...always knew you would go places!!—Avantika J [*Unrequited feelings. A lot of if only he..., we might have...had he not...it might have been... and more stuff like that.*]
- Way to go, man, way to go (double thumbs up) [*Next time, brother, next time. It will be me with the PM next time.*]
- *Kya baat boss, PM se zyaada chamak rahe ho*! [*Feelings of inadequacy rooted in a colour complex/height complex/why-should-others-have-all-the fun/get-all-the-awards complex.*]
- Congratulations!!!!!!! [*Jealousy, in direct proportion to the number of exclamation marks.*]

All in all, an all pervasive sentiment that could be pithily summed up in one of the oldest punchlines of Indian advertising—*Bhala uski kameez meri kameez se safed kaise*?

But from the face of things, people, from their very face, God was indeed in his heaven and the IAS community was once again affirming its allegiance to *esprit de corps*—that sticky glue that is supposed to bind selfish people in a zero sum game. Like that's ever going to happen!

Nevertheless, Nethra was the only batchmate who hadn't yet chimed in with her *esprit de corps* laden proclamation of pride. She had...uh...messaged him(!!)...to underscore that *he was an*

[4]It continues to be a matter of some debate as to why people post their pictures—vacationing in the Maldives/holidaying in Barcelona/receiving this or that award/hugging-kissing-doing-whatever-to one's dear spouse/partying half-naked—on Facebook. Some say it is primarily to share their happiness, most however assert it is primarily to tell themselves how much they enjoyed the particular moment; contentious, though it may sound.

altogether different case...for her? Nethra shuddered at the implication. She regretted sending the message the moment she had sent it, and a thousand times over when the two-worder-send-to-all sort of reply left her phone shattered forever. Anyway, was *this* ever going to be over for her?

Far from over! It had only begun...a day, may be the next few of days of sulk and nostalgia and that utterly wasteful Piscean ennui. It was *fait accompli*...resistance was pointless. Any number two Piscean would tell you that. So as she stealthily typed in the keywords—[PM's Award Avinash Rathore]—on the Google search pane of her office laptop, aiming primarily to get an HD view of the low resolution picture that had appeared in the newspaper, and wondering, at the same time, if the Julian Assange inspired IT guys at her office could track down dubious traffic on the office intranet, there it popped up—his image—a close up at that, a 300 dpi JPEG! Worse, as she gawked at the picture, the uber-macho smell of Hugo Boss wafted in, sending her heart leaping up from its fundamental frequency to its wildly erratic nth harmonic...her classically conditioned response to everything about him. Wow! Could it get any worse than this?

'Photographers, even those covering solemn *sarkari* ceremonies at Gyaan Bhawan have a natural faculty for beauty,' she mused, admiring the 300 dpi Eros before her. Beauty? Her mind was still struggling to churn out the right word when a polite clearing of throat broke the spell.

'Good Morning, Ma'am...the ERP people are coming today,' the ever so polite IT guy was staring at her with a look that bordered on interested.

'Yes, I know,' she replied airily, sounding almost as if it was an ERP-Advanced tutorial she had been watching with such phenomenal concentration. She did this stern I-am-too-busy-with-serious-stuff-to-be-bothered-with-lightness take every time she was busy with really serious stuff—like reading Khaled Hosseini on Flipkart Webreader or worse, checking new updates on her Facebook page—all in a day's work. But right now, she felt particularly sick that the morning news had made her forget all about her messianic ERP plans. Hadn't she resolved to transform the way SISSY (State Institute For Skill Strengthening of Youth) worked? Wasn't she going to alter the course of SISSY's destiny? Wasn't she a *truly committed officer in service of the nation*? And here she was…gawking at the 300 dpi Avinash Rathore, like some feather-brained teenager! She flogged herself mentally.

'So?' she said rather majestically, lifting up her aquiline nose and shifting her gaze to the IT guy standing in her office. She wasn't wearing her spectacles today, her usual line of defence—and predictably, the IT guy was melting in front of her.

'The presentation is ready ma'am…if you would like to look at it…' he said self-consciously, carefully avoiding her eyes.

None of the young IT boys at SISSY's office dared look at Nethra Kaul when she was not wearing her thick, dark-rimmed spectacles which she mostly wore to avoid that filmi moment when the heroine takes off her nerdy glasses and lets her hair flowing open (she also almost never let her hair open); the moment when everyone including the hero (and his out of focus sidekick) finally realize what a pretty damsel she is. Basically, Nethra Kaul didn't do pretty. But *today* was different, an *exception*, as it were.

The SAP guys (basically Vice President-SAP who incidentally happened to be a ripe-for-the-taking bachelor) were coming. She had talked to VP-SAP over the phone twice, no, thrice…he had sounded quite fine, her definition of fine, that is, and the contact lenses, you see, one gets the picture.

But honestly, even with those grotesque dark-rimmed spectacles, even with her thick black mane reined in strictly by a ruffle, most of the IT guys concurred, she looked 'cute' and as one eloquent admirer aptly summarized, she looked so '*vulnerably sublime*'. Only that these poetic musings remained strictly restricted to the younger office sections—the IT Section and e-governance section in particular—where the boys could take the liberty to jab and tease each other like pubescent girls crushing over the no-nonsense and incredibly hot head boy at school.

It was generally held that SISSY, Kisalpur where Nethra had moved in as Director recently, existed primarily as a cesspool for oddballs who valued theory above practice. That was its *leit motif*, just as the reason for the existence of a designation like OSD (Officer on Special Duty) is to accommodate 'swayers' and kingmakers till their desired slots in preferred departments fell vacant, or elbow out weak seniors in need of weeding out or *collate intelligence* or place one's own pawn, so to speak, in a nasty department…and so on and so forth. All other goals and objectives mightily professed in SISSY's Statement of Purpose (SOP) were practically incidental to this one purpose—to exist as a bloody cesspool for bloody oddballs, who, by the combined grace of the Almighty, the UPSC and government's queer recruitment policies were ever so *abundant* in supply.

As for SISSY, the institute's acronym broadly conveyed its stature with the government and consequently, its impact on the focus sector. Suffice it to say that if Project 21 was the carrot, SISSY was the bloody stick. The harder Nethra tried to push her agenda, to find the SISSY creature a pair of balls, and herself, a job, the clearer came the understanding that there simply wasn't any point. Nobody was interested in SISSY. Or in her grand plans for the cause. Or in her PowerPoint presentations. Nobody was interested in *her*. So what remained now were a never-say-never attitude, a few sundry files and lots of time and energy to squander on things of arguable relevance.

And what also remained were books, books and more books; books which Nethra swallowed in dregs, like they were some palliative, down the crucible of her aching heart…books whose men were her only real 'involvements'—bright breakfasts with Edward

Rochester, dreamy dinners with Atticus Finch –books that swelled with dog's ears, on pages that were re-read and re-thought of en route from her home to her office, books with sentences that were devoured and savoured and even furtively applied, sometimes, to her here and now—a quip here, a note there—and the *sheer* joy that followed, all vacant nods and blank stares....

No two worlds could have been further apart and yet, yet for Nethra, the two worlds merged at their seams...merged so well that she seemed to move seamlessly through; in and out of her real and make-believe worlds, the latter being so much more desirable, the former being so very imperative.

She wished she could live with them, her books. Just them. But alas, for her utterly dreary, utterly *sarkari*, utterly real world was irredeemably fulcrumized around Deenbandhu Deshmukhji—her PA, her stenographer, her comrade-in-arms, her real life *bandhu*—all in all, the only *real* involvement Nethra *really* had.

'I have uploaded a rough draft of SISSY's work-plan on our Google account, Deshmukhji. Please run it through some word processing and get me a revised draft by noon,' she told a bespectacled Deshmukhji, who seemed all geared up in a full-sleeved woollen pullover and a grey muffler in the early days of November. Deshmukhji frowned and smiled, simultaneously.

'Will you be able to do it by noon?' Nethra enquired.

'Sir?'

'Will you be able to do it by noon, Deshmukhji?'

'*Ji* Sir?'

'I have shared a document on our Google Drive, Deshmukhji!'

'Sir...*ji* sir...it must be in *dak* sir!' he said, clearly mistaking the Drive for *dak*. In any case, anything beyond office *dak* was an out-of-the-syllabus question for Deshmukhji.

'No, no, no...not the *dak*, Deshmukhji...the Drive. I have shared a document on Google Drive. You operate our Google account, don't you?' she asked cautiously, testing the waters.

He froze. He could still have weathered the gmail/e-mail nonsense, beyond the purview of his job description though it was, for he had *always* been known for his accommodating ways... but what was coming to him right here was a different ball game altogether—Google-whatever-the-hell-it-was. What was the woman even expecting? She was stretching the much strained confines of a boss-stenographer relationship like a bloody rubberband! In a place where every single apprentice had, with practice, perfected the ultimate tool of non-cooperation—the *satyagraha*?

This was downright *oppression*.

Exploitation.

Violation of the International Labour Conventions—No. 29, No. 105, No. 111 and No. 138. Nothing short of a tools-down strike would do.

Deshmukhji's lower lip quivered just as his upper lip stiffened and he looked across the room into his doe-eyed boss's blazing eyes. And just then, people, just then, the inevitable happened. It had something to do with those eyes, perhaps, or that face, maybe... but no, it had to do with the *overall* sense of whatever it was that worked for her and *something surely worked*, but eventually, like with every other civil disobedience practitioner at SISSY, something *melted* right inside Deshmukhji's heart. A safer option, a more conciliatory one, blazed across his mind at this opportune moment.

'I will get one of the computer *aaprayters*, Sir!' he quipped and lunged towards the door.

He had been gone for an hour now. Nethra was peeved.

'What have you been doing, Deshmukhji?' she drawled over the receiver.

'I got the document, Sir. Give me a day. You will find it on your table, first thing in the morning tomorrow,' he replied firmly.

For the past thirteen years, Deenbandhu Deshmukh, Stenographer to Director, SISSY had resolutely resisted the idea of getting trained in modern tools of office management. *Satyagraha* had been his mighty weapon to this end. In the spare office time that came from delegating all electronic work to the contractual IT guys (computer operators), he had equipped himself with the 'necessary' paraphernalia—he could, for instance, reproduce, verbatim, the Industrial Employment Act 1946, Industrial Disputes Act 1947, Employees' State Insurance Act 1948, Contract Labour Act 1970 and others, like EPF Act, Payment of Gratuity Act, Payment of Bonus Act, and more recently the Sexual Harassment of Women at Workplace Act (he was some authority here).

His side business (another spillover of all that delegation)—consultancy on all matters within the ambit of labour laws—had thus become a bloody flourishing enterprise. It had to be. With dedicated clientele like the Azaad Adhyapak Sangathan, Safai Karamchari Ekta Manch, Kisalpur Patwari Morcha, Bank Employees' Unions, Anganwadi Karyakarta Shakti Manch and the like, there was a strike going on each of the 365 days in a year.

Meanwhile, having stubbornly refused to learn MS Office, browse the Internet or use e-mail, the everyday survival know-how in his line of work, DDji had clung to his old typewriter like a shattered, bereaved mother who just wouldn't let go of the photograph of her dead child.

So DDji laboured on the entire day and night, carefully reading every word of printed text before typing it on paper, ensuring that there were as few whitener marks as possible. He had consulted (one of the few areas he accepted consultancy in) one of those IT boys about the Drive and the mischievous boy had got his kicks by opening the document and advising DD to get a printout (to avoid straining his eyes), do the corrections manually and type the whole damned thing out on his beloved typewriter. Like every dog has its day!

And man, he was typing in English after a really long time. IAS officers seemed to have a strange fetish for the English language. Every Director knew that all official communication had to be in Hindi, the state language. Yet, the few IAS officers who had headed SISSY in its short life of 13 years always insisted on the usage of English. It underscored the fact that they were different, and reminded them of their *stature*, perhaps, as they struggled to come to terms with the tumult of their free falling careers.

'What a pittance for solace!', he pondered philosophically, '...and these poor souls can't even go on a strike!'

One and a half hour past midnight, he typed in the last page, placed the typewritten volume on his boss's table and felt relieved. DDji's bosses had often taken pride in his perseverance—whenever *he had wished* to persevere, that is. Tonight was one such night—eighty pages of text in eight hours non-stop—DDji was mighty pleased.

As Nethra stared at the typewritten marvel that lay on her desk next morning, two words surfaced in her mind, like two people who you had known since long but only now *recognized*, and the two words were—'Trained Incapacity.'[5] Now having studied Public Administration as an optional for UPSC, Nethra had an *intellectual* understanding of the concept, but now, staring at the blue hued wonder, what she had achieved was an *emotional* understanding. And this was exactly the sort of understanding that mattered.

Quite an obituary for the Skill Strengthening in SISSY. *RIP desktop publishing*, she sighed.

'Please come on in,' she whispered now, to Deshmukhji, at the other end of the line.

'You have worked really hard! I don't know of anyone who types this fast,' she smiled.

'Thank you, Sir!' he beamed.

'I want you to do a few things more.' With this, she proceeded

---

[5]Wikipedia on Trained Incapacity—'In sociology, this refers to that state of affairs in which one's abilities function as inadequacies or blind spots. It means that people's past experiences can lead to wrong decisions when circumstances change. Thornstein Weblen invented the concept in 1933.

patiently about the wonders of e-mail, Gmail, stuff people talked about, stuff he didn't like.

'I cannot do this, Sir,' the stupefied look was back on.

'Why?'

'Because I *cannot,* Sir,' he frowned.

'Please come back at five, Deshmukhji. We will see how you *can,*' she replied firmly.

They sat together three hours every day after office for the next ten days. Nethra taught him the basics of word processing. On the twenty-fifth day, he laid the word processed document on her table. He had done it rather well.

'It would have taken much less time, Sir, had you asked any computer *aapray*...,' he said guiltily.

'But you wouldn't have learnt it that way, Deshmukhji,' she interjected.

'But it took a lot of time, Sir...the previous directors would use the *aapray*....'

'That's alright, Deshmukhji. I am happy *you* have learnt.'

'I am sorry I bothered you so much, Sir.'

'You should be happy you have learnt so much! Now you won't need to depend on your computer operators, and you can even help your grandchildren with MS Office.'

Deshmukhji smiled back feebly. The institute hadn't seen many IAS officers. Those who came were mostly bitter, arrogant and conceited. No director had been so patient with him, none had ever taught him a thing. He liked his new sahib. She was a *real* sahib. He would throw the typewriter away, he resolved.

'Ah! But why, Nethra? I see you have been missing from our party circuit for quite a while now! Not fair...you must come!' Mrs Jain's voice exuded genuine concern for Nethra's welfare. She was the wife of Collector, Kisalpur, the First Lady Of Kisalpur (FLOK), so to speak, the one entrusted with the monumental responsibility of keeping the flock together by keeping the wives together.

And how she had excelled! Thanks to her, the Officers' Club at Kisalpur was now the microcosm of an enduring carnival, some would say, a Vanity Fair, but the high point was not vanity but perpetuity. She had taken the Club from being a poor, neglected sports facility to being something of a party cruise that could, with a few tweaks here and there, serve as a venue for dinners, theme parties (purple pouts, purple puffs, purple peep toes and uh... purple brassiere), sports meets, cultural evenings, *indoor* picnics, *marathons*—yes, it was all in the mind, baby. And her mind churned out ever novel events to congregate, celebratory parties in one garb or another, for Mrs Jain lived for parties and she could as well die for them. They were *central* to her existence.

What worked for her, of course other than her husband's current designation, was her remarkable sanguinity, that cheerful, never-say-never *tenacity* that ensured close to one hundred percent attendance in every event she organized, even if there was one every second day in a goddamned working week. She was the Don Vito Corleone of Kisalpur—nobody refused her offer for a nice coffee in the evening, or spurned her friendship, or did not return her calls. She had the first allegiance of every single *sarkari* family in the district—everyone except Nethra Kaul.

'I am sorry, ma'am. I have urinary tract infection,' Nethra lied. She knew she would be found out, but she lied. Only that UTI was not a *wise* excuse, coming from a woman not yet betrothed, going to a gang of women given to dangerous extrapolations, it was a terrible self goal. Surely, enough fodder to keep the Officers' Club ladies busy and buzzing for the next ten days.

'You should accept every rise and fall in your career with equal grace and humility, Nethra,' Mrs Jain reasoned gratuitously now. The tenacious woman was of course not buying into any of the UTI business. She was one sorted person, the one with a responsible head on even more responsible shoulders. She knew, *had known* right from the outset, that the reason anyone avoided her parties had to do with things '*more complex and more basic*'[6]—like conflicts that ran deep into a person's psyche.

'A dip in self-esteem that comes with being shunted to the loop line,' was her diagnosis of Nethra Kaul's malady. Oh, she had been there, done that and she knew all of it all too well. Nothing to worry. Stuff happened. And denial was this stuff's most crucial symptom. She knew for a fact that nothing could be wrong with her parties. Could it? Just that Nethra was a poor, lost Little Bo Peep right now. She was Little Bo Peep who had lost her sheep and didn't know where to find them and all she needed was some well-meaning advice. Oh these lady officers were always so brittle—either too hard or too broken! Proffering advice to broken souls came as naturally to Mrs Jain as, 'Would you like to update to the latest version?' comes to Adobe Acrobat Reader.

To be fair to Nethra, on the other hand, stuff thus diagnosed was not the only reason for her reluctance to party. Parties and Nethra just did not go together. To her, parties stood for just one phenomena—absorption. Keeping up appearances. Absorbing nothing. Releasing nothing. Only maintaining exchanges at a cutaneous level. And she was as poor at it as one can possibly be.

All *sarkari* parties in Kisalpur, like all *sarkari* parties elsewhere started with decked up men and decked up women, arriving with decked up kids, as families, and immediately dispersing into three groups. The men, all grey and grave, sat together and chatted sombrely about government—banal talk about Pay Commissions and service conditions, about this, that and the other reform, about the latest fetishes in the Secretariat and why they were doomed to fail. Of course they never agreed. But then they didn't disagree either.

---

[6]Her words, not the author's.

If God ever eavesdropped on this tedious conversation, he would, sitting in his heaven, surely feel regretful about this bona fide blunder. Why did he even create this species in the first place? And having created them, why did he not bless them with some *colour*? Look at those poor self-absorbed souls now—they just didn't seem to know anything else to talk about, they simply went over the same things, going round and round, in circles, in meetings, between meetings, in parties, at work....

Some of the older (retired) men, of course, had broken the jinx and excelled in telling morbid jokes and everyone pretended to enjoy those. There had been some botched-up attempts to bring in cricket, but in the age of the IPL, cricket had ceased to be a subject that could hold a mixed-age group together. Only a government and its affairs could.

Of course it was in smaller groups, with familiar people, while touring in their vehicles or enjoying a drink, when such frivolity went unnoticed, that men opened up to gossip. It was then that they shared tales about other men, mostly about other men they did not like, about their illicit affairs and their shady deals and the stuff that happened in their homes and families. Women's stuff.

The women were altogether different. They huddled together, eyed each other conspicuously and chatted pleasantly about, well, eclectic things and their subjects were definitely more colourful than those of their men. But things were far more complicated and far less direct in this department, and there were lots of undercurrents, and no one said what they really wanted to say, and nothing was actually what it seemed like it was. From appearances however, one could easily glean a few salient subjects of current interest.

- Deepika Padukone's kurta-palazzos in *Piku* and Alia Bhatt's long skirts in *2 states*, the sarees and blouses Madhuri wears to *Jhalak Dikhla Ja*
- Oriflame products, Amway memberships, VLCC coupons and the end of year sale at Meena Bazaar

- Comparisons, all in good faith and in keeping with the greater Olympic spirit, of course, of marks, medals and maths Olympiad scores, all trophies for triumphant mothers...and the occasional collateral damage. To cite the latest curious case of Gaurav Agarwal who had assured his mother it was *he* who had got the highest in Maths and Physics these half yearlys, an innocent bit of information which had been dropped by Mrs Agarwal rather casually at a club meet, which in turn had made Pragya Tiwari's mom go so berserk that she had produced, as proof, Pragya's report card, in the very next club meeting; something which conclusively established the truth of Mrs Tiwari's claim (that *Pragya Tiwari* had in fact scored the highest in *all* subjects these half yearlys), which in turn had brought unspeakable mortification to Mrs Agarwal, Mrs Jain, Mrs Saxena and Mrs Srivastava, all of who had been made to believe (by their sons, obviously) that it was in fact *they* who had scored the highest in Math and Physics, that Mishra girl being no good at anything other than Social Studies and English, these half yearlys. Eventually, it was Mrs Tiwari who had emerged a clear winner and who having taken a sudden fondness for Nethra Kaul (Kauls are Brahmins, no?), had whispered in her ear with a forced intimacy—What do these Baniyas and Kayasthas think they are? Huh, bloody accountants!
- *Kumkum Bhagya, Diya aur Baati Hum, Comedy Nights with Kapil*, in that order
- Rounds and more rounds of *tambola*
- Exceptionally lame— poor husband- crazy wife—jokes; vicious elbowing and uncontrolled giggling thrown in as complements
- Fat-free, low carb, 'continental' recipes rich in exotic ingredients—brussel sprouts, artichoke, galangal, foie gras, leek, gherkin—the obscurity of the ingredient being in

direct proportion to felt pride and yes, cheeseburger and fries were alright, but no ghee on the roti please!

- Mrs Das's 3.4 year old daughter who could name the capitals of *all* 193 member nations of the UN General Assembly. Even bloody Sao Tome and Principe's whose existence, let alone that of their capitals, was a revelation of sorts for most...but the issue here was different...the issue here was that the ladies had no one to compare this girl with for most of Kisalpur Officers' Club kids were well past that stupid age now, most of them could perceive the sheer foolishness of cramming names of capitals and currencies, and were fast learning that teenage vocabulary—mom, just give me a break, ok; why don't you just adopt *her* and end the fucking story! So deep inside, the Club ladies were secretly craving for it, pining for it...more progeny, yes, just one more little Einstein Agarwal, just one more Heisenburg Shetty Jr, just one more trophy who would shoot off names of capitals and currencies and major rivers and minor millets and bloody GDPs of every nation and non-nation there was in the bloody Milky Way, thus putting that pompous little girl with her pompous little mother in their rightful place
- *Fifty Shades of Grey*
- Barcelona , where Mrs Saxena and family were currently holidaying and the fact that she had recently uploaded 437 selfies of herself—starting all the way from T3 in India to T2 in Barcelona (yes, the exact shot as in the movie *Zindagi Na Milegi Dobara*), sunbathing (yes, at exactly the same spots on the beaches of Costa Brava where ZNMD boys had sunbathed), 'enjoying' La Tomatina (yes, the same tomato festival) in Valencia and flamenco dancing (yes, yes...) in Seville—on Facebook. For the record, everyone in Kisalpur now knew how much 'black' money Mr Saxena, the Deputy

> Excise Commissioner had made and Mrs SP, EOW (Economic Offences Wing) was one particularly offended soul.

Now children, usually, pre-pubescent children didn't count much (except Mrs Das's daughter, of course). They somehow vanished miraculously at the beginning of every party, only to reappear equally miraculously at the end of the party, much like how their parents would have liked it to be. The older boys, all smug and gelled and pimpled, mingled with their cohorts—exchanging One Direction DVDs, discussing *Game Of Thrones* or the latest Christopher Nolan flick and debating if Manuel Neuer or Thibaut Courtois was a better keeper. Boys will be boys, no?

What about the older girls, you ask? Now that was a problem. The older girls behaved *a lot* older and wiser; pitying the boyish exuberance of their peers, they preferred to mingle with the ladies instead. They followed the circular conversations carefully, took in the nuances, and invariably replicated the encrypted patterns in conversations of their own. They *never* tired of praise, were all too generous with it (ABC Aunty , your clutch is soo...pretty, XYZ Aunty you look soo...pretty) and thus they seldom really meant it; sometimes they meant *quite the opposite*...but yet, the girls kept up appearances, said things for the sake of saying them, and felt terribly clever having said them. This was their essential tutoring in making dishonest conversation, in hypocrisy—the necessary 'grooming'—as their mothers liked to think of it.

So, besides the 'dip in self-esteem that came with loopline charges,' it was *all this* and more, the bloody wholesomeness of it—something like a big Sooraj Barjatya 'family' movie—juxtaposed against the daunting skewedness of her own Shyam Benegal-esque 'non-family' persona that made the whole 'party therapy' seem to her like 'a first class, one hundred percent, bonafide, total and utter *pain in the arse*.'[7]

---

[7]Quoted from *White Teeth*, Zadie Smith

Harmony Lost...

Mukhnas, 2014

Till a few months back, as Collector & District Magistrate, Mukhnas, Nethra's life and her self-esteem were on a roll. Not that Mukhnas wasn't loopline. It was as irretrievably in the god forsaken loopline as a district could be—with its forests and its tribals, with no movie halls, railways, industry or ministers. Having to stay in Mukhnas was thus, like *sazaa-e-kalapani*, like Lord Ram's *vanvaas,* the exact kind of undeserved calamity that invited sympathetic oh-dears and poor-yous apart from sullen sighs and supportive frowns from people who understood. The Germans even have a word for the support this kind of misery generates—*Schadenfreude*. Mukhnas was a district *that* feared and famed.

With its huge canopy of sal forests and a predominant presence of the Baigas , life endured with the same primeval placidity in Mukhnas as it had a few hundred years ago. A place frozen in time and all that. And it was only people who *themselves* belonged to some previous time, people who couldn't relate to the pandemonium of the present, who accepted Mukhnas and its tranquil ways as their own. And such people, though few and fickle, *loved* Mukhnas. Nethra Kaul was one such person.

They were quite an unfussy lot, the Baigas. In the hierarchy of the needy where the urban middle class would be found grumbling and pushing at the apex, the Baigas would happily, smilingly occupy the sprawling bottom of the pyramid. Because most of what they needed could be had from the forests. And forests, unlike governments, delivered.

If at all a Baiga cribbed, (it was mostly a singsong, mellifluous sort of cribbing, more like music to the ears, and quite unlike the cacophony that is second nature to the urban middle class now), it was either because their village had no '*nal*' (handpump) and the women had to walk every day for several miles with pots on their heads and babies strapped across their bodies to fetch muddied water from the nullah across the hill or if the village had no '*khamba*' (electricity) or because their sarpanch was paying them less or late wages for MNREGS' work. They could also complain if the PDS salesman was charging a few rupees extra for the subsidized rice or salt or if their *dak ghar* was some twenty-five kilometres away and the elder lot found it difficult to cover the distance on foot.

So one had to travel a mere two hundred kilometres off the state capital if one wished to time travel to a place two hundred years behind in time.

Anyway, the thing about Mukhnas was that it was *Nethra's* space, a place which allowed her to be what she had always wanted to be—*a truly committed IAS officer in service of the people*. Far from the maddening crowd of cut-throat hustlers, aggressive bullies and outright fakers, Mukhnas was her own little *territory*. And the mutual admiration showed: In long queues during *Jan Sunwai*, in the fact that people in the remotest villages of Mukhnas now knew about the new *Bai*, the *nayi collectorni* who was surprisingly approachable and much to their amazement, was keen to get *their* things done.... Never mind that she looked too young, and didn't speak like a *Bada Sahib* at all...this *nayi bai* had their *trust*—that rare and sensitive commodity ever so short in supply in relations between the governing and the governed.

Truly, then, working in Mukhnas was the only therapy Nethra

ever needed. Knowing there was so much one could do and doing it. And seeing it bloody happen. And realizing the sheer number of lives it could touch, improve, and transform. Nothing could beat that kind of *wholesome* satisfaction. Maybe, your child's wholehearted laughter after a long bout of debilitating illness, may be that, but other than that, nothing else. It was a strange peace she had found in those undulating plains, the continuum of hills covered in *kodu—kutki* and ramtil's yellow, the mud houses fenced with wooden planks, the foaming waterfalls, the glistening green of freshly leafing forests of sal and women walking along the roadside, walking back to their homes with wood collected from the forest. She was living in a rare harmony, a harmony induced by the satisfaction of doing things that needed to be done and doing them well. Her thoughts were clear, her mind was happy and her body was at peace. Nothing seemed to disturb this resonance.

Till a few decades ago, the Baigas didn't interact with outsiders. They still preferred not to, but the great wave of globalization had flattened many a barrier, even at the most unexpected of places. Thus, on her tours, while she would still find the older Baigas going on about the *nal*, the *khamba* and the *dak ghar*, the younger Baigas were different. They had studied in Sarva Shiksha Abhiyan schools and a fifth standard kid could spell a 'cat' and 'dog' after initial reluctance.

It was during one of her regular night camps that a group of Class XII students had confidently come forward with a request letter written in an illegible hand, in English. Though the contents of the letter were surely something that would have set Wren and Martin twisting, turning and twitching their deceased noses in their English graves, (the contents seemed like the ultimate act of colonial revenge, do to their language what they did to your country sort of thing), Nethra could still gather the intent of the communiqué. The letter demanded a 'tower' in the village.

'What is a tower?' was her puzzled enquiry.

The whole gathering broke into spontaneous laughter, men guffawing and women giggling with the edges of their knee length sarees drawn beneath their teeth as the *patwari* explained that the kids were demanding the erection of a telecom tower—telecom infrastructure for a cell site in a village that had no electricity! The kids studied in a government residential school some 20 kilometres away. Their hostel had a large television with a dish TV connection and several of them were proud owners of the few mobile phones in the village.

The boys wore fake Levis jeans, sported strange hairstyles (on closer examination, Nethra could also spot some well-threaded eyebrows and waxed forearms) and looked like poorer versions of the Mihirs, Arnavs and Dr Armaans of Indian television. Some of them even wore 'Being Human' T-shirts, the kind she had once watched some multimillionaire starlets wear at a charity ramp walk on TV.

If nothing else, the great wave had brought in a tide of unprecedented aspiration in the darkest and dingiest corners of the country. Aspiration matched by opportunity, she hoped. Why else would government high school students in the most backward district in one of the most backward states in the country walk around with punchlines that had nothing to do with them, their lives and identities, and with charity, the attempt at being human.

She smiled as she went about touring the village, observing the young boys flashing their Micromax phones, chewing gum and clicking pictures, the other hand stylishly tucked inside a trouser pocket, and walking in that ultimate Salman Khan stride (which naturally, is an outcome of corns or calluses on feet), aware that they were being watched, and trying therefore, to totally floor their female schoolmates who loved everything about Salman Khan as much as they did.

'People have faith in you, Ma'am...they trust you...,' MLA, Mukhnas was gleaming. She could tell he was in an expansive mood today, in the mood for some *prashasanik charcha,* administrative equivalent for lazy chitchat. He was flattering her to set the tone. Nethra half smiled and looked at him, attentively.

Under ordinary circumstances, a *sarkari* relationship between a District Collector and *jan pratinidhis* (the *more important* VIPs in the district) is expected to grow beyond the immediate and the important, and encapsulate the warm assurance of friendly gossip, settling into a comfortable, back slapping bonhomie where sessions of *prashasanik charcha* could be held over Good Day biscuits, ginger tea and giggles—standard menu—topped up with platefuls of cashews and almonds and raisins, if the given VIP was *actually* a VIP.

These *charchas* constituted what one understood were a wise Collector's 'reliance sources' of knowing who-said-what-to-whom-with-what-effect. They were a Collector's sensors to gauge public mood and perceptions, her way to collate intelligence about shady businesses of dodgy individuals whose consequence rose and fell with circumstances in a district. For no one was any cleaner than anyone else anyway. And in the insightful words of Lord Palmerston, in politics, there were no permanent friends or enemies, only permanent interests. The easiest source for obtaining clinching evidence against one politician's foibles was, thus, holding a one-to-one *prashasanik charcha* with a fellow politician from the *same* party.

The 42 year old *yuva* MLA of Mukhnas was, unlike his constituency, urbane and highbrow. He owned The Smoking Tiger Company, the leading *beedi*-maker in the state. Unlike her two other MLAs—rustic sexagenarians who were given to addressing her as *Behenjee* and *Madamjee* respectively—this one underscored his breeding by calling her Ma'am, and by speaking in soft monotones, a strangely accented English, sometimes interspersed with irreplaceable Hindi terminology.

'Is Avinash Rathore Sahab your batchmate, Ma'am?' he queried smilingly.

The name dropped with a thud, as always, arresting her in a stranglehold, throwing her off balance for several moments.

'Yes...,' she replied casually, her face not betraying the slightest hint of the turmoil within.

'What a dynamic young officer!' he gasped pleasantly.

Nethra managed a fake smile. Did she want to hear more? Wait, why had he brought Avinash in? Did he know anything? Could he? His *Vidhan Sabha* constituency included parts of Bilasar, a subdivision in Misbalgarh, the adjacent district. Misbalgarh was where Avinash had done his first charge as District Collector, exactly two years previously.

'He was Collector, Misbalgarh, you know,' he said now. Of course, she knew. How could she not know?

'He *transformed* Misbalgarh, ma'am...he cleaned it up. People there lived in awe of him, you know—they still do—like they live in your awe here, of course, of course.... People had taken to the streets when he was transferred...God, how he was loved!'

'Two girls in the Govt. Girls College had slit their wrists and written him letters, in their blood you know...it was all over the papers!' he threw up his hands and laughed merrily.

'And he is mighty embarrassed every time I mention that incident to him,' the MLA continued. 'What an extraordinary officer! He has that rockstar thing you know...that panache....'

'Yes...some are just born that way,' she shrugged lightly, smiling. What a sharp actor you are, Nethra Kaul, she told herself.

'Yeah...*bahut hi* no-nonsense *type ke adhikari hain* Sir...but then he had to deal with a lot of this, you know...he is so terribly handsome!'

Yes of course, and *I* am an all-nonsense *adhikari* listening to you rave about your man crush, she felt like saying... Wait, Handsome(?)... what did he even expect her to say? Why did he even need to mention his looks? Nethra was trying hard to maintain her I-am-too-busy-with-serious-stuff-to-be-distracted-by-lightness visage as she fidgeted with the stacks of office files on her table now.

'Yes, a very fine officer he is' she nodded grimly, shifting one random file atop one stack to the top of another.

'Very fine…very efficient…very charismatic…,' he went on undeterred. 'And so was his wife, very charismatic!' he added.

'Damn!' she bit her lip. Enough was bloody enough.

'You know her?' he enquired.

'No…not really,' she shrugged.

'She was very active, you know, even as Collector Misbalgarh's wife…very active, *bahut hi prabhaavshaali vyaktitva,*' he said. *Prabhaavshaali*—influential—that was the word he had used.

'And you had a crush on her?' she wanted to ask. The way he was going on and on…it seemed so to her.

'What a striking young couple that was!' his eyebrows were now arched in wondrous awe. 'Electrifying chemistry…such a perfect couple!'

'And I am melting with sweetness now…,' she thought, 'with this cloyingly charismatic, *prabhaavshaali* sweetness!'

So that was it. Another day had been screwed, royally screwed.

'Jab Rathore Sahab DM thay…,' or *'Rathore Sahab ke samay par…,'* were things that had been hurled at her before. That was the occupational hazard of being posted in a place bewitched by legends. Legends who left cults behind, cults that continued to worship the legend like it were some sort of chimera, throwing tales of the legend's feats at every regular mortal who ever got posted to those parts.

Mr Illustrious Rathore was *that* sort of a legend in these parts. It was another thing that those who threw around these tales weren't aware that their Collector Sahab, their legend-in-the-making had palpitations every time a mention was made, a mention of some great feat the chimera had achieved. They also weren't aware that every time, the mention *distracted* their Collector Sahab, throwing her off balance from that elusive peak of harmony she had ensconced herself so carefully upon in Mukhnas. Because despite apparent refusals and vehement denials, Nethra Kaul knew that even today, seven bloody years down, nothing, *nothing* could affect her the way 'he' did—not in as many ways, never so *intensely*. She knew this and hated herself for it.

Notwithstanding these distractions and palpitations, being in the driver's seat gave Nethra a sense of fulfillment and thrill few things could match. Though overworked, Nethra was happy that things were finally looking up in her life, that she was doing what she had always wanted to do, that things were really *so* alright—more alright than they had ever been before in her life. She was *happy*. Damn right. And contrary to her usual ways of dealing with happiness, of denying its existence, underplaying it, or attributing it to luck by chance, she wasn't really afraid to admit it this one time, to say it out aloud—YES, I AM HAPPY. YES, IT IS BECAUSE I AM DOING THINGS RIGHT.

And just then, people, just then, precisely because everything seemed so good in that moment, because some force in nature just cannot tolerate too much goodness at one place and is always working to redistribute it, because all good things must come to an end though no one can ever tell why, because of these random reasons which work only to the disadvantage of the disadvantaged, and never otherwise, Nethra was thrown out of Mukhnas and the legend that could have been never became.

She was abruptly transferred out of Mukhnas, 'shunted to the loopline' as has been so cogently diagnosed earlier, barely seventeen months after a belated posting in that district.

The writing had been there, on the wall.

Tribal Health, Upliftment and Growth Society (THUGS) had spent the last few years growing, no, swelling—in its membership base and with grants it received from governments and corporates alike. You only had to think of a powerful name and he was a member of THUGS already. The kind of influence it wielded over the powers that be was obviously, immense.

As it happened, THUGS decided to organize the largest *'Viklang Shivir'* of its kind in Mukhnas—the hot bed of tribals, poverty, and *'pichhda-pan'* in its essence and thus a fertile ground for some grassroots PR exercise. Nethra had been receiving frantic calls—frenzied politicians, frenzied seniors, frenzied notable others—and Nethra could yet not quite get what all that frenzy was about.

'The arrangements…,' everyone had gasped, 'the arrangements should be good!'

So much for a private program organized by a private organization, she had naively wondered.

It was only when the 'manager' came, with his long list of executables that Nethra finally understood what it was all about. The 50000 sq ft tent, the 201 counters for OPD/IPD/Diagnosis, tonnes of medicines, food stalls, washrooms, rent and diesel for over 200 buses that would ferry beneficiaries to and fro, and finally, the buses and the beneficiaries themselves—Nethra was expected to *'manage'* them all. Manage—that was the word the manager had used.

'Euphemistic,' Nethra risked saying, assuming that the sidekicks wouldn't understand, and she could still safely get her kicks.

The manager had walked into her office with a cocky swagger, with that air of uncrowned authority, surrounded by a bunch of tall, muscular and fierce-looking minions to up his VIP quotient and as he read out the list, his head swayed from one side to the other.

Now that kind of vanity, that kind of unnecessary confidence always irked Nethra, made her totally lose her mind.

'From where…?' she asked with apparent annoyance, 'and moreover, why?'

The manager first shot her what he meant to be a foudroyant look, then, having probably reasoned with himself that the young

Collector was a newbie, a *mahila adhikari*, and thus could be pardoned those naïve ways, relaxed his brows a little.

'That you only will tell, *behenjee*...,' he beamed gleefully.

'To each according to his *threat advantage* does not count as a principle of justice.' Nethra thought and smiled at the sample of threat advantage beaming down at her. Of course she didn't react. Shamelessness has a way of rendering you speechless.

'Or...,' the manager went on, attributing her silence to sheer incomprehension, in a tone that suggested compromise, no, a benign grant of relaxation in unilateral conditions, 'we could make all the arraynjment and you, you know, could foot the bill...*fir bhi* administrative *support* to *lagega hi*, madam.'

Nethra continued to look at him with a straight face. One's education convinced a person that there existed certain baselines to the dignity of adult conversation. Most of the times in her dealings in her job, she found, those assumptions kept getting challenged.

'But I will not advyjee you this...,' the manager was thinking aloud now, going an extra mile to help the confounded woman understand, offering her what he thought was a candid suggestion. 'You know how your people inflate your bills... *do lakh ka kharcha sarkari daftar aate aate paanch lakh ho jaata hai*...hehehe,' he giggled, 'you just tell your executive engineers, madam, they will manage....'

'Manage', again! How easily he had resolved her predicament! Why, she only had to give a '*hari jhandi*' to her EEs, '*baki wo karwalenge*' he had concluded nonchalantly. The EEs, and the engineers in general were little magic wands, next only to the Block Development Officers in a district. They could get things done. How they got them done was not supposed to be the all-white-Collector's concern. The bills produced by *tentwalas* and *buswalas* and the ilk would be 'adjusted' somewhere—in some annual maintenance head or IEC activity for XYZ *Abhiyan* head or if nowhere else, the big contractors and businessmen in Mukhnas, the *thekedaars* and the Seths would be asked to share the expenses amongst themselves, just the way adult brothers in joint families shared financial hardships, by contributing. They had to… everyone had so many stakes, afterall.

'*Ab behenjee*, you officers always have the privilege to oblyj social workers like us…,' he grinned.

Social Workers.

Back when Nethra was little, her *dadi* would often tell her a story about a huge honey lake inside a dense 'forest of bears'. The lake was no ordinary lake. Bees across the forest made honey and the big forest troll would make them deposit their honey in the lake. So, the lake was filled with sweet jungle honey. During the day, the troll would ward off greedy bears, screaming that the lake was laced with poison, that it had weeds which made the honey poisonous. The bears believed the toll, and thus warned each other never to go near the lake.

'Not only is the honey poisonous, the troll is vigilant too…' the bears would tell each other and their kids. Every night however, the troll pretended to sleep and let one bear eat honey—only one bear every night—in lieu of favours like a lamb or a rabbit. This way, the troll incurred favours and kept things in control. The bears loved this game too, because every bear thought he was smarter than everyone else, that he was fooling everyone else.

But this bear, the one sitting right across her table was a particularly shameless kind. She was slowly beginning to understand, like really understand, that unlike anything she had read in books on Indian polity, in that very crisply worded D.D. Basu for instance, government purse was precisely, a tote bag. Anyone with a *pull* had a rightful claim on it. The only difference was some did it with elegance, others were downright shameless. And rules existed only for those who followed them. For others, the only rules that existed were what they could do or get done.

'*Aur aap ye media weedia ki chinta mat kijiyega behenjee… wo sab manage ho jaega*' he kind of reassured her, the media management guru that he was, anticipating that the inexperienced lady Collector might be petrified of splurging full throttle on a private PR program and then being caught right up the arse by a scandal-sniffing media.

'I won't do it,' she said finally.

'What?'

'I won't do any of this. Leave now, all of you, please.'

Now this was unusual. He had expected negotiations, some mean-minded haggling along the lines of -'Arrey 200 is too much, *bhai sahab*, let us make it 150 buses,' he had come *prepared* for it, darlings, it was all there, neatly worked out in his mind, the pluses and minuses and the final figures...but this lady was being outright difficult.

The manager took a mental step back now, reassessed positions and switched over to Format 2. '*Aap abhi nayi hain madam... aap logon ko bahut aage jaana hai...hamari zarurat padegi, itna attitude theek nahi hai*' he said, chewing the 'attitude' surely and slowly. Then, quickly switching over to English, he added, 'Don't show me your *afsari*, madam. I know several senior IAS officers...,' and so he went ahead to drop a few jaw dropping names, '*sabhi mitra hain humare...baat karwayein?*'

'Thank you...,' she pressed the buzzer and even as he busied himself with frantic dialling of numbers of some of his friends with benefits, two guards came in and ushered the circus out. He was red all over now, howling and shaking like a leaf but the swagger was gone. The fierce looking minions looked around in a state of utter cluelessness. No templates to deal with situations like these. Sorry. They looked at each other, at their boss, and finally at Nethra for clues but not really finding much there either, stormed out sorry-faced.

Within the next fifteen minutes, calls started pouring in all over again, only this time they were more frantic, rather, peremptory.

'What. Is. This. Fuss. All. About. Nethra?' drawled a seasoned voice over the receiver now. Each word was uttered with certain finality here, like it were a sentence in its own right. 'I mean, seriously...do we have to run districts from the Capital now?'

'No Sir, certainly not, but it is a private pro....'

'Private...?' came the annoyed growl from the other end of the line, 'how could such a noble cause be *private*...how disingenuous! Isn't it a *social* cause, Nethra? It is *horrifying* to find district collectors with such a negative approach towards the social sector.'

'Err...Sir, we just don't *seem* to have the funds for such a large scale pro....'

'Funds? Am I speaking to a District Collector? You better get your act together, Nethra...you are supposed to get things done... supposed to know your way around ... stuff.'

'But, Sir the fact is....'

'The fact is, lady, (mark the gender conversion here) that *such* things shouldn't come to us in the first place! I mean, what good is it having *you* sitting right there if you cannot even *manage* such...', and a little struggle for the right word here, '... such, peanut stuff?' the voice shrank in sheer contempt for peanuts, though it wasn't clear what exactly was being referred to as 'peanuts' and owing to notions of propriety, Nethra didn't deem it fit to ask.

'But, Sir, I....'

'Oh, don't tell me I have to speak to your deputees now, Nethra... can't you simply tell any of your...*people*...to *manage* all of this?'

Manage.

Shit. No. This wasn't going in the right direction.

'Umm...I am afraid I cannot ask anyone to do something I would not do myself, Sir. Moreover, it is more of a PR exercise that THUGS should find out of its *own* sources rather than the government's....'

'Wait a sec,' the voice cut in sharply, 'are we having a debate here, Nethra? Are we? It is a *Viklang Shivir,* for the *disabled* in your district...you must go all out and *arrange* whatever you can to make this a huge success...you have no idea what it would do for your career...you know what clout the Society enjoys, right?' the seasoned voice argued.

And so it went, the voice, for precisely three more minutes.

And what did it get from the other end of the line?

What did this sabre-rattling eventually achieve?

Nothing. 'No Sir. I understand, Sir but this is not really possible, Sir. Well, you are free to think so, Sir, but I do not agree, Sir. That'll be all very unfair.'

Bloody archness. Bloody inability to say standard stuff like—

Let me have a look at it, Sir.

Oh, that's all very well understood, Sir, let me see it *now* Sir;

Please don't worry, Sir—it will be looked into, Sir;

Sure, I will take care of that sir;

No worries, Sir, it will be taken care of, Sir.

Yes, yes, yes, Sir, Sir, Sir.

Now *these* are the very elementary tricks of the trade, saying stuff in active voice and passive voice, rephrasing it and re-rephrasing it, and NEVER SAYING NO, obviously, till you have successfully confused, convinced or confounded the interlocutor.

But Nethra wouldn't do that, because she *couldn't*. Because Nethra Kaul suffered from a congenital inability to let stuff *pass*, to ignore it, to pretend she was not in the loop when she was right there in the middle of it, like an orchestra conductor. So what we were basically dealing with, here, was that woeful inability to be, to be...what is that latest axiom so much in fashion these days? Oh yes...the inability to be indifferent. *Indifference*. Bingo. The raging survival *mantra*, the spirit of the times, the Zeitgeist—Indifference.

But haven't we all seen this before, people? Don't we already know that this lady is not from our times, that she is permanently out of fashion? Well, only predictable, then.

So having duly exhausted whatever little appetite the voice on the other end of the line had for 'No Sirs' and having found all that back and forth ineffective in dealing with the situation at hand, it finally barked an '*Alright*' at her, followed by 'so we have sent you *fifty lakhs* from the Directorate *just* now. Mantriji *just* sanctioned it. All you have to do now is *just* co-ordinate, okay?'

'I will *just* do that, Sir,' she replied, relieved, sad and awestruck that the 'Manager' had short circuited her, cut through all that regular Secretariat red tape, brought the Department to its arthritic knees and got his fifty lakhs, all in thirty bloody minutes.And this was a man she had ushered out of her room precisely thirty minutes back!

And lest it should be forgotten, that belated, 'I will just do that, Sir' had *costs*.

Consequences.

Because *the people who mattered*, were briefed the very same evening about this 'situation' one Nethra Kaul, Collector Mukhnas, had spawned out of her sheer pig-headedness. There had been deep sighs and *tchs-tchs* and a lot of talk about how young officers were just not 'cut out for the job' these days…oh yes, lack of perspective and bloated egos and immaturity and stuff that goes.

On her part, Nethra too knew she wouldn't stay in Mukhnas for long. Not because of what had happened, but because of what was sure to happen, any day now. And it did happen very soon.

She had been receiving subtle hints along the lines of '*Zara wo case dikhwa lijiyega,*' from every conceivable zone of influence there was in Mukhnas, in relation to a particular case that entailed allotment of government land at concessional rates to THUGS (yes, same old). Now she had been told that the case was of interest to certain 'higher offices.' It had also been hinted to her that a favourable recommendation from her end was to be dispatched sooner than later in the case. She had also been very carefully told that the matter was in fact *very, very* important.

The only problem was that all these people were expecting her to send a favourable recommendation to the state government, justifying the allotment of 30 acres of prime government land, in the heart of Mukhnas, at throwaway rates, to a private organization, 'for educational purposes.'

Typical.

To be fair to her detractors for once, she had been holding up the case deliberately. She couldn't make a patently wrong recommendation. She didn't want to lock horns with 'higher offices' this early in her career either. Hence, following an accepted dilatory tactic in administrative circles, she had been calling for opinions and NOCs from sundry departments since the past four months.

However, as most in her line would concur, there were times when petty tactics don't work, times when your administrative mettle, your managerial acumen is put to, let us say, an *aqua regia* test, out of which only the real diamonds of the lot, the really talented truly made for the higher things in life, emerge *unscathed* at the other end.

The 'higher offices' summoned the file in the Capital with her recommendation that very evening. Something snapped inside her, and the rest, as they say, is history no one really cares to remember.

She called for the file and wrote a six-page note explaining in detail, why prime government land should *not* be transferred at concessional rates to a '*dubious*' organization. She even cited two Supreme Court rulings, her student mind always going after those extra marks that gave you the edge. Only, the sheer genius of that note pushed its writer over the edge. It sealed her fate. She received her marching orders the next morning. As for the note, the original file (complete with her brilliant note with copies of the rulings attached) mysteriously went missing in the Revenue Department. Somehow, it couldn't be found. So, another file complete with all relevant documentation and a positive recommendation was dispatched via a special messenger within a week of his joining by Nethra's successor at Mukhnas.

Now, another problem with Nethra Kaul, as one could see here again, was that she simply didn't understand how to be 'tactful'[8] in a predicament of this nature. The evening she was removed, she had a rather long and unsettling conversation with Randhir Biswas, who as Collector Mirzapur six years ago had been entrusted with training Nethra, then a probationer. As one could clearly see, a lot of Nethra' problems had to do with flaws in training and Mr Biswas had thus called with a certain sense of responsibility, and virtuosity, as in his opinion, it was every trainer Collector's prerogative to admonish erring trainees all through their careers.

'Well, I think you have to be positive, Nethra,' Mr Biswas was another never-say-never kind, the kind who was always positive about everything in general and nothing in particular, the kind who answered tough questions his probationers threw at him with, 'You better know that, you are an IAS officer!'

An officer like that.

'So be positive, Nethra, there is a lot to do at SISSY as well...,' he continued, '...but umm...I am surprised that despite *all that* training, you know, you...uhm...how could you?'

'How could I not, Sir?', Nethra said defensively, 'the same people would hang me in public if things turn nasty later....'

'That, they would, in any case, dear,' he replied, unruffled, '...but why you?'

'Sir? Uh...what else could I have done, Sir?'

Mr Biswas let out an *I-am-wise-and-I-know-it* sigh and began, 'Writing recommendations you do not want to is an *art,* Nethra! If you recommend correctly, you are never wrong!' he explained, 'I will send you some of my own if you would like to learn the nuances. I keep copies of all potentially hazardous files with me, you know,' he added.

'Surely, Sir, but....'

---

[8]Tactful—a magic word in administrative circles. Only those born this way pass the *aqua regia* test of administrative competence.

'See...a good recommendation is no recommendation. It is merely an objective analysis...listing out the *pros* and *cons*...entire facts that, you know, meaning neither this nor that, also this, also that and also something of the in between...like that. Technically, one would say that a recommendation is good if it stands the test of *multiple interpretations by multiple parties*—people can choose what they want to interpret, you know...that isn't your *headache.*'

Ah, Nethra had been waiting for this word, '*headache*'! The essence of her year-long training under Mr Biswas—though everything *looks* like your headache, nothing *really* is your headache.

Like that?

Nethra barely heard the rest of the discourse that primarily highlighted how his innate tactfulness made him a diamond that lasts forever and how her deficiency in this element made her a puny tungsten filament which nobody bothers scraping out of fused bulbs and discarded heating rods.

That evening was also one of the few evenings in past six years when she had a really strong urge to talk to Avinash Rathore. However, she didn't. She rang up Madhuparna Baruah instead.

Harmony Regained...

Delhi, 2015

Madhuparna Baruah (M.B.) walked slowly through the morning mist. The soft, wet tuft of grass underneath her bare feet kindled a tingling sensation that rose through her body. She was dreaming—a fourteen-year old girl who possesses extraordinary psychic powers, her mental ordeal in an unhappy family. The situation playing out in her mind was particularly exciting—the girl is running away from her home when she is apprehended by a middle-aged man, a bounty hunter.

Her head was this unruly creature spinning fantastic yarns in strange contexts. In her queer imagination, scenes and situations, dialogues and conversations would spring up from apparently nowhere and delight her into a smile. As a compulsive daydreaming teenager, she had often wondered if she was all right, mentally. Now, at fifty-eight, she had made peace with her mind and the daydreaming flowed naturally, without any guilt-ridden hangovers.

'Nethra madam had called. She wishes to come and see you tomorrow evening...,' the tiresome housekeeper interrupted her reverie. But it was a relief. She liked Nethra. Oh, she loved her. She had been hoping to hear from Nethra.

They had met seven years ago, at a bookstore in Dehradun—the English Book Store or EBD as it was lovingly called. EBD was one of old Doon's elite relics that had, in its heyday, seen visitors like Pandit Nehru and Dr Rajendra Prasad. It now stood as an old, forgotten building tucked away like an artefact of symbolic relevance in a street corner off Rajpur road. Nethra had found herself gazing at M.B. in the same manner wannabe models would gaze at Gisele Bundchen—a look of awe, stirred fresh with strands of jealousy. Of course, M.B. was fifty-one back then, a cotton saree-clad, boho chic with the aura of a reigning queen.

'Cleopatra!' Nethra had thought, 'ageing Cleopatra!'

Bishambar Dutt, the store's bespectacled keeper had winked at her.

'Become friends with people who aren't your age. This is how you see the world, this is how you grow!' he had said.

'Have I seen her somewhere?' Nethra had asked, still gaping at M.B.

'Perhaps...She is Madhuparna Baruah—ex bureaucrat, author. Have you read *The Mist Valley*?'

'Of course I have! I have read each one of her books...Is she 'the M.B.'? I have never seen her before, not even in pictures in newspapers or magazines!'

'She keeps a very low profile...neutral, anonymous old-world-*babu* kinds. You will see her only at her book release functions. She likes to keep it that way, low key,' Mr Dutt had whispered.

'What is she doing here?' Nethra had whispered back.

'Oh, we have a long-standing association—EBD and her—she first came to Dehradun as a probationer, batch of 1977. She comes around often, when she is in town to meet her younger daughter at Welham. Had it not been for generous donors like her, we would have shut shop long back...Kindle and e-commerce websites nearly killed us, you know,' he had sighed.

'Would she mind if I go and meet her?'

'Not likely,' Mr Dutt had smiled.

Nethra and M.B. got along like a house on fire. M.B. loved the fact that Nethra was both young and old at the same time, young in appearance and yet very straight forward in her ways; Nethra loved the fact that M.B. was both old and young simultaneously, and refreshingly *minty* in her ways.

Nethra Kaul now sat across the table in M.B.'s living room. The lights in her house had been dimmed, the way they always were, in evenings, and a warm crackle rose from the fireplace. The house smelt of coffee. Leonard Cohen's *Like a bird on the wire* played in the background. M.B.'s house was Nethra's vision of a 'home'—one that kept out all deceit, grudge and manipulation.

'So, out of Mukhnas, finally!' M.B. walked in, radiant in a purple and cream *khadi* sari.

They smiled. There was something to be said of this telepathy that always seemed at work between them.

'How do you know, sitting here in Delhi?'

'I keep track...,' M.B. said.

'I wasn't feeling great, M.B. I thought I should meet you, stay for a day. Your home calms me down.'

M.B. smiled. 'What would you like to have?'

'Coffee....'Where is Prantika?'

'In Tibet.'

'Tibet?'

'Yes, in the pursuit of truth, and happiness,' M.B. heaved a sigh.

'No wonder. She is your daughter. You cannot tie her down,' Nethra shrugged.

'I don't want to...but she is in existential turmoil. A kid with profound questions only experience will unravel. Experience doesn't come with a catalyst, you know,' M.B. turned to her. 'You seem to be in a crisis yourself!'

'Not a crisis but I am surely beginning to wonder if I am cut out for this job...,' Nethra leaned back on the couch.

'Cut out? No one is ever cut out for any one thing, Nethra... one grows, if one loves what one does.'

'Sure, but I feel like a misfit. There is no space for disagreement here, no little space of your own under the sun...it is all about subservience and career, career, career, at all costs,' she said wearily, 'if chasing targets handed down to me was all I wanted to do, if a career is all I ever wanted, I would have got a better deal selling soaps and investment schemes, don't you think?'

'Why do I feel that you are repentant, Nethra? Do you regret what you did?'

'No.'

'Do you expect the world to be nice to you?'

'No,' Nethra shrugged.

'Do you want someone up there to recognize your goodness and give you a 'good girl' medal?'

'No, but isn't it natural to feel *wronged*?' Nethra looked at M.B.

'Why? Because people did not *acknowledge* your hard work?'

'No. Because people do not like to be told the truth!'

'And how do *you* know the truth? How are you sure that your subjective perception of a situation *is*, the truth?'

Nethra fell silent.

'Everyone is driven by their own code of morality, Nethra, and most people, when they do things, do it thinking that *they are right*. Just as everyone thinks he knows and sees the truth. Personally, I think it is important to know who you are and what it is that you want, so that you choose your actions to maintain some consistency between who you are, what you want and what you do. That's the only way to stay sane, you know. You won't do any favour to anybody by doing your own thing. And you won't expect any favours in return.'

'Why did you leave, then?' Nethra asked.

'Because after twenty years, I had begun to feel that I wanted something more fulfilling...I was getting bored with meetings, and with routine. I could not find much meaning in the things I was doing. It is different when you are close to action...as a Collector, you set the course of things, you take decisions and you execute them. Things work differently in a department. You need to have maddening patience with procedure and a certain detachment...I wasn't 'cut out' for that work, you see,' she smiled, 'I wasn't growing, so I quit. But while I was there, I did my own thing. I was mad and fearless, and I look back at that time with a lot of happiness...and I am sure you will too.'

'Do you think I am afraid? That I lack conviction?' Nethra sounded apprehensive.

'Should you bother about what I think?'

'I shouldn't...but I am full of self-doubt.'

'The whole problem with the world is that fools and fanatics are so sure of themselves, and wiser people are full of doubts!' M.B. chuckled.

Nethra sighed. She knew M.B. was right, that there was no reason to feel wronged. M.B. turned to her and wrapped her arm across Nethra's shoulders.

'I tell you this from a distance of space and years, Nethra. If you were afraid, you would have stayed in Mukhnas. The greatest joy of youth is that you know less fear.... But this fire does not last forever. You learn to live with the 'not quites', the 'almosts', the 'averages'. You learn to compromise. So as long as this lasts, enjoy the pain, relish the suffering. To fear failure is human. You wish to succeed, that is why you fear. Do not ever let this fear change you—that's all,' she smiled.

Nethra smiled too.

'And be like a bird on the wire. Stay connected to the truth, just do not let the truth destroy you...,' M.B. said, as the song filled up their senses and the silence.

PART TWO

Mrityunjay Ranjan

The Simple Integer

Kisalpur, 2015

Kisalpur looked lovely in the rains. It was a beautiful, rain-drenched evening…an evening when Nethra had an unusually strong desire to sit by the river Shravani and put her mind on standby. She drove down to Kapila Gufa—an obscure cavern along the banks of the river, a place made obscure not as much by its location, as by the arcane mutterings of Pagley Baba—a cannabis-smoking, loincloth-clad Sadhu who inhabited the cavern and whose specialization lay in hurling deranged inanities at anyone who came within hundred metres of the Gufa. It had something to do with the undifferentiated schizophrenia the Baba seemed to have; that and his cannabis, the metacognitive awareness it induced, the dampening of controls it led to, the associations that his erratic brain waves in turn made with all that cannabis, that made Pagley Baba a mad seer, a crazy prophet—a hurler of profound inanities, alright, but basically, the exact kind of kickass genius modern societies do not have the time or the patience to unravel.

Pagley Baba's genius was thus deterrence enough for the ordinary mortals of Kisalpur, a class that clearly did not include in its fold, Nethra Kaul. Intrigued as she was by the mystic serenity of the place, she had simply walked into Kapila Gufa that first day in Baba's clear sight. She knew she was being eyeballed, and could be spat upon, hurled obscenities at, even pounced upon…but Nethra did not fear the abnormal these days, she only feared the normal.

She had carried on with her I-am-too-busy-with-important-stuff routine, ignoring the Baba and his 'unignorable' presence, walking around his territory like she was a regular and all Baba had done was some *harmless* eyeballing—not the lecherous, baby-let's-check-you-out kind but the curious kid kind.

Whether he had surrendered before her pigheadedness or had given up in sheer drugged inertia, she didn't know, but he had let her roam unfettered, unobserved, after the first thirty minutes of her maiden visit. From that day on, it seemed that they had reached an elusive accord—Baba would pretend that he hadn't seen the intruder and carry on with his usual cursing and spitting routine at a *safe* distance; Nethra on her part would sit *quietly* along the banks of Shravani, read a book for an hour or two, never looking in his direction, and leave soon after. No asking questions from each other. No looking at each other. No crossing of each others' paths. No truck with each other.

Today, as Nethra headed to the riverside, she saw the Sadhu lolling on a boulder on the sandy shore, rolling up a joint. Next to him sat a man dressed in formals, one of his legs resting against a large boulder as he sat on the other (the creases of his slim fit trousers crying murder). The sleeves of his shirt were rolled up to the elbows and the two men took turns at the joint. Nethra observed the other man closely. Mrityunjay Ranjan!

'Hey, Philosopher Warrior!' she cried.

The man in formals turned sharply to look at her.

His coarse expression softened—the way dry and cracked skin softens when caressed with a soothing emollient—and his eyes gleamed as they met hers.

'Ah! Katherina...what a surprise!' His eyes traced her through his rimless glasses.

'Why should you be surprised? I am now officially one of your kind, Warrior, SISSY-ing around in the loopline' she laughed.

'The Lord of Outcasts is mighty pleased! May our tribe grow!' the man laughed, his eyes fixed firmly on her.

'May our tribe grow!' she said as they shook hands.

'You haven't changed much!' he gazed at her with the same melting tenderness, the glance rendering her acutely conscious of herself.

'Nor have you…except for the beard,' she laughed, in an attempt to distract him, 'So how have you been, you *truly committed officer in service of the nation?*'

'The nation doesn't need serving, Katherina…it only needs good people doing their jobs well…' he smiled.

'And I am in top gear…counting the goats and buffaloes and fish in the state *is* goddamn awesome…. Did you know twenty-one thousand employees of the state owe their jobs and their egos to those cows and buffaloes, those royal entities lazing around in village ponds, chewing cud?'

'That's impressive! Nice that you have found your true calling, isn't it….You were always, so cut out for this Warrior!' Nethra joked.

'You are being too kind…how is your '*Brotberuf*'?' Mrityunjay asked.

'*Brotberuf*!' she laughed 'Bread job, isn't it?' she said guessing it right, 'I am loving it…it is not half as uplifting as counting cattle, though.'

Mrityunjay Ranjan was Nethra's batchmate and was currently serving the state government as Deputy Secretary, Animal Husbandry and Fisheries. A gold medalist in Computer Science Engineering from IIT Kanpur, he was set to join the Masters program at MIT when the dilemma struck—a career sparkling with possibilities or a blind gambit into a world he instinctively knew he would forever remain an outsider to. Eventually, the collective unconscious of the Bihari male clouded out individual rationality and he decided to appear for Civil Service Examinations. He topped the CSE, 2007.

Mrityunjay Ranjan had *many* problems. How does one start? Where does one even begin? Let's say he was a right-protected USB drive containing serious malware that you couldn't format with all the tips and help you get on Wiki How—something that difficult, unalterable, a coding error in the DNA, a wiring problem.

And the malware was not really sophisticated. On the contrary, it was rather rudimentary. Two simple, innocent looking words:

Truth and Justice.

Whatever he touched, wherever he went, whenever, and however inadvertently, the two words—truth and justice—went with him, promising the exact opposite consequences of tactfulness, infecting spaces they touched with utter confusion and disorder. Only that nothing of this disorder ever touched Mrityunjay Ranjan, oh not ever, for he was the one who *acted* and never got acted upon. He was the eternal mover, the eternal shaker, moving and shaking things that were neither meant to be moved nor shaken. Unruffled he stood thus, amidst all the fuss that the moving and shaking about caused—ever so stubborn, ever so resolute, in the face of what life threw at him, in the face of the consequences his character bore on his career and his personal life. He only grew more firm, more determined in his pursuit for 'truth' and 'justice' which were always chasing him in any case.

Growing up in the lawless mayhem that was Bihar; where human beings were Brahmins, Bhumihars, Rajputs, Yadavs or '*chhota log*', where *Matsya Nyaya* manifested itself in the most ruthless and rudimentary forms , Mrityunjay knew that unlike what Forrest Gump would like the world to believe, life was not a box of chocolates.

His father had been an artless and awkward puritan—a District Supplies Officer who had walked to office every single day of his thirty-five years in service since a scooter/motorcycle were too 'improper' and since he could never earn enough to own a 'Contessa' car he always claimed he would. It was a case of disproportionately high levels of pride for the given resources. While dealing with transporters, rice millers, kerosene dealers and a parent department which worked in coordinated connivance with all the above to defeat the very purpose of justice, he would quote Locke, Mill and later, Rawls and read the Rig Veda and Upanishads during evenings.

'To own things that can be bought isn't an achievement,' he would say, 'what matters is if you own things that can't.'

Mrityunjay's had been a rearing in a poverty bred by arrogant honesty, the kind that is so rare in our times that one should rather consider it obsolete, the kind that was afforded after much risk-taking in a department that enjoined upon its clan to jump into the '*sarkari raiees*' bandwagon and frowned upon innocence with condescension. But his father had survived, and retired peacefully with no pending Departmental Enquiries or recoveries and, miraculously for that day and age in Bihar, a full pension. At the time, he was the only officer in ten years who had retired with a full pension. Mrityunjay was a chip off the old block.

'This *Dharma Danda* that you wield with much valour will one day turn itself on your head.' Avinash Rathore had once warned Mrityunjay, in a light-hearted manner. Avinash and Mrityunjay had attended the same college—IIT Kanpur, and had prepared for civil services from the same room in Mukherjee Nagar, Delhi. They had hung out together at the Academy and had even landed the same cadre. It was Avinash who had named him Philosopher Warrior. That moniker had stuck and the prophecy too had come true, to an extent. After 19 transfers, each to a less important position in less than 5 years, Mrityunjay's wife had left him. Frequent transfers were not the reason for their estrangement though, it was merely a symptom.

Mrityunjay's intolerance for the ruthlessness of *realpolitik*, his frequent skirmishes with politicians and his seniors, his intransigence in the face of proposed compromise, his refusal to cower or manipulate, his sheer Nana Patekar-isms had consequences and costs that went way beyond the immediate (his career), and caused collateral damage of a scale that he, in hindsight, could only chuckle at with the satisfaction only a revolutionary could afford.

And everyone loves revolutionaries. Everyone would love to have some in their neighbourhood, to usher in a new world order and all that.

What about having a revolutionary in their own homes? you ask.

Uhm...thanks but no thanks. Who wants a revolutionary in their own home? Who wants to be a revolutionary's spouse, or parent, or child? Who wants their life totally and terminally fucked up, simply because their child/spouse/parent has *inqualab* on his/her mind? Does anyone? Really?

And if anyone has any doubts, go ask the revolutionary's mother, ask his little son or daughter—not on record, I mean—ask them in private, when no one else is in sight, when there isn't any microphone thrust on their faces, and they will tell you.

It is only the rest of the world that revels in their sacrifice, not their loved ones. Because in most cases, the sacrifice is not as much the revolutionary's as it is his family's. And no consent forms are signed here. All the loved ones consent to do is to curse themselves, curse the moment that association happened, for that association never brought them any of the *ordinary joys* that having a parent, sibling, parent or child affords. What I mean is that it takes phenomenal guts and exceptional grit to be able to tolerate all that vicarious glory.

And suffice it to say that Mrityunjay Ranjan's wife did not have in her the guts and grit of the proportions one would require of Mrityunjay Ranjan's wife. His wife, the proud daughter of a former Chief Secretary of Bihar, came from a different space, a space where life consisted of spas, picnics and movie shows. She was the kind of girl to whom austerity was going on a crash diet, who thought bad things happened to bad people and the worst thing that could happen to anyone, anyway, was their dog dying. That was the peak of human tragedy for her. Poor Bruno.

All in all, the kind of girl for whom life was nothing but a box of Swiss chocolates. Like most kids and wives of officers, she naively presumed that the perks and privileges one associated with the job were *entitlements*—that those servants, that Ambassador, those little freebies were to be had because they *were to be had*. Simple. Like most kids and wives of officers, she didn't realize that it was circumstance mandated *resource jugglery* on part of husbands and fathers that accounted for a large part of the *bandobast* they so much took for granted. For if you really looked at it, *really*, as in, there was nothing you had in *your hand*, nothing you could claim *rightfully. No.* Jugglery only became unavoidable then, unavoidable because husbands and fathers had wives and kids and appearances to keep.

But Mrityunjay would have no truck with that kind of falsity. He had no such pretensions. The first time he took his wife to the state capital, they went around the city in an autorickshaw (a veritable luxury, in his opinion, because if he were travelling alone, he would have taken a cycle rickshaw), and made *her*—the self-professed Led Zeppelin fan—relish 'nice', '*adrak ki chai*' in a tea stall outside the railway station. It was the kind of tea stall that played '*Agar tum mil jao zamana chhod denge hum*' for the general class passengers it catered to.

You are mistaken if you think she left him for this offence. No. She could do better than that and that is surely what she did. She gave it all up in the second year of their marriage, when all that deep breathing and Art of Living (oh yes, she could do a lot better than what you thought) had stopped working, when her husband asked her to move to a 900 sq ft rented flat in the state capital, without making any mention whatsoever of maids or servants to do the cleaning, washing and cooking and *when she asked*, he simply replied with a—'we cannot afford it.'

Afford? Now this was something she hadn't heard before.

'*Arrange then,*' was her reply.

Arrange?

Now this was something *he* hadn't heard before.

'You could go slow with your twenty-thousand rupee vending machine for a while,' she had whined finally. This was another story.

The twenty-thousand rupee vending machine had become a contention of sorts in their marriage. The trouble here was that ever since he had started earning, Mrityunjay had pursued a shadow profession, that of a venture capitalist. Every time he saw in a man, what a man ought to have, every time he chanced upon what he called a 'diamond in the rough', he would write out a cheque and hand it over, in most cases, to a complete stranger. The maximum amount he had written out in a single instance was twenty-thousand—and it was one time only—hence the overblown twenty thousand rupee vending machine tag had stuck.

He had spotted them cleaning tables, washing utensils in tea shacks, sweeping municipality roads, cleaning trucks, cleaning buses, carrying luggage, pulling rickshaws, breaking boulders or digging earth at construction sites...all young people with strong hands and piercing eyes which seemed absurdly out of place, because while their bodies tended to the jobs at hand, their eyes mirrored the dreams that nurtured their souls, dreams which made their hands and minds crave more.

Mrityunjay had a gift for spotting this craving, the soul's need to nourish itself, that steady glow of human spirit blazing from inside the flesh and the bones which tried, if inadequately, to keep it alive against the tempest that life was. In those days, twenty-thousand rupees meant half of his gross salary for a month.

'Keep this. And go, follow your dreams,' he would say. Some of them enrolled for BCAs and became Data Managers, later senior executives at private firms, others took up service jobs at call centres, hotels or shopping malls to later become managers, some got driving licenses and became cab drivers, later cab owners, a girl studied law and became a corporate lawyer, a boy even got placed in Google!

'Not a single year have you been able to save the admissible one lakh,' his wife had whined, 'not a single year...Don't save, don't spend, don't invest...keep writing those cheques...just keep paying taxes and keep writing those cheques!' She trembled with contempt.

Mrityunjay Ranjan's wife didn't appreciate that these diamonds were his only investments, his *real* investments, investments in hope and striving. Nothing was as valuable to him as the human spirit and to keep it alive, to keep it burning was Mrityunjay Ranjan's only enterprise.

'You are a bloody hypocrite...do you know that? You want people to think you are a philanthropist...oh you will go around town being Santa Claus, writing cheques and what does the wife get from Santa? Do you recall gifting me a single thing in these two years, honey? Anything? And now, as a final token of your love you expect me to live in this *shack*...you expect me to bloody mop the floor and wash utensils and become a bloody *bai*...' she had snapped.

'But yours is not a *need*, it is a *want*. I want money to go to people who need it, people who understand how best to use it,' he had answered, totally missing the point.

Mrityunjay's salary, the only remuneration he came back home with, wasn't enough to meet the QOL (quality of life) his wife was wont to. And she felt humiliated when ladies at the Officers' Club bragged about their spouses' accomplishments or the newest accessory they had bought. When she confronted Mrityunjay—who still possessed only six shirts, three of which were college-time and the remaining being gifts from her—with her problems, he suggested she move out.

Of course he didn't want her to move out. He was too much in love with the *concept* of a wife to think along those lines. And marriage for him was sacred, not something you could just move out of one fine day, if you didn't feel particularly upbeat about it. In his mind marriage was a thing of permanence.

So regardless of what he suggested to his wife, he wanted her to stay. He wanted to tell her to bear with him a little. He wanted to tell her to give him a little more time. He wanted to tell her what *he* was going through, why it was difficult, what he found difficult, and why things were the way they were...of course he didn't say any of that to her. Saying something like that would mean the admission of failure, or impending failure—and failure was something Mrityunjay would never accept. It was in this sense that he was brittle.

Then one fine day when his wife moved out answering the simple, 'Are you leaving?' with a simpler, 'Yes', he merely stood there, watching the process, with his hands folded in front of his chest, sipping *adrak ki chai* he had prepared for the two of them. What else was there to do? People disappoint, people let you down. Nothing much you could do about them.

'In the midst of winter, I found there was within me, an invincible summer...To the summers that warm our hearts!' he quoted and smiled at Nethra now, as he blew out white curls in spurts, as if enjoying his control over the smoke that filled his lungs. He smoked marijuana, cocaine and weed now. Till five years ago, he used to think smoking was a bad habit.

The sadhu looked from Mrityunjay to Nethra and back, with the overall air of someone watching a sequel, not having watched the prequel. He eyed Mrityunjay enquiringly.

'Katherina...IAS...friend,' he pointed at her.

'Katrina!' the sozzled sadhu laughed, his brown gums sticking out prominently as he offered her a joint.

'No, thanks,' she stepped a little further behind before turning to Mrityunjay again, 'What are you doing here, besides smoking weed, of course?'

'Oh, it is a contempt case in the High Court. Some bastard

absconding for eight years is screwing the department now. He wants his salary, arrears, increments, and pension. And as you would have guessed, we have no attendance records, he ensured we never kept any records...must have struck a deal with some menial asshole in the department....You know how it goes—I run my private business, you burn the records, together we fuck the government....'

'Someone's so concerned about the government! A change of heart, I presume?' Nethra smiled.

'My heart has always been at the right place, Katherina...only they wouldn't acknowledge...they won't come around, they won't grow up,' he sighed as he looked into her eyes again. 'They are getting mighty adventurous, by the way...making me Officer-In-Charge, in a contempt case and I am due for a personal appearance before His Honour in half an hour...that's why the marijuana, you see,' he inhaled mightily, 'How else will I kowtow before 'My Lord'!'

And then almost as an afterthought, he added, 'You know I have finally decided what I want to be in my next life....'

'What?' Nethra squinted, expecting a wisecrack.

'Judge Saab,' he hollered.

It was a cliquey IAS joke. All IAS officers wanted to be judges in their next births—judges or journalists.

'Aren't you done with blazing your ass here that you want to blaze it again as Judge Saab?'

'Judge Saab's ass is never on fire, Kate!' he said, 'it will never be.'

'But I think you would do better as a journalist...asking really tough questions...questions you know no one has an answer to.... That's what you are best at, right?' she chuckled.

Mrityunjay was a Gyaani Bihari, as deadly as it might sound, for every Bihari was a born *gyaani* (could be the left over effects of Magadha's past glory, Chanakya's gene pool or Nalanda's lost aura) and for a Bihari to be called a *gyaani* Bihari was like, drop dead, a double PhD. And to be acknowledged as so by other Biharis (who were, by no means, less *gyaani* and who, by force of socialization could admire none other than themselves) was a triumph of as much magnitude as perhaps, uh, being called a *gyaani* Bihari.

'How did you know of this place? I thought only I came here,' Nethra asked now.

'I used to come here whenever I felt fucked, and disoriented, which was all the time, so this kind of became my second home. Why second home...my only home. This shiv yogi, I owe him infinitely, he initiated me into the unfeeling ecstasy of cannabis, and there has been no turning back,' he looked into the infinity and nodded.

'I don't come here for drugs, though. I come for tranquility, for peace...,' she said smugly.

'Inner peace, Nirvana...the same stuff dressed up in obscure jargon. I totally relate to the feeling part though,' he folded his hands, 'Go on!'

Mrityunjay used to be Sub Divisional Magistrate in Kisalpur five years ago. He was shown the door for 'manhandling' public representatives during an encroachment removal operation. He wasn't given a fresh charge for a good three months thereafter.

'Do you see those crabs, Warrior?' she now pointed to a few crabs washed ashore by the waters of River Shravani. 'They struggle so hard to climb up and get to the sand...and then a large wave comes hurtling and washes them back in. I don't understand their struggle....Why do these puny creatures strive so hard against the river? Aren't they creatures that belong to it after all? Isn't it their destiny to be a part of the river? Why do they fight against their own ecosystem?' she asked without looking at him.

'Only the dead of a species swim with the current, Katherina. You see those crabs...high up on that wall?' He pointed to a few crabs that had managed to escape the river and climb up the retaining wall. 'As long as they have life, its sheer force will make them strive.'

Then at a pitch higher, he addressed an imaginary audience 'Don't bend, don't water it down, don't try to make it logical, don't edit your own soul according to fashion. Follow your obsessions—mercilessly...That's not me. That's Sartre, for you,' he bowed lightly.

'That's deep. And that's Kafka.'

'Touché! That's Kafka and you are hopelessly pompous,' he shrugged.

'And you are hopelessly insane,' she replied.

'Every great man was thought to be insane before he changed the world,' he replied.

'Some never changed the world. They were just insane, Warrior.'

'That is about as acceptable, Kate...sanity and happiness are an impossible combination,' he looked at her.

And now, for the first time, Nethra met his gaze, asking him in return, 'And are you happy?'

To which, he replied with a half-hearted shrug, 'As happy as I can possibly be.'

The sadhu now called them to his mud hut. 'Tea?' he fixed his coked gaze on Nethra.

'Sure, thanks!' To refuse him again, she knew, could be dangerous.

'So, I hear the rabbit has started growing claws these days,' Mrityunjay asked as he settled himself on the mud floor.

'Rabbits don't *have* claws, Warrior. Tigers have them,' she replied.

'Tigers! Yes, tigers mark their territory...big beasts don't fool around with them. It is the rabbits that get hunted.'

'I don't think there is a big beast here, Warrior. All we have are tigers, rabbits and hunters. Hunters kill the tigers because they are dangerous. They bring the rabbits back home for their kids to play with. The rabbits are harmless, right?'

'But tigers shouldn't try to become rabbits, Katherina...they shouldn't, merely because it is convenient,' he said.

'Convenience!' she sighed and smiled and looked at him because she knew he was smiling too.

'You have accepted that you are you, Mrityunjay. You don't fear being yourself. You are not trying to be somebody else simply because to the rest of the world, that somebody else looks better. It takes courage. And you are a Warrior!'

He smiled. A wry, melancholic smile.

The Z-Transform

Nethra invited Mrityunjay over for dinner the same evening. They sat in her study, talking about the academy days as Jagjit Singh's soulful voice filled the pleasant ambience of her dimly-lit study.

'Avinash has bagged the PM's Award for this year,' she remarked casually.

He stiffened.

'He is doing well…at least someone is!' he replied, making an effort to sound casual, his eyes scanning the bookshelves.

After a while, he turned to look at her.

'Imagine a situation Nethra, where one does not think of others….'

'It really beats me!' Nethra smiled.

'What?'

'How you make things sound so simple!'

'Are you two still in touch?' she enquired again.

'Not really….'

Nethra leaned back against her chair now, closing her eyes. Mrityunjay spoke slowly, gazing into the void.

'She was bored. She loved, had the capacity to love, for love, to give and accept love. She tried twice and failed twice to find somebody not just strong enough to deserve it, earn it, match it, but even brave enough to accept it.' She smiled, her eyes still closed, 'How twice?'

'Why? Don't you count me in?' he laughed.

She gave him a breezy, don't-you-say-that smile.

'I was just kidding,' he said and regretted it immediately. Seven years ago, during their only serious exchange, he had told her that whenever you said you were 'just kidding;' you actually meant every word of what you had said. In any case, Mrityunjay Ranjan was one of those people who always meant every word of what they said. That was his problem. Pretence was just not his thing.

She had noticed this too, because she was trying to change the subject now. 'Was this William Faulkner?' she asked.

'Yes...you are always right,' he sighed.

'And don't bring that up,' she said, without looking at him.

'What, Faulkner?' he asked.

'No, love,' she answered.

'I didn't. You brought him in first time. I tried to distract you. You brought him in again...so I was simply reflecting your thoughts.... Seven years and you are still not over it yet, Katherina? What a travesty!'

'True. What a travesty!' she wondered.

Avinash and Mrityunjay had once been close, very close. They had drifted apart now. Avinash disapproved of Mrityunjay's utopian ways, attributing a large part of his eccentricity at work to a variety of imperious narcissism that had no takers in government. Mrityunjay disliked what he called Avinash's selfish purposiveness—something he referred to as a *leitmotif* that played across all aspects of Avinash's life.

But Nethra was visibly amazed that evening—Mrityunjay's light-hearted manner, the innocence in his laughter, his ability to poke fun at his life condition bore no bitterness, cynicism or resentment as she had expected. At the Academy, he had always been the jesting philosopher, the boisterous Warrior in a closed coterie of nerdy IITians who laughed hysterically at jokes devised in their groupspeak. He called her Katherina, after the role she had essayed with great flair in *Taming of the Shrew,* a tongue in cheek satire which had won the Best One Act Play Trophy during their Foundation Course.

'What makes you hold on, Mrityunjay? It has just been three months and I'm beginning to feel hopeless already,' she looked at him.

'Reject your sense of injury and the injury itself disappears, Nethra. Do you ever regret the actions that brought you here?'

'No…I don't think so. I could not have done otherwise. It was not a choice, really,' she said.

'If you are sure you did the right thing, why do you have to feel hopeless?' he asked.

'Because I am not you. I am not a warrior. Because I cannot witness my life slipping into…ordinariness,' she said.

'What makes you think I can?' he enquired.

After a brief pause, he continued, 'I cannot say if you have ever faced it, Nethra, but I have…times when I feel that the whole world has gone nuts, *fucking nuts*. Of course, it is the whole big world minus myself. Because it beats me why everybody seems not to see the obvious, why everybody seems to pretend everything is fine, *when I can see so agonizingly clearly*, so bloody agonizingly clearly that it isn't…but nobody will say it…ever.'

'I have had it, Nethra. I cannot be the amoral salesman anymore, the *seller of glorious dreams*…All my life I have tried to avoid being the desperate salesman and all my life, I have been told that that is what the race is for—I cannot join this rat race—I had a notion that at least *this*, this will be one place where they won't ask me to straitjacket my spirit but I was wrong, my problem is that I don't belong to this time and this place, Nethra…I don't understand this time and this place…It seems like a parody to me, a funny joke… only that nobody else seems to get that joke.' He was running his fingers over his eyes now.

Nethra thought of the number of times she had cursed herself the same way and felt a tinge of *relief*…she was not alone.

'I will be quitting by the end of this year…I got a call from Harvard, PhD program. I will be one of those nutty professors in one of the US universities eventually…' he smiled. 'I won't stay here…I am not needed here…and teaching is the best thing for those who cannot do things.' He teased his brows with his fingers and looked at the floor.

Nethra wasn't surprised. It was only to be expected. The best among them was leaving. The man who solely on account of his mettle, and his character had the first right of rejection in the IAS had chosen to exercise that right. As he prepared to leave, Nethra decided she needed to say this, an advice, something she rarely offered anybody, 'Please do remember what Masood Akhtar told us Mrityunjay…. Do remember his words.'

Masood Akhtar, a 1983 batch officer from the Bihar cadre was an icon for several batches of probationers the academy had churned out. He had survived two decades of lawlessness in that state and never in those two decades, allowed law to deviate from its course where he was in charge. He lived without fear. He had no expectations.

His life or the lack of it, the raw grit it exuded, and his gall as an officer had always inspired the young birds at the academy as they prepared to spread their wings. The lecture he delivered to their batch—the only lecture in several years which progressed and ended in absolute silence, broken only a minute later to a spontaneous standing ovation, the only lecture where no questions were asked—had remained the highest rated lecture by a guest faculty in the academy's history so far. In a single sentence, the pith of Masood Akhtar's life and his lecture was this—*Never be afraid.*

Mrityunjay Ranjan left quietly.

Complex Conjugates

Mumbai, 2015

The same evening Mrityunjay and Nethra were musing about sellers of glorious dreams over Jagjit Singh's *ghazals* in Kisalpur, Amit Bhargava was in Mumbai, attending the Trendsetter's 'Leaders of Tomorrow' conclave. He was to be felicitated, as the citation stated, for 'his path-breaking leadership in drawing thousands of poor women into the fold of social entrepreneurship across the rural hinterlands of Kiritpur.' Exuding hotness in his navy blue tux dressed down playfully with a chambray shirt and a casual no-tie look, Amit Bhargava socialized about the tables set apart for the awardees, smiling handsomely, indulging in gracious small talk, exchanging phone numbers with a select few. His gelled hair was combed over backwards and his grey eyes glinted like his cufflinks as he stepped up for his acceptance speech.

'I am *humbled*. I am humbled because India's intelligentsia, the Trendsetter, has shown the courage to go beyond the glitz and glamour of big cities and acknowledged the hope of real India—the poor women from Kiritpur. You have reposed your faith in them and I, the comrade of Kiritpur's women, accept this insignia of your faith with all humility and responsibility.'

The Trendsetter was one of the largest mass media companies in the country. It ran a 24x7 news channel—OMG. The channel owed its sensational TRPs to the *subzi mandi* din of its newsroom, as also to its eyeball-grabbing presenter who was given to Freudian slips—like missing the eye in the eyeball—much to the merriment of trending panes on social networking sites. The Trendsetter also published several dailies and weekly magazines in English and regional languages besides running radio stations, an internet company and a publishing house. The Trendsetter was popular. It sold. And Amit Bhargava knew this well. His friends in Trendsetter were thus big kahunas and extending state protocol to them were highest priority interrupts in his scheme of things.

For Amit Bhargava, friends were vital inventory resources. His IRS friends, for example, were free rooms / free-dining-in-seven-star-hotels resources, those in the IAS / IPS were, inter alia SUVs / holidays- in-tourist-resorts resources, his Custom and Central Excise Service friends were Johnnie Walker Scotch / Bacardi Rum / Smirnoff Vodka resources. He mixed these resources into that vintage *Guest Of Amit Bhargava* cocktail for his scribe friends, friends who would utilize these all-expenses-paid holidays for some socially relevant reportage that highlighted how Amit Bhargava was serving the poor of this country and how badly the country needed more officers like him.

Sweet!

Now everyone needed friends, didn't they? Even scribes. And having scribes as friends was important because fortunately or otherwise and regardless of facts, it was they who decided what people saw or read these days. And what people saw or read was what they believed. And what they believed was what ought to be true. Simple!

So all you needed was to blend some facts, some fiction, lot of rhetoric and generous doses of the *Guest of Amit Bhargava* cocktail together and you had a good story.

'I do not see myself as a leader, so technically, I do not deserve this honour,' he continued, in a voice that implied nothing of the sort, 'I stand here merely as the representative of Kiritpur's women.

I see myself as an enabler who has merely unlocked the enormous potential that lay latent in these women. Today these women are proud owners of vibrant microenterprises, something that not only gives them an identity but also paves the way for their economic self reliance. We have facilitated capacity building, provided credit linkages and market linkages. *We have given every woman, the power to set the course of her destiny,*' he thumped the dais emphatically as he concluded his emancipating address.

And man, Ketaki Wadhwa was charmed. Amit Bhargava looked every bit like Rudy Giuliani on his Mayoral campaign. Ketaki was a fellow awardee, the Founder and Managing Director of Koshish, an NGO that worked 'with women.'

'Isn't he gorgeous? Doesn't have the stiffness of a bureaucrat!' she whispered to one of the other awardees.

Back from the stage, Amit Bhargava noticed Wadhwa eyeing him flirtatiously.

'Hi! Amit…' he smiled brightly as he introduced himself.

'Ketaki…Good to know about your work. It is really inspirational,' she smiled brightly too.

They talked about women and poverty; Amit about women and Wadhwa about poverty. Ketaki Wadhwa was the lone daughter of retired bureaucrats who in turn had a bureaucratic lineage. Her father had put his links in the fraternity to good use and fetched his daughter's NGO some decent grants from the Ministry of Women and Child Development. Recently, she had also clinched a hefty research grant from UN Women on the recommendation of Abha Aunty—once her father's trainee and presently, secretary in the ministry.

Wadhwa had hired a battery of dark, ponytailed men, and fair, organic looking women who liked to wear Gandhi Ashram kurtas and who liked to think of themselves as civil society—all in lieu of the fat monthly pay cheques they received for their authentic grass roots work. These eco-friendly men and women would routinely travel to villages within a 50 kilometre radius of existing airstrips and photograph poor women in dirty villages. They would document how these poor women went about all that pathetic cleaning, cooking and working on their pathetic little farms and how peeved they were with their pathetic lives. They would then visit dingy, *paan*-stained government offices and capture their abysmal sanitary conditions in photographs—suggesting how patently unfair these dirty buildings were to those poor women. They would then interview morbid, *paan*-chewing government functionaries in these dirty buildings and ask them questions that were understood to have no clear answers and document how these insensitive attitudes posed the greatest impediments to the empowerment of those poor women.

To give the whole thing a context, they would do some Google aided research; necessary copying and pasting from relevant portions of online journals, some armchair theorizing predicated on fashionable concepts like 'choice' and 'voice' and localize the content to give it something of a local flavour. These fancy research reports would always conclude on the same lofty note—some patronizing recommendations to the government on how it could learn from its failures and improve; how some South American country was doing much better (as the internet report had so cogently described), how things that were eminently doable were being derailed by politics, corruption, lack of motivation or insufficient training at the grass roots level.

It was another matter that each of these facts, ideas or problems was already known to those who were expected to act upon the research...even to those appalling, *paan*-chewing babus who always seemed to sport that know-it-all look in any case. In fact, folks in government often knew more; why each of these recommendations wouldn't work in government, how South America was different from India, and why things were the way they were.

They also knew what *exactly* would remedy the problem but it often boiled down to the same question every time—who would bell the cat?

Nevertheless, everyone understood that uncomfortable questions were best avoided and agreed that women deserved both 'choice' and 'voice' in a thriving democracy. These fancy research reports were then handed over to design artists who would work upon refining their look, touch and feel. It was this part that was most crucial to a research report and therefore, though she rarely found time to go through the content, Ketaki Wadhwa made it a point to fine-tune the look and feel part of every report herself—some pictures were to be made to look more poignant, more pathetic or more cheerful as the case may be—their positioning had to be dramatized to heighten the impact, the background colours had to gel with people's perceptions of those colours etc. *Perception is key, people*—that was one thing Ketaki could tell you. And basically because nobody had the time, the energy or the inclination to really go into things, perceptions were the only real things these days.

The aforementioned reports would be always received warmly, with grace. They would be duly marked to the library section of the department where they would go down into posterity, adorning those grand library shelves, longing through their lives that some rare visitor would open them at least once after publication. But that was not how it was supposed to happen. The executable part in the whole story was the *grant* and the content of the report had nothing to do with it. All that mattered eventually was the agency proprietor's personal equation with the Minister and to an extent, with the Secretary.

And in all fairness, Ketaki had been to a few villages *herself*, her PR team had strongly advised her to. She had cherry-picked some hygienic looking tribal villages in Kutch, Gujarat and posed excitedly with those tribal women who had giggled and looked into the cameras coyly. These photographs now adorned the walls of her sprawling office in Greater Kailash, New Delhi. Though she didn't understand either poverty or women that well, Amit Bhargava's emotive speech had floored her.

Amit Bhargava and Ketaki Wadhwa spent the rest of that long evening conferring on their mutual love for poor women. Amit Bhargava invited her to cover his work in Kiritpur to which she replied in an overall affirmative, adding that if she did indeed pay a visit, she could even make a recommendatory presentation on the subject before Abha Aunty, which in turn impressed Amit Bhargava so much that he offered her a drive back to *her* hotel which she accepted (after an initial, 'oh, that's fine'), which in turn led them to another round of discussions on poor women inside his car, which in turn grew so *passionate,* if that is a proper word to use in this context, that things did not quite go the way they were supposed to go and went haywire instead, only leading to a further and curious turn of events which are best not described in detail but which culminated anyway, eventually, in both of them landing up inside *Amit's* hotel room that night.

Now, the endgames. Three months later Amit Bhargava was in Delhi again, receiving the Ministry's annual Swadhar awards that were given in honour of good work in the field of women's empowerment. Two months after that Ketaki's NGO had won another of those hefty grants for conducting an impact assessment of work done in Kiritpur and three other places, on the choice and voice scenario of women in the community. Perfect symbiosis! And when things are so effortlessly symbiotic, a dash of harmless fun doesn't really do anyone any harm, or does it?

PART THREE

Avinash Rathore

The Atlas Who Wouldn't Shrug

Palampur, 2015

'It is only a matter of 25 lakhs, Collector Sahab...*itna to aapke excise wale hi jugaad lenge, bhai...*,' Mantriji chimed in jovially over the phone.

'I will look into it, Sir,' came Avinash Rathore's crisp reply.

Mantriji had pegged Collector Sahab's quota to 25 lakhs this year. Collector Sahab was expected to 'ask' random people—builders, businessmen, contractors, liquor shop owners—to contribute voluntarily, in cash, towards the annual *Vishaal Bhaagwat Katha* which Mantriji had been organizing for four years now.

Nobody knew who in Palampur (Urban) this *Bhaagwat Katha* was organized for. Nobody knew why. So everyone surmised it was for the under-educated and over-religious *voters* from Palampur (Dehaat) who drove into Palampur town in droves during this time, turning the tepid-torpid town into a noisy, chaotic and poster-stricken confusion for several days every year.

And it wasn't that Mantriji couldn't have managed the 'sponsorship' on his own. Oh, his minions could always be trusted to extort much more. They had their ways—bad press against targetted builders, RTI queries on construction works, all-women *dharnas* outside liquor shops—it was all quite doable, folks! But looping the Collector in made things *legit*. It made things *easier*. Such was Mantriji's thinking.

Presently, Mantriji had called Collector Sahab for 'sponsorships' which, he didn't fail to mention, District Collectors in past several years had been *'arranging'* out of their *'quota'* as a matter of *'parampara'*.

As the longest-serving MLA from Palampur, and a seasoned stalwart in party's organization, Mantriji knew Avinash Rathore all too well. Mantriji knew Collector Sahab had no plans to arrange sponsorships or to drop words. Well, any other Collector would happily do that but not Avinash Rathore. And then, Mantriji knew Collector Sahab would not clearly refuse either. Intelligent people choose their battles, you see. So Mantriji's role was to assign him a quota and loop him in. This was crucial to creating an *overall air of acquiescence* that helped everyone, psychologically. Things would get done in any case, Mantriji knew.

Avinash wasn't any less certain of his role in the situation. Things would get done, he knew. The system had a way of delivering with incredible efficiency and unprecedented initiative when *'powers that be'* had to be pleased—not professionally, in terms of how committed you were to your assigned work, but personally, in terms of how committed you were, to their personal causes.

He only had to *appear* involved, then...and not be really involved because his role expectation in the whole *Vishal Bhaagwat Katha* business was to *let things happen*, to become oblivious to the obvious and *let it pass*. That was how good officers dealt with tactical predicaments—by ducking them, by letting them pass.

And this, you could say, was another of Avinash Rathore's several talents. He could read people's minds, and situations. He could exactly tell where people came from, where they intended to go, and he could give them the exact kind of treatment they would *respond to,* not the treatment they *deserved*, not treatment as provided by law, but the treatment they would respond to.

So having muttered several half-hearted *'dikhwa lijiyega's* to concerned officials in response to endless demands which the Bhaagwat Katha Ayojak Manch chaired by Mantriji had been making over the past three days, Avinash Rathore sank back in his chair, bewildered. He hated this part of his job. Though it never seemed like he hated any one thing or loved the other, all credits to his stoic demeanour, but from the white insides of his coconut like heart, things such as these made him uneasy as hell.

Because he had never had free lunches himself, he wasn't into that terrible business of trading favours or scratching backs. He wasn't into gifts—imported watches on birthdays, 24-carat Lakshmi-Ganesha on Diwali—or into accepting free and lavish hospitality. He was very fine with whatever his salary afforded. His salary, and the regular, admissible perks that came with the job—all proper no hanky panky.

All in all, he was an officer with a clean reputation.

Speaking of which, cleanliness is best described as the mutant of honesty most acceptable in our times, the kind all good boys and girls possess necessarily, the kind that safeguards its possessor against moral abrasion but at the same time does not fetter others in the pursuit of their unclean passions.

Clean because Avinash Rathore was not in favour of disturbing the precariously balanced apple cart of interests as long as it didn't do him any personal or professional damage. Clean because he knew that as long as he didn't disturb it, it would never do him any damage. So, ordinarily, Avinash Rathore and that apple cart of vested interests co-existed as peacefully as such things could. It only took something extreme, something totally unacceptable, something that completely failed to pass his various filters of justification that made him kick the bloody cart on its bloody broken arse. That was when Avinash Rathore's pot of shit-tolerance brimmed over and those were times he turned into a tiger that *none* could cage. Every rabble-rouser, every mischief-monger, every proprietor of *gorakh dhandas* in Palampur understood this well and ensured that things never stretched too far. Everyone understood that a zoo tiger out of its cage was more dangerous, more unpredictable, and more intent on a kill than a regular tiger roaming in the wild.

Avinash returned home to the dizzying fragrance of Dior's Pure Poison that evening. His wife was where she was usually found—(before her Dorian dresser)—wearing an off-shouldered, scarlet red Forever 21 maxi dress, her filigree earrings dangling as she crooned a demure, 'Hi! How do I look?'

Some recent chartbuster played in the background.

'Beautiful!' he smiled softly, sincerely and his voice was gentle—the way it always was with Malavika.

'Where to?' he asked.

'Oh there's this art exhibition at Zephyr. Proceeds would go to Adhikaar.' Adhikaar was an NGO that worked with disabled children.

'Hmm…' he sat down on the couch and removed his shoes.

'It feels nice to do something for those children…though I was busy, the Adhikaar people were so keen to have me as the Chief Guest that they even postponed the event to suit my availability,' she continued as she brushed her hair and checked herself in the mirror for the last time.

Malavika had dabbled in modelling and had a masters degree in fashion design. Seven years back, she had chosen to get married over working as Assistant to Kritika Paul, the renowned Delhi-based fashion designer.

'Where is Ananya?' Avinash enquired. Ananya was their three year-old daughter.

'She is coming along…they had a special invite sent for her, from one of those special kids themselves…. Isn't that cute?' she gushed.

Avinash looked at Malavika and smiled. She smiled back—her coquettish smile imparting a pink hue to her porcelain skin. Malavika Rajawat Rathore was hot, smouldering hot. A trophy wife.

At 5'8" with a body to die for, she looked more like an *haute couture* model than an awfully bored Madam Collector.

Ardalis who worked at the Palampur Bangla (a sprawling 20 acre *haveli* of the erstwhile British Resident) could swear that they had not seen a more ever-so-ready-for-a-ramp-walk Bai Sahab inhabit their old *haveli* before. So all they could do was lower their eyes as their awe-inspiring Bai Sahab sashayed down the long corridors of that sprawling *haveli*, oozing charm, flicking her perfectly bonded, auburn hair off those smooth shoulders every once in a while, rolling her kohl-stained, chestnut hued eyes at silly nothings Ananya would blabber and giggling that patentable giggle…it was too much gorgeousness for any ordinary *ardali* or *aayah* to stomach in one life…and the most intriguing part was that no one had ever (not even at seven in the morning when even *the* Irina Shayk could afford to look less fabulous), no one had at any time of the day seen their Bai Sahab's fabulous self in a form less fabulous than her supremely fabulous self.

Malavika's sartorial choices were a permanent subject of kitty party musings and drawing room reflections amongst elevated *sarkari* ladies who had a flair for the finer things in life. Though they were something of an outrage (we are supposed to dress modestly, aren't we?) in the initial years, the Fab India-clad older ladies had gradually made peace with the bold bodycons, stylish peplums and pencil dresses which 'Mal' carried with immense élan. For the younger ladies, 'Mal Ma'am' was a veritable style icon who had unleashed a fashion renaissance of sorts with her classy pumps, matching totes and perhaps most importantly, that enviably chiseled body whose juvenescence neither pregnancy nor age seemed to wither.

Baby Ananya entered now, wearing a dress the same colour as her mother's and matching accessories to boot. Finding her father home, she flashed an adorable smile and raised both her hands, signaling him to pick her up. The father and the child engaged in some baby talk.

'So when do I expect the ladies back?' Avinash enquired.

'In an hour and a half, maybe. Lasagna is on the menu tonight. Wait for us!' she said breezily.

Avinash loved 'Italian' cuisine and his wife made it a point to frequently include it in their dinner menu—a meal they always had together. In fact, after Malavika's mother learned about her son-in-law's love of the cuisine, she had arranged for an Italian chef who agreed to spare an hour every evening to initiate Malavika into the culinary art. The classes went on for two months and one could safely say that the chef learnt as much about fashion as Malavika learnt about cooking in those two months.

Later that evening, as they sat down for dinner, Avinash shared with his wife how the *Bhaagwat Katha* was proving to be a pain in his neck.

'Now this guy who is some small fry in the party wants two hundred and fifty *gamlas* from our *sarkari* nursery to 'beautify' the *Bhaagwat Katha* venue! Bastard will not return even *one,* you bet...I am sure he will simply sell them off...', he muttered, 'and these bloody organizers expect us to strong-arm that Brijwasi sweet-*shopwala* into distributing free *halwa* for seven thousand people who will attend their event everyday...I mean these guys are parasites!'

Malavika's frowned in sheer contempt for parasites.

'Sheer hypocrisy!' he explained, more to himself than to anybody else, 'this is madness of the highest order, and the best part is everybody is enjoying it...everybody...not just the organizers, even our officers...they are all in it, all of them...everyone will have their pound of flesh...so there's no point...', he struggled to find the right word here at which point, as if on cue, Malavika sighed, and quickly added, 'Obviously, there is no point,' which was, in fact, the whole point.

Avinash Rathore, the one not given to speeches or diatribes, more so against the scheme of things, was speaking. And when Avinash spoke, Malavika knew she had to simply play her part. She did that meaningful nodding, the gentle holding of the hand, the looking into the eyes, the assuming of that expression of total empathy…basically, she mustered every necessary reaction that would make the subject under stress feel so completely loved, so totally understood, and so fully taken care of that he would throw open the several doors to his guarded soul upon your person, one by one, and would unburden himself upon you, by and by, and you would, very slowly, lovingly, and with utmost care, lull him to relief, or peace, or sleep. That was it.

Three terms.

Unconditional positive regard. Empathic understanding. Unqualified acceptance.

Now what more could a poor husband ask for, people?

What more than (a once over at Malavika), THIS?

If you have any doubts, get up, and ask your husband.

So.

Malavika knew that 'in all marriages, the roles must gradually come to a reverse. The one who started as the little girl *must* become the big mummy. For all men wanted in the end were mothers, not their mothers, necessarily, but mothers nonetheless. And that was also what all mothers wanted of their sons. Now it was up to you, to your skills and your talents to determine which mother your husband eventually turned to…getting the picture?'[9]

And as you would have guessed, given the above basics, Mal did not appreciate the present fuss in society. She hated what all the Sheryl Sandbergs of the world had done to the great Indian family, the family of Colgate smiles and wedding songs and Kodak moments, the family where perfect people essayed their perfect parts to perfection and everybody adored everybody else all the time and there were no role confusions or failed expectations or crazy *diljale* moments.

She didn't exactly understand why people couldn't make peace

[9]Taken from one of Malavika's several speeches on 'Marriage and You.'

with love these days, why couples were always drifting apart, why women were always complaining about their maids, their in-laws, and their husbands, in that order? Why the live-ins, why the divorces, why the extramarital flings? Where was the contentment, people? Where was the joy of giving? To cite Black Eyed Peas' famous refrain, where was the love? Why couldn't people grow in love, give in love and live happily ever after? Like she and Avinash were…[living, quite evidently, and growing (only emotionally, of course] and giving…in their perfect universe…and yes, she would always quote this only true example of a perfect marriage…) but why on earth was this whole Happily Ever After thing becoming such a Bermuda Triangle?

So to contribute her bit towards mending chaotic society, to bring in the healing touch of love and happiness, she advised. But her advice wasn't the unsolicited, government supply kind that ladies like our Mrs Jain were wont to. Oh she understood all about demand-supply and product pricing and brand building. So her advice came only during those one-to-one appointments, behind closed doors, after the subject under stress had laid her situation bare, and no, no, no hiding stuff, please, for deliverance could only be had upon total submission, and only when *that* had happened would Mal utter her first word, her 'analysis' that came from a place the subject had never been to before…which led the subject under question to her Eureka! Moment, only after which would Mal, upon being requested and prodded further, and after having paused at all the necessary places and sipped a glass or two of water in between, present her advice.

The advice that enjoined upon the young ladies of the world to get hold of their lives, to mend them and to set them rolling on the high road to Happily Ever After. She gave them an insight into the life skills young and educated women so lacked these days, in their confused and misguided pursuit of pseudo independence. And though the ingredients of her advice weren't any different from that familiar how-to tonic—'your husband under your thumb'—that generations of *dadis* and *nanis* across the Indian subcontinent have shoved in scoopfuls inside the pretty mouths of young brides, Mal liked to flavour it up for the modern palate, throwing in secular words like love and contentment and inner peace, making it more appetizing for the pseudo-liberated souls of these times.

'Relax, darling. You have so much on your shoulders,' and here she gently massaged his overworked shoulder now, 'and yet you are true in whatever you do...' and now the soft eye contact, 'I guess all we can do is put in our best...and that's what *you always do* and I am so, so proud of you,' Malavika concluded now, cupping his hands with such phenomenal care as would give Sahara Airlines a run for its money.

But Avinash was mildly irritated. Only mildly, though. Because too much of the same thing, even a good thing like sweetness, or understanding or love (yes, too much of love, even), could sometimes be plain pain, cloying and sticky, like tea too sweet or soup too creamy. Something that deserved a time-up, sometimes. But this space was not designed for any time-ups. It was an untiring effort here. Malavika had just said what she always did in situations of this nature. She repeated the same lines, verbatim, with such rehearsed intonation that the speech played out in *his* mind even *before* she spoke. Like your in-laws complaining that you aren't calling them as often as you should. Something *that* predictable.

To be fair to Malavika, she couldn't think of anything else to say. Not because she didn't understand stuff but because the stuff bored her no end, and because the stuff had long ceased to hold her interest. Now if one didn't like a place one found oneself in, one could move! One was not a tree! Notwithstanding this simple logic, she had always found the men in her life—the IAS officers—cribbing about their work, cursing the things they did and still doing the same things. Not changing them. Not doing them the way they would want them to be done. So she had long concluded that her role was that of a sprightly cheerleader for the proverbial Atlas who wouldn't ever shrug but keep complaining of the tremendous weight on his shoulders.

Her father, Vachaspati Rajawat had retired as Secretary to Government of India, Ministry of Power few years back. He was now at the fag-end of his post retirement tenure as the Chairman of National Electricity Regulation Commission. Back at her home, her father would often ponder over aloud, the roadblocks to power sector reforms or some other sundry sector reforms to an apparently 'all ears' mother at the dining table and Malavika would instinctively know her mother was more interested in figuring out whether her novel experiment with mint leaves in the *Gatte Ki Sabzi* had turned out well.

But unlike her mother, Malavika was a doting wife. Oh she was in *awe* of her husband. So to compensate for her inability to appreciate her husband's workplace woes, she indulged in promoting causes: the cause of the girl child, of 'special' children, of the poor and of every other conceivable disadvantage whose cause somebody in civil society cared to champion. For nothing—neither the encomiums showered on her million dollar looks, nor the overawed stares of Palampur's *nouveau riche* who had not seen a real memsahib before—nothing was more important to her than an appreciative word about one of her several associations in Avinash's presence.

For truth be told, she was as enamoured with Avinash's persona today, in the halcyon peace of seven years of matrimony, as she had been during the sunny days of their courtship.

Polite but Firm

Delhi, 2008—Seven Years back

It was on a propitiously pleasant evening in the sweltering May heat of Delhi that Vachaspati Rajawat got a call from his friend and batchmate, the then Chief Secretary of Rajasthan. It was an act of reciprocity, one could say, for Rajawat had helped secure a management seat for his batchmate's son, pulling a few strings, as it were, few months back, and now that Rajawat was scouting for a suitable boy for his own daughter, it was only proper that his batchmate should repay in full measure.

And his batchmate had rung in some good news indeed, a fortuitous find, as he called it. A promising Rathore boy who had made it to the IAS that year had called on the Chief Secretary during the latter's visit to Pratapgarh—the place where the boy hailed from. The very tall and very handsome boy who by the looks of it seemed to hail from a *normal* Rajput family (a plus), not only had impeccable Officer-like Qualities, *OLQs* (another plus), and spoke immaculate English (plus ++), but also had, (and here comes the deadly bit) completed *B-Tech in Computer Science from IIT Kanpur*. Now, considering the sheer fascination that Indian parents in general and Indian in-laws in particular have for the words so italicized, one can only imagine the kind of flutter all this information was creating in Mr Rajawat's heart. And if all of this wasn't incredible enough, his batchmate now produced the deal-clincher, having saved it for last, like all good story tellers do. This Rajput boy was all of 24.

'24?' Mr. Rajawat performed a mental double take.

'On record,' his friend confirmed.

Mr Rajawat, thoroughly wary that such a scenario did in fact exist (because manufacture of vintage items as these had stopped since 1957, he being the last piece, because Pratapgarh somehow reminded him of corny conmen out to inveigle decent families like his, because distrust was his first and natural response to any neutral piece of information), now sat down with his famous mobile phone in one hand and a notepad on the other and began his ultimate quest to get a low down on this chimerical entity—Whoever Rathore.

One call followed another, the old-boys networks in Rajasthan and Delhi were reactivated; former professors grilled and current neighbours interrogated, secret recces (of the boy's house) held, covert ops (on his recent movements) coordinated; the Collector and SP, Pratapgarh thus having duly deliberated, and not having found the description exaggerated; issued the NOC which when communicated, had the whole of Rajawat household truly, madly, deeply elated.

Yes, a fortuitous find it was.

And a call to the boy's father was now in order.

'It is our honour that you called Sir...' came a hesitant, gentle voice on the other end of the line. Too gentle for a public-hardened Bank Manager, ruminated Mr Rajawat even as Rathore Sr. continued, with some more hesitation, '...but I do not think Avinash is thinking about marriage right now, Sir. He is all of 24.'

Now Ranveer Pratap Rathore, Avinash's father, a General Manager with the United India Bank was quite an antithesis to his name. Tall, frail and asthenic, he spoke slowly and softly, his voice ever a caress and the gravest provocation could elicit from him, nothing more than a faint sigh of forgiveness. Thirty years of dealing with a crazy public and a crazier management had not quite damaged him the way one would expect, the way it had damaged his interlocutor at the other end of the line.

'Of course, Rathore Sahab,' Mr Rajawat let out a fruity laugh now. 'I suggest you go through my daughter's wall (obviously the FB wall though the obvious wasn't mentioned)—I mean let Avinash do that—there is no hurry.... My daughter is 23 too. And you know how kids are these days...all they need is time...so let them have as much of it as they like...I should tell you that even I got married after a two year long courtship, Rathore Sahab...it was way back in 1982,' he laughed more at this unsolicited piece of interesting information.

Sensing the loss of words at the other end of the line, Mr Rajawat ventured a little further, 'my point is we can get the kids talking...' he said as if the kids in question had fought and needed to talk, 'in any case it is always good to have the right connections in this service. That's the abstract of the 30 years I have put in, Rathore Sahab. Please tell Avinash to let me know if he *ever* has *any* problems at the Academy or in the cadre allocation business. The Academy Director and Secretary, Personnel are close friends. I will drop a word.'

Avinash and his parents broached the subject in earnest only after Mr Rajawat had called for the third time, enquiring if Avinash liked the profile. Driven to the proverbial wall, Avinash went through Malavika Rajawat's wall pictures perfunctorily that night. And what a wall that was! No less than a *Femina* portfolio complete with close-ups and long shots and photo credits to some hotshot fashion photographer in Delhi. Credits were also due, by default, to the connoisseur in trick photography—Mrs Rajawat, who had not only guided the hep photographer through some really good shots but had also run a thorough profile scan and debugged the bachelorette's profile of all potentially hazardous materials (photographs a little too bold for the current (matrimonial) context, comments (originally and unthinkingly made by her male friends) and found a little too irksome in the present light, some eyebrow raising updates made during emotional highs or lows etc.). These machinations apart, one had to concede that the girl *was* a stunner. He felt flattered (like all boys must) and mildly enthused (as those from IITs do, with stuff far inferior).

By the end of the second week, Avinash had become Avinash *beta,* and the Rathores had received a lavishly assorted consignment of Dibella's Italian cookies and Lindt and Ghirardelli chocolate and Ann's House Exotic Nuts for their twenty-sixth wedding anniversary, Mr Rajawat had shot down his wife's let-us-bedazzle-the-Rathores-with-two-personalized-champagne-bottles idea with an airy veto. Had it been a regular family, this show off of things to come would have only been proper. But the Rathores were simple people. Overdoing things could scare them.

More importantly, he had got his aspiring designer *beti* and the newfound bureaucrat *beta* to talk. During one of the calls he made to Avinash, he had casually handed over his phone to the daughter, who as baffled by the suddenness of the move, was as clueless as Avinash about the stuff to talk about.

It was, of course, another thing that Malavika who had been all marry-a-babu-at-23?-I-am-not-*that* dumb-Pa had conveniently executed a nimble volte-face and was studying the prospects of work-at-home designers after her second conversation with the Irresistible Rathore.

Cutting the short story shorter, it took Vachaspati Rajawat all of two months and two days to push his Godfather like offer down the throat of the Rathore household. It was an intelligent combination of Machiavellian manoeuvre—persuasion, persistence, sweet talk and the veneer of humility—that helped him achieve the unthinkable feat of getting Avinash to actively consider a marriage proposal at an age when three-fourths of his cohort was still struggling to find its own little space under the sun.

Mr Rajawat proposed a quick engagement before Avinash left for training at the Lal Bahadur Shastri National Academy of Administration (LBSNAA) in Mussoorie. He understood that the risk associated with not closing the deal, not taking Avinash 'off the shelf' before the commencement of his training at the Academy was too much to take.

The Academy was notorious for clinging to its old-fashioned *esprit de corps* refrain which dysfunctionally resulted in more intra batch matrimonial alliances than anything else of permanence. He was particularly apprehensive of the 'manipulative sharks'—the lady officer trainees—who would find an easy prey in the extraordinarily handsome and 'chivalrous'[10] son-in-law of his. He had always loved Mussoorie, but now, seen in this new light, from the eyes of an anxious father-in-law-to-be, he *abhorred* it.

How he wished he could cancel the training course itself... the baby with the bathwater, whatever cliché it was. Because the training hardly made a difference, did it? People already knew the academic stuff the Academy told you about and three months of conducting oneself properly wasn't going to undo a lifelong training in not conducting oneself properly, and, and, and....

Now, now...Mr Rajawat knew he wasn't being fair. The father in him having squarely vanquished the officer in him, he was seeing visions of the Himalayan trek, the village visits, Bharat Darshan... he was seeing visions of those notoriously salubrious environs of Mussoorie that offered too much of an opportunity for romance... and all its associated wretchedness, an opportunity for young lady recruits to sneak into gentlemen officer trainees' hearts.

And this heart business was all very messy, had always been, and in Mr Rajawat's current opinion, lady recruits were all shrewd, mess-loving creatures.

Speaking of his current opinion, as a matter of illustration, he

[10]Chivalry—an old world quality—now mostly found in females.

had recently advised a friend's daughter that 'clinching a matrimonial deal with a fellow trainee is the best case scenario for a lady IAS officer in this country.' The girl in question having failed spectacularly in finding a groom for herself during her two-year long probation period in the service had returned ignominiously empty-handed to her home and hearth which in turn had launched Mr Rajawat into these sagacious reflections.

'This is a fact. Take it or leave it. The matrimony market does its own price discovery. The market value of a boy freshly recruited into service soars, that of a girl falls freely.' He had gone on and cautioned the girl that she would die a spinster (the last three words, die-a-spinster, had been rather high pitched, made to sound like a death knell) if she continued to harbour exotic notions about love, liberty and choice *while still in the service.*

'Administrators cannot afford to carry ideological baggage,' he had spoken in glorious outrage, 'fashionable ideologies are for bystanders and onlookers—their business is to criticize, ours is to execute. We have no choice but to be reasonable—compromise and settle for what is rational.' Predictably, his friend had cold-shouldered him since then.

In his daughter's case however, he had taken some disaster risk mitigation measures, so to say…some spadework to ensure that Avinash's anchors remained firmly moored in the alliance even as the sharks swirled about the poor boy at the Academy. He had leveraged his good offices at the Department of Personnel, the nodal department dealing with the cadre allocation business, to ensure that Avinash got a 'comfortable' cadre, thereby precluding the possibility of him being later lured into marriage by some conniving lady OT in the prospect of moving to a better cadre. These were standard tactics in the Academy.

As a final preventive measure, even as the Rathore household failed to fathom the urgency palpable in the otherwise unhurried ways characteristic of Mr Rajawat, his polite but firm insistence on a 'quick little ceremony' made way for the big, fat engagement ceremony, seven days prior to his departure for training to LBSNAA in Mussoorie.

PART FOUR

The Academy

(Mussoorie, 2008)

Babus and Babuas

Mussoorie, 2008

Late August is a time ideally suited for the commencement of training for a fresh batch of All India Service recruits in Mussoorie. Pleasant weather, clear skies and the verdant environs provide a splendid setting for young, sprightly men and women to mingle and forge bonds. The first day of training, set apart for completion of the joining formalities was abuzz with thrill and concomitant commotion. Men and women socialized in groups, eager to make the right noises.

A day before, these starry-eyed youngsters had stepped across the threshold, that exalted threshold, and taken their first steps towards a new life. They had arrived, yes, after months and years of what seemed like indefinite drudgery, they had finally arrived. That one moment had made all the difference.

A moment before, they were all equal—aspirants—cutting *chai* sipping, *hawai chappal* clad aspirants who did a one-by-two with tiffins, notes and magazines and sustained, not their own families, but those of the photocopy *wala*, the *chai wala* and the internet café *wala* in Mukherjee Nagar, aspirants who discussed nuclear deals while cooking DBC (*dal-bhaat chokha*) together, in a single cooker and sat through those infamous six hour General Studies' sessions in the claustrophobic basements of Rajinder Nagar, without any loo breaks in between, aspirants who were conditioned to survive in what ILO would call dignity-denying conditions of living and given to walk listlessly about the congested by lanes of those IAS ghettos, with big dreams in those anxious eyes, aspirants who hurried through the normal procedures of life rather absent mindedly, with one, only one question looming large in the background—what if not this time?

And when those dreaded times did arrive, and they arrived sooner than later for most, excepting some lucky bastards about whom more shall be discussed later, when the time which wasn't the time one was hoping for *came*...one was only left wondering at the sheer resilience of the great Indian middle class...the way it overcame...some went to bars and danced to cheap songs and drank themselves to numbness, some cried themselves to numbness, others indulged in borderline illegal stuff to the point that they became numb, the more uplifted ones commenced their *n*th reading of *The Alchemist*, folding pages (already folded) along newer planes, underlining lines till there was nothing left to underline and feeling brave when the 'when you want something...' bit came...repackaging all that grief into a stoic, new resolve because one Paulo Coelho has said that just because *you* want something, the whole fucking world *must* conspire to let you fucking have it....

One only had to look at it as a disinterested third party, and one would surely fall in love with it...the sheer beauty of the Indian middle class's reset button in all its morning after glory....

All in the name of that 'charm of the civils.' The lower middle class on its eternal quest to jump over to the upper middle class... the mental equivalent of an upgrade from third AC to second AC. Same service. Same let-us-go-shitting-and-peeing-over-the-tracks loo. Same brown blankets. Same pillow covers. Just a higher price tag.

And when the higher price got its legit RFID tag, the moment UPSC came out with those results every year, the moment that 'made all the difference' as some pompous people would tell you, some lives would be thrown into a different orbit altogether;

an orbit where everybody not in it saw them with that look of *otherness*—not awe, not pride, not jealousy...no, no, no...it was not as simple—it was an air thick with *you don't belong here, mister* that moved into their lives and stayed, from that moment onwards. The moment that came or didn't, in a few marks here and there.

But all that ordeal was passé now. A new day had come, a new life. The Foundation Course for All India Service recruits had commenced.

The Academy mavens made a big deal about *Shishtachaar* (etiquette). The very first day, soon after the completion of joining formalities, a motley crowd of engineers (those from IITs and those not from IITs), MBAs (those from the five IIMs and those not from the five IIMs), doctors (real doctors, veterinary / homeopathy doctors and outright bogus PhD doctors) and vanilla arts people (the *desi* ivy league and JNU and the rest) was treated to an hour long tutorial on the bread and butter of life in the Academy—*Shishtachaar*.

Now the Academy had its own shrewd ways of stealing people's thunder...of showing people who thought they were meant for higher places the exact kind of places they were meant for. Keeping with the tradition thus, for the first fifteen minutes of the plenary session, an assortment of snapshots and videos from the previous day, the reporting day, played on the big screen at the Academy's Sampoornanand auditorium.

They looked like utterly ordinary boys and girls, all of them, too ordinary for that large, pretentious screen, that had been all keyed up to play some daunting pyrotechnics of youthful brilliance, but was disappointed with what it got instead. No makings of statesmen or strategists here, no prodigious trappings of greater glory. The video showed how the famed Academy library was gloriously devoid of OTs on the very first day—a pointer of things to come; and captured the infernal location that was densely packed with OTs instead—Ganga Dhaba. It showed OTs strolling about the Academy like footloose holidayers, chatting idly, laughing gracelessly, some zappy obscenities captured on record...one thirty something OT yawning hard, scratching his crotch, a big lady OT scuffing about in dangerously shredded jeans and a *de facto* bodycon top that...oh that just came open at the seams...shucks! A gypsy of a girl smoking away in a corner, and being checked out by few boys poking each other and choking with unexplained mirth...a fat, balding man—no he couldn't be...an OT? Oh yes...Voila! AIR 4! He, in his ragged loafers and a T-shirt that read 'I am kind of a BIG deal....'

The faculty member's eyes narrowed in amusement as he turned to face the audience. And what a dapper turn it was, what a dapper face! All salt and pepper and silver cufflinks.

'Those you saw there...' he pointed swankily at the big screen behind him, his voice dripping with theatre, 'Do they look like people who will run this nation?' he paused and deftly raised an eyebrow, 'the *crème de la crème* of our country?'

The supposed *crème de la crème* shifted uneasily in their chairs, a few of them felt like coughing for no good reason, there was a random catcall, someone snorted loudly, three people from the front row stood up and headed for the washroom, few throats were cleared.

'To me, they look like ordinary people, *the mob*.' He shrugged, unperturbed with the reception.

'The first rule of authority is that you must *look the part*, you must look and act like men or women in command. And as Ella Fitzgerald put it, it isn't where you come from, it's *where you're going* that counts...therefore, we must learn what being an officer *is* like.' He smiled slyly.

A few bored sighs. A few more throats in need of clearing. Two more loo calls.

'To begin with, we don't jeer at things. We aren't those lewd frontbenchers found in small town cinema halls, are we? So we don't jeer at things...we either accept them, as they are, or we change them...Right, Mr Samarth Chauhan?'

Mr Samarth Chauhan, the occupant of the sixteenth seat in the twenty-first row of the five hundred seater auditorium, the as-yet-undetected source of the first catcall made in the first session of the Foundation Course was now at the focus of three hundred and thirty-six pairs of anxious eyes, an unenviable position, definitely, which he only tried to slip out of, inadequately, with a lame, 'Sir?'

'All I am saying, and you being an outstanding student of Ethics must appreciate, Mr Chauhan, is that at no time or occasion should an Officer Trainee conduct herself or himself in a manner that is *unbecoming of an officer,'* he smiled, rather pleased that his eye-sight, his memory and his painstaking study of batch profiles had all held him in good stead.

And he was happy he had invoked the First Commandment—thou shalt desist from acts unbecoming of an officer—at the most opportune moment, the onset of his lecture.

'You must understand that the word 'Officer' carries *weight*, it sure has certain visual dimensions...and auditory connotations... but more than those...' he said, his hands making precise cutting movements in the air to signify the light and the sound and weight, '...it carries a certain weight and it implies certain values...now any guesses what those values are?', he looked around hopefully, as if for an answer and then like any wise professor would, pre-empted a dubious answer by supplying the answer himself, 'courtesy, decency, morality, of course...the word Officer must inspire confidence and trust, wherever it goes,' he paused, having explained the contours of that albatross which was to be hung around each of those three hundred and thirty five necks that evening, which in fact was what the ceremony was all about.

Now he came to the General Restrictions and Provisos. They were to 'speak quietly' in the OT lounge and elsewhere, seat themselves like adults, not imbeciles (never to sit in the lounge with their legs up on a table, never to sit like the lady in the fifth row, eleventh seat—'Yes, yes...Ms Vijayalakshmi R., MSc Agriculture, having a good time?'—was sitting, slouching on her chair), not to form their own parochial groups, never to talk with their hands in pockets or on hips or crossed in front of the chest or scratching any other inappropriate places on their own or on their interlocutor's bodies and to generally avoid talking shop. They were not to gossip.

'It is said: Cultured people talk about ideas, where uncultured people talk about other people,' he said, somewhat half-heartedly, faintly realizing that this was one department the Academy faculty could do with something of a refresher course on, phenomenal gossip mongers that they all were.

Anyway, OTs were expected to avoid controversial subjects which inevitably led to heated discussions. While applauding guest speakers, they were not to thump tables, 'hoot, groan or cat-call' which were all quite uncivilized and impolite forms of appreciation but had to clap, 'with your hands only', he emphasized.

They were to behave equally tolerably in hostels. Inappropriate dressing, name calling, noisy parties drunken revelries were to be avoided and music, from 2200 hrs till 0600 hrs, was to be heard through earphones only, speaking of which, no earphones were to be carried on morning jogs on which all mobile phones also were banned, the excessive use of which was strictly discouraged in any case owing to they being a potential health hazard in addition to being a nuisance. No mobiles were thus to be carried or used ever, in the academic block, or in the Library, or the Officers' Mess or in the auditoria and in the leftover open spaces lest those devices should meet irredeemable confiscation.

Next, ceremonial behaviour.

Gentlemen were expected to stand when ladies enter a room, and officers were expected to stand when seniors enter or on being introduced or when the seniors themselves stand up (which in fact meant that male officers had to stand all the time). Shaking hands on being introduced was the usual norm but not the norm with ladies unless the lady made the first move (which in case she didn't, in larger groups, created this clumsy scene where everybody stood shaking hands with everybody else, steering clear of the odd lady who had to make do with folded hands, like the carrier of some communicable ailment).

Nevertheless, gentlemen, a good handshake was important. It was supposed to be firm and continue for at least three seconds. Introductions were expected to follow a protocol: Gentlemen were to be introduced to ladies, juniors to seniors and young persons to old, with the exception of VIPs, to whom others were always introduced. The reply to "How do you do" was "How do you do" and never, repeat never, "Quite well, thank you" or "Fine" or anything other than "How do you do."

'Finally, it is only natural that intelligent men and women have an opinion of their own.' The faculty member dilly dallied with his words as he came to his concluding remarks, 'however, courtesy demands that if you *have* to disagree, you do so in an officer-like manner. Remember, brevity and tact are two keys to an educated expression of dissent,' he concluded.

The process of turning *desi babuas* to English *babus* had thus, eventually commenced. And what a painstaking process it was, how excruciatingly agonizing, for an English institution to waddle through the un-Englishness of the present times, the plebeian egalitarianism of it. And it wasn't about the language people. Appreciation of or fluency in that language was hardly a concern, the real concern was the culture around the language, the propriety, the augustness of Englishness...it was the loss of it which seemed to hurt the Academy's soul the most.

In its heyday, the Academy had seen inmates who had culture running through their lymph. They looked elegant in their rich black *bandhgalas* and thick rimmed glasses, poring over *The Discovery of India* or *Gitanjali* in the good old Academy library in a cultured quiet. They spoke with poise. They moved with grace. They ate with elegance. They apologized if you as much as threw yourself at them. They were ever so correct. Yes, that is the word. Correct. And they were every bit the intellectuals. The Liberal Elite. The English, August.

The elitism was all gone now, up the thin air, and all that was left was the slurry of liberty, an irreverent and shameless kind, the kind that had gatecrashed in with its notoriously inebriated cousins—equality and democracy—averaging everything out in the process. Averaging. The watchword of these times. Everything had to be averaged out, cut to size, cropped from the tops, made more or less equal.

So they were accepting sons and daughters of peasants, rickshaw pullers and *kirana* shopkeepers these days: those low society arrivistes who sneered at culture and ridiculed tradition for they had none, those who mutilated everything English, everything august there was about the Academy by calling it *labaasnaa*, by reading such assaults on English Literature as *My Dil Goes mmm...* (yes, that's the name of a proper English novel) while apparently attending to lectures in their classrooms, and of course, lest the unforgettable should be forgotten, by *whistling*—can you imagine people, OTs whistling, and gyrating around the stage like some small town *baraatis*—when a female folk dance artist took some creative liberties in dancing to a popular (and admittedly distasteful) Bollywood number amongst a presumed emancipated audience during one of those weekly cultural concerts. And don't you get the Academy even started about the spectacle there was on and around the stage that evening. Don't you even mention it. The very nadir was hit, people. The visuals of it were so disastrously disastrous that the Academy had to run remedial classes in *Shishtaachar* for the rest of the course that season.

The Officers' Mess too was a Hall of Shame these days. No more Excuse Mes, Thank Yous, Will you pleases here. No more niceties and throwaway phrases. The OTs struggled with cutlery on formal dinners and recalcitrant lemon tarts flying off hapless plates because their handlers couldn't cut the 'damned biscuits' was a common sight around the Mess these days. Back in 1961, this would have been sacrilege. Now it offended no one. All it elicited were a few amused snorts, or uproarious laughter, and on those rare occasions when a faculty member was an embarrassed witness, a look of helpless guilt on his countenance.

Speaking of lemon tarts, the formal dinner was a quintessentially English ceremony that had endured. The New Age OTs did not understand the rationale for this custom, just as much as they did not understand the rationale for any other. Could anything be more ridiculous than a ceremonial meal where everybody could start eating only after one of those two lamps over the Guest Of Honour's chair had turned green, and worse, just give up eating the moment the other lamp glowed red, even when three-fourths of the diners had barely managed to get that tricky piece of chicken on their forks?

But the Academy loved ceremony and the owners of Ganga Dhaba, the very *desi* eatery that served more *paranthas* to the OTs in a month than the OT mess did during the course, the place where one could pull one's legs up on the chair, even on the table and smoke like a chimney and swear dirty in Hindi, the owners of that Ganga Dhaba were the happiest people on the evenings of the formal dinner.

While the *Shishtachaar* class did not regale her as much as it seemed to have regaled the others, Nethra, as usual, felt overwhelmed. Too many people (the same kind of people). Too many assumptions (the same kind of assumptions). Too much noise (the same kind of noise). She had actually been looking forward to the Academy, to all that lay on and beyond the other side, and it had all promised to be so romantic...not the *romantic* romantic... but the elevated romantic, you know. She had been counting days, literally, and now...what had she even expected? A new world? A different planet? Suddenly it seemed like the past two months had been so much better.

She had spent the last few of what had been basking-in-the-afterglow-of-hard-earned-success months for her batchmates, in the quiet company of her *Dadi* and her German Shepherd at their ancestral home in Jammu—plucking *babugoshas*, *chikoos* and peaches from their huge backyard orchard, taking the dog for solitary walks up the river Tawi and reading old books in her *Dada's* old study.

She hadn't made smashing appearances in news channels, capturing the collective imagination of aspiring IAS families with her winsome ways, she hadn't subjected the boys in Rajinder Nagar, Mukherjee Nagar and Jia Sarai to the collective torment of longing by appearing on those 'Meet Our Stars' panels which sprung up in those IAS ghettos at this time of the year and finally, there weren't any lump-in-the-throat-inducing, guts-grit-glory dimensions to her success story either…cover story stuff…so all in all, Nethra Kaul was a pretty nondescript also-there in the fresh crop of achievers till the morning of August 27, 2008—the first day of training, and *only till that time*. For it was precisely then, as she proceeded about the joining formalities quietly, accompanied with her Tamil roommate Madhavi, that heads started turning.

'Same course?' boys asked each other in surprise, wondering internally how could something like *that* stay hidden under wraps for so long with all those modern communication modalities. Long before setting foot in the Academy, everybody in the batch had met everybody else, virtually, the assessments had been done, photogenic-ally and the ratings more or less finalized, consensually. Courtesy, Orkut. It was only physical verification that was now in progress. And not to put too fine a point on it, the pervasive feeling was one of the kind of let down which invariably comes with meeting in flesh and blood, people you who had hitherto only known online.

But now with such podium finish material making this last minute entry they were forced to reconsider the rankings again. They could do *that much* for her. They had large hearts. Hearts that warmed to visual treats like watching this epitome of human form sit in her royal blue saree, for the morning meditation sessions in the amphitheatre, against the backdrop of the snow-clad Himalayas and the spectacular green of the Kalindi lawns. Things of beauty are, after all, joy for all.

Avinash first saw Nethra sitting across the breakfast table with her roommate in a rather secluded corner of the Officers' Mess. It was that over-romantic song that was playing that moment—John Denver's *You Fill Up My Senses*, which for no apparent reason is called *Annie's Song*—and Nethra seemed lost in the rains in the forests of those springtime mountains, blissfully oblivious of the springs she was inducing in some unsuspecting hearts.

The early rays of the morning sun diffused through the large window panes to illuminate her serene face as she glanced across the window at the distant Bunderpoonch and Badrinath peaks, bathed in pristine morning sunlight. Avinash looked at her transfixed for a moment, telling himself that he was not at all transfixed by shoving more *moong* sprouts and baked beans into his mouth every once in a while, but his eyes were hell bent on insubordination that morning, they kept wandering back to the same corner of the mess, and then, as it must happen, by force of telepathy or by the script of the Hindi film scriptwriter, she looked up, only to find him gazing at her and thus their eyes met…a full two second mutual checking out was followed by an equally mutual and deliberate looking away, aimed at trivializing the moment as just another of those harmless, perfunctory glances.

And did anyone hear that rumbling in the lady's heart? Did anyone see that tiny thaw in the little mound of ice?

In her twenty-three years, manoeuvring through the tumult of teenage and a relatively placid college life thereafter, Nethra had been thoroughly disappointed in men. Most she crossed paths with did not 'measure up' to her construct of 'the perfect man'. They were all either too self absorbed for her 'pride' or too 'shallow for her intellect', and in most cases, devoid of that 'force of personality'. It had happened to her, what too much reading of English classics could do to people, the irreversible damage of woolly-mindedness.

'Do you have a boyfriend?' This was the third question Madhavi had asked her as they introduced each other in their shared room.

'No,' Nethra had replied, almost guiltily.

'Thank goodness!' Madhavi had cried, almost ecstatic, 'I have had so much of that love struck roommate ordeal that I now dread having one….'

'What? A love struck roommate or a boyfriend?'

'Both!'

They had laughed smugly and in that moment, Nethra had known that she had found her perfect partner in crime, a straight-out-of-a-Jane-Austen-novel character who, like her, suffered from the great social impairments of modern times.

They 'couldn't just try boys on, casually…' Nethra shrugged, '…like on-sale clothing at a Westside store or something,' Madhavi added,

'…or have careless, offhand, irresponsible affairs,' Nethra added further, '…with not-bad-but-not-so-good-either men,' Madhavi completed, gesturing the so-so-ness with the top of her palm, 'something that a lot of the girls in the engineering college,' Nethra had attended did.

'Yes, exactly, same with,' Madhavi's college!

In less than half an hour, they were completing each other's sentences. These Soul Sisters quite simply lacked the moral courage much needed for the afore-described risk taking prevalent in present times. Basically, that familiar *I-am-so-good-that-the-world-doesn't-suit-me* situation, multiplied by two. Basically, two *very* good girls.

'How can one inflict such an outrageous insult upon oneself… and on the self esteem of another person?' Madhavi, the eldest daughter of a cooperative bank manager in Coimbatore, would wonder.

So they hadn't yet found the perfect men they had been looking for—men who would enthrall them, men who would be as men ought to be, men who would hold them in awe for the rest of their lives, men who did not exist. Nethra and Madhavi were hopelessly hopeless romantics.

And then, when it happened, whatever 'it' was, 'it' took her completely, like a raging storm that swallows everything, obviates the need for reason and makes everything look small and insignificant before its power. After that brief visual encounter in the OT Mess, Nethra realized she was subconsciously looking for him everywhere... at breakfast for which he would breeze into the OT Mess sharp at 8 every morning, or during tea breaks between classes when he would be found nodding importantly at one of the seven nerds in his coterie (which seemed to be perpetually discussing important things anyway), or during lunch break, in the newspapers and journals section of the library where she would spread the no-nonsense pages of *The Hindu* before her person, even as he fixed his dour gaze on the orange, business-like pages of the *Economic Times* sprawled before him, or at the gymnasium which he would hit at 7:00 PM IST, every evening, come hell or high water, after his hour long squash session in the sports complex.

There was something strongly magnetic about this man—not merely his sharp, angular face and deep, dark eyes—there was something more, something on the inside, something she had always looked for and failed to find in an Indian man before... something Madhavi strongly felt was the, 'Piscean female's natural and irresistible attraction for the Scorpio male.'

To make things worse, he was that rare commodity amongst men in general and engineers in particular—a spectacular orator. A rare commodity that Nethra along with the rest of the batch plus three female members of the faculty and their five teenage daughters had totally fallen for, all over again, after the second week's course debate; the debate audience had been so perplexed as to what to attend to—that voice, that logic or that presence. It had been *that* overwhelming.

And his charm was precisely this. He could floor you from the podium one moment and completely forget about it the next. He remained utterly oblivious to the spell he cast around, speaking little, laughing lesser and never so much as crossing that fine line that separates pride from hubris.

For the first time in a long time thus, Nethra Kaul was consciously experiencing that natural female desire—the searing desire to attract a man, to hold his attention and the fact that he was one of those rare men who did not appear to notice her at all was turning out to be all the more overwhelming for her.

And then, if there wasn't enough on the plate already, Avinash played the guitar too, and (don't kill me, people, fiction is what this is), he played it well. Girls and music buffs would hover around a shy Avinash in the OT lounge, where he played select renditions during the weekend musical evenings organized by the Performing Arts Club. Though he mostly strummed the guitar, sometimes, he would sing too, and his favorite piece was Falling Slowly by Glen Hansard.

Now the predicament before Nethra Kaul was this—she had to be at these events and not be there too. She had to come because not coming was not an option. She longed to see him, hear him, and watch his long, shapely fingers string at the cords. But she was too much of an Elizabeth Bennett to give herself away, so easily, so unilaterally, so without that Victorian wooing she considered compulsory. She had to put up a deliberate act of indifference thus, an indifference matched by his.

So during those weekend evenings, as his audience swooned wow-Avinash, once-more-Avinash all around him, she would absorb herself in reading *Poor Economics* or writing her law assignment on Torts and Civil Wrongs (her *n*th attempt, for the record) at least fifty meters off the event site in the OT lounge, donning her I-am-too-busy-with-serious-stuff-to-be-bothered-with-lightness look with all the imperviousness she could muster, trying her best shot at not seeming like a part of his swept over audience.

And he would reciprocate in equal measure, never looking even perfunctorily in her direction...but then, as it must happen, the farce would give itself away soon, as soon as he began to sing *Falling Slowly*, because invariably then, at some point into the song, their eyes would meet in a momentary gaze...before they broke it again, preferring the convenient cloak of indifference for as long as it could veil them from each other.

Ethical Dilemma

Their first real conversation literally happened at the discussion table. It was the fourth group discussion panel which both of them along with five others got grouped for. Now GDs were troublesome things. In the mental cartons of OTs, they were items marked FRAGILE! Because you either got through them *safely*, or you didn't get anywhere at all. In between these extremes, you always ran the risk of slipping through the crevices of illogical reasoning, grammatical gaffes, that last minute usage of Hindi phrases, pronunciation blunders, and such other grotesquerie that qualified, that went down into posterity and that your batchmates *remembered you with* through their lives; stuff that would throw up enduring epithets for its victims and fables that would remain alive in the batch's collective memory, inducing nostalgic laughter during reunions.

The discussions were moderated by V. Ravi, the lone Keralite in the Academy faculty and an iconoclast of sorts, particularly notorious with the touchy how-could-he-speak-like-that OTs for his unabashedly sly, some would call risqué, sense of humour.

'So *gurrrls* and *bowiz*, the *sub-juct* on *tay-bre thiz yeevening*', V. Ravi rubbed his hands in glee, '*yis—Aii-Yaay-Yess: ya* career or *ya* service. The *pa(rn)el musta rimumber* it *huz wall of tuandy mi(rn) udes.* No *yextra poyinds* for *stray-(rn)ing yuar vocarl courds. Yiffucktive* or *uderwise yis* for the *djury* to *dis-cyde*...for *stardurs, yid (rl)ooks (rl) ike a veesual treada* for *oll ov* us!' V. Ravi smiled meaningfully as he announced the names of panelists for the evening's discussion. OTs hooted. A visual treat, for sure.

Nethra's heart missed a beat as her name was called out immediately after Rathore, the Invincible's.

'Relax, you've been a *great* speaker all your academic life, Nethra,' Madhavi, ever the coach in this relationship, said with a conviction one would not ordinarily expect from a month-old friend.

'But are you really prepared for this? To take him on, here and now?' Another voice, startlingly husky and coming from somewhere inside her head, teased gently.

'Weren't you telling me about that Doon School debate, Nethra?' Madhavi continued on her bucking up spree, 'where you had trounced former PM's…or was it was former President's…well somebody's grandson? That was national level *ya*, this is like…' Madhavi struggled for the right word here, attempting a recall by feeling air with her fingers, '…what is that North Indian concept?… *chhawanni* right, this is such *chhawanni* stuff, *ya*.' The misapplication of the North Indian concept and its majestic pronunciation had Nethra in splits for a moment. But just then, the *chhawanni* stuff in question took his seat on the stage and all hilarity went up in thin air.

She had expected Avinash to lead the discussion, and to open it, something he had always done on previous occasions. He didn't. Instead, he gestured an all too eager Gopal Krishna to take the lead.

'Hi friends!' Gopal Krishna waved generally, with the air of someone opening an entertainment show discussing celebrity affairs. 'I don't see much of a point here, really…IAS as a career is meant to serve, I mean…serve the citizens and all…' he shrugged and smiled witheringly and then, as if struck with some sudden realization about his current location, added, almost as an afterthought, '… of course we must serve the poor people of this great country who look to us for…rural development…poverty alleviation…and women empowerment…is the only way…to end poverty.'

This turn to the argument, unexpected as it was, raised quite a few eyebrows. Where was this even coming from, like? What was happening? Wasn't this supposed to be about some career-service dichotomy? Was this creature nuts?

But no. Gopal Krishna wasn't nuts. He was a *P Hech D* in Crop Science, the sort of crop doctor who knew that words like poverty alleviation, women's empowerment, grass roots issues and human resource development were like tea, you could serve them anywhere, anytime, and generally, no one would mind.

But of course, here, people did mind. An eerie silence followed the opening remarks. Panelists looked at each other quizzically.

Thankfully for everybody, the eye candy stepped in now, to save the day and the discussion.

'Now *that* is pretty…tangential, I would say…' Avinash smiled now, '…off by a huge margin,' he smiled fraternally at Gopal Krishna who smiled back conspiratorially even as the audience swooned and laughed, respectively, at either pair of feet. Adorable adorableness.

'Because if you ask anyone walking down the street,' he cleared his throat gently and continued, 'beyond hundred mmetres of this Academy, I am sure he will tell you that IAS officers are narcissists with little interest in anyone's welfare other than their own….'

'He will tell you that they are *ruthless careerists* who will sell everything there is to sell about themselves—sometimes, even their conscience, just to keep moving up…' he narrowed his eyes darkly.

For no apparent reason, Cadbury's Dairy Milk Silk jingle was playing out in Nethra's mind at this moment when she quickly paused it and added thoughtfully, 'But are we discussing perceptions around here? Are we discussing what a man down the street thinks we are? I guess we ought to know first what we think we are, what we are all here for?'

'Touché!' Avinash cocked his head in Nethra's direction, looking into her eyes, 'the man down the street isn't important…but if a perception exists, someone ought to have created it!'

'Is it your argument that *all* IAS officers *are* amoral careerists…

out there to sell themselves cheap?' Nethra returned his gaze, brazenly, brave-heartedly.

At which, Avinash Rathore smiled his mysterious smile.

'*My* argument is that each one of us is a selfish and rational person...and what each one of us *wants,* more than any fancy poverty alleviation nonsense we dish out to *please* an audience,' he paused for a deliberate moment, 'is to be seen and be known and be talked of as powerful and successful bureaucrats.'

She noticed he had honest eyes. With his square jaw and chiseled face, the overall sense of his face was strongly masculine, but his eyes were beautifully kind. And man, she had *time* to notice all these things!

'Do you mean that each one of us here seeks success *only,* at the cost of doing the right thing?' she asked now.

'What *is* "the right thing"?' he retorted.

'You want me to *explain* what things are right things, for an IAS officer?' she asked back further.

'Yes, I am curious...', he shifted in his chair a little, like he was really curious, 'and hopelessly ignorant, enlighten me please,' he said faux deferentially and all she could see was that faint smile on his lips.

'Well...to let truth prevail, to be just and honest *in every situation*...these things would be the right things for me.'

'Truth, justice, honesty...all relative concepts...and all very fickle...variable with time, place and...circumstances. Don't you think truth for one man could be untruth for another? What seems like justice to me might look unjust to you. Then how would an ignorant officer like me, you know, know if a thing is the right thing to do?'

He looked at her indulgingly, 'Wouldn't I be better off getting my career right, with all the truth, justice and honesty I can summon? What do you say?'

'You seem to suggest a contradiction between being ambitious and being good…' deterred from her objectives by his constant gazing, Nethra now pulled out the most offhand face she could.

'See…now we have another concept, being good, what is good? Would you please elaborate?' he shrugged.

'Why do you talk in absolutes? *There are no absolutes!* Everybody here is fighting his own battle…with his own premises…and everybody here is intent on winning it.'

'Oh really!' she snapped back, 'do we have a battle going on? That's news! Because I was told this was peace time. I was told we were all supposed to be working together,' she turned to look at Gopal Krishna now 'as he rightly said, to serve the people of this country….'

'And you *think* we all are doing that, right?' he asked with a look of intensity only Shahrukh Khan, in all his glory, could match.

'May be we aren't. May be, you are right. May be, there is actually a mental battle going on here,' she said, marvelling at her own underutilized talents for hyperbole, '…a battle where everything's fair and *veracity* is the last thing on people's minds… but if battling each other was all we had to do, if a single-minded pursuit of professional success was all we had to offer, why did we even come here? I mean government is the last place you come to make a glorious career, right? All of us had *options* if all we wanted were glorious careers…so why are you and me stuck here, then? In a place this unrewarding, a place as, dare I say, indifferent to competence as government?'

'Indifferent to competence!' he raised his right eyebrow deftly, 'that's quite a judgment, I would say. Do you mean that government doesn't reward efficiency, that it has no place for competent people?'

'Quite the opposite…I am curious why would a go-getter waste himself in working with an employer who doesn't even pay him ten percent of his market price…this isn't smart, this isn't clever… and we all are rational people…aren't we?' Nethra looked at him.

'What could be anyone's problem with smart and clever

go-getters working in government, delivering results and being successful too?' he looked right back, his voice a clear baritone.

'Delivering results is a relative term...like truth, justice and honesty are...' she retorted.

'Yes it is...but far less relative...because results, unlike justice, can be defined and measured,' he smiled.

'And fudged too...' she replied.

'Yes...but not as much as truth and justice *are* fudged,' he replied.

She took a full two seconds to recover.

'This debate is not about *whether* we deliver results,' she said in the most presidential tone she could manage, 'we *all* deliver results. It is about *how* we deliver results...whether it is only power and privilege and career growth that drives us...', yes, yes, she knew it, she could see it clearly now...she simply had to drive down that high road of self-righteousness now, '...or whether we feel driven by something *more*, something *different*...do we feel driven to act because we *actually* want to serve?'

He was quiet for a moment, not in awe of that little motivational speech, but apparently, in admiration of the full, peach crush lips which had collaborated to deliver it so succinctly. People surely had a sense of timing around here.

He looked away quickly, and narrowed his eyes into near slits, 'the how is not half as important as the what—the result—if you do not get results, you do not count because you do not make a difference...and you are here to make a difference, right?'

'Right! We exist for results...the IAS exists to achieve that elusive ideal called 'Results'!' she said, imparting a definite momentum to each of the above words, 'I concede, but while you achieve your 'results', what is the template you work on? What are the values that guide you?' Oh there was to be no stopping the high priestess of righteousness now, she was on a roll.

'Alright, tell me, what was your motivation to join this service?' she asked now.

'My motivation was the same...' he replied.

'Same as who?' she asked almost simultaneously.

'Well...same as most of us.'

'Speak only for yourself, *Prince*!' she snapped back.

That was bad. The 'Prince' elicited quite a few hoots and it delighted one and all, because it had sounded so un-Nethra-like. The only one not delighted was Nethra. *What was wrong with her*?

Avinash tried, inadequately, to ward off a smile. He had just been coronated the *'Prince'* of Foundation Course, an epithet that was to stick to him, just as Philosopher Warrior would stick to Mrityunjay, and Ice Princess to Nethra.

'Thank You,' he smiled in acknowledgment of the 'Prince'. 'As for the boring subject of motivation...well, the power to influence and bring change...the kind of exposure and decision-making...it comes very early and expands as you grow in your career. That is what drove me towards this service,' he looked at her engagingly, his cool eyes studying her.

*You would look even more awesome with a stubble, Prince...*a voice in her head observed. Nethra pressed her lips firmly and made a really stern face.

'You sounded like that good boy facing the UPSC interview, Mr Careerist,' she said with a strange mixture of sombreness and iciness only she could pull off, 'you know my question—what is that one factor that guides you when you take your momentous, change inducing decisions?'

'Rationality...cold logic!'

'Rational for your personal interests or rational for public interest?'

'Public Interest! Here goes another unguided missile...the most heinous acts in history have been committed in the name of public interest, Princess!' he replied.

Nethra ignored the volley of hoots and upped the severity of her expressions.

'So you are driven by rationality that suits your personal interests?' she enquired.

'I did not say that,' he replied.

'But you said you did not believe in whatever passes off in the garb of public interest,' she half-smiled.

'That does not mean that I subscribe to decision-making to promote personal interests...' he retorted.

'What do you *subscribe to*, then?'

'I have already said that—logic and rationality.'

'And I asked you a supplementary you have been evading.'

'I do not see any contradiction between that which is rational and that which is in public interest.'

'Oh, you do! You can't be so naïve. And supposing that you are, let me show you the contradiction right away,' Nethra could take the narrative from here, people...she could just see the future from here.

'Imagine a situation where the Minister in your district, a strongman, the don of land mafia is constructing an upmarket mall that violates land control and development regulations...imagine that you know it is an unauthorized construction and you also know that he is the most powerful minister in the Cabinet. Imagine that he has requested you to lie low...the relations between you and him have been pretty cordial thus far,' she spoke slowly now. 'Imagine all this and now tell me, will you lie low, Mr Careerist?'

Avinash looked at Nethra with no decipherable expression in his eyes. And then she saw in them, stainless steel. No, he will not do a lose-this-to-win-that *Bazigar* he had been trying till now with her. He will not give her a walkover.

'I would proceed as per rules...if something is illegal, it is illegal,' he said eventually.

'Which means that you will bring that Mall down?' Nethra looked at him for corroboration.

'I would proceed as per rules...and if the rules require me to tear it down, I will,' Avinash looked right back.

'But don't you see a contradiction here? If you bring it down, you incur the wrath of a notorious Minister who will, you know, nip your career in the bud a risk no careerist would take....'

'There *is* no contradiction. Rationality doesn't mean committing flagrant irregularities for the furtherance of one's ambitions.' Avinash Rathore retorted, apparently without much conviction.

'Flagrant. Furtherance', Madhavi whispered into her neighbour's ear, 'big words to defend the indefensible. Hah!'

Nethra looked away, at the other panelists now, 'Well the reason I brought this situation in was because I wanted to highlight the conflict between personal ambitions and public good that we face in decision-making every day,' her voice that of a scientist explaining the results of a highly successful experiment to high school students.

'And the way we resolve this conflict defines whether we are careerists or public servants...public servants who are expected to have the courage to stand up for what is just and fair, even if it isn't the easy way out, even at the risk of their career graphs missing the desired trajectory,' she said smugly, confident that she was going to have the last laugh.

The other panelists had been watching the volley with much interest, and at the cost of their own participation in the event. V. Ravi was observing, amused.

'We seem to be losing sight of the *object* of the debate here,' Avinash came back, 'the question here is not what the IAS ought to be or what it should be, something you have been intent on discussing, the moot question is *what is it* about today? When I say we are careerists I am not saying it is good or bad to be a careerist. I am saying that a majority of us *are* careerists today... and it is a fact...take it or leave it...a fact which you, unfortunately, choose to ignore in an irrational quest for moral upmanship. Only for the sake of elegance, you are trying to sound morally pure,' Avinash frowned.

That last line was Marcel Proust's. And she loved Marcel Proust. Nethra bit her lip.

And he had frowned. It was a first in his three debates. No one had ever been able to unsettle Avinash Rathore. Imperturbability was his strength.

And unfathomability was hers.

And the two, like gin and tonic, worked best when together.

And now, Nethra Kaul had unsettled Avinash Rathore's cool visage…what a relief!

Or was it relief?

'Alright…I am being theoretical…what's your practical point?' she asked coolly.

'That this service has produced dozens of powerful bureaucrats who have made glorious careers out of clinging to powerful politicians—they are the role models, you see—those who have done nothing remotely akin to 'public service' as you define it, but nonetheless have outshone their sober peers…. foreign assignments, stints in international organizations, the best and most powerful positions…you name it and they have had it.'

'Likewise, there have been several remarkable officers too…' she reasoned.

'Yeah…those who compete for the lifetime achievement in observing elections award, I am sure…', he continued amongst supportive chuckles. 'Let's not cheat ourselves, alright? We all know it is the powerful bureaucrats who become the face of this service—role models for the younger lot who are keen to tread the same path—because it is glamorous, convenient and an ego booster like no other,' he said.

'Well that brings us back to square one—the question I had put to you at the outset—what brought you here? A quest for glamour…convenience…fame…power?', she looked at him darkly.

'I agree that a large number of us do regard intellectual honesty as irrelevant, but the reason why we *still* exist, Mr Careerist,' she said, looking at him, 'is because of those lifetime achievers in observing elections, because of those strong though powerless people who cannot bring themselves to be indifferent...and it is this irreverent minority that has managed to retain the hope and faith and expectations of those who look upon us for justice, Mr Careerist, despite quite a few gnawing at the roots of this very faith. It is easy to be a careerist—you stand to lose nothing. It is because of those 20% who do not care about losing, who do not fear losing most of what they have that the institutional faith hasn't *plummeted* to *abysmal* lows it would have otherwise.'

Plummeted. Abysmal. Oh the grandiloquence of morality!

With the ringing of the fifteen minute alarm, this soliloquy came to a much deserved halt and as was the norm, V. Ravi entered the scene with his signature look, that of inquisitive amusement.

'And never shall the twain meet!' he smiled beatifically, rubbing his palms together.

Fixing his gaze on Nethra, he added 'And now that you have identified yourselves as one of the silent minority and our Prince as the microcosm of all that has gone wrong with this service—you are representatives of the 'intellectually dishonest' majority as you very conveniently desrcibed him, let me suggest a tentative conclusion that brings the Prince and the Princess together'.

Sexual undercurrents were always pervasive in V. Ravi's jibes at his panelists. A pro at detecting budding amorous interests as he was, the chemistry between the two had ignited his curiosity.

'To wrap up the panel's unfinished business, let me say that the IAS is a service dominated by careerists. At the same time, let me assert categorically that it is a place that also allows modern day Knights and Spartans to exist—and sometimes, given a bit of luck, to grow in its fold,' he signified the growing, not very accurately, by some rolling motion of his palms, 'further—and I would like Ms Kaul to please give it a thought—a careerist is not all black, a Spartan not all white. We come in several shades of grey and we change our shades with time, experience and circumstances.'

'And on this note,' V. Ravi concluded, 'Waste no more time arguing about what a good-man should be. Be one...any guesses?'

'Marcus Aurelius,' Nethra and Avinash replied, at almost the same moment.

The jury adjudged Nethra as the 'Speaker of the Week.' Like they had any other choice. Out of five, Nethra got three votes, Avinash got two. As the gathering dispersed, batchmates thronged to congratulate Nethra, and Avinash disappeared in his important looking coterie once again.

'Speaker of the Week! *Aiyyo*! You trounced the invincible Prince, *da*!' Madhavi rushed to hug her.

But Nethra wasn't all that elated. Rather, a sadness was slowly growing on her. Merely for the sake of elegance, she had tried to sound morally pure, and expectedly, she had won. Now, she felt strangely unsettled, she felt anxious, she felt lost. She had never found herself so arrested in anyone's presence before and this unnerved her all the more for it was grossly dissonant with her self concept—her self image of a strong, self-willed person.

Back in his coterie, Avinash felt uneasy too, and it had nothing to do with his loss at the debate, or with the fact that he had been unsettled at a debate. It had to do with the fact that *she had unsettled him*. Worse, the only thing that calmed him down these days was her mere presence in his vicinity. It was, as if his existence and her presence were coeval and coterminous functions. In the moments she was around, when they shared the same space, he lived; in all other moments, he merely *waited*. Nethra was a mystery and the more he tried to pull away, the more she pulled him towards herself.

A fortnight into the Foundation Course, Avinash had casually requested Mrityunjay, his closest friend, and the only nerd in his coterie hitherto privy to the fact of his engagement—to keep that knowledge to himself.

'Nothing, man...I just do not want to be labeled, you know... would-be son-in-law of a powerful bureaucrat...you know how the stereotypes operate here...' he had explained casually.

But Avinash was *unaware* that he was merely a puny *pyadaah* before Vachaspati Rajawat, the *badshaah* whom he could never transcend. The very evening of their engagement, Mr Rajawat had called the Academy's Director—his batchmate—to break the news and to request that his son-in-law be taken good care of. Not mentioned but implicitly understood was the embedded request for surveillance, whenever deemed necessary.

The Director was cooperative. He had congratulated Avinash in the very first Counselor Group Meeting, spending a large part of that hour long 'interaction' in heaping effusive praise on select players of the illustrious Rajawat *khandaan,* with terms which normally went with such praise—Mr So-and-so Rajawat was an outstanding officer and a very dear friend, Ms. Someone-or-the-other Rajawat was a remarkable lady, very graceful and very competent, etcetera and had welcomed him to what he sinisterly referred to as 'the gang.'

The two lady OTs in the audience had exchanged looks and appeared visibly crestfallen for the rest of the meeting, with the immediate consequence that within the next four hours, the whole clan of outraged sharks was cursing the mean *jaat* of Indian men—gutless, greedy, pliable invertebrates who weren't men enough to take on similar-statured women as wives, of course. Most of them had sobered down by the next morning though, and accepted this mini-heartbreak as an inevitability—it wasn't really possible to attend the same course as Avinash Rathore and yet not be smitten by him. That was that.

And yet, because there are always a few who somehow manage to stay in this small world and still not stay in it, the only girls who missed the news that day, the only girls who missed every other news flash anyway were Nethra and Madhavi—the outsiders.

As for Avinash, he did not quite know why he had asked Mrityunjay what he had asked him. It seemed ridiculous to him, plain irrational. For he knew that he was engaged to be married, that this detour, this fixation…well, this whole *thing* was nothing. *Nothing.*

He knew that he would outgrow it, like one is supposed to outgrow things like these, the way these things are meant to be grown out of…he knew that six months down, or may be six years down, he would look back and laugh about it because none of this would matter *then*, and none of this was thus supposed to matter, *now*.

He knew that he could never, not that he wanted to, go back on what had been done. He knew it had been done. And that it was all quite simple. And that there was no reason to complicate it. No reason whatsoever. He had been talking to his fiancée every day, thirty minutes of honey-dipped conversation twice a day, apart from several messages and e-mails they exchanged on a daily basis. Basically, he was too *involved*. There was no space for confusion.

But without his knowing it, the virus of confusion had struck. And with the group discussion, the first symptoms had made their appearance. He now feared that he might discover in this woman something he should not, he ought not to if his life was ever to settle in the placid calm of matrimony with Malavika.

For even if everything went as planned, this discovery would make him regret the choices he made and the 'might have been' would haunt him forever. He ardently wished that this woman would turn out to be a disappointment—that apart from her entrancing aura and quiet charm, apart from those mysterious, black eyes and that majestic aquiline nose and those tantalizingly full peach crush lips, there would be nothing in her for him to want her. He wished she would let him down. He did not wish to want her.

Little Women

As would be clear by now, within the conch shell that LBSNAA was, Nethra and Madhavi lived in an insulated shell of their own. Both of them were lucky rookies—academy slang for those who cracked Civil Services Examination in their first attempt—and for all practical purposes, fresh out of the academic oven. They had been brought up not to *live* in this world but to *excel* in it, and *only* to excel in it. Their rearing had happened in *anticipation* of that eventual triumph, in terribly protected, extremely artificial environments that only allowed bookish values and ideals to seep through, and none of the regular crudeness, thus leaving them terribly ill-equipped to deal with the routine-ness of a routine world.

The Academy was only a continuation of that protection, that artificiality. For where else could you have nature treks and "morning reflections"[11] embedded into life's routine? Where else would they serve you memos for missing PT sessions?

The two girls loved the regimen. They were those unbelievable species (found in every batch) who were perhaps born with the queer ability of getting up early on weekends when they loved to set out trekking on hitherto untrodden trails, inhaling deeply,

---

[11]Morning Reflections is an Academy ritual which consists of practices like the batch sitting around an open air theatre in the morning, listening either to fairly loud but heavily soul stirring classical music gleaned from the internet by keen type OTs (the only loud thing allowed on campus) or doing a meditation routine steered by some awe inspiring Yoga teacher dressed all in white or similar cultural stuff aimed at generally elevating one's general state of being.

taking the sylvan sights in with their breaths. On some evenings, they would walk down to Happy Valley—the Tibetan settlement nearby—or relish Tibetan Thukpa at Kalsang, the famous Tibetan eatery down the Mall Road. On some Sunday mornings they would trek up to Benog Hill. They would first walk down to the Tibetan monastery in Happy Valley and then take Hathipaon road to reach Cloud's End.

Cloud's End offered the setting (the mist, the mountains, the clouds and the valley) where they could sit at the edge of a precipice, feeling the wind on their faces. They would read, talk to each other, and listen to Aruna Sairam or Nithyashree Mahadevan or Sudha Raghunathan—all Madhavi's favourites who Nethra had only heard of before, and now come to like.

On other mornings, they would jog up to Lal Tibba, have a plate of freshly cooked and deliciously served Maggi at a makeshift tea shop and take a lazy walk back thereafter. Mussoorie was dotted with these Maggi points, little teashops sitting enroute hillock tops. The shops sold chips and biscuits and tea but more importantly, they served hot and spicy, 'double masala, tomato special' Maggi which could send tears running down one's cheeks.

They had so much to tell each other, so much to experience that they never felt the need to socialize with others. But even when they had not deliberately planned it, they already had a gang—the Tamil gang. The 'gangs' would invariably emerge within the first month of the beginning of every Foundation Course. The emergence of primordial clannishness was only to be expected in a group where people as different Parmigiano Reggiano and snake gourd were tossed together for a shared experience.

The most unabashedly cliquey and internally egalitarian was the Tamil gang. This gang enjoyed friendly relations with neighbours—the polite and mild-mannered nuns and monks from Kerala, the Secret Society of extraordinarily clever, all male Andhraites and the perpetual right-of-first-refusal claimants over Cauvery waters, the Kannadigas. Several members of these primary groups had regrouped into smaller sub groups—the Anna University group, the IARI (PUSA) group, Nairs-in-Chennai, Naidus-in-Coimbatore sub-cliques, the Ilayaraja fan club.

The thread that bound them together, and this thread held the Tamilians even stronger together, was their shared dislike for the Academy. They hated the place, the regimen, the weather, and most of all, the food. They missed their *sapad,* and curd rice, which made them querulous and they cribbed. The Tamilians dwelled in reveries of good old Chennai, the taste of *aapam* and *adai*, the tamarind rice at Annalaxmi's, the idlis and gun powder at Murugan's and they consoled each other over packets of *murukku*. They debated the state of Karpagambal Mess and whether Harris Jayaraj or Ilayaraja or AR (Rehman) was the best music composer of our times.

Just as North Indians couldn't do without that mindless stereotyping of all things that lay south of the river Narmada (and geographically speaking, south of the river Mahanadi and the Vindhya ranges too) into the *Sambhar-Idli* omnibus, the Tamilians too *loved* to typecast things that lay north of those rivers and mountains into that ignominious omnibus—*North Indian*. It was an insult, if you asked Nethra, within that group—the very term, the monstrosity of the things it implied, the utter lack of refinement it stood for—oh, it was so far beneath them as to not even discuss it properly.

Yet, this communal contempt for North Indian-ness was what kept them warm through those notorious Mussoorie winters—this cultured gentry that knew how to say what it wanted to say without actually ever putting it into words. And the general drift of what they wanted to say was this—North Indian men were basically quite lecherous, weak-minded, and on a perpetual lookout for women to rape or berate; North Indian women were all, well, Punjabis—fat, fair, loud, showy, and not quite educated.

But all this and more was more than made up for by the

simple fact that the Tamil boys *loved* Nethra for more or less the same reasons that they loved Tamannaah (Bhatia). This made the Tamil girls a little anxious, but true to their values, they stayed always ever-so sensible, ever-so dour, and always too wise to take offence at such little frivolities.

Despite the intellectual snobbery and cultural warfare, it was the Tamil subgroup that Nethra and Madhavi eventually got co-opted into—Madhavi as an authentic Tamilian and Nethra, as Madhavi's 'plus one.' And this was one thing about the gang—once they issued an OK Tested certificate, once they let you in, they were a very *fair* lot.

They who conferred on you, the privileges of being one of their clique, they stood by you, tall and firm in times of need, they were those whose true temporal value, only circumstance and time revealed.

The Marathis [*Jai Shivaji!*] were the most clannish by far. Every Marathi *Manus* (who could speak Hindi with an equal eloquence and pidgin English too) insisted on public usage of their *maatrubhasha* in mixed groups, at dining tables, in cafeterias, throwing all *Shishtachar* mandated caution to the winds. If you had the misfortune of finding yourself at an intimidating all Marathi table in the OT Mess, and looked around in incomprehension as they traded cliquey jokes in Marathi, all you could expect to get was a brief, '*Kaay Zhaala*?' You were obviously expected to know what that meant. The '*Kaay Zhaala*' was to be responded to with an innocent shrug and, '*Kaah Naahii*!' (nothing!). God was indeed in his heaven and all was fine with the world.

The other group was that of *jholachaaps* from JNU. Comprising severally of sulking communists, habitual critics and perpetual agitators with bleeding hearts, the 'intellectuals' as they liked to think of themselves, nursed the grandiose notion that somehow, they understood everything better than the rest. The deeper, more complex, more humane, more philosophical aspects of every issue with its myriad socio-cultural/politico-economic/psychological ramifications were clear to them simply because most of them had read The *Communist Manifesto*, *Second Sex* and *The Algebra Of Infinite Justice*, and could of course, speak in English about obscure concepts they themselves did not quite understand, in a manner that others too could not quite understand…what if they did not know what Laplace and Fourier Transform were!

One of Madhavi and Nethra's daily rituals was the post dinner walk to the Company Garden. The weather at this time of the day would usually be pleasant, with a mild breeze blowing through the *chirs* and pines. The close to two kilometre-long stretch of road leading from outside the Academy gate to the Garden was an idyllic track lined on both sides by tall pines and lit inadequately by the moon. The tourist traffic to and from the place would ebb by this time and the tranquility of this boulevard would be disturbed only occasionally by some native of a nearby village whistling blithely as they cycled past. The only sounds would be those of crickets singing, the only glimmer that of fireflies playing hide and seek with each other.

'Let's go out for a walk,' Avinash nudged Mrityunjay, seconds after spotting the two girls walking towards the Academy gate.

'Walk? Are we really getting *that* old, Avinash?' Mrityunjay seemed baffled, but agreed nonetheless. Avinash proposing a walk was a product of probabilities, an event so rare as to deserve a little investigation.

Fifteen minutes into the walk, having summoned to his "RAM", associated events of the past four weeks and having arranged them into logically consistent permutations, Mrityunjay achieved the desired mental clarity. So, this was it. He took a deep breath and shook his head lightly.

'An 8 AM breakfast, gym after squash, don't-tell-anyone-about-the-engagement, and now this…a quiet walk amidst the pines…all is not right with the world, partner!' he remarked casually as they strolled down the street.

Avinash shrugged.

And then as if on cue, the two girls appeared on the horizon, on their way back. Things fell silent. Paths were crossed, glances were avoided deliberately.

'Shall we turn now?' Avinash asked Mrityunjay after a while. His friend smiled at this display of innocence. Of course they could turn now. The purpose of the walk had been served.

'From a certain point, Prince, there is no turning back…', he turned to look at Avinash now, 'that is the point that must be reached.'

Avinash was quiet. They stood like that, facing each other, man to man, for another few seconds.

'You are reading too much…into things' Avinash replied, without looking at Mrityunjay.

'Should I not?' Mrityunjay asked.

Avinash looked away. The last thing he wanted at the moment was an insight into his state of mind.

'This is what…like our sixth year together?' Mrityunjay said, clear in *his* mind that an insight was what was now in order, 'and this is a side of you I haven't seen before, Avinash…I have never seen you melt the way you do when *she* is around.'

'I *melt* before her?' Avinash said, offended, apparently not at the '*her*' but at the *melt*.

'Of course…you did melt down at the G.D. last week, didn't you?'

'We've barely exchanged a *sentence* beyond that G.D.' Avinash blurted out disbelievingly.

'And you would like to…very much…because you are so… irretrievably attracted to her.'

'*Irretrievably attracted*…where do you even find such words Warrior…in the *Amarkosha*?' Avinash said, alluding to the current joke about this Sanskrit thesaurus that Mrityunjay's father had gifted his son upon his selection, presumably considering its undeniable suitability for the kind of stuff his son was destined to be up against.

'And I am *not* attracted to her...' Avinash continued his protest, 'I mean, not in the way you suggest...yes, she is different, a little mysterious...that is all. I mean it is just a silly, fleeting crush that will...get crushed...the way all crushes do,' he said. In doing so, Avinash verbalized for the first time, the line of reasoning he had been invoking in self defence.

'Now come on, Warrior, men committed into a relationship *can* have an occasional and harmless crush!' Avinash said in a failed attempt at sounding very reckless, very casual, quite unlike himself.

Mrityunjay, whose face now wore a look of solemnity far in excess of what the occasion demanded, saw herein the necessity of inserting one of what was famous all over IIT and now the Academy as Mrityunjay Ranjan's Everyday Moral Lectures.

He commenced thus, 'I won't advise you, Avinash, because you are more—let's say—*worldly wise*—and you haven't sought my advice either. But I would rather speak once and for all *today* and *never* bring up this subject again...', (now this last bit was to be proved wrong precisely a week later, not that it mattered right now), '...I have observed both of you for *over a month* now and I hope it is just the way you describe it...' he let out a half-sigh here, though it must be mentioned that he was not at all the sighing type.

'The woman in question here is,' he turned to look at Avinash, 'or at least *seems to me* a little different, a little more...sensible and... quite possibly, very sensitive too. If you ask me, she seems to be going through a similar, silly crush herself...so,' he exhaled again, 'I trust you would do the right thing, Avinash.'

'Philosopher Warrior's grand take on sense and sensibility!' said a smiling Avinash, as he wound his arm around Mrityunjay's shoulder. Mrityunjay smiled too. And he let Avinash digress to other mundane stuff—Fannie Mae and Freddie Mac and the global economic crisis—on the rather longish walk that night.

Back in his room, Avinash tried to put his mind off what Mrityunjay had said but he couldn't. Was his attraction towards her that obvious? Was she too going through something similar, as Mrityunjay had just observed? Beyond a point, there was no turning back…Mrityunjay had said. Was he moving towards that point? What would happen if he did? Did he even want to do so?

As believers in Fate often say, everything that appears random in life is simply part of a grand plan that moves you inch by inch, towards your destiny. In large part this would stand true for the lives of these three individuals.

In the long haul, things would have turned out very different from the way they eventually did, if the random events that happened at this point, had simply not happened. It's amazing, if you think about it, how one stray event, sometimes contained in not more than a fickle minute, alters the course of not one but several lives—meticulously planned lives, elaborately thought over lives. Even unconnected lives. It's a shame, if you ask me, our sheer powerlessness in face of the random…the indiscriminate power that the two words—"If Only"—continue to enjoy over human lives.

Things would have happened very differently indeed, and their lives would not become what they eventually did, Nethra's and Mrityunjay's at least, had Avinash and Nethra not been grouped together for the second time, for something that was to bring as much joy and longing to their beings, as pain and resentment in their later lives.

The Twain Shall Meet

The Foundation Course (FC) at LBSNAA is designed not from the point of academic rigour but with the purpose of instilling *esprit de corps* in an eclectic group of young recruits into the All India Services. The activities that constitute the core structure of this course are designed to inculcate a *sense of belonging to a structure*, of being members of All India Services who shall stand tall and firm with each other, through their careers. The inter service networks forged during the FC, the camaraderie between batchmates from different services is what is supposed to help the big bureaucratic structure buttress its reach and power with the sturdy scaffolding of informal bonds. It is the flexibility and informality of human relationships that is supposed to help the big bureaucratic beast wriggle through the narrow alleys and difficult corners of the grand administrative maze.

Well, that's the concept. Is this how it *actually* works?

May be it does. And then may be it doesn't. Whatever.

Going back to the structure of the course, the fifteen day long Himalayan Trek (HT) is one of the salient features of every FC. While OTs do get curtain-raisers with the weekly treks to Mussoorie hills, nothing can match the thrill of a fifteen day-long Greater Himalayan retreat. Over the years, certain trek routes have come to be labelled as 'soft', few others as 'hard' and still fewer as 'challenger'. Every year, groups of fifteen to twenty OTs each set off for the Himalayas, with nothing more than backpacks stuffed with Cuppa Noodles, Ready-To-Eat MTR packets, a few rugged clothes but most vitally, a muscle relaxant gel.

Amidst the shared travails of inclement weather and mountainous terrain, between sore feet, hypothermia and searing back pain, when food goes basic and ankles get sprained, it is only true and lasting bonds of friendship that come to sustain.

Speaking of friendships, HT and Bharat Darshan are also two reputed features of every training program that invariably throw up interesting tales of intra-batch flings, some of which later materialize into marriages (hark, sharks!) while others, you know, just fizzle out…leaving the…*participants*…cold as an open Coke…in the refrigerator…on the fifth day. Something *that* cold, and *only* cold…and may be too sweet as well, but nothing. This whole precariousness stays…but only for a few days…after which, the Empire strikes back with a vengeance.

Vengeance.

The role that the random had played in bringing Avinash and Nethra together again must be discounted here a little. It was actually the agent of the random, V. Ravi, who in all his romantic excitement about the potentially sparkling pairing of the lovely ice-princess with the 'soon-to-be-married Prince,' (oh it can't be put in words, how far his imagination had guided him into the possibilities of this particular case…), it was he who had this great 'cohabitation' brainwave in the first place, the Hindi soap opera junkie that he was. And since it was he who happened to be the Faculty-In-Charge, Himalayan Trek, his heart glowed silently as the mouse pointer dragged N. Kaul in the group where A. Rathore sat waiting with open arms, in Ravi's imagination.

And was he lovin' it, people! Scripting a fairy tale romance, set in the lap of nature, right here on this 'HT-2008' MS Excel worksheet. The fun didn't end with the lead pair, obviously. He went ahead, in his casting director role, and blessed the group with a few more 'pieces', all stalwarts in their own right, all thought fit to play the roles V. Ravi had assigned to them in the little romcom incubating in his mind ever since the last group discussion.

For example, Devyani Mukherjee, Indian Foreign Service, was his thoughtful choice for the Group Leader (GL). A hypochondriac and habitual defaulter at the morning PT sessions, Devyani spent most of her time at the academy *sighing*, or, saying 'What the f***?' and such other delightful variants of the forbidden word or rolling her eyes or doing all three together. When she wasn't doing any of the above, she pored over Nietzsche's musings or Sartre's phenomenology.

The 'I rebel; therefore I exist' shibboleth she liked to throw into her several discourses delivered on several occasions inside and outside the Academy had earned her the moniker Devyani Existentialist Mukherjee abbreviated as DEM and pronounced as 'Dame' by her batchmates.

So the only thing Dame loved about the Academy was the weather and its liberating romance. She hated the 'institution', its 'dichotomous legacy of autocracy and subservience' and its 'irrational, almost fascist insistence' on physical training of OTs. All she wanted was to be left totally alone, with her existentialist literature, her pack of Marlboro and her coffee.

And then the day came, the one prior to the day when trek groups were to disperse on their routes. Because everyone loved briefings, everyone was once again summoned for a formal briefing on 'Officer Like Conduct and the Himalayan Trek—Expectations and Mismatches.'

The Academy has some very firm convictions regarding seating arrangements. Because OTs in a group must bond well, because they must all feel the centripetal pull of team spirit, every group had to be seated round a circle. A circle to each group. Each group in a circle. Circles arranged around a circular briefing hall, V. Ravi beaming at the centre of the circumscribing circle.

Seated diametrically opposite each other in their circle, Nethra and Avinash did their best to avoid looking at each other. Avinash appeared unusually chatty and socialized with group mates including the three other women in the group who in turn were buoyed by the prospect of things to come. Nethra remained unnecessarily solemn and attended only to Dame's sighs and ****—swear words—answering her enquiries about 'how to distribute group stuff between backpacks' in profound monosyllables.

Later that evening, Nethra and Avinash crossed paths again on the Mall Road. Much of the batch was out on the picturesque boulevard that evening. Mussoorie knew that OTs were preparing to leave for the trek and had come out to help with a fresh stock of wares as always—sweatshirts, sunscreen, sunglasses, trekking shoes, track pants and torches.

As Nethra and Madhavi walked past the important looking coterie, Avinash and Nethra inadvertently looked at each other and immediately looked away. Both Madhavi and Mrityunjay noticed that. Mrityunjay slowly wrapped his brotherly arm over Avinash's shoulder, a gesture of between-you-and-me solidarity.

'Why do the two of you behave as if you don't know each other?' Madhavi asked Nethra.

'Do we know each other?'

'Well I hope you get to…now!' Madhavi smiled happily, putting her arm over her friend's shoulders.

Back in their room, Mrityunjay felt tormented by the familiar itch that torments too many of us too often—to become light just when you had decided to be nothing but sober, to renege on your word and your logical resolve to let go, to bring back to consciousness something you had decided to erase from it. We are too easily tempted by fallibility. We are truly a masochistic species.

Mrityunjay and Avinash hadn't talked about Nethra since their last conversation about her; not even in the manner of good humoured banter when the trek groups came out but Mrityunjay couldn't hold himself back any further.

'So who all are in your group, Prince?' he asked.

'Don't ask as if you don't already know,' Avinash replied, 'I am sure you found that out before you got to know about your own group.'

'Notwithstanding, I would like to hear you deliver the good news,' Mrityunjay smiled mockingly.

'You expect me to blush?' Avinash smiled and frowned simultaneously. After a minute of silent contemplation, he turned to Mrityunjay, 'Well now that we are at it, any parting thoughts on how to deal with the situation?'

'Do we have a *'situation'* here?' Mrityunjay was thoroughly enjoying it now, 'last time I checked, we were only dealing with… what was that…err…a harmless crush?'

'I am just a little confused, that is it.' Avinash replied.

'Ah! As Kafka would say, "you are at once both—the quiet and the confusion of my heart"' he sprawled lazily on his bed now, gazing thoughtfully at the ceiling, his hands crossed behind his head.

'"Thou art to me, a delicious torment",' he went on, without looking at Avinash, 'that's Emerson!'

Avinash stood looking at this picture of poetic flourish, waiting, for the advice he knew would come trailing towards the end.

'15 days is a long time…' Mrityunjay said finally.

'A long time,' Avinash replied.

'I would tell you the way it works for me. The best way to demystify a person is to speak with them. Silence and absence tend to make the heart grow fonder.'

'But in this particular case, don't you think it might be counter-productive?' Avinash asked, barely convinced.

Mrityunjay thought for a moment.

'That depends on how you define productive, Avinash.'

'You are having the time of your life…aren't you?' Avinash said, smiling back faintly, 'I don't think your demystification theory will work here…speaking to her will only worsen it.'

'It?'

'Yeah...*it*.'

'In that case,' Mrityunjay shrugged, 'don't speak. Just play *it* on...the old fashioned game of glances and sightings...of weaving charms and getting charmed,' he said, sinking back further in his blanket, 'Speaking of charm, here's this last one for the day, from Camus again.'

Amidst mild protests from Avinash, the last one for the day was duly delivered at his feet, 'You know what charm is—a way of getting the answer yes, without having asked any clear question...'

Both men lay examining this last one for the day, on their respective beds, for some time.

'And who holds the charm here?' Avinash asked finally.

'Obviously, she...she could get that yes from *anyone*,' Mrityunjay replied, before switching off the lights.

The Himalayan Trek

The tranquility of a late October Mussoorie morning was broken by the din of excited OTs preparing to embark on their first independent outdoor activity together. The misty morning air smelt of thrill, expectation, and buses. Backpacks and hold-alls were being loaded atop buses, crates of mineral water bottles and breakfast packets were being shoved inside, roll calls were being carried out, delightful pronunciations of 'Present' filled up the air, and missing OTs were being dragged out of beds....

Strips of Avomin—a compulsory keep for mountainous travel—were in great demand. Group Treasurers (GTs) were busy pooling group funds out of reluctant pockets and Group Leaders (GLs) were bringing the excited herd together so that they could finally push off. Amidst this flurry, Nethra had found Avinash looking at her twice or maybe, he had found her looking at him and had become conscious! Nethra wasn't sure.

As things fell into place in the next half hour, Trek Group No. 7 came together for a group photograph, with their nausea-inducing bus looming large in the background. To the Academy's credit, the buses which ferried OTs to the last motorable points in the higher Himalayas were not the ubiquitous, Volvo coaches but sturdy Road Transport Corporation buses. And while a separate novel would be in order to describe the machinations of their unpredictable drivers and high-strung conductors, one could only assume that this was all in keeping with the general and overarching spirit of adventure, the thrill of the unexpected.

Because some rebels are always scouting for causes, amidst weary 'Ughhs' and death stares, Dame now stepped to the front of the bus aisle, and read out a commencement-of-trek pledge from the Leave No Trace movement. The pledge enjoined upon backpackers to, 'leave nothing but footprints, take nothing but photos, kill nothing but time, keep nothing but memories.'

'Words!' someone from the backseat cried out.

'Someone's taking the GL thing to a whole new level,' another voice from the backseat joined in, in the backdrop of a '*Humaara GL kaisa ho…Dame madam jaisa ho,*' chorus.

Those who have travelled in the mountains know that mountain travel can kill people, even without the bus falling into the deep gorge below. One only needs to sit inside one of those clumsy RTC buses that seem to lean over ominously while negotiating the endless hairpin bends on a mountain road and feel one's cerebrospinal fluid spin up a whirlpool. Add to that the ordeal of an overwhelming, retch-inducing air fresher, a *tum to thehre pardesi* on the rocks, and the stench-sound-sight of fresh puke flying straight out of one of the front windows and landing bang on yours….

The first wicket to fall to the cruel spins of mountain-bus sickness was Dame's. Sixty-five minutes into the journey, she was already feeling like her gut was about to fall out of her mouth, her brain out of her cranium, and life force out of her body. She had caused the bus to halt twice already, with oh i am going to puke false alarms. As a consequence, the bus driver and conductor were now giving her one of their signature you-better-get-on-with-it looks. Sick and harassed, her face bore a haggard look and her body language suggested anti-existential resignation to fate. This lead-a-trek business was turning out to be such an anticlimax! It was such an unedifying start, such an oppositeness to her assumptions that....

Yes, that was that. She had to rebel. Only then could she exist. She would not assume a responsibility by assignment. She despised treks and equally so, the despicable task of keeping the herd together. Leading a group trek was fundamentally inconsistent with her beliefs. In the second hour of the first lap of their first day's journey, the decision was made and the leader having rebelled against her own group, Trek Group number 7 suffered a subsonic implosion no one heard at the time and only suffered later.

From that point onward, all they heard from the GL were these two words: I dunno (pronounced *Ayerno*, accompanied by a shrug).

Where do we stay, GL?

I dunno.

When do we start GL?

I dunno.

Is something the matter, GL?

I dunno.

Will you marry me, GL?

I dunno.

And no points for guessing, the new Group Anthem was,

Humara GL kaisa ho?

Ayerno, Ayerno.

Back in the bus, Nethra was seated next to Nesan G. Kandiyar, an adventure junkie from the Indian Forest Service. He was a buddy from the Tamil gang and the only person in the group Nethra could ask to sit next to her. Having spent a large part of the last one hour in giving a live tutorial on the various functions of his latest Nikon DSLR to a borderline enthusiastic Nethra, he had now segued effortlessly to his favourite subject—birds. He went on and on and on, about their wondrous hues and scientific names, habitats, food habits and vocalizations, their mating patterns and such other trivia which had fittingly earned him his Academy epithet—National Geographic Kandiyar.

Six hours went by—*antakshari*s petered out, jokes fell flat after a point, people dozed off and woke up and dozed off again, and then woke up again, to do milestone countdowns to kill time which music alone could no longer kill. Life returned to the group again when the bus finally halted at Rudraprayag—the confluence point of the rivers Alaknanda and Mandakini. What a solace it was, to breathe in the fresh air! The serenity and panoramic view of Rudraprayag, perched prettily in the lap of the Holy Mountains cast a spell on everyone.

What particularly caught Nethra's eye was the footbridge over the river Mandakini. The old wooden structure was held in place by steel ropes that joined together to form a crescent. The crescent along with the wooden base was suspended along the two ends by huge rocks that provided support to the massive structure. There was something mystic about that bridge, sitting tranquil over the eager confluence that made it look exalted, and fragile.

As everyone in the group settled down for a late afternoon siesta, Nethra kept looking at the footbridge from the window in her room. She knew she had to touch it, feel it, talk to it in some privacy and listen to the stories encrypted in the roar of the waters gurgling below and in the winds blowing across its steel ropes.

Avinash couldn't sleep either. He sat on the floor, facing the balcony at the threshold of his room and talking to Malavika as a chirpy Alaknanda flowed past. Rudraprayag was one of the last locations served by the National Telecom Network. The next location would probably be Badrinath, which was six days away.

He was still squatting lazily on the floor, talking to Malavika when he spotted Nethra moving towards the wooden footbridge along the pebbled bank of the Alaknanda. Wearing a yellow T-shirt and denims and sporting her ponytail, she looked like a young girl drawn towards an interesting looking giant wheel at a fair. His eyes followed her as he talked over the phone, his muse clearly unaware of this unsolicited intrusion. She jumped lithely over the boulders, sweeping her face clear of strands of hair that kept playing with the winds, obstructing her view of her destination.

It was a moment that was to remain etched in his memory till his last breath. She stood over that mystic bridge, feeling the winds blowing through it, the sun kissing her lovely face with its gentle evening rays. With each breath, every cell in her body seemed rejuvenated. She felt weightless as she spread her arms out along the wooden rails, lifting her chin up and closing her eyes to internalize everything in that moment into her being. Her face radiated bliss. Pure Joy.

Avinash disconnected the phone and picked up the DSLR Nesan had carefully kept on the table before dozing off. He clicked close to twenty pictures in less than a minute. Hard as he tried, he simply couldn't take his eyes off the lovely young girl who lingered about the bridge that evening. If there was innocence, it was this. If there was joy, it was this.

If there was love...

Well, he knew that it was, quite simply, an infatuation...he kept reminding himself, all through that evening, it was nothing but a seriously silly infatuation with someone it was impossible not to fall absolutely in love with, if only....

Later that evening, the group visited the Rudranath Temple, an old Shiva temple that stood at the confluence of the two rivers. It was during the Sandhya Arti that their eyes met again, not once, but again, and again, as if there was something that needed to be told. Amidst the gleam of a hundred lamps that illuminated the *deepshikha* and the space between and around them, they stood avoiding that which so obviously existed, without either of them knowing exactly when it had come into being. They stood apart—yet held together by an invisible thread, as the pundits recited age-old chants to the rhythmic music of cymbals and conch shells—and the golden reflections of the holy fire swept merrily over a dark Alaknanda, flowing quietly by.

The destination for the road trip next day was Gobindghat—the base station for their first trek up to Sri Hemkunt Sahib and the Valley of Flowers. Gobindghat was a scattered, temporary settlement with narrow roads lined with small eateries, economy motels and makeshift shops selling walking sticks, canvas shoes, yellow raincoats and golden souvenirs.

A large, white gurdwara loomed ahead as the group crossed the suspension bridge across the Alaknanda. Gurdwara Gobind Ghat was clean and surprisingly spacious for an edifice in the hills. Trekkers, pilgrims, and tourists, the SUV *walas* and the bus *yatris*, all lay on its cool marble floor catching some rest before setting off for the eighteen kilometre long trek to Gurdwara Hemkunt Sahib.

Nesan Geographic Kandiyar had taken over as the *de facto* group leader and declared that the group would travel up to Ghangaria that very day. Ghangaria was twelve kilometres from Gobind Ghat and was the base camp for two distinct treks upto the Valley of Flowers and to the holy shrine—Gurudwara Hemkunt Sahib.

It was already two in the afternoon when the group commenced its onward journey. Distinct subgroups had appeared within an hour on the winding mule track, each clustering around a mean age, BMI and kinesthetic quotient—the ascent up the trail in inverse relation to modal BMI of every subgroup. The only exceptions were the tailenders, Dame and two other ailing OTs who more than made up for their low BMI by a heightened reluctance to contribute bodily to any activity at hand.

Though steep in the beginning, the slope gradually straightened through an ascending valley of terraced fields and vegetation. Deep down in the valley, the river Laxman Ganga came hurtling down, eager to meet the Alaknanda. Leading the group were the avid trekkers—Nethra, also the first to complete the first three kilometres, alone—followed by Nesan Geographic and Avinash. The scenic splendour of the landscape, a steady supply of chocolates and her favourite tracks playing at a high volume on her iPod—Nethra could have easily scaled the Banderpoonch with her soaring energy levels.

Three kilometres into the route, the track led to a small but picturesque hamlet, Pulna, the winter retreat of the local people. Rhododendrons were in full bloom, peeping from a verdant thicket of trees and tufts of white and pink roses blossomed in rows of shrubs. A few metres from Pulna, the terrain grew steeper and the blazing rush of the Akash Ganga could be heard above the music playing on the iPod. Distant snow-capped peaks could be spotted behind the shoulders of the younger, greener mountains on the horizon.

Nethra had just spotted a tentative mud track that diverged stealthily from the body of the mountain she had been climbing. Though clearly quite steep and tricky, it looked like a sure shortcut to Bhyundar, the next village uphill, some seven kilometres from Pulna. It was a gamble she could afford as there were still two clear hours before it got dark. She had barely walked some two hundred metres up the track when she was apprehended by a strong arm on her shoulder. This not only brought her upward clamber to a sudden halt but also almost threw her off balance on the slippery, narrow track.

It was Nesan. While the loud music prevented her from discerning his words, the convoluted frown on his face and the amused look on that of his partner made it clear that she had misjudged the shortcut.

'Do you wish to go down in history as a trek martyr?' Nethra finally heard Nesan say.

What embarrassed her was not Nesan's minute-long diatribe *per se*, it was its sharp delivery in the presence of a thoroughly amused Avinash.

'I was just checking…', Nethra shrugged, 'if there was a way up…' she looked fixedly at Nesan, completely ignoring Avinash and his obvious amusement.

The three trekked down the trail, Nesan slipping thrice, barely missing the deep gorge below. They had walked together for some distance—Nesan sandwiched between them—when someone called out to him in Tamil.

'Nesu…*Poramboku*!'

It was one of his friends from the trailing all South group who, annoyed by his prolonged absence, had peremptorily summoned him by way of a mild insult. Nesan left in haste, promising to join Nethra and Avinash soon.

It was still early evening and the last convoy of mules was on its way up to Ghangaria. The mule drivers had decked up their animals in bright tassels that dangled precariously around their ears and necks. The string of bells around their necks would jiggle as they moved, filling the valley with euphonious sounds audible from the furthest reaches of the hills.

'You aced in the last GD,' Avinash began. He was the usual polite but frigid Prince, polite because that was the way he was, frigid because he wasn't sure where *this* trail was headed.

'Oh *that*…', Nethra looked for the right words, for she had a special talent for messing things up at crucial moments as these, '…that was…well, like you put it, only for the sake of elegance, I was trying to sound morally pure…and it is inelegant to snub the morally pure…right?' she smiled as she turned to look at him.

He smiled at the ground beneath him.

'Have you been here before?' he asked, still addressing the ground.

'No, you?' she asked.

'Me neither…but you seem to be in love with the mountains,' he said rather grimly.

How can one speak of love so technically, like one was speaking of Schrödinger's wave equation, she wondered but immediately added, 'Yes, I am…The smell of fresh mountain air…the morning mist…cascading springs…beautiful valleys…I could spend my life here…' she inhaled deeply.

'Consumed by wanderlust you must be, then?' he asked, rather poetically.

'Consumed in my imagination, yes!'

'You must have travelled a lot, then!'

'No.' she sighed, 'but I really want to….'

They walked in silence for a few minutes.

'All I have done in my life so far is study and make a place for myself under the sun.' she said, as if an explanation were required, she added, 'There have been practically no deviations from the standard trajectory of a good student so far….'

He was listening, with an appearance of politeness and sincerity, without a hint of emotion in his eyes. It was impossible to decipher what was going on in his mind.

'Which is the place you want to visit most?' he asked her now, fixing his unsettling gaze on her. Though that gaze was soft and arresting, his expression was grim, the kind of expression people wore to solemn conferences and boardroom meetings.

'Nordic countries…Ireland in particular!' she answered.

'What is it about Ireland?' he asked, his mysterious smile making its much deserved appearance on his lips now.

'I want to meet Irish people.' she answered matter-of-factly.

'What *about* Irish people?'

'Well there is something about them…the men, basically. Look at all the Irish actors…every actor I have ever fallen for is Irish, or of Irish descent or half-Irish-half-something…so there has to be something about Ireland,' she looked at him and smiled.

A full smile escaped his lips now, as if setting itself free, against his volition.

'I went to Italy for the same reason,' he cocked his head to face hers now, looking momentarily into her eyes.

'Monica Belluci?' she chuckled.

They laughed lightly.

'But seriously, you have been to Italy?' she asked.

'Yes,' he pressed his lips together and nodded gently, 'and to Ireland as well.'

'Ireland as well? Did you go on a world tour?' she gasped.

'Not a world tour, but I have seen much of Europe...I went to Germany for my industrial training in the third year of college and then to Finland for the final-year internship. After college and before appearing for CSE, I took a few months off and visited some places I had been interested in—Southern Europe and South America mostly.'

'Places like?'

'Barcelona, Tirana, Lisbon, Santorini in Europe and then Puerto Rico, Quito, Cusco...' looking at her wide-eyed glance, he broke into another of his epic smiles.

'Few months off...all by yourself?'

'Yes...It was a great learning experience. Gave me the space to reflect and make my own choices' he replied grimly.

'Neato!' she said. There wasn't much else to say.

Few more minutes of silence passed between them.

'Where did you get the money to travel so much?' she asked now.

'There was some scholarship money and royalties...My father asked me to do what I wanted with it,' he replied.

She noticed he was walking at a *safe* distance from her...and that as they walked, their steps synched with each other. Very rarely did her steps sync with that of others. This was one of the first things she observed whenever she walked with people. Her eyes had now settled on his arms, strong, sculpted arms, and just as they moved up to rest on his face, she realized the cop had caught the burglar red-handed—and because the courteous cop wouldn't embarrass the burglar, his eyes were now scouting the ground... for pebbles, perhaps.

'So you have covered most of Europe which means…', she said quickly, switching back frantically to the subjective comfort of travel, '…not just Switzerland or Paris but the whole of Europe. You mentioned Albania, right?'

'In fact I haven't seen much of Paris or Switzerland. These places are way too…out there before the world. I prefer the smaller places—some far off Scandinavian village with its sprawling meadows…speaking of which…I am reminded of Reine.'

He looked at her. She was listening with rapt attention.

'I had read about this fishing village in Norway, in Lofoten archipelago to be precise, in one of the tourist manuals…' he said. He took out his tablet from the rucksack and the most amazing sights of nature played out in the slideshow right before her eyes—sapphire bays and dramatic cliffs surrounding towering mountains of granite.

'It didn't seem like a place here on this earth,' he scrolled through the images, one after the other, and crossed the imaginary *laxman rekha* he had marked out between them, so that she could look at them. The delicious smell of his cologne (and sweat) wafted up to her as he moved closer. Sweat and cologne. Keenly alive to the sensations within and around her, Nethra stepped away a little.

'They have remodelled some of the fishermen's cabins right beside the Norwegian Sea into cottages for tourists. I had booked one of these cottages,' he continued, pointing at one of the pictures now, 'It was summer and I could gaze at the midnight sun sitting in my balcony right beside the sea….'

Swept away in the specifics of Reine's beauty, without so much as realizing and having made no deliberate effort to, the two had once again come quite close to each other, something they both realized, when his hand brushed against hers.

'By the way, there's something strangely familiar about your cologne…' she said, stepping away a little, and with the seriousness befitting a forensic expert, 'which perfume is this?' she added in a very just-asking way.

'Same as yours,' he replied in the same vein.

Nethra flushed conspicuously. She was wearing Hugo Boss Woman.

'Hugo Boss, I mean,' he smiled daftly.

'It seems you have a lot of experience with Hugo Boss Women,' she said equally daftly and immediately regretted it.

'Were *you* not the one who said Hugo Boss smelt strangely familiar?' he said, without looking at her.

She kept quiet. The cologne, the sweat and the Norwegian Sea…it was way too much for her to handle.

'So you read about all these places first?' she veered back to the subject, keen not to mess it up with this odd interruption, 'Anyone would go to Paris…but Reine is something that would require some prior research.'

'Yes…Travel books and Internet, mostly' he nodded.

'And you did it alone?'

'Yeah…I like it that way…' he shrugged and then, as an afterthought, added, 'unless there's company I am comfortable with.'

Company I am comfortable with! Nethra pursed her lips, *how very vain of you, Prince!*

'I…interrupted you. You were talking about villages. Tell me about some more…' she looked at him. He had crossed over to the other side of the *lakshman rekha* but their steps were still in sync.

'Manarola…It was one Italian village I had visited…It was like CGI animation…brightly coloured, multistory blocks emerging out of a terraced hill. I stayed at a small guest house there….This place was at a walking distance from the sea and one could go sightseeing in the hills and vineyards nearby…Speaking of sightseeing, one shouldn't fail to mention Italian women.'

She looked at him, surprised.

'*La Donna Perfetta*…' he continued, pronouncing it the Italian way.

'What is that?' she furrowed her brows.

'That, is Italian for "the perfect woman".'

'So you speak Italian?' she asked, trying to pull a very straight face.

'I don't. But this extraordinarily beautiful woman on one of those beaches in Manarola came to me and...', he took a moment to look at her, '...You know, among other things, she told me that she was my *Donna Perfetta*. She proposed to me, basically,' he spoke, as if she had co-authored a research paper with him.

'Yes, sure!' she threw him a mocking smile, 'and you must have refused her, saying Monica Belluci was your *Donna Perfetta*!'

They laughed. He told her of fantastic places, of villages and towns, their men and women, the food they ate and the way they lived, all in the same sombre vein.

'Most cities are similar...or are becoming so. Similar malls and fashion, the same brands...it takes you in for a while but the thrill recedes equally soon...small towns and villages give you the real flavour of a place,' he said.

Nethra knew the truth of that. All malls were the same, more or less. How they bored you with the sameness! Places good only for walks, her father would say.

Nethra's pace had slowed as her mind and body stood tethered to every word he said. The breeze that caressed her bare hands made her shiver. The air she inhaled felt chillier. She untied the sweatshirt wrapped around her waist and pulled it on, expecting its warmth to steady her pulse.

'Seems like you need something hot,' Avinash said, noticing her chattering teeth. She pressed her lips together to suppress a smile. Of course! Something hot *was* what she needed. Only if she had had the necessary courage, she would have carried this last sentence to its logical conclusion. *If only....*

But Avinash seemed not to have noticed Nethra's silent enjoyment. In all earnestness, he pointed towards a makeshift tea stall, several of which lined the trail upto Ghangaria. It was a temporary structure made of wooden logs and branches, roofed with plastic sheets over bamboo poles. They settled themselves on the opposite ends of a little bench outside the tea stall.

'Cheeni Kam Rakhiyega Maulana Sahab!' he called out softly, reverentially.

'Itni nazakat se jo kahenge ghol denge, janaab' the old man with his flowing beard grinned as he peeped out of his little kitchen.

Nethra smiled again.

They were quiet for a while.

'What are you thinking about?' he asked.

'Nothing…' she shrugged.

'What are you thinking about,' he leaned in and smiled softly this time.

The moment was so strangely intimate that she had to break into it.

'You are fortunate, Avinash—you are living according to your choices,' she said, in her effort to spoil the mood.

He realized she had addressed him by his name for the first time.

'Everyone can…you just have to make that choice.'

They were sitting quite close together, close enough for her to smell the cologne and notice the light two-day-old stubble on his face, close enough to make her acutely aware of the sensations within her own body.

'Is it that simple?' she asked, bringing her mind back from its wild ramblings.

'Which is the difficult part?'

'We are in this *service* now…It drastically reduces our choices. Plus, there is always a financial side to a choice. You know how well we are paid…and then there are rules. If I plan to travel the world, for example, Department of Personnel would have to permit me first.'

'The only rules which matter, Nethra....'

'Are what a man can do and what he cannot,' she completed his sentence.

'Right!', he smiled, 'If you decide now, you *can go* and visit Reine by next week...as a probationer who is not yet confirmed in service. It is quite simply, a function of your choice. If you need money, take it from me,' the unexpected hint of personal warmth took her by surprise.

'Do you have certain undeclared sources of income?' she laughed lightly.

'I have savings—royalties from a patent I own flow in quite regularly. I will be happy to lend some,' he answered.

'Patent?' she pouted skeptically.

'Yes, college time....'

'On?'

'Semiconductor device fabrication.'

'Ah! There's Intel inside...' she shook her head, 'Engineer is a rather generic term, don't you think? Both of us are engineers. You are the patent kind and I am the BPO kind....'

'You have a tendency of self deprecation...' he said, the muscles on his face growing taut.

'What rate of interest will you charge?'

'No interest, no collateral...custom option for you,' he replied, glancing at her.

Maulana Sahab cut into the scene now with steaming tea in conical glasses and a plateful of Parle G biscuits.

The plate of biscuits was complementary, a random act of elderly affection. Nethra uttered a grateful *shukriya*. Then she lifted her glass up and looked at Avinash.

'Here's to a trip to Reine!'

Avinash smiled back, raising a toast, 'Here's to several such trips!'

As they sat sipping their tea in silence, Avinash wondered why they had not met earlier. He could see through that aura now, he could see a mystic purity, a poetic serenity.

There are very few occasions when two professionals in a trade, especially bureaucrats, converse sans mental filters. Their conversation had more passion than logic, it came straight from their hearts—a warm emotion gushing through their veins, effusing out of their beings and entwining them together. They talked about travel, music, and themselves. There had come a point in the conversation, when under ordinary circumstances, Avinash would have spoken of his marital commitments. He did not. He simply convinced himself that she knew about it already. She must know. Everyone did. However, deep down, he knew that she didn't; he knew that if she had known, she would force herself to let go of him—she would hold back instead of giving in—and he didn't want her to hold back. The more time he spent with her, the more he wanted to delve deeper. They found themselves in Ghangaria a lot sooner than they liked and the haggard group trailing behind joined them soon after. The simple fare for dinner at the Ghangaria Gurdwara tasted better than any meal that they had had in days. By eight in the evening, twelve out of the fifteen in the group had already slipped into the sleeping bags lined across the dormitory at a *dharamshala*...groaning and grumbling and cursing the Academy, the UPSC and the doomed day they had decided to take the CSE. They were already debating the prospect of a group bunk. They could head back and chill out in Rishikesh, go river rafting....

'Thankfully, the academy hadn't got GPS installed on our heads....'

Yet the idea seemed quite preposterous to some of the more conscientious participants. Someone suggested that they could stay back at Ghangharia and catch some rest instead.... As it is, it didn't matter that the buses didn't have GPS navigation, the conductor-driver duo was a live GPS transmitter—hard core V. Ravi loyalists who everyone knew would betray even if bribed heftily...the way Indian voters do....

But where was the risk taking, folks?, others averred, 'weren't treks all about risks...if only they all stuck together...they could....'

The aimless chatter went on for a few more minutes, till no one had the energy left to carry on any further. The debate ended in a very bureaucratic (and convenient) let-us-see-what-can-be-done situation and everyone knew in that moment that there would be no escaping the six-kilometre steeper climb that lay ahead of them the following day.

Nethra couldn't sleep for obvious reasons. She felt famished despite a filling meal and gorged on chocolates for comfort and clarity. She loitered about the maze of makeshift shops, her mind buzzing with myriad thoughts and emotions. There was still an hour before the small market settlement wound up for the day. Sikh families were out in *dhabas* for a noisy meal and *kirtans* set to tunes of popular Bollywood songs blared out at the eateries.

The ever enthusiastic Nesan had dragged Avinash to the Ghangaria bazaar too. As Nethra rambled about the settlement, gazing at the pretty little souvenirs in brightly lit shops, Nesan's cheerful voice apprehended her.

'Looks like someone's painting the town red!'

Nethra turned sharply to find Nesan beaming at her. Next to him, Avinash looked grim as ever, his eyes fixed firmly on her, his guitar strapped across his shoulders.

'Hi!' she smiled at them both.

'We were thinking of visiting the riverside. You game?' Nesan asked.

River Pushpawati met the Akash Ganga at Ghangaria. On a full moon night, the lush green mountains emerging from the meadows provided an ethereal setting to the pretty rivulet and its softly flowing waters were rendered white with the multiple reflections of the star-lit sky. The riverside was serenely quiet when they reached—Nethra and Avinash sat listening to the sounds of silence, sipping hot coffee.

Nesan leaped all over the place with his DSLR, hopping enthusiastically over rocks for better shots of the night scenery.

'You play that guitar very well!' Nethra picked up the conversation from where they had left off earlier in the evening.

'Thank you,' he replied without looking at her. 'You have a…' he pondered, as if looking for a word, '…good voice too.'

Good voice. Goodness Gracious! She thought.

'Will you sing for me?' the abruptness of the question, and the intimacy woven in it startled her. Her smooth cheeks flushed red, a colour that matched her scarlet sweatshirt, and she slowly adjusted the few strands of hair sweeping across her face, tucking them behind her earlobes.

'Will you?' he turned to glance at her.

Nethra was stupefied. Sing? *Before him*?

'No! I can't…I just…never have…and…' she fumbled nervously, 'I haven't ever, before/I mean, I can't sing.'

'If you never try, you will never know if you can.…Of course, that goes for most things,' he said dourly and looked away quickly, realizing that his last was open to several not very decent interpretations.

A few moments passed—then suddenly, the moment of deliverance. She pressed her lips together. Avinash knew she was ready.

'I am going to sit behind you,' he said, getting up, 'you could sing like you were sitting here alone…' he whispered, his breath grazing her ear.

She sang *Aree Ali Piya Bina, drut bandish* in Raag Yaman.

Avinash was quiet for a long three minutes after she had finished.

'Will you sing *Falling Slowly* with me tonight?' he asked finally. His eyes gleamed with a delicate hope—like he was offering elements from his innermost core to her—like he had always dreamed of making this offer to the one woman in his life, to his *Donna Perfetta*.

Nethra's palms had got unusually pink and she could feel warm blood gushing under her skin, rushing all over her face. They both were *falling slowly*...after all!

'We don't have a piano...like Hansard had...but it doesn't matter...as long as we do it together,' he said, readying himself with the guitar.

And then they sang. Nesan stopped in amazement. He could hear joy. Love.

Nesan had taken quite a few photographs while the two sang by the riverside, landscape photographs which looked sublime in the ambient moonlight. As soon as they had stopped singing, Nethra grabbed Nesan's DSLR to downplay the situation between Avinash and her. She was flipping through the pictures when her photographs on the wooden bridge struck her.

She looked at them, surprised. Her beauty, so effortless, so natural, spoke through every picture. There was joy written all over her. This was a far cry from how she looked in her regular photographs—utterly self-conscious and ill at ease. These were pictures that flew in the face of her self-deprecating notions. It had probably to do with the photographer....

'When did you...?' she paused midway through her query to Nesan.

She clearly remembered that she had visited the bridge alone. No, there had been nobody from the group in sight that evening or she wouldn't have let herself go that way. Had someone clicked her from the room in the lodge? Nesan? Or his roommate?

As she pieced things together, she instinctively looked up at Avinash. He was looking at her too, wondering how he had forgotten to delete those photographs after transferring them to his tablet. His face bore no embarrassment and he looked at her evenly, softly; the inside of his cheeks pressed against the jawline, making it all the more prominent. Nethra looked away.

They didn't talk much that night. Nesan made up for their verbal inactivity by supplying abundant factual information about species of birds that had an active nightlife. It was past twelve that by the time returned.

Dawn broke with the chirping of Himalayan birds and a thick cloak of mist enveloping the village. The climb up to the shrine was very steep and the *kucchha* path was interspersed with large stones, painstakingly cobbled in loose earth. Nethra, Avinash and Nesan moved together, walking sticks to their aid, spotting narrow trails that cut their journey short by several hundred metres at a time.

Gurdwara Sri Hemkunt Sahib was a lofty pentagonal building sitting in the lap of snow-clad peaks amidst the pristine beauty of nature. Mosses, ferns and flowers greeted visitors at an altitude much above the Himalayan tree line. The holy lake Hemkunt surrounded the Gurdwara on three sides and the seven snow-clad mountains fenced the lake, almost two kilometres in circumference. Amidst this virgin divinity of nature where nothing but the purest elements of life existed, Avinash acknowledged to himself that he was wrong. Looking at her, here, he knew that he was falling in love with her...there could no longer be any denying it. The seven mountains seemed to smile at him in agreement. He felt pleasure and peace, an imperturbable peace that grew out of the warm assurance of love.

Ruminating in the flowery wilderness of the Valley of Flowers—crossing streams with water so sweet and walking past meadows draped in pink, yellow and orange, he ardently wished that life would come to a standstill.

For the next ten days, the group continued on its trek from

Hemkunt Sahib and the Valley Of Flowers to Badrinath and then the Mana Pass—Avinash, Nethra and Nesan would wake up early in the morning and head for explorations into the wild. They discovered salubrious valleys, frothing waterfalls and pretty little hamlets perched in the midst of mountains. Sometimes, Nesan would stay back to sleep longer. On these occasions, Avinash and Nethra would proceed together on quieter walks through sylvan forests bathed in sunlight.

And then one morning, Avinash was finally confronted with the inevitable, 'What next?'

'What next?' he asked himself, looking at the washroom mirror of the *dharamshala* they were staying in. They had to go out for a walk by themselves that morning—she and he. Nesan had excused himself from the walk on account of M.V. Samantha's high temperature. Avinash had spent the previous night like most other nights in the past few days: waiting for dawn, when he would see her again. It no longer bothered him, this near obsession he had for her. He indulged in it.

And only now had the fullness of the situation he had helped spawn, presented itself before him, that, and the question—what next?

Walking with her along the narrow alley that ran through the forest with that question still hovering in his head, he turned to look at her.

'So what is this concept of 'One Man' you were referring to?' he asked her.

Nethra was surprised to find that he remembered something she had referred to in passing, a few days back.

'It is the idea of a person I wish to spend my life with, someone I would dwell in awe of...all my life...' she replied, striding regally, without looking at him.

'And you really believe that is possible, is it? Dwelling in someone's *awe* for your life?' he looked at the ground as he spoke, 'awe is a function of distance and relationships ought to be close. Don't you think it is more of a romantic projection...your 'One Man' thing?' he asked.

'Romantic projection? And what do you think *Donna Perfetta* is...?' she jabbed and smiled.

'Very dear to me,' he said, looking at her, and looking rather glum at the same time. He seemed lost, Nethra could feel that... and she could perceive sadness, a hint of *fear*, even pain, in his eyes. She could not understand it. He quickly looked away.

'We are young and hopeful creatures, Nethra...', he continued, in an effort to rationalize the situation, not for himself, but for her, '...We see the world as a place full of possibilities. We hope to find joy and love and peace and we project this intrinsic need for love on these imaginary concepts—the one man or the one woman who will contain that love or joy or peace...our equal...our ideal...but nothing is ideal', he faltered. '...All of us are merely human, Nethra... we fall...we are inadequate, and we are too imperfect. *Imperfect.*'

And just then, as they walked, their fingers brushed against each other. He stopped and turned to face her. She was nervous.

'Is something bothering you, Avinash?' she asked him.

He said nothing. His eyes didn't leave hers.

If there was ever to be a *moment*, this was it, Nethra felt.

But Avinash said nothing, he did nothing. He didn't touch her. He didn't hold her hands. He just kept looking at her.

'Nothing,' he nodded then, apparently in response to her question.

'Are you alright?' she asked again.

'More than I have ever been,' he replied in the manner of bookish characters.

They walked in silence for a little longer. This was normal now, the warm affinity of silences.

'You might be correct...about the projection thing, Don't you think this one person could help you discover yourself fully? She or he could help you experience the full force of your existence, like travelling does…or music,' she said.

'Or love?' he said, without looking at her.

'See…we are on the same page now,' she smiled.

'Eventually, all you need is the key to that space where you are what you can be, where you can bloom to your potential…and love is the key,' she said dreamily.

'Who said this?'

'Nethra Kaul, of course. Didn't you know?' she asked, faux surprised.

He looked at her with the same vulnerable air—a smile played on his lips, fear lurked in his eyes, his reason and will standing firm against his desire to kiss her immediately.

'Have you ever seen married people in such a…state, Nethra?'

Reason and will finally having won, he said, 'Have you seen a married couple deriving joy in their existence out of a shared co-existence?'

'I haven't but I am sure they exist,' she answered.

'Where? In novels? Or movies? Like happily ever after? I read this somewhere—"if two people love each other, there can be no happy ending to it".'

'But why should one *look* for happy endings? The joy is in the process, not in the end. Nothing of what might happen in the end deters my quest for it. It keeps me happy and full of hope,' she said.

'You belong to some other world,' he shook his head.

'No…a different age, I belong to a previous age…my friends in college felt I would look best in old age. That *suits* me,' she giggled.

Avinash looked at her and the corners of his eyes lit up.

'You would look as beautiful in any age…because you are a beautiful person…you have a lovely soul,' he said.

Nethra blushed.

Avinash watched the colour suffuse her cheeks.

'So you still haven't found *L'uomo Perfetto*, have you?' he asked.

'*L'uomo perfetto*?' she looked at him.

'The perfect man...your perfect man?'

Nethra didn't answer.

As they walked through the forest, smiling to themselves, they wished for time to stop, there and then, and for things to perpetually stay the way they were, in that moment.

And even if *that* was not to be, so thought Avinash, nothing of the aftermath must prevent one's quest for love, especially when one was *this* close to it.

The Weight of Sanity

Camping at night on higher altitudes, in the midst of craggy ridges, the group would cook on their own, on wood gathered from the forest. They would later sit and eat around the bonfire—Avinash would sit with the rest, playing *Falling Slowly* on his guitar. He would savour the sight of her, her occasional acknowledgement warming his heart more than the bonfire warmed his body. Avinash knew he had to talk to her before they went back to the Academy. He would then speak with Malavika and her parents and call off the engagement.

It was the last day of the trek, and the group had halted at Rudraprayag where they would stay for the night. They would return to Mussoorie the next morning. Having postponed his next steps to the "what next" till the last day, Avinash had now decided to take this fairy tale in his hands. After dinner, he would walk up with her to the Rudranath Temple where he would tell her everything.

Back in her room, Nethra was taking this fairy tale to the real world *she knew.* She had so much to tell Madhavi, and so much more to ask from her. Someone had to confirm *this,* after all… confirm that all of it actually meant what she *assumed* it meant… someone had to listen to all of it and tell her in that all-knowing, I-told-you-so vein—See, I told you so! And then of course she had to ask Madhavi about the text message she had received from her a few days back…a strange text message which went like this, 'Know it's awful, *da.* Forget it. Tried your number but network is bad. Will talk. Chill for now. So much more to life than this!'

So as soon as her phone detected network, she called up Madhavi.

'What's supposed to be awful, Madhavi?' she asked her over the phone.

'Ah! That this Avinash guy is engaged to be married...we are such hopeless morons, Nethra! Seems the whole Academy knew about it from day one...*atai vittu*...You okay, no?'

Nethra was stunned. 'Yes...!'

Not one to bother much about reactions, Madhavi continued, 'That is probably why he would stay so aloof *na*.... He is going to get married in December? Or January? Whatever. And did you hear about his fiancée? Jaideep was saying that the girl is very hot...what an obnoxious lech Jaideep is!... Bugged me throughout the trek...he only told me about this girl...she is obviously the daughter of some Secretary in GoI, and all her uncles and aunts and cousins and second cousins are in the services, apparently... anyway, why to....'

'Who told you this?' Nethra interrupted her, barely able to mask the consternation in her voice.

'Hey!' it was Madhavi's turn to be taken aback, 'did you not know, Nethra?'

And now, as if on cue, there was a soft knock on the open door. Avinash stood before her, waiting. She looked right back at him, at those honest eyes, that lovely face. She could not quite believe this was happening. She hung up on Madhavi abruptly and walked slowly to the door.

Of course this was wrong—a terrible miscommunication. He could not be getting married in December, or even January, for that matter, and be doing what he had been doing with her in October. But hey, was he even doing anything with her? Of course they had taken some long romantic walks together, said the unsaid with their eyes and all that...nonsense...but had he actually done anything? As in the *real* done?

Unable to resolve this herself, she looked straight into his eyes and asked, 'Do you have anything to tell me, Avinash?'

Before that sunk in, he had shrugged a no.

'Nothing?'

'What....'

'Nothing at all?'

'But....'

'Are you are engaged to be married, Avinash...in December?' she interrupted him, her voice cold as steel.

His face went pale. He had feared this. He had taken too long. This should have come from him, not from anybody else.

'See you have to....'

'Are you?' she cut in again.

'Nethra, please....'

'Are you?' her voice, choked with emotion as it was, almost broke down this time.

'I *am right now* but....'

'Avinash! Will you please allow me to steal Nethra away for the evening? If you haven't already planned a silly walk or something? Nethra, Is that okay with you?

Dame's well-timed query from across the verandah now interrupted the conversation, if there was going to be one in the first place.

Avinash first turned to spot the source of this interruption and then turned back to find its reaction, losing too much valuable time in the process.

'Yeah sure, Devyani! No plans here...' Nethra called out loudly, the steel in her voice ready to slice anything now offered by way of explanation into two. And now of course, tears were welling in her eyes and she was turning into that miserable picture of feminine misery she had so hated all her life and all she wanted now was to vanish, as a consequence.

But of course, there was no such need. Female solidarity was at hand. Dame had now made her appearance on the scene and

Nethra had decided to ignore his existence altogether. A quick gulp and Nethra looked ready as ever to accompany Dame on a trip to get herself something. Nethra didn't bother finding out what.

She slipped back into her shell. She blocked him off from that moment, using Dame as a smokescreen to hide herself from the world, from him. And wasn't this peculiar?

Some people seem to hold post doctorates in feeling ashamed about hurts *caused to* them...not the hurts they cause, but the hurts they suffer. Funnily enough, this felt shame brings them more hurt than the hurt itself. They would go to any extremes to avoid people who hurt them thus, feeling anxious and awkward when confronted with the one who hurt them, going red all over and fumbling and not knowing what to do or say...such *pure pain personalities*. Feeling and thinking too much about too much all the time. The *feeling warehouses* of the planet.

Being one such warehouse, Nethra did not have the *courage* to face the world, *to face him*. It was as if she had romanced him into deceit. And no, one couldn't make such people see the illogic of their behaviour. They understood everything and yet, and yet... when it came to the bottom line, it was always this. Had *she* been too naïve to read too much into an innocuous companionship?

Had Avinash only been flirting with her?

Had it only been the case of wanting female company and having it?

Had *she* mistaken him for someone he wasn't?

Had *she* this...he that? The endless questions to a single, universal answer—may be, may be not.

Things didn't quite improve at the Academy. They worsened. To protect her friend against any further physical, emotional, or mental damage, Madhavi turned into a Z plus security cover. She was all one could see if one wanted to as much as look at Nethra these days. And talking to her was like...next life baby, next life!

But Avinash was to be hoodwinked no more. He was not

much of a stalker by design, but if this fairy tale required him to play one, a shameless one at that, he was more than willing to oblige.

Thus began an emotional hot pursuit that started with phone calls that went unanswered. Then came messages that were left unreplied, along came e-mails that were simply not responded to. This eventually led to the adoption of that centuries old recourse—a letter, written by hand, duly delivered at the lover's doorstep.

The letter that read thus:

Dear Nethra,
If you have ever believed in me, meet me at the Happy Valley Street behind your hostel, tonight.
Love,
Avinash.

Predictably, this worked.

When she finally appeared out of her hostel late that evening, a woolen stole wrapped around her shoulders, her thick black hair falling in soft, long curls over her back and her eyes, pained and parched, devoid of the regular kohl, she looked so lovely that Avinash wanted to hold her forever in his arms. He watched her descending the hill using the steep stairs and when she reached the foot of the hill, he walked up to receive her, the way grooms walk up to receive brides in weddings these days. But of course it was all quite serious.

'Yes?' she asked.

He said nothing. He merely held his hand out for her.

'What?' she asked.

'Come with me,' he said.

'Oh really? That's a nice back up arrangement you have, Avinash,' she said tersely.

'Nethra, I....'

'No really...is your fiancée having some trouble coming to

the Academy? I can understand the trek, you know, you were so deprived of female company you so much needed not to miss her… but now? I mean do you really think I am *that* available Avinash?'

This little paroxysm did not so much as deter Avinash, for he had come prepared for much worse.

'Yes. I think you are *that* available, Nethra. I know you are *that* available…and since you are, now, *you will listen to me,*' he said, with an authority he didn't quite possess yet.

Often, when you are too furious and the one with whom you are too furious says something totally, outrageously ridiculous, you are rendered speechless, quite like Nethra was.

She looked at him disbelievingly even as in all his glorious self confidence, he utilized this moment to reach out and hold Nethra's hand—first one and then the other—

'Please, Nethra, listen to me, once….'

'Why did you not…?' she asked, gently releasing her hands from his.

'Let me explain myself once, Nethra.'

They walked towards the Company Garden, their steps, much to Nethra's agony, still in sync.

Though Avinash hadn't planned a ceremonial speech for the occasion, what came out eventually was something quite like it.

'I wasn't prepared for this, Nethra,' he began, 'I hadn't expected that you would move into my life at this juncture and change everything so completely…My heart knows how much it resisted, how much it tried to rationalize this, but I couldn't stop myself… The past few days have been the loveliest in my life…Not travel, or music, or anything else…*nothing* does to me what your mere presence does…I experience that joy of existence you were talking about…I love myself more when I am with you, Nethra,' he gently slipped his fingers into hers as they walked.

'As for hiding the fact of my engagement, I am at fault. I was afraid…I was afraid of losing you, of never getting to know you fully. We wouldn't have ever come this close Nethra. Never...*You* would never have let me.... I know this is not a plausible explanation but this is the only one I have.'

When they reached the Company Garden, it was already dark and the usually crowded gazebo overlooking the valley looked beautiful. They walked towards the edge of the structure and stood there beneath a star lit sky on a full moon night.

He was gazing at her, his body facing hers, his arms slowly enveloped her body in a warm embrace. He gently caressed her jaw and cheeks with his thumb. He kissed her—a soft, lingering kiss—a kiss exactly as Nethra had imagined it would be. As the moon peeped into the gazebo and the stars smiled in joy, he pulled her closer to his body just as she wound her arms around his neck. They could smell each other, feel their warm breaths on each other's skins, and because nothing could now be said, it was only another kiss that could convey what remained to be said.

Next day, he brought her a bracelet with bright red, yellow and blue beads.

'This is a Venetian glass bead bracelet...' he said, holding it up to her, 'I got this from an old lady's shop at a street market in Rome. I was walking past her when she pinned me down with her eyes.... The most piercing eyes I have ever seen....'

'She put this in my hand, "Give this to your woman", she said. I was surprised that she spoke in English. I was more surprised that she chose me, of all people,' he smiled,

'I believe that was a message. This has been with me for three years, and now, this is where it belongs...' he said, slipping the bracelet on her left wrist.

Two more weeks went by. By this time, the more perceptive observers—discerning faculty member V. Ravi, for instance—could see that something was cooking indeed. Something was spluttering under covers. However, given the secretive dispositions of the ingredients, their extreme aversion to PDA, to not changing FB statuses every now and then or sitting together or holding hands or indulging in such other little things that give one away—no one could exactly tell how much of the cooking was done and how much more remained. It was the kind of information even a RTI query couldn't fetch.

The only way forward was to put the cooker back on the stove and let it sit longer. Things cooked better that way. They became nice and tender. V. Ravi surely had the hang of such intricacies. In the interest of better cooking, therefore, and to give the world a clearer picture of how and where things stood, he decided that Avinash and Nethra must be grouped together for a third time—this time for the Village Visit.

And they did cook better. By the last day of the Village Visit, everybody was telling everybody else, a secret that was not to be told to anybody else—Avinash and Nethra were now an item!

An item that was not to be. Because all things good must come to an end, even if all things bad do not. Because in the intervening weeks, things had been cooking elsewhere too, and had just come to a full boil with Avinash having missed Malavika's calls on not one or two but five consecutive occasions!

One simply could not do this to Malavika. One could not miss her calls and not call back, something Avinash was to truly understand and appreciate, only much later. This was because beneath the several layers of L'Oreal and LV, Malavika was at heart, a Gestaltist—she could always see the whole as much more than the mere sum of its parts. She knew that these missed calls were merely symptomatic (just as the increase in Avinash's response time for her messages, the new distance in his voice, the steady decline in the mush quotient of their conversations were symptomatic) of a deeper problem. And she had considered the problem serious enough to be tabled before a full house, with her father as the chair.

Her father had in turn called up the Academy's Director, who had more or less confirmed his worst fears—certain stories about

Avinash's quiet camaraderie with one particular 'shark' had been doing the rounds on the Faculty grapevine, though, of course, the Director was yet to formally confirm it.

On hearing the Director say thus, the muscles on Mr Rajawat's face had grown taut, marking out the severe lines on his severe face and his mouth had twisted in displeasure. This was distasteful. Disgraceful. Sitting in the anteroom of his office, he had pondered over the situation. He could not let this slip from his hands. He could deal with it.

Out came his famous mobile phone then, and with it, Vachaspati Rajawat in his famous riot control mode.

Three days after their return from the Village Visit, Nethra was summoned by Suranjana Singh, a faculty member and an officer whose two years' sabbatical at the London School of Economics (LSE) had given her nothing more than a severe British accent.

'He is engaged, Nethra,' she commenced, as if they had been discussing this issue since the dawn of time and thus a preamble wasn't necessary.

'Ma'am?' Nethra asked, doing the necessary double take here.

'He is *engaged*, dear!' she looked at her and smiled, a wide kind of non-smile managed without a single tooth showing.

Nethra kept quiet.

'And home wrecking isn't merely a moral issue,' she added, matter-of-factly, 'I am afraid it won't bode well for your career either.'

Nethra kept quiet.

'And, Rajawat Sahab you know...' she said in her singsong voice, throwing her hands expansively, leaning back on her chair and studying her subject with cool, calculating eyes, '...he is an *extremely* resourceful bureaucrat. You know what I mean, dear... very very resourceful....'

Nethra kept quiet.

'And if you ask me, like ask me *in private*,' she added, mock-whispering the last two words, 'he could get quite *vindictive* too. So, if you inflict personal harm, *deliberately*, you do it at the risk of a career...', she paused here a little, 'that hasn't even started.'

Nethra wondered how that little face could contain so many expressions and convey so many emotions, at the same time.

'You are *such* a young girl after all...look at you!' she continued, looking at her as if she were really looking at her for the first time.

'...And you have to go so far. And every single step counts, darling, every little decision. And *no one* can afford powerful enemies here...you see? Many of us have silly misconceptions about...well, whatever...but when things unravel....you know, when they *really* unravel...our careers simply go...down the drain.'

At this point she used her hands to mime a disappearing act, '...whoosh!'

Nethra kept quiet. She hadn't had the opportunity or even the mental acuity to ponder over the dimensions which Ms Singh was dissecting with such surgical precision before her.

'And as a lady officer,' she said finally, invoking an obvious spirit of fellowship hitherto untapped, 'I thought it was my duty to *warn* you. I thought I should at least do that much. And I am sure you will take the right decision, Nethra,' she beamed, nodded and politely, asked her to leave.

As she returned from that disturbing encounter, anxious to discuss the whole home-wrecking angle with Avinash she saw him walking towards his hostel carrying two large luggage bags. He escorted two women, both wearing swanky sunglasses, both looking supremely chic. The younger one caught her attention immediately—her auburn blonde hair, oversized watch and glares, drop shoulder, boat neck mauve top paired with shredded pencil jeans, and her extremely envious frame. Could that be her?

Now we all know what social and moral pressures are to the eccentricity of free will. They are the forces that have guarded civilization from the disruptive entropy of free will. We also know that they are always applied in that order. Social pressure first, moral pressure later. Most rational people with reasonable stores of free will are known to succumb to variants and varying intensities of this combination.

So even as Suranjana Singh explained the demerits of home-wrecking to Nethra, Malavika and her mother were greeting a surprised Avinash at the Academy gates. They had dropped in for his birthday—a full ten days in advance—and in relaxation of the Academy's otherwise stringent rules, they had been graciously allowed accommodation in the Kalindi Bhawan, an officers' rest house that stood next to the hostel where OTs were lodged.

The three walked past Nethra, Avinash looked at her as their paths crossed. Mrs Rajawat noted the intense exchange of glances, and also that the much discussed, never before-glimpsed entity that had been giving her sleepless nights looked way more attractive than in her awkward I-teach-mathematics-at-a-public-school photograph in the Batch Profile.

'But *humari Malvika ke saamne to bilkul phikki hai,*' she later reported to her husband, over the phone.

Given that humanity generally tends to have a greater collective interest in good-looking people, given that we find their tales somehow more exciting, their struggles somehow more heroic, their pains somehow more elaborate, in a mere twenty-four hours of her show-stopping debut at the Academy, Malavika Rajawat had already turned into something of a cause célèbre and her cause, an imperative subject of public interest at the Academy.

Because here, we had not one but three beautiful people, enmeshed in an equation so tantalizing that it was impossible not to follow their story episode-by-episode, it was impossible not to put them on 24x7 surveillance or to discuss their actions, reactions and inactions threadbare, as if they were not people with lives and consequences, but characters who did not quite deserve the luxury of being ignored, let alone be left alone.

But the vivacious Malavika Rajawat wasn't complaining. Oh not at all. In fact, she was savouring every bit of the attention. It was, as if the public gaze had reacted with her adrenaline to make her something of a celebrity. It was as if some hidden cameras were tracing each and every of her several dazzling moves to determine if she could be declared the hottest live-wire on campus. She was on that sort of an inexplicable high. She accompanied him to the Officers' Mess—all smiles and giggles—cracking jokes at the dining table, hitting it off with his important-looking pals. She was his constant arm candy at cultural events, compensating for all the PDA that had hitherto been missing. At every possible opportunity, she could be found cheering 'Go, A, go!' from the stands in the squash court.

All in all, the more Avinash tried to play things down, the more Malavika played them up.

So far, so good for Mrs Rajawat. She had been successful in making a statement—loud and unambiguous. Avinash Rathore was out of bounds—conclusively and irreversibly.

And poor Avinash, duly overwhelmed as he was, the darling that he was, the thorough to the power thorough gentleman who didn't yet know how to say no—he quite simply did not have a plan in the face of such well crafted, full blown propaganda.

Mrs Rajawat was now in charge and her only agenda was to steer the ship of her daughter's marriage, as far away from those shark infested waters as possible. She understood that infatuation happened and men were infatuated all too often, for different psycho-hormonal reasons, at different stages of their lives.

She did not wish to delve too much into the whys. She was concerned only with the hows. It was now her job to bring her son-in-law back to the fold of reality, the way she had, time and again, brought her husband back. It was now her job to help Avinash appreciate the larger picture.

In the fifth hour of their arrival, Avinash had confronted Malavika's mother in private, confirming her worst fears.

'I am quite surprised, Ma'am—the whole timing of this visit—I am surprised I wasn't told...,' he had stammered.

She cut him short, 'Surprise is what it was all about, *beta*! A birthday surprise... and no more ma'am-sham, *beta*! Call me "Mom", the way Malavika does. *Ab to tu hi mera beta hai....*'

Avinash cleared his throat, and commenced on a speech he knew was going to be difficult.

'See, Ma'am, I mean, uh, well, Aunty, I have the greatest regard for all of you, and Malavika is a wonderful person. I like her. She is a very nice person. But here's something I want you to know now, before....'

'If there's anything that needs to be known', she interrupted him again, smiling, 'it is that Malavika loves you more than you can ever imagine...we can't wait to see you two get married' With this, she had touched him witheringly on his cheek, her face swamped with emotion and made a quick, convenient exit.

The Director's moral abutment only buttressed her case. Two days following the duo's arrival, Avinash received an unexpected invite signed by the Director, requesting the 'pleasurable company of the soon to be married couple' for High Tea at their residence. While several of the Academy's Directors had invited OTs to their residence once in a while, the incumbent Director had broken with tradition in the two years at the helm. His ancestral roots lay somewhere in the Royal Family of Bikaner and the noble lineage had rubbed off on all other dimensions of his life as well.

That very evening thus, Avinash and Malavika were ushered onto the lush green lawns of the Director's Bungalow by old royal servants who had served Raja Sahib since before he joined the service. The Director was sipping green tea perched on his majestic rocking chair. His wife, Her Highness Tejaswini Devi, an erstwhile princess from the Royal Family of Jodhpur, gleaned photographs from an old, bulky and equally antique album.

And what an epitome of grace she was! Tall and svelte, she wore a sea blue chiffon sari which highlighted her curves perfectly. Her pallu was fashionably draped just to cover her low bun, and never seemed to fall off its place. She chatted affably even as the Director retained his regular aloofness, nodding occasionally, preferring his Cheddar cheese sandwich over customary enquiries.

It was only when Tejaswini Devi had left with Malavika, leaving the two men behind that the Director opened up, speaking slowly and softly, relishing every word he spoke.

'Feedback about you is good. You hold promise' he said, furnishing an assessment not explicitly solicited.

'Why don't you tuck in?' he added, waving at the assortment of homemade cakes and pastries spread out before them.

Avinash smiled and waited for what he knew was coming.

'Your career is simply a series of decisions, each propelling you further up or dragging you down', he began now, gazing into the void regally as he spoke, 'Most of your batchmates will retire as forgettable have-beens, or worse, frustrated never-weres', he paused deliberately for effect and continued, 'some, of course, will matter.'

'Vachaspati Rajawat has been my buddy since the Academy days. We used to go horse riding together. His personal influence is phenomenal. *Phenomenal,*' he repeated.

'He has cultivated a large network of friends—politicians, bureaucrats, mediapersons, corporate leaders, academia, builders—you name them and you'll find them in his phonebook....'

He shrugged, shook his head, and smiled into his teacup, 'You will inherit them!'

'Being a son-in-law of the Rajawats, you have everything going for you, lucky man!'

Avinash was sickened. Mr Rajawat had gone too far. Avinash disliked the old school's propensity to hard sell in cover. He disliked their propensity to assume that everything and everyone could be manipulated. Mr Rajawat had always assumed so. Now, it was the Director.

'I understand that the whole conversation has a context, Sir' Avinash spoke in a low, deferential voice, 'But somehow, I have never felt the need to depend on somebody else to steer the course of my life, or my career, for that matter. I am quite assured of myself and my capacities, Sir.'

The Director looked up, a streak of surprise in his eyes, 'Of course, you understand the context!'

He paused for a moment before speaking again, and his voice was gloomier, more ominous this time.

'We are supposed to act like men, Avinash. A man lives by honour for a commitment made. A man lives by pride for a word given. We are not creatures actuated by fleeting feelings. We are not animals. Deceit is for lesser forms of life. As for love, take my word for it—fidelity of body might be a fact, but fidelity of mind is a myth. The mind never stops craving, never. Five years down the line, can you say with absolute certainty...,' he paused here to look Avinash in the eye, '...that your heart will not find itself infatuated with someone who...,' he frowned a little, '... mystifies you as much as this lady does today? What would you do then? Ms. Kaul is not the end of mankind's search for the ultimate woman. That search is interminable.'

The Director reclined in his chair, observing his wife and Malavika strolling in the garden at a distance.

Avinash kept quiet.

'My wife is an exquisite lady—*exquisite*!'

He continued, 'Do you think my mind has never wandered off in these 32 years? Eventually, one has to understand that as a responsible man, one cannot be selfish. Look at the innocent girl, she seems so fragile! One has to be mindful of one's obligations, Avinash. Dishonouring a commitment made is highly unbecoming of a proud Rathore, more so, of an officer of the service who is expected to lead by example...,' he said as he put his cup and saucer back on the silver tray.

'We know you will not disappoint,' the Director said sombrely before Avinash left his bungalow that evening.

The Director spoke to Malavika's mother the same evening. Dangling the carrot was pointless, she was told. She should emphasize the moral dimension. She was a poor mother after all. A night later, Mrs. Rajawat walked into Avinash's room at a time she knew he would be alone and gently took his hand in her own.

'I have something to tell you, *beta*...' she settled herself into a chair and said, '...and what I say now should remain between us...,' and with this, the thinnest preamble to tears had appeared in her eyes.

Avinash looked at her, perplexed. All of them had so much to tell each other that the sequencing had all got mixed up.

'*Meri shaadi me mai kabhi khush nahi rahi, beta,*' she began, nonetheless, 'Malavika's father never cared for me...*kadr hi nahi ki unhone meri kabhi*...,' she said in a choked voice.

'He could not understand me. I could not understand him. *Chala rahi hun bas is rishte to kisi tarah*...,' and here she let out a burdened sigh, '...*ab to Malavika hi meri iklauti ummeed hai*...she is my only silver lining, *beta. Usi ke liye jee rahi hun bas*...,' she wiped her tears.

'I was very anxious when her father started looking for a match for her in the services. *Mere pitaji ne bhi yehi kiya tha*...*IAS ke chakkar me*...no one asked me then....'

'*Lekin phir tujhse mili*, and Malavika fell in love with you—*kaise bataun beta tujhe kitna chahti hai wo—phir laga ki zindagi me ab bhi*...,' she broke down completely here, '...*kuch hai*!' she took several seconds to recover.

'I keep thanking God...I keep praying,' she muttered inaudibly, her voice choked in sheer emotion, '...*ab to bas yehi dua hai ki tum dono ki acchhe se shaadi ho jaye aur mere dono bacche khushi se eksaath rahein*...,' she said, wiping off the steady stream of unabated tears.

Avinash was perplexed. This emotional turmoil was unsettling, and so was the realization that *he* had caused this to happen—by agreeing to marry her, by kindling in her and her mother, the hope for love and joy and peace that one keeps looking for in one's life. How could he betray her now, now that she had chosen him as her One Man. How could he do this to her, to a person so *thin, so hopelessly thin?*

But then, how could he do anything other than that?

He could not think. He had to see Nethra, he knew. It would settle him down.

It was half past twelve at night when he knocked at her door. A bewildered Madhavi stared at him as he asked for Nethra, sounding distraught. Nethra came out and led him towards the balcony.

'Come with me,' he pleaded.

Nethra stared at him, confused.

'Let's get married. Let us go to the Bhadraraj temple in the morning tomorrow and get married there,' he said.

Nethra was bewildered. She could not imagine herself getting married—this way, at such short notice.

'They won't understand, Nethra. Their tenacity is beyond words, beyond argument. I know this is not the best way but for now, this is the only way.'

Nethra considered the prospect—she and him, getting married at Bhadraraj, the following day. A chill ran down her spine. Then came images of her family, her Dadi in particular…the hands that she could only associate with weaving freshly-plucked gurhal flowers into pooja garlands for Devi Kheer Bhawani every morning, those frail, bony hands…she could see them, covering her face in utter disbelief.

'This is all that these 23 years meant to you, Nethra. This is all our love ever meant to you…,' she could hear her father's disappointment.

'How we lived every single day of our lives for you…', she could see the sorrow in her mother's eyes.

Nethra could feel guilt rising from inside her chest, all the way up, to clog her throat. 'This is it then…you have shamed us Nethra…. Wish we had died before you did this to us.'

Nethra was her parents' only child. Her father sat for CSE in 1978, 1979 and then finally, in 1980. He hadn't made it. He had lost five years of his youth trying to chase his dream. To make up for it, right from kindergarten, Nethra was told that she *had* to be an IAS officer.

A *peer* had once come to their door while Nethra's mother was pregnant with her. He had told her mother that the girl—the *peer* had said it was a girl—would be a *yashaswini*, born in the raj yoga. Thus, the heaviness of being good, the enormous weight of the expectation of goodness had always lain over the dutiful daughter that Nethra was.

It was Nethra's Dadi, who had slowly and resolutely, ingrained the awareness of a Kashmiri pundit identity in her—this was despite Nethra's convent schooling, despite her Communist father's relentless propaganda, and despite Nethra's tenacious sense of independent opinion. It was Dadi who had told her about Kouls, the followers of the kaula system of Kashmiri Shaivism, and also that her forefathers had been highly regarded scholars—mathematicians and grammarians—whom every ruler of Kashmir had held in great regard and honour.

Dadi had told her that it was Nethra's great grandfather who had migrated to Allahabad, which was why her dada and her father had little perspective of Kashmiri Hindu history and glory. But she had spent her early years in Jammu, the paradise it was then, Jammu and Kashmir. She had told Nethra stories about Kheer Bhawani, the sacred spring at the mouth of Sindh valley in Kashmir, and about the Martand Sun Temple. She would claim that women were not as free anywhere in the world, nor was their education as emphasized, as by Kashmiri pundits.

After Dada's demise, Dadi had moved back to their home in Kulri, their ancestral village. But then the killings had started and in 1988, Nethra's father had risked his life and brought Dadi back to Nazira in Sivasagar, Assam—that is where he had been posted as an engineer in ONGC at the time. Dadi said it was only the 'shadeless green' of the vast tea estates in Nazira that had given her the solace to tide over her sorrow back then.

Dadi was rigid in her notions of caste and custom, especially those pertaining to marriage. All through her childhood, as Nethra hovered around a busy Dadi, listening to her impassioned recitals of vakhs by Lal Ded or shruiks from Nund Reshi, she would wonder how much Dadi had to say about the sanctity of their 'kula' and the necessity of its preservation. Though Dadi understood Hindi, and a bit of English and Assamese too, she would never speak in any language other than chaste Kashmiri.

'I live for the day when you will dress in the pheran, wear aath, dejhoor, and tarang,' she would say.

'I will sit with my friends, singing Wanvun, sipping sheer chai ...the day you will become a Dhar or Bhat or Kachru or Mattoo or a Tikkoo,' she would laugh and her eyes would water.

That was Dadi's propaganda. On some days, she would tell her that nobody in their extended family had ever married outside of their caste. On others, she would wonder if Kashmiri pundits, with all their liberalism and openness would even survive as a community. She dwelled on it thus, with her righteous sense of victimhood, willfully twisting every fact she chanced upon, to fit into her subjective perception of the past, the present, and the future.

'May be, you have a foreboding...,' Nethra would often tease her, '...that I am going to become a *malecchha* someday.'

For Dadi, any Kashmiri pundit who married someone who was not so became a *malecchha,* an outcaste who deserved to be ostracized.

Nethra knew that getting her parents, specially her Dadi to agree to her marrying a Rathore, a Rajput, would take months, if not years. She knew they would come around, eventually, but she needed time. She couldn't shock them into it. They were brittle, especially her Dadi, and would break down. It had to be a slow and resolute tempering, the kind her Dadi had resorted to, to make her understand the immutable fact of her Kashmiri identity.

'I will wait for you outside the hostel at five tomorrow morning… Is that alright?' he looked at her now.

'But…I…cannot,' she replied.

Avinash's eyes narrowed. 'What?'

'I cannot Avinash. Not like this.'

'I love you Nethra…you know that.'

This was it. He had said it, finally. Only that the situation now was not even remotely close to how she had always imagined it would be like. She broke into tears. How she had wanted to hear this…how ardently she wanted to go with him…and to tell him that she loved him too.

Then again, the burden, the heaviness, the weight of sanity…

'I know that Avinash, but this isn't….'

'This is the only way right now….'

'No, there has to be another….'

'We don't have time, Nethra….'

'But I need time… at least a few months…I cannot betray my….'

'Even I will be betraying people, Nethra…you have to trust me.'

'I trust you Avinash, more than I trust anyone….'

'Then come with me…trust me, we will pull it through…we will convince everyone in your family later…*I will*, I promise…trust….'

'Please Avinash, it isn't about trust….'

'It is…if you love me, you have to trust me….'

'Please Avinash….'

'You have to understand my position, Nethra, please….'

'Please!'

Two mountains and a sea of "pleases" between them—unable to budge, unwilling to stay, looking only at the sea at their feet, to do for them what they themselves could not.

'Think about it. I will wait for you tomorrow morning'. Those were his last words. Then, he left.

Nethra did not meet him the next morning. He waited outside her hostel for an hour and a half. He called her thrice. She did not reply.

Malavika's mother was reading the situation closely. She had this knack—to be a part of a situation, and yet, to be able to appreciate it from a distance. In one week, she had realized that this girl-shark was not a *real* fighter—she was a dolphin—a harmless, endangered dolphin. She did not expect her to rebel—not owing to weakness, but to that weight, the weight of sanity.

She watched Avinash leave his room that morning, and return ninety minutes later. He looked so dejected. She was relieved, vindicated. How she had dreaded this other woman before coming to Mussoorie, and how pointless her fears had been!

Nethra waited and waited. She couldn't run to Bhadraraj and get married, but she couldn't give it all up either. She waited for Avinash to call her again—to tell her that a solution could still be found. Every minute of the four days that passed was a nightmare. She checked her e-mail every five minutes, her phone every minute. She kept hearing knocks on the door which Madhavi dismissed every time. Nothing happened.

In the morning of the fifth day, as Nethra and Madhavi brushed their teeth in the washroom, Malavika's giggly squeals erupted from somewhere in the hostel's sprawling frontage.

'Bimbo on a prowl,' Madhavi rolled her eyes and sighed.

Now, there are some people who always know exactly what you need to hear in certain situations. They always say that. They say the exact words you want to hear. These people are your best friends.

'No one's ever a bimbo…you said that, remember?' Nethra rinsed her mouth and peered out of the window to find a perky 'Mal' flicking her long, bonded hair back over her gleaming bare shoulders and flashing her eyes at one of 'A''s friends.

'She is so shiny, a shiny little plastic Barbie…' Madhavi screwed up her face.

'The way she throws her hands as she meets Avinash's friends and cries...,' she mimed with her hands, 'Hey! that's amazing... and *that's* one word she overuses...everything 'A' does is *amazing*, all of 'A''s friends are *amazing*, their cryptic jokes I am sure she doesn't even get are *awesomely amazing*, the weather is *amazing*, the food—imagine the Mess food is *amazing*, Nethra!' Madhavi scowled.

'...And then she says *wanna*... I mean can you believe it?'

'I *wanna* do this 'A', I *wanna* see that 'A'...I so *wanna* blah blah blah...God! God save 'A'...who does she think she is? Posh Spice?'

'So now you are trying to placate me?' Nethra asked with a deadpan face.

'I am *not*—trying to placate anyone. I am simply saying that she is an incredibly shallow and scatterbrained girl... a doormat...a....'

'What is it Madhavi? Tell me; whatever it is.... You have built up a good preface.'

Madhavi breathed out, 'So she is throwing a pre-nuptial party... Ugh! The whole batch has been invited. I tore off your invite because I didn't want you to...Pathetic PDA *baaz aurat*....'

'What party?' Nethra asked, genuinely surprised.

'*Pre nuptial*,' Madhavi answered, mimicking Malavika's cut-glass accent, and then, twisting her face into that Malavika-like poshness, added, 'Not many of *our* friends would be able to make it to our mid-session wedding, you see...so here's this little celebration with all our *amazing* friends.'

Nethra shrugged lightly and slumped on the armchair. She flopped back as heavily as she could on her seat, hoping that it would break but it only creaked annoyingly. There were not many people Nethra Kaul *abhorred*. And she *abhorred* Malavika Rajawat—form, content and concept.

While Madhavi wouldn't give her more details, that there was a party that evening settled one thing.

The marriage was on.

And Avinash hadn't called her again; but Nethra was waiting. Of course, she had told herself and Madhavi, quite categorically, that she wasn't waiting and what she was doing, in fact, was quite the opposite of waiting. She was putting herself through the inconvenient process of starting to put the 'whole chapter' behind her and 'getting over' it and high sounding stuff like that. But just as everyone else who knew her knew, she knew too that she was still very much waiting. She was counting every minute that ticked by, for him to call or e-mail or message.

Anything, something, just a sign, a quarter of a signal…that was all she was living for, like her life hanged on it.

Poor, poor woman, not yet alive to the fact that often in life, when we really want something, not generally but want *really*, the whole of the universe conspires to show us a big, cosmic middle finger.

Anyway.

The party that was thrown for 'all *our* amazing friends' turned out to be quite amazing indeed. Malavika planned it to the last detail. She even baked a 'dancing couple' cake which was obviously the cutest thing ever and everyone seemed to have totally enjoyed themselves—everyone, minus Madhavi and Nesan and practically the whole of the Tamil gang which abstained in solidarity for *their* Nethra (though everyone stated different, unrelated reasons, obviously) and who, in the spirit of solidarity, threw their '*Tammannah*' their own little party the same evening.

Not a grand, JW Marriott's pool-side thing like 'theirs', but a local, in-house thing—an impromptu party at Madhavi and Nethra's room where they laughed and laughed and laughed, even when there wasn't anything funny about the same old jokes, where everyone, including the ordinarily uptight M.V. Samantha and Vijayalakshmi N. grew so boisterous that Nesan had to record the whole event for evidence's sake, and where everything and everyone right from the recording to the recorder were mercilessly ridiculed and secrets of their unspeakable exploits laid bare, amidst frantic protests, before a greatly tickled audience.

It is incredible how human beings become so utterly lovable sometimes, even the ones we ordinarily do not think much of, even the ones we ordinarily assume incapable of things deeper than their frivolous indulgences.... How even they can, at the most unexpected of moments, and in the times of direst needs, delight you with abundant stores of both enormous love and unplumbed wisdom. It is in times like these that despite one's disappointments, one falls in love with the concept of human creation.

After everyone left, the two girls cleared the room of chocolate wrappers and disposable plates and empty cold drink bottles. Then, they cried—Madhavi and Nethra—they cried, and cried, and cried.

Madhavi kept telling Nethra that Avinash would come back, that he would realize it was she whom he loved, not Malavika, that it was yet not late, that it would never be too late. But that's where the similarity ends, between real and reel lives. Because God doesn't plan lives along the plots of *My Best Friend's Wedding* or closer home—*DDLJ*, howsoever much one would like for it to be so.

God's plans seem a lot more random, more inscrutable, less logical, and almost never, repeat *never*, accompanied with the background music to set the tune for things to come. For if we did indeed know what these plans were, those plans would never go as planned, would they?

The wedding day came and went, without any of the last minute twists Madhavi had been predicting for more than a week. The only new e-mail in Nethra's inbox that day was a group mail from V. Ravi, requesting early submission of law assignments and the only message on her phone was a reminder to pay her post paid phone bill—both of which were accorded undue, detailed and disproportionate attention by Nethra.

A day before the wedding, Avinash sent a single liner that, in Madhavi's description, didn't even 'qualify as a proper message.'

It was the only communication from him in the month following their last meeting and it read: 'I love you. I am sorry.'

As simple as that.

On the wedding day, as Nethra lay back in her room, examining the nuanced wording of Avinash's message for the fourteenth time, Mrityunjay Ranjan (of all people) dropped in for a casual chat.

'Hi, Katherina,' he began in his baritone, holding on to the only thread that connected the two—Petruchio and Katherina.

'Hi,' she replied, surprised, confused and a little disoriented at the same time.

He stood before her for a while, examining the room in general and the wall behind her in particular, quite unsure of what he wanted to say, now that he was here.

'Umm...why don't you sit?' she offered.

'Yeah...oh...of course...' he sat on the chair close to the bed she had been sitting on.

A few moments of silence passed between them.

'So, all well?' he mumbled. 'Yes...pretty much,' she replied, her face belying her words.

'Good!'

'Yeah....'

'Uhh...I was...I was just, you know,' he began again, looking nervously at Nethra.

Nethra seemed to be following his words quite seriously.

'Um...I was going through the...literature section in the library...looking for this book...*Of Human Bondage* by Maugham. I couldn't find it,' he trailed off.

'Oh...' she nodded gravely, 'I had it till sometime back, but I couldn't....'

'Oh so you too were reading it?'Mrityunjay feigned surprise, because he had been right behind her when she had had it issued from the library.

'Yeah...I'

'And how did you find it?'

'I couldn't read it. Not couldn't, I mean I didn't....'

'Oh, alright. But, anyway, could you suggest a nice read? I hear you are quite an authority...' he said, hoping that this, at least, would be a subject of common interest upon which a reasonable preamble for what he had to say could be prefaced.

'Yeah...sure,' Nethra replied tentatively, 'What...what is the kind of...what do you like to read?'

Mrityunjay looked at her for a moment. It wasn't fair, he thought, going round and round in circles. How did it matter what he liked to read, in any case? The thing he had to ask her was if she could like him, if she could bring herself to love him even, simply because he did.

Hence, without much of a warning, Mrityunjay dumped the whole literature angle and said, 'I hope this...this whole scene... hasn't impacted you very much,' thus jumping right into the middle of a whirlpool of feelings and pain and suffering and chaos—things he had never been quite adept at handling, things he generally preferred to keep at bay, for as long as, and to the extent that he could keep them at bay.

Struck by this sudden turn to the conversation, Nethra took a moment to collect herself. Oh, how could she miss it? The entity before her was, first and foremost, Avinash's friend, in fact his best friend and he surely deserved his own little share of the much deserved verbal assault.

So she asked quite casually, 'Which whole scene?'

'Uhmm...the scene between you and Avinash...and his wife?' he said, in all his Mrityunjay-ness, about which much has already been said, though of course, much more could always be said.

Nethra bit her lip.

She could have obviously said something sharp and smart here, something like, 'But I didn't know I was playing *with* them...I only knew I was being played upon....'

She could have said something like this to shame the interlocutor but she didn't. All that she said instead was a simple, 'Yes, it has, impacted me, very much.'

A simple answer to a simple question. And it was this simplicity that Mrityunjay loved the most.

'Of course it has. It must have...I...', he tried desperately to look for words that could convey what he wanted to convey—just that, nothing more and nothing less, but then, Mrityunjay could not find those words.

'I am sorry...I mean' he fumbled again.

'Don't be, please don't worry. I will be fine, I guess...' she said, sensing the loss of words at the other end, '...Thank you for coming. That was really very nice of you,' she said.

'I...I will...' he looked around nervously, '...write to you shortly.'

And then he got up, and left.

Two days after the wedding, Nethra finally saw Avinash's wedding album—done by some really hep Mumbai based event photographer—and splashed across Facebook by an excited Malavika for an equally excited audience. The album had garnered some 1899 likes and 462 comments when Madhavi hovered over and then clicked on the album with Nethra as her I-am-simply-not-interested audience.

He was looking like a handsome prince in his wine-coloured *sherwani*, which obviously Malavika had chosen for him because it matched with her wine-coloured, Ankita Mogre *lehenga*—a mention of which had been made in one of her *amazing* thank-you-people comments. He was *smiling* in exactly twelve of the fifty plus photographs—looking at Malavika and smiling. He had even posed for those classic couple poses—a romantic hug, groom asking for the bride's hand, a close dance of love....

'Seriously! How pathetic...and how North Indian, really,' Madhavi gasped, contorting her face badly.

Nethra looked at Madhavi, poker-faced.

'I mean you would never find Tamilians doing such nonsense.... Thankfully they have not smooched in public, or may be, you know....'

'There's nothing North Indian about it,' Nethra snapped back at Madhavi, on this issue for the first time.

'All these cool professional photographers these days...and a lot of them are Madrasis, you know,' she said, emphasizing the *Madrasis* unnecessarily, Madhavi thought, 'they get you to pull off these miserable stunts...nothing *North Indian* about it really.'

Madhavi looked at Nethra who pushed back her chair and closed her eyes.

'I am sorry,' Madhavi said.

'I am sorry,' Nethra said. 'This so totally looks like that Barbie doll's idea,' Madhavi said, sitting next to Nethra now, 'Let's get a little naughty before the camera, 'A'! What a pathetic PDA *baaz aurat*.'

Nethra had told her several times that *aurat* was not an abuse in Hindi. But Madhavi wouldn't listen, just as she would never really acknowledge that the Prince could do something this cruel to his Princess.

The Prince and the Princess did not speak again for the next seven years. They met each other again, after seven long years, at A.N. Bakshi's air-conditioned office in the State Capital.

PART FIVE

Amit Bhargava

Men and Women

Fizapur, 2009

Almost a year later, as Assistant Collector—Under Training in Fizapur, Nethra had fallen victim to the inanities of solitude, that fickle companion whose romance she had once been so much in harmony with. She had tried to forget the past and outgrow her pain, but that was in vain. The only things she had outgrown instead were her jeans, and some of her tops. She had been eating and eating, and eating—the fattier the food the better—to fill up the permanent cavity inside her that needed filling all the time these days. The bingeing wasn't bringing her any of the comfort she had hoped it would. It was only making her feel worse, which in turn made her eat more which in turn made her feel worse and thus the cycle.

While she still had her moments of peace—on those halcyon mornings when sunlight would sieve through the window mesh and fill up her room with its gentle warmth—she knew it was transient peace. She had a heightened sensibility for all kinds of pain these days, and a magnified empathy for all the suffering that the world around her had always carried but which she had grown to truly perceive and feel one with, only now. She had also begun to understand the true meaning of songs and lines that dealt with suffering, a meaning that sunk in either in moments of nostalgia or regret, bringing both peace and pain, a meaning that even you, once out of the scene, would never again decipher.

During those long nights when the speakers in her room resonated softly with Adele crooning *Someone Like You*, she allowed herself to feel sad, to *really feel* sad, and to cry, a few silent tears for love—the true nature of which she had only begun to understand now.

Her parents called her every evening—The conversation followed a standard pattern.

'Did you find out, *beta*?' her father would ask.

Her father had researched on past five years' IAS/IPS Civil List for about a year now. Madhavi had been a willing accomplice, equipping him with lethal stuff like backgrounds, marital statuses and phone numbers of eligible IAS/IPS bachelors. Nethra's father would forward these to her after careful caste-religion based culling and with great hope.

'Did you find out? What do you think?' he would ask.

'I don't really know, Papa…I am only twenty-four. I need time,' she would answer.

His daughter never "really knew". His daughter always "needed time". Good thing was that after a year-long exercise in reality check, her *Dadi* had grudgingly conceded to allow non-Kashmiri Saraswat, Gaur and Kanyakubja Brahmins through her caste filter which was an entry level vetting ground for all proposals. She had an elaborate pecking order among the permitted categories of Brahmin castes, speaking of which, Chitpavan Brahmins were permitted too.

But Nethra's parents weren't very excited. They were deflated instead. They had not reared their lone daughter for marriage. They had always walked the extra mile to ensure that as a student, she had an edge over her peers—the edge of parental guidance and concern. In the school and then in the college thus, it had always been EXCELLENCE. Nothing was ever allowed to come between their daughter and excellence. And now that she had in fact excelled, in some sense at least, one could say, the goalposts seemed to have shifted suddenly. Suddenly, finding a boy and getting married and having a family (if one didn't have one, already) were the things. Now, it wasn't that ABC's or XYZ's daughter had made it to the IIT, or had got a job offer from Google, or had scored a 99.9 percentile in CAT, it was that ABC's or XYZ's daughter had just got married to a boy from MIT who had a seven figure income and a house in GK.

While they searched for a suitable boy, Nethra's parents had fervently hoped that she would choose some 'decent Brahmin boy' from her own batch. They had been dropping increasingly less subtle hints to this effect, though none of these had had any impact on their daughter.

Towards the end of her district training, as she dreaded a fast approaching Phase 2, an end-of-training stint at the Academy—Avinash would invariably turn up with his *PDAbaaz aurat*—Her irritability peaked. She couldn't concentrate. She couldn't read a book beyond the first few pages. She avoided talking to her parents, feeling all the more annoyed when she did.

She wasn't unwilling to get married. It was only that every time she tried, it turned out to be a huge disappointment. And every time she had concluded that it wasn't going to work, she ended up hating herself, for having tried, for having exposed herself, for being desperate enough to have come to the table with a person she knew she would turn down eventually. Mostly, she ended things without a preface, abruptly. She couldn't even summon the courage to be nice.

'You are looking for him in everyone,' M.B. had told her.

'It is probably this…this bracelet. He has bound himself to you with this. Throw it away,' she had said, pointing at her Venetian glass bead bracelet.

But she knew she couldn't throw it away, ever. And M.B. was wrong. It was not only about Avinash. That bracelet meant a lot to her. Avinash had only been a medium. Every night she slept with the bracelet clasped firmly in her hand. In the light of the day, when she was confident and self-assured, the bracelet would stay locked in her drawer. But as she settled down to sleep, she rooted for that bracelet, not because it reminded her of him and she was still dwelling in the past, but because it had come to symbolize hope, love and warmth. She pined for it like a little child reaches for its mother's breast at night, to put away the tiredness of the day and retire to the warm comfort of night, suckling at its mother's breast, for reassurance and comfort.

Into this scene came Amit Bhargava, four years her senior from the Nagaland cadre. When Nethra remained indifferent to his Facebook overtures, he approached her parents directly. In a twenty-minute conversation with her father (a first for Mr Kaul who couldn't go on for more than five minutes with his own wife), Amit Bhargava hit bull's-eye, rolling out pithy couplets from Firaq Gorakhpuri and Faiz, (having figured out the sweet spot in the first five minutes, the floor was his thereafter) and the coup-de-grace, of course, was his response to Mr Kaul's statement that his was quite an enviable job.

Hum to maloom hai jannat ki haqueeqat lekin,
dil ko khush rakhne ko, ghalib, ye khyaal accha hai....

He spoke with such withering charm that made the Urdu poet in Mr Kaul's petroleum engineer heart quiver with unspeakable delight. Duly charmed with the bright officer's *tehzeeb,* he called his daughter forthwith, his voice keen with excitement.

'You have to take this seriously, *beta*. Look at his credentials, impeccable! Most importantly, he comes from a decent Brahmin family. It is a rare combina....'

'Really, Papa? I was given to understand that you are a Communist, at heart...'

'Yes I am,' he shot back, fuming. How much one's kids can hurt one, how much and how often, he wondered, adding, '...but this is a stand-alone matter.'

'Seriously...?'

'Are *you* ever going to take this seriously?'

'I do not look at people this way, Papa...' Nethra replied testily.

'Which way do you look at people, then?' he said, baffled *'Ye kya tareeka hai, Nethra*? All our lives, we worked hard to bring you up well. We never went out on LTCs like our friends did. We didn't socialize. We didn't go out every second day because we feared it might impact your studies. We...'

'I know, Papa, I know how much you *sacrificed...'*, she said, emphasizing the 'sacrificed' a tad too much. I have been told this too many times for me not to remember. I know I will have to live with this *guilt* all my...'

'Guilt? Guilt! You surely use the choicest words, Nethra! Instead of being thankful, instead of showing some...'

'Respect! I know... I should show some gratitude. And I should behave like a good, grateful girl...but tell me, Papa, honestly, I mean, hasn't my life *only* been an *epic* on gratefulness....?'

This last bit of grandiloquence totally pissed her father off.

'What are you trying to say? What is your point?' he fumed, 'and whatever it is that you are trying to say, it will NOT undo what we have done for you. It will not! It will not diminish the efforts that went into...' he grumbled, '...one bit.'

'Papa, I do not wish to argue....'

'No, you will have to answer. Where did we go wrong, tell me? Didn't we work hard, didn't we try? What was our fault? Was it that we wanted you to grow up into a successful and responsible person? Was that our fault?'

'Please, Papa, I don't want to...'

'Yes, yes, I know you don't want to have this *conversation...'*, he said, imitating her accent, 'did we ever tell you which *conversations* you were allowed to have with us?'

Here, of course, he had a point.

'Please, Papa, Don't extrapolate. Marriage is not an assignment that your good girl must finish on time, just like every goddamn assignment she *has finished* in her life....'

'Enough, Nethra, *Bas!* I have just three years left to retire. We still do not have a roof to call our own, you know all about my lipid profile and your mother's blood sugar and yet...*Yet,* Nethra Kaul—the dutiful daughter—is too engrossed in her existential confusions to think of anything other than herself! You are a selfish person, Nethra...an arrogant and selfish person. Go and do whatever you wish to do with your life. I have nothing but regret for the way I have brought you up and I will die with this regret,' he said, his voice breaking down in anger.

Nethra fell silent.

'And do not call me again...DO NOT!'

He hung up.

Nethra was shocked into silence. Her mother was wont to occasional, thyroxin-induced outbursts of this nature, not her father. Mr Kaul was a reasonable man, had always been. And he had always been a proud and confident father.

The two didn't speak for a week—the longest in the past twenty-four years. On the eighth day, Nethra accepted Amit Bhargava's friendship request on Facebook. They started talking on a daily basis by the next week.

The one thing Nethra immediately noticed about Amit Bhargava was that he could not listen to others. The moment he stopped speaking, he'd start fidgeting with things, his eyes would glaze over and his body would show symptoms of unrest. If ever the arc lights drifted from him to any other person, it would make him restless and impatient.

Nethra could also see that his mind naturally lent itself to setting and achieving targets. His current target seemed to be to wow her by his sheer knowledge, and to sweep her off her feet, with his sparkling intelligence. As for the stuff he talked about, it sounded like a sales pitch, always. From the sub-prime mortgage crisis to the physics behind the latest Christopher Nolan flick to his latest stunts in the district, things he said always had to do with how *he* was NOT an ordinary person, how *he* was very important and very intelligent and how it was *he*, and *he* alone who was moving things around, despite everything that stopped them from moving around. As Mrityunjay Ranjan would have described it, Amit Bhargava took himself way too seriously.

Nethra Kaul and Amit Bhargava got engaged a month later. As an experience, it was for her, the exact antithesis of how she would have wanted it to be—hope replaced with numbness, excitement with indifference. Her joy was mingled with a generalized, undifferentiated anxiety—it was akin to sleepwalking—you knew where you were, where you were headed, you knew all the facts all right and just those and nothing more, the perception of feelings having been blocked, logic having yielded to nothingness. An emotional exhaustion had set in inside her, and she had let herself adrift on it, flowing with the flux of events, observing them but not attempting to influence them, as they moved to shape the course of her life.

A fortnight after their engagement, in one of those too sudden to be pleasant surprises that only end up in more confusion than pleasure, Amit Bhargava turned up at Nethra's doorstep in Fizapur, unannounced.

'Hello, sweetheart!' he said, flashing his million dollar smile and practically thrusting a bouquet of deep red roses on her face as she opened the door.

Before she could recover from this and say hello, he slipped his arms around her body and gave her a full-body squeeze fulcrumed at the bums, much to the silent mortification of the circuit house manager, the *chowkidar* and two other room attendants for whose bedazzlement the whole scene was in fact being played out.

This was how it was with Amit. It was, as if great, big cameras suspended from the sky were perpetually recording his moves in slow motion; twenty four by seven. It was, as if, walking into and out of places, taking the microphone or a garland of marigolds, inspecting schools, hospitals, sewer lines or now, his fiancée's room, there was a parallel theme always playing in his head, a theme set to the background music of *Mission Impossible* or *Skyfall*. It was this larger than life, his life. In his life he was Shahrukh Khan, with arms wide open.

For the next half an hour, after the door had been closed for the audience—saying appropriately sweet things all the while and blowing titillating kisses in the air between them every now and then he casually inspected Nethra's room in entirety. He did not do it blatantly, only casually. It was born out of an excitement and curiosity that comes naturally to all fiancés. He opened and then closed her wardrobe, the drawers, and most leisurely, her laptop. It was obvious that he was looking for signs of something romantic—a photograph, old gifts, cards, letters, dried roses—that people like to retain from old lovers. The absence of anything remotely associated with a previous romantic relationship in her room appeased him.

'I would like to meet your Collector and Commissioner while I am here,' he announced now.

This was his first visit to her place, and he wanted to meet the Divisional Commissioner and the District Collector. ('As if he isn't going to have enough of them all through his life,' thought Nethra).

'Okay,' she half sighed. 'But before that, I wish to speak to you about certain things. We haven't talked about it much, so....'

'What sort of things?' he asked, almost suspicious.

'I wish to know...', Nethra hesitated because she knew she was going to sound very theoretical in front of the entity before her, 'What...are your expectations from your partner?' she looked at him.

'Partner?'

'Yes....'

'You mean, my wife?' he asked.

'Yes, your spouse,' she nodded.

'Ah, I do not have any expectations, *per se*...she should just be a nice woman,' he shrugged.

'Nice, as in?'

'Why do you ask? People have got married to perfect strangers and lived together for their lives! Your parents did. My parents did.'

'Yes. They did. But it is important for me to know,' she said.

'She should generally be caring and respectful...and bring up my kids well,' he said, studying her face for a reaction.

'Oh!' she said, listening to him intently, quietly.

So Amit Bhargava had an audience now. How could he not speak? How could he not turn this conversation about certain things his wife-to-be wanted to speak about into some sort of a preliminary coaching in the art of being a 'good wife'?

'See Nethra, a woman, even while she works outside and contributes to the family income, *remains* a woman...' he said pacing up and down the room, his hands making random gestures in the air.

'The division of labour in human society is one of the simplest things to understand. Man sustains a family and a woman maintains it. The role of a man is to work hard, earn a living; that of a woman is care-giving and of course, creating life. That is how it was designed to be. Even where women work outside of their homes to supplement the family income; their primary function remains the same. That is why they have to work twice as hard. That is why we have superwomen, like you,' he glanced at her, smilingly, offering her you-better-be-a-superwoman trophy.

Nethra only listened.

'Take culture for instance. One of the duties of a woman is to instill culture and tradition in the progeny. She facilitates this by adopting the accepted mores and values of our culture into her own being. With her mild and kind temperament, she infuses warmth and relieves stress from the lives of others in the family. She shows how to respect the elderly and tend to the young ones.

She sacrifices and accommodates, even when she knows she isn't in the wrong. That is why we epitomize women. She is unselfish, altruistic and puts the needs and desires of others before her own…' he said, continuing his pacing.

Unselfish. Altruistic. Nethra could feel several weights being piled upon her chest now. But Amit hadn't finished yet.

'I have great regard for women. My mother has been the bedrock of our family. She dedicated her entire life to bringing up her kids and taking care of my father. She is a double gold medalist from Allahabad University, mind you, very efficient, but she never complained. I have never heard her argue with my father, you know, she had held his ego in its proper place…', he said gesturing how egos could be kept in their rightful places, with external reinforcements, 'This is why my father holds her in the highest regard and…'

'Do you think *she* is happy?' Nethra interrupted him.

'What do you mean?' Amit arched his brows.

'Do you think she is happy?' she repeated.

'Of course she is happy. She has everything she ever wanted. Her kids have done well, her husband….'

'Sure she has raised her kids very well…', she interrupted again, She should be a proud mother…but is she, as an individual, happy?'

'What could bring more happiness to a mother than the happiness of her children? As long as we are happy, she is happy!'

'I am just curious…so please don't mind my prying into things but what you just mentioned is *one* dimension of her life. There has to be something *more* to her life, a space where she isn't a mother or a wife, where she is just another person with needs and hopes. Do you think she is happy in *that* space in her life?'

'She ought to be!' Amit seemed flustered now.

'Why?' Nethra asked softly.

'Why should you be so concerned about my mother's happiness?' he asked, a touch of sarcasm in his voice.

'Because I think happy women make happy mothers-in-law too,' she made a forced attempt to sound pleasant.

'Ah! As if women these days give a damn about the happiness of their in-laws!' he chuckled.

Nethra ignored this comment.

'Amit you must appreciate that a person who lives by choice is a person who is likely to be happy. If I live by my choice, I will hold fewer grudges, less remorse, less baggage...and I would be a positive person. If I play a second fiddle to people I think, or am made to think of as superior all my life, I will be a miserable person. I might still make a proud wife or a proud mother, but I will a miserable person. Everyone has an ego, just about the same size.'

'Ego? What kind of language is this? How can you speak in terms of ego and second fiddling in context of a wife, a *mother*?' Amit was not even looking at her now.

'Why? Aren't *mothers* regular human beings?'

'Ah! That is so *primitive*! While I am talking of those sublime values that a woman is capable of...while I am highlighting what makes a woman so worthy of respect, you still operate on that primal plane of needs and wants. It is such a pity that those who clamour for liberation do not understand that it is love, caring and giving that liberates; not strife, not confrontation....'

'The same is applicable to men too...' she said, forcing herself to stay calm.

'Of course not!' he argued, 'Because I am a man, I will exhibit masculinity and traits that go with it. I own up to those values. Why should you feel so ashamed of owning up to the traits of a woman? Why do you women want to become more and more like men? Aren't we different? Your defensiveness only underscores the point that liberated women, educated women look down upon the very values that define femininity.'

'May I know the *values* that define femininity?' she looked at him, surprised.

'Compassion, warmth, tenderness....'

'By corollary, men should not be compassionate or warm or tender?'

'Some men are! Metrosexual men!' he smirked 'I have never understood what good would ever be achieved by blurring those gender boundaries!'

'Gender stereotypes, if I may correct you, Amit. This whole construct of femininity and gender roles is a smart ploy that supports and sustains patriarchy. Glorifying the supreme sacrifice a woman is capable of only reinforces the society's ignoble insistence on more sacrifice,' she said.

Amit Bhargava only stared at her.

'Every human being is as much capable of compassion as they are of aggression, Amit. There are occasions that demand tenderness, just as there are occasions that call for a certain emotional ruthlessness and trust me, you will gradually realize that in life's most decisive moments, a woman is often more capable of exhibiting virtues you attribute to masculinity than a man himself is. Just as a man is naturally capable of tenderness, care and compassion, if only he allows himself that...' she said, settling down on the couch.

'As for your mother, I think it would be a good idea if we all let her love herself first, if we let her put her needs above most other demands and let her take decisions that are important to her. And we can do that even now. We need not make her the sacrificial lamb, we need not stunt her growth—her mental and emotional well being. We should do this if we want our mother to be happy, and not weigh her down with that unbearable burden of a deity on the pedestal.'

She looked down at her engagement ring as she spoke.

'We cannot force her to subservience and beseech her to revel in her sacrifice. We need not institutionalize this subordination of mind and spirit, by devising fancy schemes of false glorification, or by devising the most elaborate, mundane rituals to keep her engaged. To be divine is painful, one should learn to be human first. One should learn to weather one's share of misfortunes—the threats and dangers we are perpetually pretending to be guarding her against.'

Amit Bhargava's annoyance was foaming at the brim by now, and he was annoyed not only at what his fiancée was saying, but at the unperturbed ease with which she was doing so.

'Ah! So I am a hidebound MCP and you are a bra burning feminist...interesting equation!' he exclaimed

Smiling expansively, he continued, 'But tell me, frankly, if it is as you say it is, why should women, including self-styled activists,' he said, pointing towards her, 'expect men to be chivalrous to carry their luggage, to vacate space for them in overcrowded buses or bear the general physical hardships they are too tender to bear? Why this hypocrisy then?'

'I do not burn bras, Amit, and I didn't use the word MCP. I am neither a chauvinist nor a feminist and that is exactly why I know how to carry my weight—I am strong enough to stand through a journey and I earn enough to be able to afford helpers for tasks I alone cannot physically accomplish. My argument is only for rational behaviour, just relationships. It is simply that every person is an "I" and ought to enjoy complete control over the "I".'

'Ah! That's so Ayn Rand,' he laughed. 'Have you been reading any of her...eh...*fiction* recently?'

She grew quiet now. Something inside her wilted. It had never been blooming in the first place, but now it decisively wilted.

'No—but I have read most of it', she replied. Almost as an afterthought, she added 'I don't want to stretch an argument too far, Amit but I just want to know—when do the women in your home eat?'

'Eat! Why? They eat like everybody else. I can assure you the women in my home aren't deprived of food!' he laughed lightly.

'Does your mother sit at the dining table and eat with the others?'

'No. She eats with the other ladies, in the kitchen. The women eat together, after the men have finished. But that's how they *choose* to eat. If you so wish, you could always be an exception!'

'Which means I could eat with the men, at the table with the other women serving us?' she asked.

'Would *you* want that?' he asked.

'That is not important,' she sighed.

'Well, we will cross the bridge when we come to it,' he smiled, reaching across to her shoulder and pressing her tightly against his frame.

The Inevitable Recoil

Fizapur, 2009

They met the Collector and the Commissioner the same evening. At the party hosted by the Collector, Amit was the epitome of affability. Deft as he was in the diverse arts of blatant flattery, fake deference and empty mendacity, he knew the exact things to say to everyone. Everyone thought of him as the charming, interesting man who had something for them—the officers, their wives, even the children. The chivalrous offering of his chair, his hand and his shoulder to the 82-year old Mrs Dasgupta, the honey-dipped baby talk with unknown little children, and other seemingly random little acts of contemplated sweetness made all the ladies go so, 'Awww!'

'You are so lucky, Nethra…', exclaimed one,

'He is so handsome *and* he is so nice…so *genuine*!' offered another as she elbowed her.

Nethra smiled vaguely. She closely observed the man on the prowl.

Amit Bhargava *looked* handsome. He smelled of cologne and his gelled hair was neatly combed back. He was the embodiment of every girl's dream—a tall, broad-shouldered, well-mannered, well-dressed hunk with a handsome face. Why couldn't she like him then? Why couldn't she simply *bring herself to* like him? And just then, looking at him nod and chat pleasantly with someone even she didn't recognize, Nethra had the answer—Amit Bhargava had dishonest eyes.

He was always trying, trying very hard to play to the gallery all the time. But Nethra could understand the effort he put behind this cloak of all consuming geniality. He had several fancy tools in his toolbox; the sentences, the punch lines, the little stunts and tricks he employed to make that remarkable first impression, the tools that came in very handy in his profession. He had used almost all of them with her. He had tried hard, and like with most of the other things he had tried his hands at in his life, he had 'got her'. She had heard those jokes before, run through the profound, pseudo-intellectual discourse about the scheme of things, but she could see through that now.

It was probably Faulkner who had said something very close, wasn't it? Something like, *the next time you try to seduce anyone, don't do it with talk, with words...women know more about words than men ever will...and they know how little they can ever possibly mean.*

She smiled quietly as the lines came to her. How little can they ever possibly mean! How little!

On their way back from the party, Amit was unusually quiet. Aware of government drivers' compulsive tendencies to eavesdrop, he was basically trying to convey his displeasure by way of a tense silence.

Once inside her room, he began, quite curtly, 'What is wrong with you, Nethra? Why can't you behave normally? What is the point of appearing so aloof?'

'Aloof! I am sorry but that's how I am. I am never the life of any party!' she retorted.

'Please stop being so smug, Nethra. You know you are attractive. Women like you do not even have to exert that much. You just have to be nice and sociable! Is that too much to ask for?'

'What do you mean "not exert that much"?' she asked, disgusted.

'I mean you appeared so aloof! You could have mingled with

the ladies, the Commissioner's wife. Most of them are housewives, right? But intelligent people can mingle with just about everyone, can't they?'

'Even if I were a housewife, I would have been like this, Amit. Being a housewife doesn't make you dumb. I am the way I am. I do not wish to change anything about myself...and I will not feel guilty about this,' she retorted.

Amit stepped back mentally, his voice was a shade softer now, 'You have to understand darling that we are a couple now. When we socialize, we should make the right moves and network with the right people. You told me your Commissioner is leaving for the Government of India deputation soon. He could help us with the cadre change business; you know. It's only your social network that counts!'

'I can't build social networks, Amit...not when I do not feel sufficiently connected with the person I am supposed to spend the rest of my life with. I am not used to living a life which is all on the outside. I cannot live with so much pretence,' she said.

What Amit Bhargava singularly disliked was anyone, especially a woman, challenging his authority. He had been raised to believe that every woman had a 'place', and it was important to keep her in that place. Nethra had been getting on his nerves lately. She was clearly unaware of her place.

So Amit calmed his nerves now. He had to handle her with kid gloves, the way men handled cute little puppies. Switching to a more cordial tone, he moved towards Nethra with an indulgent look, his hands reaching for her waist, 'Alright then, let's go beyond pretensions...let us *really* look at each other...', he said.

Pulling her towards himself, he said, 'Tonight...It's a beautiful night, don't you think? And we will make it one to remember. So now, please smile and change into something nice.'

The ground beneath her feet sank. Did he intend to stay for the night? She quickly removed his hands from her waist and turned towards the washroom. She needed to clear her head. She had booked the adjacent room in the Circuit House for him. She wanted him to go, now. Why was he then taking off his shoes and unbuttoning his blazer? Why was he taking out the shorts from his suitcase?

'You had asked me to book Room number 4 for you. I have…' she swirled back and said, somewhat hesitantly.

Amit chuckled in amusement. 'Yeah! I don't want people here to know that we are sleeping together which of course we are. This is a small town honey! People talk.'

His voice had acquired a strange, sexy tone and the way he looked at her made her uncomfortable.

Something had to be done, she knew, and soon.

'Amit, we aren't married yet. I feel we should wait for this… whole thing…till after marriage,' she parried.

'Which age are you living in, my Gloria Steinem? My…' he moved to grab her waist again, '…Virginia Woolf. We are engaged to be married, right?'

'I am a little old-fashioned, Amit. I am not very cool and I am not comfortable with this,' she said, firmly pulling his hands off her waist.

'I see you have an electric kettle here…can we have some coffee? A shot of caffeine to add to the fun?' he said, pointedly ignoring her discomfort.

Nethra's face grew stern. She looked away.

'All right, sweetheart. No fun stuff! But we can sip some hot coffee together, right? Also do a bit of "networking" before we call it a day?' he said, making inverted commas in the air with his fingers.

He hovered around close to her as she prepared coffee. She could clearly smell the alcohol on his breath. She went inside and changed into a cotton nightdress—a loose, pale blue T-shirt and pajamas. She sat sipping her coffee across the table from him. It was half past eleven and there was nobody else at home.

As she turned to put the empty cups back in the kitchen, Amit grabbed her from behind, holding her from the back, fingers moving around her waist, and then caressing her hips.

'Are you a virgin?' he asked, his voice raspy and hoarse.

Nethra didn't answer. Her patience with him was fast receding and so was the dignity of the conversation. He repeated himself.

'What difference does that make?'

'A lot!' With a sharp jerk, he twirled her around, her body now facing his.

'Take off your clothes,' he ordered.

'Amit I have made it very clear that I do not want this…' she responded in defiance.

She had barely completed her sentence when he pushed her on the couch. What followed was not an act of love but of aggression. It had no trace of warmth or softness. He pounced on her, his hands groping, squeezing her breasts and his mouth opened wide, his tongue pressing hard against her mouth in a bid to subordinate it.

She was alarmed. She resisted fiercely. His response to her resistance was more force, and aggression. She couldn't stand this violation. She was disgusted. She bit his hand hard, the entire force in her body drawn into this action and slapped him right across the face with all her might.

'Get off me!' she shrieked, 'You stink!'

Amit Bhargava sprang back in pain, staring at her in shock and anger.

'Ah! So you haven't gotten over him yet! Avinash Rathore…' he hissed, spitting out the words

'I should have expected this.' His face was red and his voice full of hatred as he arranged his clothes back together.

'Get out of my home right this moment!' she hissed back, her voice quivering with wrath.

'You cannot get over the fact that he fucked you at his will and then dumped you big time….'

'Go away or you will get killed today!' she was shaking wildly now.

'Was he really so good, honey, that you won't let others touch you now?' he gnashed his teeth, 'Or are you a bloody whore, still craving to be fucked by happily-married man?'

Nethra closed her eyes. She would not cry. She wouldn't let this filth see her shaken. A sudden calm filled her head. She could breathe. Yes, she hated him. It was precisely this—hatred. *Hatred.* She felt relieved.

'Yes, Amit Bhargava. I have had the *best* time of my life with Avinash Rathore and I will always love him immensely. *Always.* He is every bit a man, and I realize this all the more when I deal with shrimps like you. Yes, he left me, and yes, I am shattered. But this is not reason enough for me to commit the wretched sin of marrying you. Your weakness is repulsive. You are a despicable piece of scum,' she said, her voice surprisingly even.

'And let me give you some parting advice—don't try so hard. It shows. And you might not know it but it looks ugly. Now, leave at once. I have nothing else to offer. I know it is the cadre you are interested in, not me. Go and buy yourself a slave because women for you are either slaves or whores.'

'I am doing you a favour, you slut!' he was furious.

'No officer with a morsel of dignity will ever marry you because you are a second-hand product with a fast approaching expiry date. Respect me for the favour!'

'Respect too comes with an expiry clause, Amit Bhargava, and you lost it from the word go. Good for me that you got down to the brass tacks this soon. I am spared the suffering of being your wife!' she said, pushing the ring off her finger and flinging it across the table.

'Now fuck off before I call the police and get you booked for molestation!'

She announced her decision to her father the next day.

'Don't explain yourself, Nethra,' said her father, 'Age is clouding my rationality. It was not a good decision.'

Nethra's mother took longer to come around. A girl walking out on an engagement or marriage was unheard of in their circles. She continued to dwell on the ignominy their irresponsible daughter had brought upon their respected family.

Apocryphal stories started floating around a fortnight after their break-up. Amit Bhargava had broken off the engagement when he discovered that Nethra and Avinash were carrying on an illicit affair. The two had been meeting clandestinely, in shady hotels, and she had also had an abortion—Amit had seen the medical papers—Nethra was also generally quite licentious, abusive, alcoholic and in general, "of loose character."

This being the original version, the versions that reached Nethra via some of her Tamil friends made her seem like a deranged prostitute.

Demonizing a working woman is, in fact, one of the easiest jobs in the world, next to writing her off. It is easier than sipping a lazy cup of tea over mindless gossip. People are primed to readily take to stories of her sins and failures, and to fabricate and circulate them, with glee. I guess it's ingrained in the human DNA—that subversive wish to see a woman in her 'place', and her being put in it.

Nethra and Avinash maintained a studied silence over the stories. When they reached Malavika's ear from some of her concerned friends—officers' wives who on their part had contributed generously to their wider circulation—she did not bring it up with her husband. She knew her husband had been faithful. He hadn't left her alone a single day or night in the past year. His phone had carried no suspicious content—ditto for his mailbox.

Amit Bhargava married an IPS officer from the same state a few months later.

The Man In The Arena

Barela, 2010

Amit Bhargava spun his Parker Premium pen between his fingers, rocking a little in his chair. He said in a measured tone, 'So, who do you think is your boss?'

The mining officer and mining inspector stood in horrified consternation, blurting out timid little denials, trembling. The stenographer was summoned for dictation.

'An enquiry team headed by the ADM is hereby constituted to investigate the complaints of extortion, willful delay and corruption filed against the Mining Officer by 1) M / S Aramco Mining, 2) Shramjivi Patrakar Sangathan and 3) Barela Vikas Evam Samajik Utthan Samiti. The team shall enquire into the substance of allegations and submit a factual report in a week's time,' he read out without a pause.

'Now you will know...' he glared and with a wave of his hand, motioned them out. The mining officer was due to retire in six months. The mining inspector was a 24 year-old probationer who hadn't, as they say, tasted blood yet. Even before the enquiry orders were served, they knew they had thrown themselves into a tornado of professional calamity. The officer might have to spend the rest of his retired life cooling his heels in *sarkari daftars*, sorting out a departmental enquiry before retirement claims could be settled. The probationer, he could never get to taste blood after all. A single show cause notice could end his career.

If only they had not responded to the Sub Divisional Magistrate's commands, if only they had known who their boss was, they would have been safe. Their boss liked to kill—with his Parker Premium pen—on paper, in cold blood.

Mrityunjay Ranjan, the new, swashbuckling SDM of Barela had resolved to play the Dark Knight for his Gotham City by locking horns with Barela's notoriously ruthless mining mafia. In an overnight raid conducted simultaneously across seven locations in his sub-division, he had seized 43 dumpers loaded with high grade hematite apart from several excavators, Poclain machines and earthmoving equipment. At 4 a.m. when Amit Bhargava received the first SOS call from the ruling party's *zila adhyaksh*, Mrityunjay had already completed voluminous paperwork to nail the culprits.

'Why didn't you inform me about your plan beforehand?' Amit asked irritably over the phone.

'I...wasn't required to, Sir,' Mrityunjay replied.

'Who tipped you about the locations?'

'That...I have completed the paperwork, Sir. I am forwarding them to you with recommendations as to the quantum of monetary penalties,' Mrityunjay replied, clearly ignoring his boss's question.

'It is 4 in the morning. When did you do all the paperwork? Who are with you?' Amit asked peremptorily, this time.

'The mining officer and his team, plus my revenue team, Sir. The *tehsildar* is on his way to deliver the files to your residence, Sir,' he said.

Amit Bhargava was piqued—one, Mrityunjay Ranjan was acting smart—two, Mrityunjay Ranjan was trying to outsmart his boss—three, while doing so, Mrityunjay Ranjan was being unrepentant and insubordinate.

'You should have consulted me,' he said, and though his voice was quite even, Mrityunjay could sense the brute force in it.

'Something like this, of this scale cannot be carried out so stealthily. We could have had discussions—sorted things out—now,

I want you to hold on to the files. I will assess the situation and instruct you about the future course of action,' Amit said with an authority he knew he must now assert over his subordinate.

'Discussions? With whom, Sir?'

'With people who you have unnecessarily dragged into a totally avoidable controversy, Mrityunjay! You have no idea what sort of press this is going to generate.... That's what happens when you skim through the surface of problems, without understanding them,' Amit said with the air of an adult whose patience with juvenile levity had just brimmed over.

'You mean we could have had discussions with the mining *mafia,* Sir?' he asked, harping unduly on the word mafia.

'I believe mining regulation is a magisterial exercise, Sir, as against a *panchayati* one...' he half-chuckled.

If this chutzpah wasn't enough, his voice glowered with the hair-raising intensity of the Dark Knight as he added, 'You will have to take a call on this, Sir. Forty-three dumpers carrying over one thousand metric tonnes of illegally mined hematite have been seized for unauthorized mining on government land. The market value of seized mineral is over two and a half crores. The penalties could go up to as much as twenty-five crores. We have the entire gamut of evidence—fake transit passes, mining operations way beyond the prescribed area...I want you to take a call, Sir,' he insisted.

Amit Bhargava took the call, in a manner that was quintessentially his. The cases were referred to the ADM who in turn colluded with affected parties to drill holes in the cases and passed orders exonerating the defaulters on one frivolous ground or the other. Amit Bhargava didn't bring himself into the scenario. The cases never came back to him. It was the ADM who passed the orders in lieu of a decent pay off of 20 lakhs. Local reporters and those from Barela Paryavaran Jagran Manch were also suitably appeased. Amit Bhargava parted with a lion's share of the one crore that was paid off to push the cases under the proverbial carpet.

Amit Bhargava shrugged helplessly as he signed departmental enquiry orders against the Mining Officer with Mrityunjay Ranjan as his audience. He said, 'You need to hone your drafting skills, Mrityunjay. The lawyers could nail you down with technical loophole in every instance. You need to have your basics right before you venture into something like this....'

Amit Bhargava was a fighter. When he was five years old, his father, an Assistant Engineer in PWD bought him a schoolbag as a birthday present. It was muddy brown in colour, and the panel on its top flap glistened with the words—'I can't help it. I am a born loser...'—written in flashy red. His father had either not understood the message or had not found the time to read it before gifting it to his son.

He had hurriedly picked up the first thing he saw at the retail store and paid the shopkeeper, his mind still busy figuring out how much different contractors owed to him for works in his area. This was one hell of a business...keeping track of due payments. He maintained a small spiral diary to record the "cuts" due to him. He would extract these from conniving contractors before recording his valuations in the Measurement Book, in lieu of more sand, less cement, flaky metal and reduced thickness of iron reinforcements.

Amit's mother had instantly disapproved of the message on the bag, and of the bagmaker's mental bankruptcy. How could she not? She was a double M.A. in English from Allahabad University, after all. What sort of person would print such horrible things for young children, things those little kids would lug around on their backs? Her annoyance however, was an internal musing, an unuttered thought. The bag was a gift—the first from a busy father to a grateful son—and a mother had no business poking her ignorant nose in it.

Something about that bag stuck. Those words stuck to that

child, like an extension of his name. Children in his class giggled and pushed and called him a loser. Every passing year, he struggled as one of the weakest boys in the class, a loser, bullied by his peers and sneered at by teachers for his querulous and jaundiced ways. His life had been a struggle against those voices—the mean laughter, that wicked contempt, those cold and condescending stares from teachers.

Throughout his childhood, he struggled to get rid of that bag on his back, to prove to the world that he was not a loser, to claw his way out of the trap that those words had become for him.

It was only in college, that he realized that even though he couldn't become strong, he could still become popular. If he talked of things people wanted to hear, pandered to their insecurities, to the Lowest Common Denominator, if he played to the gallery and lied without a care, people would like him. In fact, most people hated strength and truth, just the way he did. It made everyone feel weak and helpless. He also knew that perfection or excellence were skewed attributes, they rarely instilled harmony. And worse, they made both—people possessing them as well as those devoid of them—feel inadequate and insecure.

Lightness relieved people.

He freed himself of the bag on his back the day UPSC allowed him into the IAS. He shot ahead with a vengeance. There was no stopping him now. His childhood became a cold and distant memory, repressed in the dark corners of his mind. The only scar that remained and showed was his intolerance for children. He felt like choking them, hitting them hard on their faces, and hanging them upside down. He hated children.

Amit Bhargava loved the way his life looked at present. It had only been a year since he had joined the cadre, post his marriage to an IPS officer three years his junior. He had already landed his first charge as District Collector, as DM and Collector, Barela. His palatial bungalow had become something of a ecosystem these days and as any description of an ecosystem must begin with water, the water supply department had recently installed a 24x7 solar water heating and pumping system in the bungalow which in turn nurtured the wheat, pulses, fruits and vegetables growing on a 'demonstration organic farm,' courtesy the agriculture department. The farm produced enough green feed for 3 cows and 4 buffaloes which were looked after by the veterinary department and which in turn generated sufficient organic manure to nurture the maize which in turn fed the chicks and hens and goats which in turn were consumed in various forms as instructed to cooks who worked in the kitchen and prepared tea eight times a day for all the other *ardalis* and peons who worked elsewhere, doing something or the other, in the bungalow, parts of which were being remodeled along the lines of *Mannat*—SRK's home in Mumbai.

Things were moving with perfect harmony in Barela, and Amit Bhargava was in full control—and then—Mrityunjay Ranjan happened. He had been granted a second chance. Having been shown the door from Kisalpur in an unceremonious manner, he had subsequently been shunted to inconsequential positions in the Secretariat till some kind, condescending *babu* in the General Administration Department decided that he deserved a second chance.

The first thing Mrityunjay had noticed as he stepped inside Amit Bhargava's office to 'call on' his new boss was a wooden plaque. It hung on the back wall and was set in an ornate, wrought iron frame. It carried a few lines from Theodore Roosevelt's famous speech, 'The Man in the Arena.'

It is not the critic who counts; not the man who points out how the strong man stumbles, or where the doer of deeds could have done them better. The credit belongs to the man who is actually in the arena, whose face is marred by dust and sweat and blood....

Mrityunjay's boss, Amit Bhargava, looked every bit like a man in the arena; except that for a man actually in the arena, a proclamation of intent was quite unnecessary. On his work desk directly facing him sat another plaque, considerably smaller and Mrityunjay could guess that it read 'Liar, liar, pants on fire,' in different fonts, colours and sizes. He laughed silently. He stole a curious look at the other plaque the next day, when his boss was in the washroom. It read—*Never attempt to win by force, what can be won by deception.*

So much for the gladiatorial arena!

Mrityunjay instantly decided he could not like his boss. The man was a demagogue.

The boss did not like his subordinate either.

In bureaucracy that thrives by subservience to the hierarchy of authority, Mrityunjay Ranjan was an unruly exception. He conferred his regard on excellence, not on position. From Day One therefore, Mrityunjay Ranjan's presence made Amit Bhargava uncomfortable and this discomfort quickly grew into a strong dislike.

'I don't find you at our weekly *nashamukti* motivation workshops?' he once asked Mrityunjay.

'I do not find much of a role for myself there, Sir.'

'And you are usually missing from our monthly *mahila sashaktikaran sammelans* too…actions speak, Mrityunjay. People form opinions too easily. I have not been able to trace you at our environment awareness drives either….'

'Why do you keep looking for me, Sir?' Mrityunjay wanted to ask. He kept quiet.

'Same with the Rotary's Youth Sports Camps, Mrityunjay… You must understand that we are public figures…the community looks to us for social leadership. We must show the way forward. Our conduct has to be impeccable, we must espouse good causes.'

'Sir,' Mrityunjay replied coldly, his standard response to most things he thought best not to answer. Obviously, he couldn't tell his boss that *mahila sashaktikaran* doesn't come from *sammelans* which the women attended only for the hot *samosa-chai* in any case. Likewise, the youth cannot be *made* to arise and awake by treating them to pseudo-speeches at Sports Camps. Haven't we been doing this for a hundred years?

Though Mrityunjay was not doing so overtly, Amit could feel that he was laughing. He wanted to punch Mrityunjay in the face. There was something about Mrityunjay that made Amit Bhargava experience a definite loss of control, every time they met. He felt helpless and angry whenever he realized this. This incommodious coexistence that had in a few months become a permanent subject of speculation in Barela's *sarkari* grapevine eventually reached its tipping point with the Raj Vilas Resorts case.

Raj Vilas was a sprawling 90 acre farmhouse owned by the Home Minister's nephew, a local overlord and one of the biggest civil contractors in the state. He was redeveloping this estate into a lavish, 7 star tourist resort and his *yuvraj* credentials had ensured that RVR was seen as the 'First Project' in the VIP-philic work culture of rural Barela.

Everyone in Barela knew well that the 90 acre farm house stood on tribal land, misappropriated unlawfully some fifty years ago, in fraudulent deals that the district administration had conveniently chosen not to take note of. Within a month of assuming charge, Mrityunjay Ranjan registered 42 cases of unauthorized dispossessions, put every single case on fast track and in a matter of a month, put out orders that the entire land be transferred back to tribal families.

Amit Bhargava knew very well that for one, his subordinate was walking into a predicament that impulse alone couldn't resolve. One tactless action in this case could seal the coffin of Mrityunjay Ranjan's career. Therefore, Amit Bhargava had chosen to remain silent, to observe and enjoy the increasingly muddled spectacle as political interests coagulated against the recalcitrance of a '*sanki*' bundle of whims that the new SDM was.

'*Aap chinta mat karen, Sir, main hoon na,*' he had to assuage the home minister who was getting increasingly concerned about the inexplicable obsession the new SDM quite clearly seemed to have for RVR.

'Main hoon na...!' was what he would also tell the several *jan pratinidhis* who swarmed his office with representations against the naye SDM sahab.

'Ab kya batayein, vidhayak ji...wo kehte hain naa...adhjal ghaghri chalkat jaay.'

But as we all know, the aforementioned *adhjal ghaghri's* cup of shit tolerance was brimming over perpetually.

So on being enquired about his plans for RVR, Mrityunjay had told his boss quite clearly, 'Individual conviction to act must prevail over collective consensus to act helpless.'

And Mrityunjay was right. He had observed the dispossessed farmers who showed up on court hearings, old men with hollowed cheeks, wrinkled foreheads, pencil thin legs and sharp eyes—sharp eyes that nursed a dying hope for justice. They would sit in silence, sometimes muttering to themselves, and staring into the void. They would huddle together at the far end of the courtroom, never quite looking *yuvraj* or his counsel in the eye and leave quietly after every hearing. But none of them ever missed a court hearing. Somehow, the *naye sahab* had kindled something in them—a faint ray of hope. Somehow, Mrityunjay felt responsible for keeping it alive.

Thus one fine morning, in a brazen act planned in absolute secrecy, the Sub Divisional Magistrate of Barela connived with his Sub Divisional Officer of Police, a young recruit into the IPS and a justice lover his parallel, and laced every inch of RVR with a truckload of dynamite. The issue of eviction orders, serving of notices and the subsequent seizure of RVR premises, all had happened in a matter of the preceding 36 hours.

'We will blow it up,' he told his batchmate on phone, just after signing the eviction orders.

His batchmate breathed out. He smiled. 'Give me a day. Also, summon the telecom exchange incharge in your office. The exchange has to be shut down immediately.'

The telecom networks in Barela were jammed and in a post-midnight swoop down, every staffer of RVR was picked up and hauled inside a police *chowki* outside the town limits. This, while the District Collector and Superintendent of Police were blithely unaware, and touring the rural wilderness on a two day long *Adivasi Samman Yatra*. Amit was travelling with a few close friends—renowned journalists and social activists, and his core team of reporters and photographers was covering all the right photo opportunities and recording all the right sound bytes.

In several powerful explosions spanning over ten minutes; RVR came hurtling down to the ground even as thousands gathered to witness the unprecedented spectacle in overawed disbelief. A thing like this had never happened, and never would it happen again, they knew. Young boys hooted and howled in exultation, the older and infirm, those who had learnt to live with RVR over the years gaped in bewilderment for nothing in their collective experience had prepared them for this outrageous act of contemplated chutzpah.

As the dust settled and the explosion expert declared the site safe, people ran in in hundreds, collecting what they could out of whatever was left. Many of them simply collected debris that would be preserved in their homes over the years. In the past 70 or so years of them becoming free, they had never seen freedom face to face as they did today. It wasn't about a piece of land. It was about courage, and truth.

Mrityunjay Ranjan and his batchmate from the IPS were put under suspension the same evening.

'It was not only brazen, Mrityunjay, it was foolhardy. Who do you think you are? Superman?' Avinash was the first to call, post his suspension.

'No. A Warrior. A Philosopher Warrior!' he laughed. 'Ah! What could have been a wiser way, Prince? Well, before you enlighten me, let me lay it out for you.... Pass the order, appease one party. Withhold its execution, appease the other. Bide your time. Do nothing. Simply bide your time. Let the buck pass to whoever comes next. Or smarter still, ask the wronged to go to the courts. The Courts shall instruct you to carry out your orders. You will lest you should be held for Contempt of Court. You shall carry out your orders not because you passed them but because the Courts ordered you to. Oh hypocrisy, thy name is tact! What have we come to, Prince?'

Avinash was silent. Mrityunjay was right.

'But you cannot be an extremist and stay in the system, Warrior,' Avinash retorted.

'What should we be then, Prince—Moderates?' Mrityunjay laughed aloud. 'Dear Buddha, I would rather die an extremist than get moderated to inconsequence....'

'Extremism will drag you to inconsequence, Warrior. To make a change, you have to stay here. You will not stay here if you do not change yourself, if you do not become more reasonable,' Avinash reasoned.

'Change? Does the Prince ever bring change?' he laughed. 'I am a Warrior, not a Prince. The Prince, the reasonable man, adapts himself to the world; the Warrior, the unreasonable one, persists in trying to adapt the world to himself. Therefore just as all stability belongs to the Prince, all progress depends on the Warrior,' Mrityunjay replied.

'You may think so, and your thinking may have no correspondence with reality,' Avinash said grimly.

'And *that* may still not limit my freedom to think so,' Mrityunjay replied.

'Be reasonable, Mrityunjay. Please try to understand.'

Mrityunjay ran his fingers over his wrinkled brow.

'Prince, I live a life which is not circumscribed by a career. My self esteem is independent of the vagaries of office. In my list of concerns, which is probably not half as long as yours, postings and transfers, intrigues and networks, understanding of and influence with the Who's who, don't figure. Any work given is work that needs to be done. Whoever cares if you are Deputy Secretary, Finance or Controller, Govt. Press or Director General, Foreign Trade or Commissioner, Handlooms? You are just another cog, not even a man, just a cog; as replaceable, as dispensable,' he scoffed.

Avinash was quiet.

'You must meet the Chief Secretary, Mrityunjay. Explain your side of things and if necessary, acknowledge that you acted on impulse,' Avinash insisted.

Mrityunjay swallowed hard. He stiffened. 'No one can persuade the other to change, Avinash. Each of us guards a gate of change that can only be opened from the inside. We cannot open the gate of another, either by argument, or by emotional appeal. That's Marilyn Ferguson.'

'I am not fooling around Mrityunjay…this is not some joke!' Avinash was getting impatient now.

'I know this is not a joke, Avinash. Do not bother your utilitarian mind with issues pertaining to me ever again. We have long ceased to operate on the same page.' He disconnected the phone.

It was only after four years that they spoke again, over the phone again, and this time, it was Avinash Rathore and not Mrityunjay Ranjan who was at the receiving end of justice.

PART SIX

The Sale

Jal, Jungle, Zameen

Palampur, 2015

Amlai Thermal Power Plant (ATPP), a 1080 MW PSU of the State Government was situated in the Majra subdivision of Palampur district. ATPP had commenced operations in the year 1982, and it sat over a sprawling 2700 hectares of prime government land, most of which still lay undeveloped and underutilized. Beneath the land lay coal. Several coal blocks had recently been allocated to power, iron and steel, and aluminum majors in Majra and concomitantly, a mad rush for land had ensued.

To transform Majra into the nation's power capital was one of Mantriji's most fervent wishes. The only 'roadblocks' to its transformation were the forests and the tribals and these roadblocks were looming large with the growing and active involvement of environment watchdogs, tribal welfare warriors and promoters of several eclectic causes and persuasions.

Land purchase for industrial projects had become a strife-ridden enterprise. A whole new class of middlemen (part-time political workers, RTI activists, '*patrakars*', '*samajik karyakartas*', permutations and combinations of the aforementioned) had sprung up to make easy money as huge investments poured into big-ticket projects in Majra. These messiahs of the Project Affected Persons (PAPs) were phenomenal nuisance mongers—they knew how to distort facts, fabricate dark stories of dispossession, get them flashed in the media, and then sit back and watch in glee as microphones were hurled at the sorry faces of nonplussed officials who would stammer their way through excuse and evasion, in standard officialese.

On the sidelines, these messiahs were always cracking deals with the other party—the industrialists and their middlemen—the grimmer the story, the higher the price to clean it up.

A renowned Indian industrialist had once aptly remarked, 'You will never reach your destination if you throw stones at every dog that barks. Better keep biscuits and keep moving.'

Industrialists in Majra kept biscuits, lots of them (feasts of mutton and alcohol, drugs, women and small cash) in their bid to keep nuisance out of their focused pursuit for land. Of course, talk of PAP Welfare was hogwash, nothing more than a must-have slide in PowerPoint presentations, just as Corporate Social Responsibility (CSR) was.

If all of this was not interesting enough, Earth Age—an international environment organization renowned for its propensity for 'direct action'—had recently opened its office at Majra. Earth Age was playing a seminal role in inciting anti-establishment feelings, stoking discontent among the locals and mobilizing 'independent media' to bring the harrowing tales from Majra out before the world.

It could be some sort of residual wiring, but the Indian mind was primed to sanctify anything associated with fair-skinned, English-speaking sahibs. The farmers in Majra particularly enjoyed watching the *gori mems* exhorting them to fight for their rights in their broken, accented Hindi interspersed with English words and *'bhaiya'*. The men would tease each other and wink at dirty jokes as the 'madams' socialized with them, smoking their *bidis* and chatting away in a bid to experience and internalize the great Indian rural agony.

Till recently, coal had been the greatest curse in the lives of Majra's peasants. Its murk had eclipsed their *jal, jungle, zameen,* and their livelihoods too. Then in the past decade or so the same coal had turned into gold. Companies were now willing to pay liberal prices for their barren land. They were promising employment, pensions, gratuities and attractive compensation packages.

Earth Age however told them that they were being robbed—that these were vacuous promises the companies had no intention of honouring once they had wrested control over tribal land. The companies never employed PAPs, the land being sold was an asset and the packages offered were peanuts compared to the mammoth profits these companies would reap from their *jal, jungle, zameen*. Mindless industrialization would destroy Majra and the sons of the soil would never partake of any benefits. Any package should offer them a solution—a long-term remedy to the age old maladies they had suffered from for generations.

The poor PAPs were confused. They didn't know who to believe. The speeches on exploitation tickled their hearts while the companies' offers tickled their minds. So the PAPs chose to be loyal to both.

They would sincerely attend the numerous *dharnas* and *andolans* outside the Collectorate or the Tehsil office chanting '*Jo humse takrayega....mitti me mil jaega*' or '*Band karo bhai band karo, taanashahi band karo,*' their pitch and volume in direct proportion to vicinity of cameras or senior officials. They would sit idle for hours, half-attending to impassioned diatribes against company raj and their hand-in-glove *sarkar.*

In the evenings though, they would also negotiate with the corporate middlemen. And it was all quite fine, with everybody. People here understood the whole 'open relationship' concept rather well. So the evening deals were crucial and were mostly brokered by the rural elite—the ward *parshad* or *sarpanch* or some local *seth* cum small time politician cum civil contractor. NGO's middlemen could also intermediate sometimes, in cases of their specific interest.

In Majra, thus, it wasn't only land that was up for sale, it was people, their mercurial allegiances and these subsidiary transactions that bought or sold allegiances were most crucial to every added stamp paper that legalized the surrender of agrarian land to industrialists, inch by inch.

Whatever the amount they got for their land, the first thing PAPs did with the money was buy a brand new Scorpio SUV from the Mahindra showroom in Palampur. Natives of Majra were obsessed with the vehicle. For years, they had seen the vain village *sarpanch* or the *sahukar* or the *thekedar* boss around in their flashy Scorpio. They would even have flashlights mounted on top to give it the impression of being a 'VIP' vehicle. Now all of a sudden, Majra was witnessing an unprecedented deluge of flashlight mounted Scorpios and the dejected *sarpanches* in the sub-division felt as resigned to their destinies as the erstwhile *zamindars,* post the abolition of *zamindari.*

All in all, Majra had become a fireball with its heady cocktail of tribals, forests, industry, NGOs and coal. It had transformed into an epicenter of statecraft where an interested administration had to appear disinterested and mediate between business interests, rights of the PAPs and the tremendous popular pressure of the voluntary sector and local media. Every decision the Collector took, including conscious decisions not to act in certain cases, was subject to intensive scrutiny and media trial.

Majra was one of the factors the Chief Secretary had in mind while posting Avinash to Palampur. His decision had been vindicated. Avinash had walked the fine line with great dexterity and tact so far. The industry reps considered him dynamic, pro-active and industry-friendly and the PAPs had faith in his sense of justice and fair play. The NGOs and local media swore by his exceptional positivity—he listened patiently, responded frankly, and accorded them a standing, unlike the peremptory or calibrated way in which bureaucrats usually responded—and he sometimes flashed that rare smile which made the suave ladies in Earth Age go really weak in their knees.

Hard Work Paying Off!

It was in this context that during one of his visits to Palampur, Mantriji had a brainwave.

While purchase of private land for projects had become both conflict-ridden and expensive, ATPP was a gold mine with 2700 hectares of prime government land.

'Can't this land be put to more efficient use, Mantriji?'

'*Waise bhi*, ATPP is in red, Mantriji…sooner than later, it will have to be closed down.'

The power lobby had cautiously planted the idea. Selling off the 'white elephant' would make him the poster boy of economic reform; boost his 'image' as an industry-friendly go-getter who had the guts to kill 'too much government.' They had even suggested a punchline—'Minimum government, maximum governance'—with which Mantriji could commence his Cabinet speech on the subject.

Mantriji knew it would be a political gamble but his mojo was on a major reformist streak these days. In any case, ATPP Township was not his 'area'. Its voters were not his voters—had never been, were not likely to be.

Mantriji discussed the idea with Avinash. The rationale was strong—ATPP was in dire straits. The plant load factor had fallen to a poor 30%, ATPP employees were always on a strike, and senior-management was always too busy in intrigue or corruption to bother itself with falling production. It must be sold off. Avinash concurred.

Within two months, the State Cabinet passed the ATPP Strategic Sale Resolution and a High Power Committee (HPC) was constituted to oversee the process. The HPC was headed by A.N. Bakshi, a senior hawk whose stature as one of the state government's key door openers had risen steadily over the years. His core competence lay in his ability to get things done—by manipulating inept ministers, piloting influential dealmakers and playing mind games with the powerhouses that mattered.

In the capacity of Collector Palampur, Avinash Rathore was co-opted as the convener of HPC. The Cabinet note also provided for an Officer On Special Duty (OSD), ATPP Sale who would liaise between the Department of Power (which owned ATPP), the Department of Industries (which had to organize the sale) and ATPP management.

The first meeting of the HPC was convened to mull over the options for the post of OSD. Several names were considered. The job was unenviable—one that required an officer junior enough to accommodate the egos of behemoths in the HPC and mellow enough to coordinate actions of the two big silos that the Department of Power and the Department of Industries were. Avinash proposed two names—Nethra Kaul and Mrityunjay Ranjan. The HPC rejected Mrityunjay point blank calling that choice a self-goal; Nethra Kaul was a low profile greenhorn but given Avinash's strong pitch in her favour, she could be given a chance to claim her own place under the sun.

The transfer orders stated that Nethra Kaul was to report as OSD ATPP Sale. When she reached the State Capital to call on A.N. Bakshi, her new boss, Avinash was seated opposite him in the latter's chamber. Several voluminous documents flagged with orange, yellow and green tags lay on the table and tables of statistics flashed across two laptops adjusted precariously between the documents.

'Ah, Nethra Kaul! welcome aboard...' A.N. Bakshi eyed her

tentatively, 'I believe this is our maiden meeting. Haven't seen or heard much about you around here.'

Avinash looked up at her for a moment before directing his attention to the papers again. Everyone was awkwardly quiet for a while before Bakshi spoke again, 'As Collector Palampur, Avinash is the convener of the HPC handling the strategic sale process, the youngest convener I have seen in recent years!'

He turned to Avinash now, 'I believe the two of you are batchmates?'

'Sir…' Avinash nodded grimly.

Nethra knew that her heart was throbbing heavily inside her chest. She wished her boss would not ask her to say more…her boss's arrogance was rather comforting at the moment, for silence had a way of obfuscating fault lines and her fault line was sitting right before her. She hated herself for the way her body reacted to his mere presence even after all these years.

'Well then I leave to you the task of explaining things to her. I have a meeting to attend,' said Bakshi, looking at Avinash and grabbing few of his files before casting a final glance at Nethra.

'I am sorry we have little time for preliminaries, Nethra. I expect you to put up the basic drafts in the next thirty days.'

Then glancing at Avinash again, he added, 'Avinash would help you with things. He is our Mr Bankable! Count on him for everything….'

He patted Avinash on the shoulder and left the chamber in a hurry.

'Sir,' she forced herself to smile.

Though the moment was awkward, it was of his making. He had waited for this for the past seven years but he avoided looking at her, now that she was finally before him.

'I will give you a brief background of ATPP and outline the plan we have so far,' He commenced without a preamble, his face dour and his eyes carefully avoiding hers. His manner was professional, his speech lucid. Nethra fixed an unflinching gaze on him, listening intently and sombrely as he spoke. She had to match him in the act, and she did.

He spoke for about 15 minutes and concluded the monologue with the customary query, 'If there's anything about the project you want me to clarify further....'

'There is just one question I have,' Nethra interrupted him, 'are you responsible for my landing this assignment?'

He twisted his mouth in the same way that made his jawline appear all the more prominent.

'That is besides the point,' he said.

Oh really? What is the point, then? That you plan to have a casual extramarital fling with an ex even as you pack your punches here for the Project 21 trophy? That is how you intend to use me now? Do you think I am that foolish, or is this some sort of a professional favour to absolve yourself of the guilt of the past? How on earth can you sound so bloody callous? So cold? With me! When I have been...like some silly....

All this and more is surely what Nethra wanted to say, which of course she didn't. What she did in fact say was this, 'Alright, but I still insist on knowing.'

'I am only discussing the project with its OSD right now and everything else is in fact besides the point.'

Ouch!

Nethra twisted her mouth, picked up her bag and said, 'Alright then...I get the point!'

How disappointing could he be? What had she been expecting? How she hated him! How she wanted to hurl choice words at him—words that had been inside her for years but seem to have curdled up now. How she hated herself for having thought of him way more than what he was, and for having loved him way beyond he deserved.

At the outset A.N. Bakshi had clarified that state bureaucracy wouldn't rely on consultants for 'handholding' in the sale process. To Bakshi, consultants were 'modern day Brahmins'—out to 'inveigle and exploit' an ignorant system in the garb of ERP and BPR.

'What do they do,' he would ask, '...other than tell you stuff you already know in fancy language!'

No hands were thus required to be held. The dependence on Brahmins for achieving salvation had to end with this project, so Bakshi had declared.

Every document, as a consequence, had to be drafted, amended and finalized by the HPC members themselves. Nethra, given that she was the junior-most, was tasked with preparing the basic drafts—the RFP (Request For Proposals), the information memorandum, bid pack, share purchase agreement, shareholders agreement and draft contractual documents—in thirty days.

For the next month, Nethra's world contracted to contracting parties and plant load factors of power plants. She hadn't slept in days and her back burned with pain after remaining hunched up before her laptop in sedentary perusal of manuals but her mind was at peace.

With the help of ATPP's IT wing she coordinated the launch of ATPP Sale Automated Contract Administration Portal (ASACAP), complete with a Web GIS and a virtual data room—the first of its kind in a government PSU's disinvestment. Avinash put the NIC staff in Palampur at her disposal. Truckloads of files containing vital information about the power plant were digitized and organized into modules for access during the due diligence process.

Nethra delivered on all of her targets before time. On the twenty-fourth day of her assuming charge as OSD, the HPC reconvened to consider the entire bulk of documentation she had drafted. Her drafts were near perfect. Bakshi was surprised at this impressive spectacle of workmanship and efficiency. The RFP was floated on the twenty-sixth day. Documents were flowing in and clearances were flowing out—without red tape or avoidable objections, and with clockwork precision.

She did bank upon 'Un' Bankable Rathore for refining some elements of her drafts. She shared her drafts with him, a feedback mechanism, as Bakshi liked to call it, over e-mails which she purposely drafted to read like Second World War telegrams. His return mails were not as uptight but were scanned scrupulously for any hints of human bonding—he never missed deleting the 'Dearest' before 'Nethra' and the 'Yours truly' at the end—before sending these e-mails.

It was the evening before the day HPC was scheduled to meet to vet Nethra's drafts. Nethra had been working round the clock since the past 40 hours and the draft shareholders agreement still needed a final review. Avinash had flown in from Palampur that evening. He knew she would still be in her office, ensuring everything was in place for the next day's meeting. He could *not* see her at this time.

'Trust everything is ready,' he walked into her chamber, coolly, sounding as matter-of-fact as ever.

She did not look up from her papers or acknowledge his appearance. She had been expecting him.

'May I have a look?' he asked.

'I think I sent you the final drafts yesterday. There are no further corrections,' she answered without looking up.

She looked tired, probably because she hadn't slept in days. Her face looked exactly the same as the night she had walked down the hostel stairs, without the kohl that usually kissed her eyes, her thick black hair let lose...the night he had professed his love for her. How could he ever have walked away from this woman? How could he, when despite the seven years' weathering, the gossamer threads that tied him to her were still the brightest tassels in his vanilla life? How when her thoughts and her memories were still, his only solace, could he have forsaken her?

He was sitting facing her across the table and as she perused the files, he continued to gaze at her, the same old gaze....

'You want something?' she looked up from her papers.

'Nothing...You seem tired.'

His voice surprised her, because it reminded her of the old Avinash.

She went back to her files again.

'In case you need to catch some rest before the meeting, you may....'

'I am perfectly alright,' she replied tiredly, without looking up.

'How have you been?' he asked her.

Silence.

Five minutes ticked away. He kept his eyes trained on her.

'I had hoped to find anger, even hatred, what I find is indifference,' he said.

'I do not think I have even room for that,' she replied.

'Which means you are oblivious.'

'Perhaps...or that I am at peace with myself?'

'That is an actualized state of being.'

'It is a matter of semantics.'

Another couple of minutes passed. She continued to sift through her papers as he sat looking at her.

'I do not seek clarifications Avinash,' she said finally, looking up from her papers. 'I look for no explanations. I do not want anything from you. I have nothing to give you either. You may please leave now.'

'What more can you give me, what more than what you already have...' he thought silently.

'Alright,' he heaved a sigh, 'All the best for your presentation tomorrow,' he said as he left.

The Simple Present Tense

The State Tourism Corporation's sprawling rest house atop the hill at Sulepur had been finalized as the venue for HPC's fourth meeting which was convened to formally approve the bid documents for ATPP's sale. Sulepur was a hill station, some 170 kilometres off the state capital, and was renowned for its handicrafts and handlooms.

Nethra had reached a day early and was busy revisiting the bid documents in her suite when the Reception called to announce that Collector Sahab, Palampur had requested her presence in the lounge, if she wasn't otherwise occupied. Avinash had turned up a full 22 hours early!

'Yes?' she looked surprised. Avinash was seated on one of the sofas at the far end of the lounge.

'Hi,' he stood up, looking at her, as she walked across the lounge to him.

'What is it?' she enquired.

'I want to talk to you.'

'About?'

'You know that. This is a request. It is long overdue.'

When they stepped out of the rest house late that afternoon, the gray sky and heady winds that blew through the avenue palms portended rain. The path that led downhill to the town below was a cobbled boulevard lined on both sides by splendid palms. On one side, the idyllic town of Sulepur could be seen perched in the lap of the hills. The wind was cool and the placid quiet of an unhurried evening was broken only occasionally by the chirpy din of parrots flying across the sky.

Downhill, almost three kilometres from the rest house was the street bazaar of Sulepur where merchants sold their wares—Sulepuri saris, wooden dolls, cushion covers, table runners, lamp-shades and terracotta figurines in their brightly lit, colourful marquee shops.

'How have you been?' Though his question was addressed to her, he wasn't looking at her.

'I am fine...' she paused, 'at peace with myself.'

'It must feel good.'

'Yes...' she shrugged lightly. 'There are always minor aberrations—little things one sometimes wants and sometimes doesn't—barring those, I am pretty much fine.'

'How have you been?' she hadn't intended to ask this.

'Good...' he stopped, as if as an afterthought. They walked in silence for more than five minutes.

She didn't understand this. He had said he wanted to talk. And here he was, walking with her silently, as if time didn't matter, and nothing needed to be said.

'Do you still play your guitar?' she found herself asking.

'Guitar!', he paused a little before adding, 'That light has long gone out of my life, Nethra. There's no music. There is no more dreaming. I live with facts, in reality.' He looked at her. She was listening.

'The person you knew is dead. ...He died the day he left you, the day he surrendered. Much of what made me died on the way as I kept closing my doors to it.'

His honest eyes carried a strange melancholy, she noticed.

'The Best Performing Collector of the state, a successful man with a beautiful family and a slew of recognitions—aren't you misrepresenting?' she chuckled lightly.

'Successful!' he chuckled too.

'Yes, I am a successful man, and therefore, I am a happy man too.'

'You ought to be...you have everything you ever wanted.'

'Do I?' he looked at her, surprised.

'The choices I made were conscious choices Nethra—Nobody forced me into them. These choices have put my life along a path which is all sunny and rosy but it is not a path I wanted to take. I feel inadequate....'

'Inadequacy is a sign of hope, of ambition and progress; all of which comes from a basic sense of contentment,' she reasoned.

Avinash fell silent. His eyes told her she was wrong. She dropped the subject. He spoke again after a few minutes.

'What have you been doing all these years?'

'I read a lot and travelled...' she replied.

'Travel?'

'Yes, one of the things I—picked up from you. I save for a year and then splurge it all in a matter of seven days. A fifteen-day long annual tour has become a ritual now. We are a group of five, all from different countries and we manage to get together annually for this *amazing* experience...', she paused and smiled lightly, '...last year we visited Reine!' 'Did you go to Ireland?' he asked suddenly. He remembered Ireland.

'Yes...' she smiled, without looking at him.

'And?'

'And nothing...I came back.'

'So nothing really happened?'

'Nothing ever happens, Avinash...not with me,' she laughed.

'How long have you been doing this? How did you all meet?' he asked.

'This is going to be the third year. We met in Venice. I was pretty low at the time and was travelling alone; trying to make sense of things. This fortnight means a lot to me now. It fills me with hope and love, for life.'

'I am happy to know that...' he smiled.

She didn't want him to enquire about the bracelet. She didn't want him to know. She did not want him to think that while he had moved on in his life, she was still clinging to that piece of jewellery, that he was complete and she, incomplete in some way. Suddenly, she wanted him to feel forgotten and unimportant. So when he asked her if she still had that bracelet, she merely shrugged and put up a deliberate act of uncertainty.

'I think I do,' she said, looking doubtful.

He said nothing.

Then she remembered about the muffler, the only thing she had left him with. It was her father's muffler. Would he still have it? She wouldn't ask. How could she reveal that she still remembered a trivial occurrence that happened on that cold night, when his hands had become very cold and she had offered him a muffler— Her father had forced her to pack it in her luggage. He had taken it quietly, and wrapped it around his neck. Would he still have it?

'Do you know that footbridge over Mandakini got washed away in the Uttarakhand floods,' he said seemingly without a context now.

And with this, the ease with which he had recalled *that footbridge over Mandakini* now, some seven years later, she knew that the thing between them could never ever end...not because of his marriage or any number of other relationships that kept them apart.

'Yes, I know,' she replied, her voice reduced to a whisper.

'I miss you, Nethra. I miss you badly.' He said now. 'Tell me the truth...do you really carry nothing about me in your heart?'

She breathed in, a slow quiet breath.

'I am not the same person I used to be, Avinash. I have learned to live in the moment and I do not harbour any regret, none at all, about the time we spent together,' she said.

'I value the time we spent together greatly. I would have retained the anger or vengeance inside of me if I had loved you with a purpose—if my love was conditional and marriage was an expectation in return. What has helped me come through is perhaps the simple fact that from the word go, I didn't have a purpose in mind. It was a simple feeling—true and absolute—an end in itself. I liked being with you and I look back at that time with a lot of joy, not with regret,' she continued.

'Yes, it did hurt at one point of time because we are all selfish, we wish to monopolize. But with time I have realized that we cannot keep looking for meaning, happiness, fulfillment or purpose outside, in other people. I could not have lived my life through your love. I have to love myself first. Only then, would I enjoy people and relationships without the baggage of pain or jealousy or expectation.'

She looked at him. He was quiet, looking at her. Their pace had slowed down considerably. His eyes carried an expression that beseeched her to continue speaking.

'There was a point in my life when I was this very Victorian one man woman who dreamt of *L'uomo perfetto*,' and here she turned to look at him and smiled.

'Whatever romantic crap it was...it was pure and honest. Since then, I have realized that people can't be perfect, nobody is perfect and even if at one point you have a notion that you might have chanced upon the perfect person, time disillusions those notions. Time and circumstance tend to make routine...' she breathed out.

'...Everything that at one point seemed perfect, too perfect to be true!' she smiled.

'So in a way I feel good that I never got together with my "one man." It at least left me with the imagination of things that could have been and a faint hope that I might still chance upon someone close, the hope that keeps Romance alive inside me,' she said.

'But you cannot keep hoping forever,' he said, slightly anguished.

'I think I can...an escapist dreamer with twisted notions about love and commitment can...', she chuckled.

'So you are trying to tell me that you do not wish to commit yourself to a relationship now?'

'Commitment is not only about that one fleeting moment when you experience pleasure or look into each others' eyes, Avinash,' she said.

'It is the routine one has to live with everyday, complete with its dejections and disappointments. You see a person you once thought perfect in forms less tasteful, as a human being much more vulnerable, much more fallible than you ever thought and...' she swiftly pulled herself out of the reverie she seemed to be falling into.

'Are you seeing someone right now?' he felt compelled to ask.

'No.'

'Is that a choice you have made?'

'No! I just don't seem to *have* anyone to see...as desperate as that might sound,' she exhaled lightly.

'I think I am simply not cut out for the day to day life of a relationship. I would rather be on my own,' she shrugged.

'As much as I know you, you are the last person who would dread routine or be unsure of commitment, as long as you love somebody, Nethra.'

'Exactly...' she sighed, realizing how exactly he understood her. 'It is not commitment that I fear. It is the lack of love. There has to be something more to love than mere commitment or worse, the dreadful surety of routine. There must be someone you love beyond a mere need to commit or a desire for stability. And sadly for me, I haven't been able to love again,' she said.

It started raining.

He was looking at her those dark eyes and the thicket of lashes that seemed to stand guard to the secret world of dreams inside, the purity in that face, those soft and delicate lips, the hollow under that neck, and he knew again why he had fallen in love with her. It was impossible, not to, as much back then as it was now.

They stood waiting at the roadside gazebo, waiting for the rain to stop...the gazebo was a viewpoint overlooking the Sulepur valley and several such structures lined the stretch down to the Sulepur town below.

'I often have this dream, in the wee hours of the night...you and I are standing together at the edge of a cliff. You are wearing something yellow, and your eyes are closed as you soak in the mountain breeze. You look lovely...', he smiled softly,

'You seem to be dreaming and I am looking at you. Then you open your eyes, and tell me that you want to fly. I hold out my hand, ask you to close your eyes again, and come with me. You close your eyes again, step ahead, and then suddenly, I cannot see you anymore. I hope you haven't fallen off the cliff, I desperately pray...and I look for you but you are nowhere to be found...' his voice cracked a little.

She gulped hard and tried harder to hold back her tears. She couldn't. She felt ruined and lost and wanted to cry. Gradually, she let the tears flow out, without any restraint, silent tears.

'Do you remember that night, Avinash, the night in the Company Garden on the gazebo where we stood gazing at the skies for the longest time?' Reverie, she knew, was the best distraction for regret. She wanted him to indulge in it.

'I remember that night better than any other in my life so far.' He said. 'And the sort of love you are talking about, I haven't experienced anything like that in a long time now, not since that time in my life. Those memories are my anchor, they keep me steady.'

'Even I think I put all of my romanticism, all of my tenderness into that one night and I have never been able to feel the same way again....'

He wished he could hold time back. He knew she would be gone again and that he too would return to a life very different from this. He still hadn't fathomed what it was about her that completely obviated the need or effort for any explanation or pretence. He still hadn't understood what it was about her presence that made everything so pure and bright and...happy. Perhaps, this was love.

At the Sulepur bazaar, Nethra stood admiring the brightly lit, iridescent displays.

'Pick one from here,' Avinash was pointing at a display of Sulepuri sarees.

'Do you want one for your wife?' she asked.

Avinash knew this question was deliberate.

'No, she doesn't wear sarees much.'

'Then delight her with one,' she said.

'If I pick one for you, will you take it?' he asked her.

'No, I won't. But I will help you pick one for her.'

She chose a blood red saree with a beautiful golden border.

'This is for you,' Avinash insisted.

'This is for the woman in your life, Avinash. The woman you live your life with,' she smiled.

As they walked back towards the rest house later that night, she eventually turned to ask him, 'Why didn't you call me after that night, Avinash? I might still have asked you to do what you eventually did. I might have still asked you to marry her. But why didn't you ever call again?'

'Because if I did, I probably wouldn't have done what I eventually did,' he said.

'And?'

'I would have convinced your Dadi, your parents and we would have got married.... We might have had children by now and you might have got lovelier, a little chubbier....'

Both looked at each other and smiled.

As they walked, their steps synching as always, their fingers brushing against each other every now and then, Avinash slowly slipped his fingers into hers and turned so that their bodies faced each other.

'I love you,' he said in his sonorous voice, looking into her eyes for affirmation. His eyes carried the same kindness, they carried life.

Nethra was silent. She smiled feebly.

He now pulled her close, to the same range that had always helped them *really* look at each other, smell each other, and feel each others' breaths on their skins, the same range that had always made them realize that they were one.

'I am sorry, Nethra…' he buried his face in her neck, the words blowing against her skin made her shiver slightly.

'Do not be, Avinash,' she whispered softly into his ears, 'and do not ask me if I *still* love you…love has only one form…the simple present tense.'

The Really Good Officer

There had never been a state PSU's sale of this scale before. The organizers had no templates. They were creating one. Four out of the five companies notified as pre-qualified were seen as serious bidders.

ZMD group—the leading business conglomerate which manufactured everything from paperclips to apparel and car bodies to electricity was the acknowledged frontrunner. Its Chairman, Vishwajeet Prajapati was known to share a strong camaraderie with the president of the ruling party and no other bidder could possibly match ZMD in its sheer financial muscle and exceptional political clout.

Trailing close behind in bets was Synergy Power, an infrastructure major that had recently made a Big Bang foray into the power sector by trouncing ZMD to bag a major PPP power project.

Alpha Energy, a relatively new player could be a dark horse. While its management had deliberately maintained a low profile, it had learnt the ropes rather well. There had been no sponsored news and no advertising blitzkrieg but they had been meticulous in their core work; hobnobbed with the state politicians, and networked with State Government's key deal makers, essential elements of the steep learning curve of dealing with government. Sridhar Bhanot, Alpha's Chairman and Managing Director had once been a hi-flyer with ZMD but had later had a falling out with Vishwajeet Prajapati. Alpha had also bagged a coal block in Majra, and had been prospecting the area for its first solo venture.

Finally, the Avon Group. Though its presence had remained restricted to the aluminium sector and the only power plants it held were captive units, this was the first time Avon was looking at an independent power generation project.

The pre-bid and due diligence meetings foreboded a corporate clash of a scale no one had anticipated so far. ZMD, Synergy and Avon had put in specialized bid teams with smart blends of negotiation experience, financial, contractual and technical skills. During due diligence meetings in the capital, their corporate teams would turn up like slick Men (and Women) In Black—exchanging sharp glances, raising intelligent interjections and attending to every word uttered in the proceedings with hawkish calculation.

Alpha participated in pre-bid meetings but unlike its rivals, Alpha was fronted up by one man—a huge, balding man dressed in algae-coloured shirts which he never bothered to tuck inside his filthy brown pants. Bakshi liked to call him Shrek. Shrek would sit sprawled lazily on his chair, bored and distracted, playing on his mobile phone or staring at Nethra, point blank. He would not listen, he would not speak, even as the two arch rivals—ZMD and Synergy—fought over every paragraph in the Draft Share Purchase Agreement and as every Term of Reference laying down the representations and warranties of contracting parties was hotly debated.

Veterans in HPC had unanimously agreed to put Nethra at the Forward Line of Own Troops—to resolve impasses, to handle queries, to avoid traps—aided by her marathon guzzling of Contract and Company laws and contract administration manuals. She was clear-headed and took quick, rational decisions to which the HPC appended its formal seal of approval.

While the young unsung heroes were up to their neck in the perilous and untrodden waters of disinvestment, it was Bakshi who was basking in the golden haze of media attention. He had given exclusive interviews to national channels and written articles in the Trendsetter, articulating with great reformist passion how government needed to focus on simpler, doable things while leaving complex issues like electricity or telecom to the great sleigh of the invisible hand. Neither Nethra nor Avinash had found an honourable 'also there' mention in his several articles and interviews about the great team that was out there, working round the clock to prove to the world that the government meant business and reform.

It was one of those hectic days when Avinash had just wound up at a late evening site interaction with ZMD representatives at Palampur when Bakshi summoned him to the State Capital.

'Mantriji has indicated his preference for Alpha Energy,' he said.

Avinash was not sure if this piece of information was meant to be an instruction.

'This is an open competitive bidding process, Sir,' he said.

'A good officer never explains why not, Avinash…he always shows how. Mantriji wishes so. He trusts you to work it out. I am sure you don't believe you were put here for writing tender documents. Any boy from one of those pricey firms could do that. You have been assigned a very vital responsibility, Avinash, very early on in your career. Don't squander it.'

Avinash's face went pale.

'Well if I were you, I would have clearly seen the perils of letting ZMD into the price-bidding round. It would be a cakewalk for those giants. Technical evaluation is the little window you could look at,' he said, drawing out a window with his fingers.

Disqualifying ZMD on technical grounds? Did it even sound credible? His mind could think of only one word: Preposterous.

'But that barely sounds credible, Sir,' Avinash muttered.

'That is what you are here for…to make things sound credible…to dress up that old bitch!' his left incisor stuck out as he flashed his wolfish grin, leaning back in his chair.

'People from Alpha will meet you.' He reached out to the buzzer on his table. The buzzer always signalled 'end of conversation.'

'As I always say, Avinash, a fine line separates good officers from really good ones.' Bakshi had uttered his parting lines.

Two days later, Avinash walked into Nethra's office. 'A substantial error has crept into the bid document,' he said.

'Which is?' she asked.

'We are selling off a power plant and we haven't considered existing coal linkages. We haven't assigned weights to existing coal block linkages in Majra. We haven't factored in the transportation costs,' he replied.

'But it is a pit head TPP and the National Coal Company mines in Majra. ATPP has a live coal linkage with National Coal,' she reasoned.

'Think, Nethra—ATPP's FSA (Fuel Supply Agreement) with National Coal will lapse with its sale. The new entity will need a fresh FSA and you know how dilatory a coal linkage approval can get. We ought to have preferred bidders with an existing coal block in Majra. The costs of transporting coal from outside would be exorbitant otherwise,' Avinash argued.

'But I do not see the rationale of a front-loaded preference for an existing coal block allottee. We should start with a level playing field. The new entity can always have a FSA with a coal block allottee post the sale.'

'That's theoretically correct but where is the risk mitigation? We simply cannot hand over family silver to a complete blow-in with no presence, with no backward linkages...assured fuel supply must be a determining factor in technical evaluation of bids,' he argued.

'And...have a look at this!' he slid a bunch of papers towards her on the table.

'National Green Tribunal's ruling...Industrial activity aimed at power generation must minimize the environmental impact of fuel transportation. We are bound by the NGT's rulings.'

'We do not have an option at this point, Avinash. The RFP has been issued. Final bids will be submitted in the next ten days.' Nethra reasoned.

'We do have an option,' Avinash looked at her. 'There is nothing that bars us from partially amending the technical evaluation criteria till we receive the final bids. We simply have to inform interested parties and give them an opportunity to reframe their offers accordingly.'

Nethra wasn't convinced.

'Please go through the GFR (Government Financial Rules) and contract guidelines. I do not see a problem there. We will have to put up the draft amendments before the HPC in the next two days,' he said.

A footnote in the Guidelines for Government Contract mentioned that minor, non-substantial amendments could be made in the RFP till at least a week before submission of the final bids under written intimation to interested parties. Alpha Energy was the only coal block allottee amongst the four serious bidders.

Avinash knew that irrespective of whatever weight the HPC agreed to assign to a coal linkage, it would still not suffice to skew the odds decisively in favour of Alpha. It was the Business Plan that held the key. And this was the most Avinash was prepared to do. He was confident that despite the insertion of a front-loaded preference clause, the technical evaluation parameters were still rugged enough to deflect any artificial tweaking that such a preference could induce.

When the file moved to Nethra for notings, she observed that 'while there is merit in assigning a front loaded preference to an existing coal block allottee, an amendment should be avoided at this stage.' If Avinash was really keen on an amendment, he could go ahead and trash peer opinion. It was her duty to her opinion.

Avinash did just what she had expected. Not only did he expressly counter his peer on the file, citing the holy GFR with all of its profound, capable of multiple interpretations verbiage; he went a step ahead and issued the amendments in anticipation of HPC's final stamp of authority.

Nethra was surprised at this curious bypass.

'Approve and issue the amendment notification in the capacity of HPC Convener,' Bakshi had instructed Avinash over the phone. 'We shall clear it in the next meeting. We have no time to waste....'

Avinash proceeded on Bakshi's oral consent. The HPC didn't get convened again. Bakshi flew out to Delhi at the eleventh hour, ostensibly to attend an 'important' summit that hadn't been all that important so far. The file proposing the amendment somehow went missing in the department and no one in the HPC thought of bringing it over again.

Shrek-ified

It was Alpha Energy's Business Plan presentation that stopped the fiesta in the tracks. Khalate, Alpha's out-of-the-swamp Shrek who had contributed to the deliberations only by way of blank stares and bored yawns until this time suddenly metamorphosed into a raging bull, tearing through ZMD's business plan, pointing out its pitfalls and offering tenable solutions. Khalate made coal linkage his trump card and cogently demonstrated how every other strategy was contingent on it. Alpha's business plan was perfect. Disturbingly perfect.

Something hit Avinash. He moved uneasily in his chair. It seemed that the advantage accorded to Alpha by an amendment he thought as important but not pivotal had somehow been dramatically magnified by a dubiously perfect business plan. Khalate had met him once, the day after his meeting with Bakshi, and it was he who had lobbied for a coal linkage preference. Avinash hoped he was only seeing things with a magnifying glass.

The coffin of ZMD's business plan had just been sealed with its final nail. ZMD's representatives had argued like a querulous bunch of juveniles, caught off guard but their theatrics couldn't puncture Khalate's arguments. Alpha had decisively turned the proverbial tables on its flabbergasted rivals. Nobody had anticipated this.

The results of the Technical Evaluation round were sensational. ZMD's dream run had come to an abrupt and ignoble end. Alpha, Avon and Synergy were to slug it out in the final round. As the evaluation team gingerly rechecked the calculations, A.N. Bakshi sneaked out of the conference hall, motioning to Nethra not to declare the results till she got the go ahead.

'Looks like ZMD is not even making it to the final round, Sir,' he rung up Mantriji.

'What do you mean, "not making it"? What are you all doing there? If ZMD doesn't, who does?'

'We really do not have an option at this point, Mantriji. ZMD's business plan has been shredded to pieces.'

'But what will I tell Prajapatiji?' Mantriji was nonplussed.

'I need five minutes to explain the whole thing, Sir. May I see you at your office?'

At Mantriji's Office, A.N. Bakshi explained in detail why maintaining a semblance of fair play and transparency was key to the success of this great gambit. ATPP's sale was a personal risk Mantriji had taken—so perception management was crucial. It was a PR time bomb which could go off at the slightest hint of manipulation. The other bidders would surely take to the courts if the organizing team messed it up.

On the other hand, elimination of the frontrunner would mean that the project would go to an underdog—a competent underdog. This would be an immutable proof that the organizing team under his leadership had been above board and let due process take its course. It would also silence Mantriji's critics who had been projecting the fate of the deal—ATPP going to ZMD—as a foregone conclusion. Some upstart bagging the deal would have tremendous PR spillovers for Mantriji's image. Twenty-five minutes into the persuasion and after a call to Prajapati, Mantriji relented.

The financial bid evaluation was to be held in the form of a public auction. Unlike others who were dressed in formals, Khalate had turned up in a full-sleeved cream shirt and dark brown trousers for the auction. He moved about with a disregard characteristic of his grotesque presence, checking out the female representatives in rival teams with a look that bordered on the prurient.

The air inside the conference hall carried anxiety. As the proceedings commenced, the auctioneer opened the sealed envelopes containing the offer price quoted by the bidders. The auction would commence at the highest offer price. HPC had pegged ATPP's reserve price at Rs. 2500 Crore.

'Synergy group has offered the highest starting price at Rs. 2450 crore,' the auctioneer declared.

Bakshi, Nethra and Avinash heaved a collective sigh of relief. The auction had commenced in the ballpark of the reserved price. It could only be an upswing from here.

Avon Group opened up first with an ascent to Rs. 2500 crore. Synergy came after with Rs. 2520 crores. The bidding was slow and careful in the beginning. Alpha had still not made an entry. Khalate slouched on his chair and stared at Nethra.

Avon Group continued to lead the trail and Synergy matched up in measured pursuit. Bid number 11 upped the offer to Rs. 3000 crores. Chameleon Khalate now changed colours. He rolled up his sleeves and unbuttoned the first three buttons of his shirt revealing a hairy interior as the lines on his pug-like face grew tense.

'3100,' he thundered.

Team Avon and Team Synergy went into a minute long stupor. The matador was back. Avon stepped back mentally, reflecting, even as Synergy growled back with a spunky Rs. 3150 crores. The ambience in the conference room grew uncomfortably tense as Alpha and Synergy threw themselves in to a Who Blinks First session, growling back numbers at each other. In a mere seven minutes, they had pushed the price through the 3500 crore barrier. The only ones pleased in the room were Bakshi, Nethra and Avinash. Bid price had upped 140% of the reserve price.

At bid number twenty five, Avon struck back with Rs. 3600 crore, as if trying to close the game. It was to be their last throw of the dice.

It was not to be. The bids went higher and higher and at one point when Khalate had raised the game to Rs. 4200 crore, Synergy reps seemed stuck, apprehensive. An SOS call to its base camp and Synergy came thumping back, ramping up the stakes to Rs. 4250 crore.

Khalate was adamant.

He fired again, '*Chawalees Sau!*'

Synergy's team lead looked around quizzically.

'That's Rs. 4400 crores only...', Khalate smiled beatifically.

There was silence. The auctioneer glanced at Team Synergy, 'May we have the next bid?'

Synergy's team lead threw his hands up, and clicked his tongue, finally giving it up.

'ATPP is sold to Alpha Energy! Congratulations Mr Khalate,' Bakshi declared.

Khalate let out a big growl and thumped his chest. At a majestic 4400 crores, Alpha's price was almost double of what had been anticipated by the advisers.

'We have set a precedent with the ATPP sale,' Mantriji declared triumphantly. 'I will ensure that the proceeds are utilized for the development of the State.'

Mantriji became a reform messiah overnight. Several cover stories, editorials and guest columns were written about the historic sale. IIMs built out a case study for their Public Policy courses and Mantriji also bagged the Trendsetter's 'Man of the Year' award.

Avinash was named the maiden CEO of Project 21 within a month of the ATPP sale. The assignment marked a change of orbit in his career trajectory. He was now the youngest and one of the most powerful bureaucrats in the state. Nethra too was 'sent back to the field,' as they would say, this time to Piprali. Piprali was a new district that had been carved out of the Capital, a mere half hour drive away.

PART SEVEN

The Fallout

Public Accountability

State Capital, 2015

It had been three months since Avinash's elevation to Project 21. It was a fine sunny morning when the first chips started crumbling. Avinash had received a few calls pertaining to the ATPP sale in the past few days. A news reporter from *Jan Jagriti*, the highest circulating Hindi daily from the Trendsetter Group had been quizzing him rather dubiously. Avinash hadn't given much thought to the enquiries till he saw the headlines in *Jan Jagriti* that morning.

The cover story carried a picture of him with the Chief Minister, the same picture where the CM's arm rested on his 'solder.' It carried the title—'ATPP Sale Scam—The Biggest Scam in the History of the State—How Few Babus Made Hay While We Slept!'

The cover story that ran into two broadsheets was shocking, lurid. Proclaiming itself as the 'Truth behind the ATPP sale,' the piece described how Avinash Rathore, the 'chief handler' on behalf of Mantriji colluded with officials in Alpha Energy and twisted government procedure to secure a windfall for the nascent company.

It rued that ZMD would have quoted a price much higher than Alpha and that apprehensive of this possibility, Avinash had single-handedly altered tender conditionality to change the game in favour of Alpha. HPC members 'weren't aware' of 'last-minute, game-changing conditions,' Avinash had inserted in the tender—an HPC member (requesting anonymity) had been quoted as saying.

Replete with innuendo, the story suggested that the state government's decision to sell off ATPP was motivated by an unholy deal Mantriji had struck with Alpha—family silver had been sold for peanuts while Mantriji earned his big bucks to fund the forthcoming elections.

For the next three days, *Jan Jagriti* went hammer and tongs with the story. It reproduced official communication, file notings and proceedings of HPC to establish that extraordinary decisions were taken to actively preempt ZMD's progress further in the deal. It compared business plans of Alpha, ZMD and Synergy to bring out startling similarities—suggesting that someone in the know of things had actively assisted Alpha in its Business Plan documentation.

Nilay Mohanty, the scribe behind the ATPP Scam story explained in accurate detail how the single, 'last-minute' criterion Avinash had introduced into the document had altered all equations, leading to the eventual disqualification of ZMD, and paving the way for Alpha's ultimate victory. Implicit was the conclusion that it was his felonious sledgehammer tactics as the ATPP sale convener that had ultimately fetched Avinash Rathore the hottest assignment under the incumbent government—Project 21.

Nobody understood how Nilay Mohanty cracked it. The volume and nature of confidential documentation he had been able to access was startling. The precision with which his arguments punctured the big government bluff about ATPP was stinging. It couldn't have happened without an insider's active direction.

Nilay Mohanty abhorred authority, probably because he craved it and the IAS 'lobby' was his *bête noire*. His repeated failures in CSE and the success of those he thought inferior had left him bitter and paranoid about civil servants. As *Jan Jagriti*'s senior scribe and a self-proclaimed anti-corruption activist, he had dedicated himself to exposing the diabolical underbelly of an arrogant establishment.

Nilay Mohanty did have a few friends in the IAS. Smart bureaucrats understood pretty early in their careers that manipulating perceptions was the elusive key to 'being a great officer.' PR was important. More important than work, sometimes. And mind you, one had to work a lot harder to develop good PR.

Nilay Mohanty was accordingly, one of Amit Bhargava's 'good friends' from the Trendsetter Group. Amit would often invite Nilay to cover his numerous public awareness / mobilization / sensitization events and Nilay would oblige. Amit made Nilay feel comfortable. It was easy to be friends with him, to exploit his good offices and still hate him.

Four years ago, during one of his several visits to Barela, Nilay had run into Mrityunjay—the only man Amit Bhargava had ever spoken unfavourably of. This antipathy had stoked Nilay's interest. Therefore, soon after his mining raids and the aftermath, Nilay had sauntered into Mrityunjay's office.

'I have come to interview you,' he had said very casually.

'I do not give interviews,' Mrityunjay's eyes hadn't moved up from the files he had been working on.

'I am not some yellow journalist!' He thrust his visiting card rather brashly on Mrityunjay's table.

'I don't discriminate on the grounds of colour...and I don't read newspapers,' Mrityunjay snapped back.

'That's unusual for a public servant. You ought to keep yourself informed.'

'Those who do not read the news are uninformed, those who do are misinformed,' Mrityunjay chuckled.

'Mark Twain was jealous...' Nilay retorted flatly

A local journalist cracking his quotes! Mrityunjay was curious. He looked up.

'So am I!' he laughed.

'Civil servants of today have ceased to be both civil in attitude and servants of the people, it seems', Nilay settled himself into a chair in front of Mrityunjay's desk.

'You are judging the whole buffet from a bad salad dressing,' Mrityunjay sighed as he bent over the table, 'I am sure you find your other friends quite civil and servile.'

'Do not digress. You are a public servant. You are accountable,' Nilay tried to curb a smile.

'To who?' Mrityunjay asked.

'To the public at large. They seek answers. Your office runs on public money.'

'Who is the public at large?', Mrityunjay chuckled.

'I know my job. I do it to my satisfaction…which is why I don't entertain intermediaries.'

Rookie arrogance, Nilay smiled to himself. 'I am a journalist. I hope you have been told that it is the media which enforces your accountability to the public.'

'I don't recognize it,' Mrityunjay replied.

'What? Your accountability?'

'Your authority to enforce it. Please leave. I have more important things.'

'What could be more important than…?'

'My interview?'

'Communication—putting your perspective across—people should know your side of the story before they judge you. People should know why you felt the need to conduct raids in such a sinister manner, without keeping your boss in the loop,' Nilay lit a cigarette.

'I do not care about anyone judging me.'

'Administration cannot be irresponsible. It cannot haul people up for no reason and then refuse to answer well-intentioned questions. Your evasiveness proves there are skeletons in the closet, that you are afraid will tumble out,' Nilay said, letting out a curl of smoke.

'If I were, I would have offered you an explanation and along with it, a nice cup of tea to go with the smoke. You are free to publish your views. I won't humour you,' Mrityunjay leaned forward in his chair, looking right into Nilay's eyes.

'Perhaps because you don't have answers…perhaps because your seniors could see through your sinister plans and averted a major wrong, leaving you shame faced.'

'Now that you have unearthed the devil, please go and write about the discovery,' Mrityunjay said coolly.

'Why are you so bitter? You have a long career ahead. Shouldn't you be worried about your impression?'

'Over whom?'

'Over people, your seniors in service, politicians who write your destiny…they will judge you, label you.'

Mrityunjay Ranjan smiled.

'Your concern for my welfare is phenomenal, my friend. I must assure you that I wouldn't delegate the task of writing my destiny to anyone else,' he paused for a moment.

'I only know of one way to do things—the way they seem right to me and I keep it simple. I do not compromise and I cannot manipulate. As long as I am here, I will continue to do what I think is right. I do not fear loss. I have nothing to prove. I do not seek popularity and my ego doesn't feed upon recognition from others. You might not like it but it is your concern, not mine.' Mrityunjay said.

'Then why are you *here*?' Nilay Mohanty didn't know why he had asked that question but it was the most spontaneous query that had flashed across his mind.

Mrityunjay smiled again, his usual, sardonic smile, 'Isn't this ironic?'

Now that he had lapped up the opportunity, he banged his parting shot, the words winding into a deliberate drawl, 'I seldom end up where I want to go, but almost always end up where I need to be. That's Douglas Adams for you, Captain!'

Nilay was quiet now. He looked at Mrityunjay for a moment and got up to walk away. Somehow, he couldn't hate this man. Ordinarily, his retribution for this impertinence would be a professional obituary written in his tongue-in-cheek style.

But this encounter was not to be written about. His mind was filling up with a pleasant, warm emotion and on his way back, he skipped Amit Bhargava's office. He wanted this warmth in his head to stay. Nilay didn't meet Mrityunjay in the next four years. They only talked once in between, when Mrityunjay was put under suspension. Nevertheless, Nilay ensured that with his season's greetings and formal calls on new postings, he always kept in touch with this strangely dear acquaintance of his.

Schadenfreude

The edifice of Avinash Rathore's success was fast crumbling. *Jan Jagriti*'s 'expose' on the ATPP sale had induced a devastating earthquake in the power corridors of the State Capital. It had come at a time when the Legislative Assembly was in session. Opposition had been quick to demand its pound of flesh and had stalled Assembly proceedings till a CBI enquiry was instituted into all dimensions of the deal. Friendly media groups had succumbed to TRP pressure and had either joined in the mudslinging fest or were trudging along a 'balanced reporting' format, much to the opprobrium of their readers.

Mantriji's moral authority had received an inexorable setback. Organizations supported by his detractors in and outside of his government had commenced a 'fast unto death' outside his bungalow demanding his resignation. Labour Unions and employee welfare organizations were quick to grab this opportunity to up their ante for 'renationalization' of ATPP.

Marxist-Leninists, environmentalists, neo-socialists and the associated league of agitator-activists who had decried everything about the sale its intent, process and purpose from the outset—had found a fortuitous cause-to-die-for in the scam mish mash. Ergo, the hitherto moderating issues of deprivation and denial, state sponsored infringement and institutionalized injustice had now been reinstated to the periphery of a raging storm that had hit the state's public relations team the hardest.

The CM's aides advised him to distance himself from the matter, and a press conference was hurriedly convened.

'My government has only served the people of this State,' he said. 'The government is setting up a three-judge committee comprising former High Court judges to enquire into the substance of the allegations. If the allegations are established, I promise strictest action against the guilty.'

Avinash Rathore was put under suspension the same evening.

While the Chief Secretary and the Chief Minister heard him out and advised him to be patient, A.N. Bakshi refused to give him an appointment, apparently owing to an exceptionally busy schedule that week. Others shrugged and judged, and some even avoided him. The very people who had once sung paeans in his praise were now silently reveling in a vicious schadenfreude.

His suspension orders came the same evening Malavika announced that she was expecting their second child. Annexed to the orders were supplementary instructions requiring him to vacate government accommodation in Palampur forthwith and hand over possession to his successor in the next two days.

'Sir, all I am requesting for is a transit accommodation till the time I find a rented one in the Capital. My wife is pregnant and has been advised bed rest for two months. I have to shift out of Palampur by tomorrow,' he pleaded with Secretary, Establishment.

'I am sorry, Avinash but one is not sure how long your enquiry will take…plus there is a lot of unmet demand we have to cater to. Please let me know if there's any other way I could help.' The Secretary hung up on him. This was the first time someone had hung up on him. The very first time!

'You and Ananya must go and visit your parents. I should be able to sort things out in a month or so,' he told his wife.

'I am not going anywhere. We will go with you wherever you go. We will stay in a hotel till we find a rented place. We have savings,' she said reassuringly.

Mrityunjay Ranjan called the same evening. He had called a full four years after their last conversation.

'Just saw your orders.'

Avinash remained silent.

'I read the cover story. They set you up. When can we meet?'

'I have to vacate by tomorrow.'

'Are you moving out with family?'

'Don't know.'

'Do you have a place to stay here? This is going to take time.'

'None so far.'

'In that case, put your stuff in my place. It is not nice enough to be a home but it might just do for now,' Mrityunjay offered.

Suffer with me

It was a second Saturday, a *sarkari* holiday. Avinash, Mrityunjay and Nethra sat in pensive silence around the solid wood coffee table at Mrityunjay's office. Avinash had arrived a week previously, with his family and was staying at Mrityunjay's place.

'It was only the amendment. I had a 10 minute long meeting with Khalate. A.N. Bakshi had sent him to meet me. He was very persuasive. He explained why it was important to prefer an existing coal block allottee if ATPP had to be turned around. He wasn't hard selling. His arguments were logical. I understood his rationale and I was convinced.' Avinash didn't say that he did it because he wanted to prove he was a 'really good' officer. Both Mrityunjay and Nethra understood it.

'Frankly, I do not understand the fuss around the amendment either. Preferring an existing allottee makes sense. The panel must understand this. But there's too much ambient noise right now for even a sane mind to understand this,' Mrityunjay said. He was rarely grim.

'The fuss is not about the content of the amendment,' Nethra said coldly. 'It is about its timing and the procedure; or the lack of it!' Both men could sense the terseness in her voice.

'I have had a lot of this procedure bullshit Nethra…', Avinash argued. 'You know well that if we had left it to the HPC, we would still be quibbling over the sentence construction in the tender documents. You know we went beyond our stated briefs on several occasions. Even you did. And we did that because we wanted it to get through! Of course, I could have always acted like a bureaucrat and waited; waited for procedure to kill the deal…'

'But you ARE a bureaucrat! Aren't you? You aren't running a privately funded company that has the luxury to toss the form and go for a kill!'

'I think his only fault was that he went beyond his assigned role because the situation demanded a firm decision when nobody else was willing to take it,' Mrityunjay intervened.

'He went for it and went all out to ensure he did his job well. It is the same way I went after RVR. When examined from the point of technical purity, these decisions may expose several holes but we took those decisions because those decisions were necessary and nobody was willing to own them, Nethra.'

'And that is precisely why both of you screwed up—you, on several occasions and he, on his grand performance on the way up to that mountain top!' she snapped back.

'You haven't been riding a feather either, sweetheart…You just missed it by a whisker this time. And you never know…the judges might drop a bomb on you too, anytime. So I would say you are as terminally screwed up!' Mrityunjay said passively as he looked at Nethra.

Nethra glowered back at him. She could see that both of them were smiling, perhaps as much at their own follies as at hers.

Late in the evening, Nethra stood up to leave.

'Stay back. Stay for today. We still have a guestroom, unoccupied,' Avinash said hastily, unthinkingly, as if her presence around him was his only hope.

An odd silence followed as Nethra quickly tore her surprised gaze off Avinash, and looked at Mrityunjay who expectedly, was smiling.

'Well, come with us. You could leave after dinner…your place is just half an hour away,' Mrityunjay added.

The two men convinced her to stay for dinner at Mrityunjay's home. Malavika had been busy in the kitchen all day, putting together an elaborate Saturday dinner. She had tried her hands at white chocolate cheesecake after a long time. Her husband loved confections immensely, and only when he was under stress. Mrityunjay's house looked very different, very warm, and homely. There were lights, flowers, and good food—things Avinash liked—things she had carefully and finely put together so her dear husband would relax. She had chosen the right music as well—Avinash's current favourite—*Agar Tum Saath Ho* from *Tamasha*. She had been working all evening, arranging flowers and furniture, lights and music, preparing dinner.

And then the car stopped and she saw Nethra emerging. A stab of pain rose in her chest. They were moving towards her. She forced herself to smile even as her heart throbbed in agony.

Tum saath ho ya na ho kya fark hai,
bedard thi zindagi bedard hai...

What an anticlimax!

'Ah! Nethra. We haven't met before. How have you been?' she asked as they hugged.

From the corner of her eye, Malavika observed her husband.

'How have you been?' replied Nethra and smiled. She recognized the soundtrack in the background. *What on earth?!*

More smiles all around.

They settled on the couches. 'Now I know why you have so many secret admirers! You are beautiful—too beautiful to be an officer!' Malavika smiled, and looked teasingly, not at her husband but at Mrityunjay.

'Minefield,' Nethra thought and smiled softly.

Mrityunjay rubbed his molars hard against each other. He looked at Nethra, then at Avinash. Nethra had a plastic smile pasted on her face, while he sipped his drink coolly.

'Don't say a thing...don't you say a thing,' he prayed, and cursed himself silently.

'Of course, my husband *also* appreciates you a lot. He really admired the hard work you put in for the sale...' she nodded and smiled, looking immediately at her husband, who, quite unwisely (for in the given situation, wisdom required looking *only* at his wife with the moon eyes of a new lover) had chosen this exact moment to steal a glance at Nethra who was not looking at anyone in particular but who having found Malavika looking at her husband who in turn was looking at her, thought it best to look at Mrityunjay who was also basically looking at Nethra but on being found out, quickly shifted his glance to Malavika who having noticed the full circle of following eyes was now looking at Mrityunjay. So Mrityunjay began looking at the white tiled floor instead.

The previous evening, Mrityunjay and Malavika had talked for a long time. They were looking at old pictures, and laughing at how different everyone looked back then. Both noticed that the trek and the village visit photos had Nethra and Avinash together, quite noticeably together.

'It seems they were good friends,' Malavika said casually, trying hard not to make it seem like a leading statement.

'Yes,' Mrityunjay replied.

'Is she still single?'

'I guess so.'

'I haven't met her but she looks so...so sorted. She has that look of a quiet, green lake guarded by snow-clad mountains,' said Malavika while looking at one of the pictures from Hemkunt Sahib.

Mrityunjay smiled at the use of colour green. He remained silent.

'She is a mess of gorgeous chaos...and you can see it in her eyes,' he said gazing at one of the pictures. The photograph was a close-up along with other lady OTs of the trek group. The words had spilled out of his mouth, almost involuntarily, as if he had no control over them.

Malavika was startled. She looked up at him.

There! How could she have missed it? Here he was...a poor,

lovelorn lover. Here was another tale of unrequited love. A sweet pain of sympathy ran through her heart, sympathy and relief.

'So you love her!'

'Did I say that?' Mrityunjay was surprised, and embarrassed.

'Yes…you just did,' she affirmed.

Mrityunjay had given himself away. He could no longer bring himself to lie about it.

'Well…yes' he said, 'Yes, I love her, "I love her as certain dark things are to be loved, in secret, between the shadow and the soul".'

She shook her head. 'Don't play these games with me. Who is this?'

'Pablo Neruda.'

'Never mind… Haven't you told her?'

'I did. Seven years ago. The two of you had just gotten married then…' he looked straight into her eyes. She shifted uncomfortably in her chair.

'I wrote her a long e-mail. I wrote that I understood her, and loved her. I also proposed marriage…in the same e-mail,' he laughed.

'That was so naïve…so so naïve,' he pressed his lips together and shook his head.

'She replied after two days. She had written that she feared I had mistaken pity for love. According to her, what I felt for her was compassion, not love. She didn't want any compassion, she wrote. She was hurt, and bitter and my timing wasn't right. But I was hurt too—the way she had dismissed my emotion as pity—when I had suffered as much as her and since an earlier point of time. I got married in retaliation. It was an act of impulsive vengeance, that marriage, my revenge against the snubbed sincerity of my love,' he said.

Malavika listened. How much more hid beneath these laughing eyes, she wondered.

'But you can talk to her now…' she suggested.

'I won't.'

'Why?'

'If she wants to, she will come on her own. She knows that I love her. She knows that very well.'

'But she might not be sure of your feelings now, you know… she might be hesitant to initiate such a conversation. She is a woman after all!'

'Don't be a hypocrite Malavika…. You cannot choose to claim the privilege of "being a woman" when it suits you and lay claim to equality with men when that is convenient. You should make a clear decision—are you equal or not?'

Malavika rolled her eyes. 'How long will you wait?'

'I am not waiting. I love her but I am not waiting. It is the kind of love that needs no waiting.'

There was an awkward silence in the living room. Avinash was paying too much attention to his drink and Mrityunjay was staring unseeingly at the tiled floor of his house. Malavika had dropped another bomb, no, she had just served another ace.

'Don't you plan on getting married, Nethra?' Malavika had just asked.

Nethra was stumped. 'I…am still thinking about it,' she said and wondered if there could have been a wiser answer.

'Where is Ananya?' Avinash interrupted.

'So, the father finally thinks of his daughter!'

'Ananya, Papa is home,' Malavika called out dramatically.

'I see you have already transformed this house…' said Nethra, admiringly. She stood up, admiring the little artifacts on the mantelpiece. She wanted to digress to less sensitive subjects. She wanted to appease Malavika.

'This living room looked more like a garage earlier—grey and austere. Now it looks alive—with these flowers, chimes, candles…'

The two men breathed out.

Malavika shrugged and smiled.

The caretaker gently pushed Baby Ananya into the living

room now. The little girl stopped at the doorway, hiding one half of herself behind the curtain, as she peeped out from there. Her eyes were fixed on Nethra, who was watching her as intently, and smiling.

'Hello…' Nethra whispered and waved at her.

It was love at first sight. Ananya was a quiet child. She had always maintained a safe distance from her mother's friends, preferring her toys and caretaker to the company of her mother's friends. But now, the ease with which her daughter slipped her hand into Nethra's, and the warm smile with which she met Nethra's eyes, surprised Malavika. She was now sitting beside Nethra, on the sofa. Her eyes were still fixed on the guest, lips moving slowly in response to the guest's gentle questions.

Avinash noticed that Nethra did not make Ananya sit on her lap. She shook hands with the child and offered her a seat beside herself.

'Children don't like to be treated as things, as dependents,' she had once told Avinash. 'Children want to be loved like regular adults.'

'Looks like everyone here is equally charmed by you, Nethra!' Malavika smiled.

In another fifteen minutes, Baby Ananya was chatting excitedly with Nethra. Her eyes carried wonder, and her voice was no longer a whisper, but clear, baby-like and perky as she told stories about guava-eating monkeys who teased lazy bears and ran after cuddly rabbits.

'What would you like to become when you grow up, Ananya?' Nethra asked the child.

Ananya pondered for a while and looked at her father.

'A bird,' she replied firmly.

'A bird! That's lovely! Will you take me along on your flights?' Nethra asked her.

'You can be a bird too, if you like, when you grow up,' Ananya answered.

Nethra smiled. She wanted to be a child again, a young girl

who could say something like Ananya had just said, with as much hope, and as much certainty.

A few months before her *Dadi* died, the last time Nethra saw and talked to her, she had asked *Dadi* a similar question,

'What would you want to be, *Dadi*, if you were to come back again on this earth?'

'A free bird,' *Dadi* had said.

There was something amazing about children. They seemed to intuitively know most of what man understood after a lifetime of experience.

The evening was replete with innuendo. Malavika was marking her territory, showing her adversary the place where she belonged, and driving home the point that she and her husband were a not-to-be-disturbed, much-in-love couple. Nethra listened quietly, nodding and smiling occasionally.

As the men slumped into the couches towards the end of the evening, Nethra walked into the kitchen where Malavika stood preparing coffee.

'I have something to tell you,' Nethra said.

'Yes?'

'Try not to mind.'

'I am all ears!'

'Do not feel threatened, Malavika. I am not taking anything away. We could waste a lot of time, and energy over this mental wrestling, but it would all be very pointless. There is a life growing inside of you. It is a blessing. Spare yourself this pointless suffering.'

Malavika was staring at the pot of brewing coffee. The smell made her sick. The whole afternoon, she had fought nausea and cooked, cleaned and dressed the flowers. She couldn't stand the smell of *tadka* in the dal so she had thrown up but had kept cooking. The first trimester was taking a heavy toll on her. Her legs had swollen up in places, her breasts had become way too tender and she felt like peeing, every ten minutes. She felt exhausted. But she had worked and worked through the day, for the evening. In the evening, after she had cleaned the kitchen and laid the table, taken a bath and dressed herself in his favourite evening dress, her husband had turned up with an arm candy.

And the lady was telling her not to mind any of it.

Suddenly, she exploded. What had been brimming inside her, came out like hot blood gushing out of an artery slit open.

'I too have something to tell you…' she stuttered.

Her breath was irregular now.

'Mind if you will, I do not give a damn…I can see you are desperately trying to take advantage of my husband's present condition—you are trying to exploit his weakness—but I must assure you that I will not let that happen. Howsoever hard you try, I am *not* going to let that happen…' she exhaled mightily.

'Just because you go to an office, you don't become any smarter, or wiser…so spare yourself this sympathy. I don't need it, least of all from you,' she almost spat those words.

Over the years, Malavika would often wonder what had made her erupt like that. It was unlike her to be so blunt, and she had always been very good at playing those little games women play, games that were played with eyes and pleasant words. She concluded it was her wild baby, the anxiety.

The pitch and volume at which Malavika had hissed back at her guest were high enough to convey to the men in the couch that truce had been breached. All four of them sipped coffee in a tense silence. Then, Nethra left.

It was 11.45 at night. Nethra lay on her bed, holding her phone in her hands, crying.

'Suffer. You are a part of me, so suffer. Suffer with me,' the message read. It was a text from Avinash.

Nethra cried through that night. Surprisingly, it was not Avinash who kept coming to her mind, it was Malavika. The pain and the hurt in her eyes, the hatred. Nethra felt hated, scorned, despised. She felt helpless.

Avinash too couldn't sleep that night. He stared at the ceiling as he lay beside his wife who pretended to sleep. He had spent several nights staring at the ceiling, back in Palampur and before that as well. Whenever he had her on his mind, he could not sleep.

Sometime after Nethra had left Mrityunjay excused himself and retired to his room. Avinash and Malavika stood at the dining table, clearing the dishes away, when he asked her what had happened.

'I don't like her,' she had said. 'I don't want her in this house. I hate her.' Soft tears had flown out of her chestnut eyes.

'All right.' He had acquiesced, 'Now that you have told me, I will take care.'

He had offered no excuses, asked for no explanations. He had simply accepted his wife's verdict.

And then he had pulled her close and wrapped his arms around her, hugging her tightly. She had rested her face against his chest and smelt him. It always felt good to smell him, to smell his warmth and strength.

'I love you, Avinash. You are all I have. Stay like this, always,' she said. He kept her like that for several minutes, stroking her hair gently, kissing her forehead and whispering softly in her ear, 'Don't worry. Everything is fine, don't worry at all...I love you.' She felt comforted, consoled.

Later as she lay on the bed, her eyes closed, her mind clearer, she thought about what Nethra had said. Worry is pointless. May be she had meant it. May be she actually did not intend to take him away. Without any reason, she felt better. Slowly, she fell asleep.

Nilay Mohanty sat opposite Mrityunjay Ranjan in the restaurant of a five-star hotel in the Capital. With his white shirt loosely tucked inside grey pants, his disheveled grey hair and greyer sandals,

Mrityunjay stood out like a wet warbler amidst fancy peacocks. But that was besides the point. Nilay Mohanty was curious. What had Mrityunjay called him here for?

'What do you think of my ATPP story?' he was anxious to start the conversation. It had to be about his scam story.

'Well…' Mrityunjay rubbed his temples.

Nilay Mohanty was piqued. Everyone knew that with his latest story, Nilay Mohanty had finally arrived, Mrityunjay was just trying to be pricey.

'People have liked it a lot…Even the judges in the enquiry panel are going by my arguments!'

'Sure…' Mrityunjay kept rubbing his temples.

'What have you called me here for?' Nilay was now sitting on the edge of his chair.

'I read your story,' he looked at Nilay, '…not very convincing' he frowned in a bored way 'At this point it looks half-baked, too simple to be true. It seems to me that you were simply presenting content manufactured elsewhere and delivered to you.' Mrityunjay looked into Nilay Mohanty's eyes.

Nilay rolled his tongue inside his mouth, 'At this point! Really? What, in your opinion, would be a more realistic representation of truth?'

'I do not know. I thought I should let you know. The whole thing looks very…well-orchestrated. It is like someone fixed the end and is weaving the story over backwards. You will appreciate it if you step back and look at the complete picture.'

'How does it look like, your complete picture?', Nilay looked curiously at Mrityunjay.

'And besides, what gets you so interested?' Nilay asked.

'Curiosity, and of course, general interest in people's welfare,' Mrityunjay smiled.

'I doubt that. Are you batting for Avinash Rathore?' Nilay smiled.

'You must be joking... He is a batchmate, for heaven's sake! Besides, I operate at too conceptual a plane to advocate for individuals.'

'What is your story?' Nilay's curiosity had been duly whetted.

'I don't have a story; just a few questions.'

'Like?'

'Well the first question I would think of is this,' *Quo bono*? Who benefits? Mrityunjay shrugged.

'From?'

'The story's fallout. *Your* story's fallout. You might think you have put a full stop to the story. You might actually only be a semicolon in it,' Mrityunjay smiled slyly.

Nilay ignored the comparison.

'Who do you think benefits out of the fallouts?'

'I don't think, I see. I see they gave you a story with a purpose. I see ZMD winning ATPP—by the orders of the Courts or otherwise—in a fresh auction, maybe six months from now; obviously at a price lower than ZMD would have ordinarily quoted. I also see Alpha going bust.'

Nilay Mohanty was silent. He pondered for a while. Not possible.

'Even if you do see the complete picture, what do I get from writing about it?'

Mrityunjay smiled, 'Journalistic satisfaction of having told the truth...of having enforced public accountability on uncivil unservants!'

Nilay Mohanty smiled, 'That won't pay my bills, Mark Twain. I don't work for money but *Jan Jagriti* pays a pittance. I have been looking for a change. Do you have an offer?'

'Not right now but I will come to you with one,' Mrityunjay promised.

Women!

It was a lazy Sunday morning. Nethra and Malavika sat sipping tea in the balcony, listening to the sounds of chirping birds; sometimes indulging in small talk. It was Malavika's second visit to Nethra's place. Her first visit had been forced upon her by Ananya who seemed to have fallen in love with Nethra.

Malavika had never imagined doing this. A part of her was surprised when she accepted Nethra's invitation to be her guest. But then, Nethra had been genuinely warm, and her warmth seemed to have no correlation with Avinash's presence. Nethra had even visited Malavika twice, despite the sting of her first visit, when Avinash and Mrityunjay had to leave the city in connection with the case. She had stayed back with Malavika overnight.

'Why are you doing this?' Malavika asked Nethra.

'What'?

'This! Being so caring and…nice…' she paused for a while, 'you still love him, don't you?'

'What are you talking about?' Nethra frowned.

'Let us drop the pretence, Nethra. You are honest. Be honest. I am strong enough to face the truth.'

'The truth is before you, Malavika. You wouldn't have asked me this question if I were married to someone or were in a romantic relationship with someone already. A woman needs a man in her life to prove she isn't looking, isn't it?'

'I would have still asked you this question,' Malavika replied evenly.

'Love *cannot be* transitory, Malavika. It has mellowed within me and I simply carry it, accept it as a truth, as a part of my existence. I do not need an external reinforcement now. To me, love is not about indulgence, it has never been about indulgence.'

'What is it about, then?' Malavika asked softly.

Nethra breathed out. She leaned back in her chair and closed her eyes. 'I am not having an affair with your husband, Malavika. I do not intend to have one. I am not working towards securing physical intimacy with him. I do not seek his attention or his appreciation. Even if he offers it to me now, I wouldn't have it.'

Malavika gulped a little.

'I am relieved that I have been able to free myself of the compulsive need for a justification, Malavika…I am pretty happy with myself and my life. I want nothing—from you, your husband or anyone else. The moment you feel uncomfortable, the moment you feel manipulated or taken advantage of, I would advise you to exit.'

Malavika understood what she was saying. She too leaned back on her chair, caressing her belly.

'I must admit, Nethra that one of the reasons I came here to stay with you is that I wanted to see how you live. I have never felt Avinash dwell in such awe of someone. He has never said it but he is obviously totally besotted with you. There is such a gentle expression in his eyes when he talks about you. He probably wants to reassure me that he is all mine and that you are just a 'wonderful officer and a very nice person' he happens to know… yet I feel it in my bones whenever he mentions you—that warmth, that softness, a side of him one rarely gets to see otherwise....'

'Do you not feel secure in his love for you?' Nethra turned her head to face Malavika.

'I am sure of his love for me. It is his unfulfilled love for you that disturbs me,' Malavika answered.

'Why do you think about it? Does it matter? You are an

independent person capable of steering the course of your life and you have chosen to raise a family with your husband. You are your family's lifeline. They can't do without you.'

'Oh, they can! Everyone can. I am not that important. I am not very intense or sharp. I am not very intelligent or capable. I am quite simply, a housewife!'

'So?'

'I cannot match up to people like you!'

Nethra sighed.

'You might not go to an office everyday but you do things which nobody else does or can do—you make your home, a home—imagine if no one in a family were willing to do that, if nobody had the strength or the inclination or the time to make that effort....'

'That sounded like an uplifting sermon to a second-hand life, Nethra. I am just another housewife. I do not get paid for loving or caring. I do not run my family. My husband has loved me too gently to ever subject me to this truth but this theme has played out in the life of every woman I have known—my mother, sisters, cousins. None of them held down a job and none of them was ever respected. My husband is an exception, which is why I love him too much to afford losing him, Nethra.'

'I am glad that your husband understands this, Malavika. Yet if he were to ever fail you, he would stand to lose a family too, he would stand to lose you! He loves you. Why should you fear losing him?'

'Try being me for a day. Try seeing yourself only in relation to others; not as just yourself. Try it. You wouldn't last beyond a week, Nethra.'

Malavika kept caressing her belly and said, 'For people like you, independence is a given fact, a habit. Imagine being dependent on others for your life and well being and then try to enjoy it. You are human, you won't.'

'You would complain of minor material aberrations, knowing well that nothing material ever causes that discomfort. That discomfort is in the mind, rooted in emotional emptiness because you know your happiness is borrowed, not owned. You will always be judging—yourself and those around you because you feel insecure—you are insecure that your paradise might not last, that somebody might snatch it away from you, leaving you marooned and rejected. You have never lived a life of choice and you do not feel good when you find others—especially women very similar to you—live the way they want to.'

Malavika paused for a moment.

'Isn't it a travesty, Nethra, that after seven years of relentless effort to pull him away from you, physically and mentally, I find myself brought to your very door?'

'Isn't it ironic that we exaggerate the significance of things we find missing in our own lives?' Nethra retorted.

'There's so much fuss about independence, about being on one's own…I have always striven to own my life, to be self-sufficient. I am largely self-sufficient but do I not miss being in love? When I see your child running up to you, don't you think I crave that experience too?'

'One never enjoys too much of a thing, Malavika, nor too long. You might think it is a travesty that you had to land up at my place eventually but I am pretty sure you still wouldn't wish to trade places with me and go through all of that…or would you?'

'At this point, I am as incomplete as you are, my life as imperfect as yours. But I have started to love life the way it is. It feels tremendously better this way. Trying to have it all and expecting that all can be had the perfect way is a recipe for disappointment.'

'But I feel I must do whatever I can and go to whatever extent that I can to secure a sense of fulfillment for myself, first and foremost. I strive for that, every moment. Ask yourself what gives you that fulfillment and go for it. You would never need to fill your head up with things you cannot control when you are preoccupied with things you can, things you would love to do. Ask yourself, what gives you that fulfillment?' Nethra asked.

Malavika pondered for a while.

'I fancy having a fashion line of my own someday. That is what gives me a high! I love fashion…it is therapeutic! It brightens up your spirits, makes you feel strong and confident,' Malavika beamed, 'it gives you a tangible means to deal with lows. I also want to study applied aesthetics in the context of interior design. I had plans to…but then I got married.

Malavika felt light. She wondered why she had not shared this with any of her friends.

'That's cool! I see you have a project waiting for you six months from now!' Nethra said, putting an arm around Malavika's shoulder.

'I have put my past behind me, Malavika. There was a point in time when I disliked you, probably because I saw you as a competitor. Now, I do not. I know that Avinash loves you and he loves Ananya—that you two constitute the core of his life and I cannot have anything but love for you two as well. The only way I could resolve this mental conflict was by accepting this truth,' Nethra smiled.

'And now as I talk to you, I admire the remarkable openness of your mind, the courage to speak of your fears aloud. You say you suffer from insecurity and low self-worth but you are one of the most secure people I have met. Insecure people are afraid of exposing themselves; they always masquerade in deceptive covers…' Nethra said.

'I would think about you often in these seven years, try to find out more about the past and the more I knew, the more I dwelled on it. Frankly, Nethra, I hated you. I couldn't stand the mention of your name. Now that I am talking to you, I do not feel that anxiety. I actually feel comfortable. I like you.'

Malavika turned to look at Nethra and said, 'I feel the reason why anyone likes you is because you make people look at themselves and love themselves that way…I have been carrying the guilt of giving up my job for years now…you are the first person I have actually discussed it with…it is strange, isn't it?', she smiled, 'I am happy that I could connect with you in a way that is far more fulfilling, for me.'

'Women understand each other better, I think. Only if we could stop forever looking at each other as people with competing interests…' Malavika said, smiling at Nethra.

And Nethra was smiling in agreement, 'Yes! There is so much more to life than the things we choose to keep in our heads.'

Ananya now appeared on the scene. She tugged at her mother's shirt, beseeching her to play with her farm animals. 'The joys of your kid's childhood, for instance,' Nethra hugged Ananya tightly. Malavika beamed.

Later, Nethra drove them back home, Malavika seated next to her. On the way, Malavika turned to Nethra, 'Tell me, if you had a choice, Nethra, what would be that one thing you would wish for…the thing that would give you a sense of fulfillment?'

'I want to be a mother. I want to have a child…' Nethra said.

Malavika's heart wobbled inside her chest. She looked away.

'You can have a child, you can get married…only you don't want to. You know Mrityunjay loves you. And you know the sort of person he is.'

Nethra was quiet.

'Mrityunjay is a very dear friend…but I don't want to get married,' she said finally.

'Why?' Malavika asked.

'I don't know why. I only want to be a mother. I want to love a child, to play with her, to put her to sleep, to feed her. We grow ungrateful with age. We become selfish and insensitive. A child is sensitive, she loves you back…' Nethra said.

'Mrityunjay will love you back. Don't close your eyes, Nethra.

He will love you back. Don't withdraw…don't close your eyes.' Malavika pleaded silently as she looked out of her car window, leaning back on her seat, closing her eyes.

Esprit de corps

Mrityunjay had been thinking hard.

'Everything that happened was part of a plan. They nailed you down on paper and circulated it as evidence so that every other manipulation could be attributed to you. The Business Plan, for instance. Quite clearly, ZMD's plan was leaked to Alpha. Because you made an error that was captured as evidence, all other manipulations naturally came to be attributed to you,' Mrityunjay told Avinash.

Nethra pitched in,

'Our only defence is that you acted with bona fide intent, that assigning preference to an existing coal allottee made sense. There is still little evidence beyond that amendment you issued without sanction to implicate you as the chief conspirator. Much of Nilay Mohanty's argument is unsubstantiated allegation.'

She was right. Legally, his case wasn't as weak as it appeared. Everyone seemed relieved.

'But I am still not sure what this is all for? It never seemed as if we were being manipulated, that things had been planned to pan out the way they did...and if someone actually did conspire, as you suspect,' she looked at Mrityunjay, '...what are the endgames? What does all of this lead to?' Nethra was thinking aloud.

Mrityunjay smiled. Someone was finally starting to see things his way.

'I met Nilay Mohanty today,' he said.

Avinash and Nethra looked at him. They were surprised.

'A lot of what I have been thinking seems true. There has

to be a mole. ZMD must have planted a mole,' Mrityunjay said.

'A mole?' Nethra wondered.

A stubby face with ruddy eyes flashed across her mind. It was staring at her, point blank and she was looking back at him. She looked up at Avinash and she knew he was thinking of the same man—Khalate.

But why?

'What are you thinking?' Avinash asked.

'ZMD has been on top of the game from day one,' Mrityunjay laughed, something that seemed quite inappropriate at this moment. 'And of course, whoever the key planners were, including Avinash's nemesis, the idea was to fell multiple targets with the same shot—Alpha, Avinash, ATPP—all as in one shot!' Mrityunjay said.

'I was doing a bit of research on ZMD's owner, Prajapati. He had a big falling out with Alpha's owner, Bhanot. Bhanot used to handle ZMD's most sensitive businesses and kept some of its dirtiest secrets till he marooned Prajapati and took a good chunk of ZMD's business strategy, its connections and even members of its core team along. Prajapati would go to any lengths to destroy Bhanot—as long as he is still doing clever business,' Mrityunjay concluded.

Avinash mulled over it.

'So you are saying that ZMD deliberately let Alpha resort to illegal tactics to bag ATPP, and Khalate was ZMD's mole? ZMD leaked its business plan to Khalate, colluded with someone in government to devise a trap and kept collecting evidence which could be used against Alpha later, in courts of law?'

Avinash spoke slowly, 'That way, Alpha would be doomed. It has taken perilous market positions. It sits atop huge loans it had raised to revive ATPP. Infact, they had put all their bets on ATPP. The price they had quoted, ZMD would have borne it happily but for a company like Alpha, the money is huge. If the deal goes *kaput*, Alpha will go down with it.'

Avinash shook his head.

'Right! And with a mole right inside their den, ZMD could maim Alpha in an irredeemable manner. Prajapati plans to kill Bhanot with the same gun Bhanot had once pointed at him. Now, in all probability, the government would scrap the deal before the courts chip in. There might be a second sale and obviously this time, it would be ZMD all the way—the price they pay will be much lower than what they would have originally paid for it,' Mrityunjay grinned.

'Avinash, you must spare some thought for your plight and try to figure out who got you into this and why. It is clear that Bakshi was in the know of things from the very beginning and he might have been an active member of this unholy alliance. But he would not go to such lengths to damage you. He might have consented because of the anticipated windfall from this deal. I am quite sure there was another eager participant here, one of our *esprit de corps* driven friends who did all the dirty work while Bakshi smiled at you,' Mrityunjay grimaced, looking at Avinash.

'I don't know who it could be. I have not harmed anybody. The timing of this story suggests it could be any of those who were vying for Project 21. Harming me now would mean one contestant less, forever,' Avinash said.

'And who all were 'vying' for that project, if I may ask?' Mrityunjay asked sardonically.

'Amit Bhargava!' Nethra blurted out, looking instinctively at Avinash for a reaction.

'Yes. Amit Bhargava,' Avinash agreed, speaking slowly.

'Oh, the same Amit Bhargava who broke up with you,' Mrityunjay smiled jokingly at Nethra, 'because you and Avinash were still meeting in shady hotels and having....'

Nethra and Avinash looked at Mrityunjay incredulously.

'Having?' Nethra asked finally.

'Nothing. Just a story I heard,' Mrityunjay replied sheepishly.

'And you totally relished the stories, didn't you?' Nethra asked, seething in anger.

'No. I killed them, Nethra. Unlike the two of you who chose to remain silent about them, I fought with everyone who carried them…till they stopped bringing them up.'

There was an awkward silence.

'Anyway, I am sorry for this…', Mrityunjay paused, looking for a word.

'Digression,' Nethra offered.

'Digression,' Mrityunjay looked at Nethra evenly and continued,

'Amit Bhargava is a dangerous man, Avinash. He is boiling with potential violence. He fears competence. He must have felt threatened with your involvement in ATPP,' Mrityunjay said, cracking his knuckles, 'and then of course, he had old scores to settle….'

Both Avinash and Nethra ignored the last bit.

'All of this amounts to nothing more than speculation. Even if we do lay our hands on the whole story eventually, even if we corroborate it with evidence, who will believe it? And why will people believe this?' Nethra mused.

'Nilay Mohanty will spill the beans. He will yield, only if we find him a better job. And then, we will have to find a credible voice to tell the complete story.'

Nethra thought of someone who could do this. She knew someone who could nail it all in one stroke—the most authentic person she knew, the most credible writer in all of India—Madhuparna Baruah.

'We will find him a job. We will also get a very credible person to tell the complete story.' she offered, smiling to herself.

….

'But I am not a regular journalist! I am a fiction author and… yes, I do occasionally write for dailies, but it is mostly on policy matters.'

Madhuparna Baruah was unsure. With a solid twenty-year

reputation as a celebrated writer, she couldn't now dive into something so unusual; something (she was afraid to openly admit) so basic.

'I will help your friend with his job. I will talk to a few people. Rest assured about his job, but the story…', Madhuparna trailed off.

Avinash, Nethra and Mrityunjay had come to her with their story. Though the idea of getting M.B. to do a story on the ATPP sale had sounded implausible, everyone had averred that if M.B. could be convinced to do that, Avinash's career would be saved. Why, his life would be saved! In case she didn't, Plan B was to convince her to put in a word with some top notch journalist, most of who loved her too much not to oblige.

M.B. told them she needed time to think clearly. Then one fine morning, she called back.

'I will do it, Nethra,' she said.

They were overjoyed. They had to give her whatever facts they had and she would do her own research. They were told not to interfere. Nilay Mohanty joined as Senior Editor at *JanSatta,* a distinguished Hindi daily with a reputation for real journalism. The day he signed his three-year bond with the daily, he finally confessed to Mrityunjay that a friend of his who was an IAS officer had put him in touch with some handlers from ZMD.

'I have got you a story that will turn your life around,' the friend had claimed.

The documents had been delivered to him in a briefcase—photocopies of classified files from the Industries Department, note sheets on the ATPP sale, confidential proceedings of the HPC—all neatly arranged, flagged and highlighted.

Precisely 22 days after she agreed to do the story, the first part of her expose on the ATPP sale appeared in the *New Delhi Times*. Madhuparna Baruah had not only made it national; she had laid bare a wicked corporate battle that had caused serious collateral damage to the government. Nethra, Avinash and Mrityunjay read the story only after it appeared in print. It hadn't been written in the conspiracy-sniffing, browbeating style characteristic of corporate-phobic, Left-leaning writers. It was uncoloured, matter of fact, utterly believable. She had told a story her audience had believed every word of.

The article was shared and circulated widely on social media by Mrityunjay, Nethra and a core group of friends from IIT and LBSNAA. It went viral on WhatsApp. By the time her next article was published, the one that contained more gruesome details about how Khalate colluded with ZMD's henchmen to nail Alpha, three-fourths of the world was already gushing about how bad they felt for the poor, good guy in the story. Avinash Rathore was suddenly a martyr. Mrityunjay nudged some of their common friends from IIT to launch an online voting platform begging the question, 'Do you think IAS officer Avinash Rathore has been unfairly persecuted in a corporate battle?'

The first three thousand votes for 'Yes' were cast overnight using fake names and ids by the core group of friends. After that, of course, everyone cast a 'Yes.'

An online petition asking the government to cancel the deal, reinstate Avinash Rathore and ban ZMD from all government procurement was drafted by Nethra and floated online by DD Deshmukhji who had recently retired from SISSY. DDji was a full-time online career counselor now with a rock solid following of 1.2 million hardcore Hindi belt wannabes and given the aforementioned credentials, DDji was quite an authority on social media marketing now. His petition garnered 11.5 million views and was shared by 1.5 million users in a fortnight. It appeared on trending panes of all major media sites and social media kept buzzing with it for a full seventy-two hours!

In less than a week, perceptions changed directions like the pointed head of a wind gauge. Everyone knew Avinash had been unfairly persecuted because everyone else was saying so.

Born Loser?

Kiritpur, 2014

Amit Bhargava's phone rang. It was Piyush Pandey, head of the utilities division, ZMD, and one of Prajapati's trusted lieutenants in the company. It was Amit's third tenure as a District Collector and he was thoroughly enjoying himself at Kiritpur. Piyush and he were good friends since his Barela days.

(ZMD had forayed into the power sector in the state by commissioning its first power plant in Barela, five years ago. Amit Bhargava, the then Collector of Barela had been instrumental in facilitating the process. He had sent in Tehsildars and Police Officers who threatened gravest consequences if the land owners did not concede to the company's offer prices. Barela had had no brushes with industrialization till that time, and land owners lacked the ability to bargain collectively. District Administration and ZMD had struck like blitzkrieg; a total of 2500 hectares of agricultural land was acquired in a record time of 144 days. Later, during the construction phase, Amit had helped them with labour troubles that ensued from time to time. Local administration had mediated in and resolved each of the dozen plus sit-down strikes, sick-off strikes or general strikes that happened during its two-year construction period.

Of course, Piyush had been quick to acknowledge Amit's efforts and had gifted him a 2300 sq ft, lake facing flat in their housing project in Pune which Amit had accepted after initial reluctance. The flat was booked in the name of his brother.)

Piyush Pandey expressed his wish to meet Amit Bhargava. They met at 'Istanbul,' a posh restaurant run by ZMD's Hospitality division in the Capital. Piyush looked relaxed, and talked about a dozen random things before he dropped a reference to the ATPP sale. Amit had seen that coming.

'Mr Prajapati is quite interested in the ATPP sale,' Piyush said, sounding casual.

'It is a very promising project,' Amit nodded.

'He is more interested in the sale,' Piyush emphasized.

Amit waited for him to explain.

'The project is good and our sources tell that some of our competitors are also very keen.' Prajapati had referred to ATPP in an interview the previous day, saying it was an important project and private industry was very positive.

'What does he want? You can trust me, you know,' Amit took his first step forward.

'Our people had sent out word that ZMD is going to bag it. Now Bhanot is making it personal. Mr Prajapati likes to mind his own business. He dislikes face offs. But Bhanot wouldn't understand... so I guess Prajapatiji wishes to wind up his unfinished business this time,' Piyush explained.

'*Unfinished business*?'

'They have a history, you see...Prajapatiji wants Bhanot to push hard, so hard that it goes beyond his control. This is why he is showing a lot of interest in the sale. Bhanot thinks he is going to clinch it right from the jaws of ZMD,' Piyush chuckled.

'From the jaws of ZMD? Bhanot will get pulverized...he doesn't respect relationships, and Prajapatiji doesn't pardon ungratefulness,' he added.

Amit Bhargava listened. He saw a role for himself here, a very important role. He immediately thought of Avinash Rathore, then, A.N. Bakshi.

'What does Mr Prajapati want—Alpha or ATPP?'

'Alpha and ATPP, in that order,' Piyush smiled at Amit Bhargava's intelligence.

'Are you prepared to throw in money?' Amit cocked his head to one side.

'Oh! Lots and lots of it!' Piyush smiled.

'You will get that, in that order,' Amit threw his head back on the chair and grinned.

All he had to do was to get Bakshi and Piyush Pandey to talk, set a mole in Alpha and throw in a lot of money. He knew this was a rare opportunity—his only chance. He couldn't live to see Avinash Rathore become the CEO of Project 21, something he was sure to, if he carried off the sale on his shoulders.

Then suddenly, the words started ringing in his ears, haunting him. He remembered every word of what she had said to him, *verbatim*. He remembered her mouth, twisted in hatred and contempt, calling him a 'shrimp,' a 'despicable piece of scum.'

'Don't get mad,' he had consoled himself then, 'get even. Get even with her man!' Cold anger ran through his body as he thought about that day, and about Avinash Rathore. This was his only chance.

'You will see who is strong—the man or the shrimp, you will see,' he muttered.

His Brown Muffler

State Capital, 2016

'But this is the most important day...the judgement day—the D day in your trial! You cannot not be present! This is absurd!' Mrityunjay paced across the living room, bewildered.

'I want to be absurd, Mrityunjay. I haven't gained much in my chase for rationality. Much of what I have lost, I have lost to rationality, and fear.'

Avinash was calm.

'Birthdays come every year. You should tell Malavika how important this is,' Mrityunjay reasoned.

'I have been with her every year in the past seven years, and I have put her through so much in the past eight months, the time I should have taken care of her and ensured that she was at ease—I have remained unavailable, I have neglected her—she hasn't insisted but I know I must go. I must learn to keep relationships,' Avinash said calmly.

'That's all right, but this is not the time! Tomorrow is the day for which you have prepared every single hour in the past eight months. You have been through hell, Avinash. I have witnessed it. Tomorrow, those judges will read out the verdict...You must stay...' Mrityunjay was perplexed.

'Let him go Mrityunjay...' Nethra intervened now. 'He cannot change the verdict now. It has been written. Let him change the things he still can, things he wants to change.'

Avinash looked at her.

Suffer—you are a part of me. Suffer with me.

Mrityunjay sighed, throwing up his hands, 'So when do you start tomorrow?'

'In the morning at six. I should reach Jaipur by noon. Call me if the verdict is favourable. Don't, if it isn't. I will be back by the day after. We will then look at it,' Avinash breathed out.

So on April 7th, the day his verdict was to come, the day his wife was born, some thirty years ago, Avinash Rathore set out to meet his nine-month pregnant wife, and daughter in Jaipur. An hour before noon, forty-five kilometres before the city limits, a petrol tanker came hurtling down the road and smashed into his car.

MLB Hospital, Jaipur.
1.45 pm

Avinash Rathore's phone rang.

'Hello?'

'We did it, Avinash! It is a complete acquittal on each count… They have found you not guilty, on each count…the Chief Secretary was trying your number….'

'Hello? Who is this?'

'Avinash? Who is that? Oh! I wish to speak with Avinash please….'

'Who is this?'

'Tell him it is Mrityunjay. Tell him that we won….'

'This is Thana Inspector, Narela, Sir. There was an accident. We have informed the family in Jaipur,' the voice on the other end said.

'Accident? Where is he now? How is he?'

'Sir, he is dead. He was killed on the spot.'

MLB Hospital, Jaipur, 7 pm

His cold body lay in the hospital's mortuary. Three-fourths

of his car had been squished flat. Rest one-fourth, the side on the back, opposite the driver's seat was relatively intact. Police had retrieved a birthday cake box, a few toys and a blood red Sulepuri saree with a golden border from that part of the car.

In the ICCU of the same hospital, Malavika lay unconscious, sedated. Next to her bed sat Nethra. Nethra was cold. She was shivering wildly. She felt she would die of cold. A few minutes ago, she had seen him in the hospital mortuary, dead and cold. Wrapped around his neck was the brown muffler that Nethra had offered to him some eight years ago on a cold night during the Himalayan trek. The muffler was soaked in blood. It probably couldn't bring the heat back into his body now.

In the million dreams where she had seen herself with him, had she ever dreamed of him like this? A swollen face—cuts across the face, blood. Could he die? But the muffler was wet with blood. *He had died.* Her hands trembled but she unwrapped it, held it in her hands—her bloodied hands—and stared at his cold blood on her hands. Then quietly, unthinkingly, she put the muffler inside her bag. Her body had performed these actions automatically.

Now in the ICCU, she stared at Malavika and reached out for her hands. Malavika's hands were warm, reassuring. She clasped them tightly and slowly, she put hers on Malavika's belly—his blood on her hands, her hands on the belly, the baby inside. Something inside her belly moved, it could be an elbow or a knee. She could see it from the surface of Malavika's skin and touch it as it moved—a small, rounded elbow, a beautiful elbow.

'Don't you fear my baby...Everything will be fine...Don't you fear,' she whispered and sobbed.

'Don't you fear at all!'

PART EIGHT

Malavika Rathore

I will take care

Seven days had come and gone. The baby, a girl, was birthed via C-section on the fourth day. In the 41st week, the umbilical cord had slipped through the cervix and the prolapsed cord was threatening to cut off oxygen supply to the baby.

Malavika hadn't spoken a word. She hadn't cried. She had not touched her baby. She hadn't looked up at her parents, siblings, friends, her father-in-law—people who had come to reason with her and convince her to cry. For seven days, she had lain on the hospital bed, staring into the void, her face expressionless, her eyes dry.

Only Nethra had not visited her. Nethra had been with Ananya. Ananya had been gently told that her father had gone somewhere far off, to attend some important meeting, and that he won't be around for a while—an explanation Ananya seemed to be increasingly growing suspicious of. Nethra had held Ananya close to her body all through, more in order to comfort herself than to comfort the child. The child needed no comforting. The warmth of her hands had stabilized Nethra's breath, and her shivering.

On the seventh day, as doctors threatened Malavika's parents with dire consequences, Nethra walked into Malavika's hospital room, and sat on her bedside, taking Malavika's hands into hers.

Malavika's eyes moved to meet her. She kept looking at Nethra for a while, 'Tell him I am calling him…he *has* to come.'

Nethra clasped her hands firmly and stroked her hair. Malavika's eyes looking into Nethra's, her face stricken with despair.

'He is gone, Malavika. He cannot come,' she whispered.

'He is dead, Malavika. He is dead,' she repeated, crying.

Had she been waiting for Nethra's confirmation?

Because only then did Malavika shut her eyes and let the tears roll out. Soft tears, moans, wails…crying, more crying….

The woman who had lost it all held the other woman in her life and cried.

'I killed him…*I killed him*. If only I had known…if only he had hinted. If only there was a sign…some sign…Nobody hinted… nobody told me he was going to go…I killed him.'

Nethra held Malavika firmly as her arms flew around, her hair got undone, as she cried more tears, bitter tears.

Tears were flowing out of Nethra's eyes too. If only she had known, if only someone had hinted, given her a sign, just a hint…. Nethra had thrown him to his death. She had allowed him to leave—she had given him the permission….

Late that night, before leaving for Jaipur, Avinash had called Nethra. He said he couldn't sleep. The verdict would be out the next day. He was anxious.

'Should I go'—these had been his last words to her.

'Should I go?'

'Don't worry. You go. I will take care of everything here…' she had told him.

These had been her last words to him. 'You go. I will take care of everything here….'

Suddenly, she felt lighter. That eternal sunshine—the weight of sanity—it was clearing out the muddled skies, bringing solace. She had a reason to live, to love, to give love, as much as she could, as much love as lay locked inside her and as unconditionally.

'You cannot go on like this, Malavika. We cannot go on like this,' she told herself.

Ananya had to join back at school. The as yet unnamed baby that lay in one of the baby warmers of the hospital's SNCU had to be brought back home. Parents had to be looked after—Avinash's,

Malavika's. The death of a child was not an easy experience to have for a parent unfortunate enough to experience it.

For several years to come this was to be Nethra's world—its beginning, its end—a world of drained hopes and pain and anguish, a world like the dark night sky, lit only sporadically by the starry smiles and merry laughter of his two daughters, a world where her only solace was that eternal solace of sanity.

Avika

Mumbai, 2019

'The Zeitgeist Award for the best fashion start-up of the year goes to—Malavika Rathore—for Avika!' Priyanshu Mehta, one of the country's finest fashion designers announced with a smile.

Malavika was numb, and Mrityunjay was giving her a big, tight hug. Hard as she tried, she couldn't prevent her verklempt heart from giving in. She had tears in her eyes as Mrityunjay let her free, prodding her towards the stage.

This was the moment. Her dream had been realized. She had founded her own online fashion boutique with an independent label—Avika. She was now at the Zeitgeist awards which she had watched every year on TV and was actually receiving an award from Priyanshu Mehta, with the likes of Alex Pinnata, Ali Fazal and Babul Gidwani in the audience.

Was it a dream?

Slowly, she walked down the aisle, attempting to take it all in. She could see them all—the A-listers—Alex Pinnata, Ali Fazal, Babul Gidwani...even Lopamudra. Some of them even seemed to be cheering for her. She was breathing heavily now. It was too much for her to take in. Too much to take at once.

'Here's to a woman who pieced together the broken shards of her life—after her soulmate's untimely demise in a shattering accident. A mother of two little girls who resolved that she wouldn't let pain get the better of her, a woman who gave back to life, all that she had, with all the creativity inside…' the emcee sounded a tad too maudlin as she delivered the welcome address.

'Please welcome the budding entrepreneur who gave us the Riverleaf—Malavika Rathore!'

Malavika accepted the trophy with grace, and then, the breathtakingly handsome Priyanshu Mehta thrust the microphone at her. She was supposed to deliver an acceptance speech. Best start-up award was one of the most coveted honours of the annual Zeitgeist Fashion Awards.

In her bones, Malavika had known that she would get the award. No one else could have. So stupendous was the response to her boutique website in a mere ten months of its launch that the win was a foregone conclusion. Malavika had vaguely thought of what she would say, she had rehearsed the words in her head but they had all sublimated now.

'This is for Avinash, my husband,' she said. A slight pause and then, 'Thank you, Mrityunjay—my friend, my website designer, creator of the Riverleaf…it's all yours.'

Her voice quivered as she paused for more than five seconds, making an effort to gulp down the emotions that were meddling with her speech.

'But most of all, thank you Nethra…' she paused again, 'for everything….'

She couldn't say more because she was choking with emotion. As she walked back from the stage, she watched the A-listers stand up, row after row. With her trophy in her hand and tears in her eyes, she could feel a hall full of people according a standing ovation.

'She did it!' Mrityunjay texted Nethra.

It was 9.45 p.m. Ananya had been fed and put to sleep. Nethra was now pacing back and forth with Niramaya in her lap, humming a lullaby. This was the way Niramaya always fell asleep, in her arms. When she read the message, she too had tears in her eyes. She kissed a sleeping Ananya on the forehead and pressed Niramaya to her chest.

'Congratulations!' she wished them silently.

'Congratulations, Avinash…hard work paid off!' she whispered to his picture in the room, wiping tears off her eyes.

It had taken Nethra and Mrityunjay two years to pull Malavika out of her grieving, and to bring her to consider her life independently. Once Malavika relented, there was no looking back for her—she threw herself into Avika, hook, line and sinker.

Mrityunjay became her website designer. Along with three of his juniors from his Alma Mater, he designed the Riverleaf, an application that brought together parametric technology and three dimensional imaging to simulate an online, virtual fitting room. Riverleaf was a high-tech mirror that showed how clothes looked on an online buyer who simply stood in front of his LCD monitor. It also allowed buyers to have a virtual touch and feel experience with any product they were ordering online. The 'Get My Riverleaf' button on the Avika website had also been voted the 'Coolest New Website Application' by Digitech magazine.

'So it runs in the family….' Mrityunjay smiled as he hugged Malavika again, 'this whole business of getting awards!'

'Guess it does…' Malavika smiled back and wiped off her tears. The only thing she wanted right now was to be with her daughters, and Nethra at their home in the Capital.

Mai and Dada

Mussoorie, 2029

The two girls stood smiling and waving at the door. That was the way they always received him. Niramaya ran through the front porch, crossed the little garden, leaped over the hedges and threw the gate open before throwing herself into his open arms. He gave her a bear hug.

'Here's my wild child!'

Niramaya was a young and hardy girl now, an outdoor person who loved trekking up and down Mussoorie hills. Her tenacious control over the horses in the Academy stables was already the 'stuff of legends,' as the Risaldar Major in charge of the riding establishment liked to say. As a thirteen year old, she had performed thrice at the end of the course horse show with Officer Trainees and taken Mallika (her favourite black mare) on weekend rides to Dehradun.

Niramaya's laughter, *Mai* said, was like a huge waterfall—engrossing and spectacular—but she had none of the softness of her sister or the gentleness of her *Mai*. In her sober moments, *Mai* said, she looked exactly like her father. One evening, *Mai* had walked in to Niramaya's room to find her studying at her table. The look on Niramaya's face had completely startled *Mai* and it had taken her a good fifteen minutes to be back on her feet again. *Mai* said she had felt as though Avinash had been sitting and reading at the table that evening.

Ananya watched this reunion intently from the door of their home. She smiled softly. The bond she shared with *Dada* was a subtle one, one that didn't entail an overt display of affection, the kind her younger sister was wont to. He hugged Ananya gently and smiled into her eyes.

'You must be triggering "heartquakes" around here!' *Dada* teased Ananya often, to watch her blush red with embarrassment.

Ananya was a beautiful sixteen year old now—tall and slender, her mother's frame and her mother's long, flowing auburn hair. She had the dark eyes and sharp, hooked nose of her father. Rest of her was her mother's.

'How are you all doing?' *Dada* enquired.

'We are all good…how about you?' Ananya asked.

It was only when Ananya talked that one could see her *Mai* in her, in her expression, in things she chose to say and things she did not. It was only in her very palpable, very precocious savoir faire, the words she said and the things she did that one could see this little woman move inch by inch towards acquiring that unmistakable weight of sanity, the weight her *Mai* had carried with such aplomb all her life.

As for sanity, it had weighed Mrityunjay down too, eventually. It had been actuated by Avinash's death, and later propelled by Malavika's. It had come wrapped in the role of a proxy father which Mrityunjay had assumed with great readiness in his alacrity to aid and assist Nethra—*Mai*, the proxy mother.

Nobody had asked him to take on the role. The kids always called him *Dada*, and somewhere unexpressed between them, driven as much out of willingness as by necessity, was that bond between a father and his children. For the past thirteen years, as Nethra shifted base from Piprali to the State Capital to New Delhi and now to the Academy (where Nethra had moved in as Deputy Director some four years back), Mrityunjay had visited them every weekend.

Ananya and Niramaya loved their weekend expeditions with *Dada*—treks, picnics, or visits to Dehradun where they would drive up and down Rajpur Road and sometimes, stop by a multiplex to watch a movie. Mrityunjay was a loving parent. *Mai's* eyes would swell up every time she watched him stroll down the Happy Valley road, holding two little hands, narrating interesting stories of real people and real places—unlike the kind of stories that *Mai* had, often in their childhood, lulled them to sleep with.

This was a specially awaited visit. Mrityunjay had returned from Harvard after eleven months. He had enrolled in a doctoral program at Harvard Business School. His role as a father had kept him from joining Harvard some thirteen years ago, but now that his girls had grown up, *Mai* had pushed him to it.

More importantly, in another ten days, Ananya was to leave for Cambridge, USA where she had been selected for the BSA (Bachelor of Science in Architecture) undergrad program at the MIT School of Architecture and Planning. She planned to go on to the Graduate School, to earn an M-Arch from MIT.

Mrityunjay had come to say goodbye, and to tell her more about HBS, another place she had obsessed about a lot in the past few years.

'Where is *Mai*?' he enquired.

'She is running late. She is the Course Coordinator for Phase IV and they are having a seminar today…she must be back soon,' said Ananya.

'Shall I ask you a question, *Dada*?' Niramaya chirped.

Ananya grimaced. Her younger sister was given to verbalizing her live stream of consciousness thoughts, something that made her ask seemingly bizarre, irrelevant questions, at the most unexpected of times. Ananya braced herself for one.

'Yes?' he looked engagingly at Niramaya.

'Who is your best friend?'

Ananya sighed.

'Best Friend?' Mrityunjay pondered over it.

'There is nothing like a best friend, if you ask me, I have a few very close friends…your father was a very close friend.'

'Hmm…' Niramaya looked thoughtful.

'She put the same question to *Mai*,' Ananya intervened now. 'A week back. You know how Niramaya's mind works, *Dada*. She has been ruminating on this subject for a while. By the way, *Mai* said that you were her best friend.'

He shrugged and smiled softly.

'Did she say that?'

'Why didn't the two of you get married then?' Niramaya continued.

Ananya grimaced harder.

'Who told you that best friends should get married? We have all we need, don't we?' he smiled gently. 'We have each other and we all love each other…that alone matters!'

White Chocolate Cheesecake

State Capital, 2023

Six years back, exactly seven years after Avinash's death, Malavika had been diagnosed with Stage IV colon cancer. She had been experiencing persistent abdominal discomfort for four months but had chosen to ignore it because she had been very occupied with Avika and with her kids.

When the test results came, the prognosis was poor. Cancer had metastasized to distant organs, far from the primary tumour site. Surgery was ruled out as an option because the cancer cells had travelled through her blood and set up shop in her liver and her lungs too. At this stage, their doctor told them, the five year relative survival rate was 11%. She had roughly six more months to live.

In the five months she lived thereafter, she was intensely alive. Though in great pain, she laughed and played with her kids and dressed herself in the best clothes and filled her house with flowers and lights and candles and terracotta figurines, things she had always loved.

Then in the fifth month, when her stomach bloated and water started filling up her lungs, she passed the baton to Nethra.

'Is it very painful?' Nethra was at Malavika's bedside. She had been admitted to the hospital again.

'Yes. But it is a sweet pain…this is the least I must go through…before I meet him again.'

Nethra looked away. She was angry. And she did not know why.

Malavika smiled weakly.

'I understand,' she said telepathically, 'but I don't have an option now. I could either die with remorse or with hope.'

'I will die with the satisfaction that my kids have you, Nethra. My kids will have the kind of mother I could never be…I grant you your wish, Nethra. In my death, I make you a mother.'

'And get married, Nethra. He is a good man and he will make a loving father,' she paused for a few moments.

'I have always been so selfish, haven't I?'

'I always knew that my husband loved you and that you loved him. I knew it the day I first saw you—in the Academy. Yet, I married him. I knew that the day of the verdict was important for him, and yet I fought with him, I blackmailed him with my tears…and I killed him. Now, in my death, I am taking away your freedom to choose the course of your life…I am making you a mother,' Malavika said.

'I am sorry…I am so sorry Nethra,' Malavika was crying now. Tears were rolling out, tears she had held back through the brave days of her toil, and through the braver days of her sprightly walk towards death.

Once she calmed down, she started smiling again.

'But do you know something, Nethra? I beat you to it…again.'

'You beat me to what?' Nethra asked.

'I got to him while you were still thinking—Things repeat themselves—don't they?' she smiled.

Nethra bit her lip. 'You are such a bitch!' she laughed weakly.

'But we will meet again…half a century later, may be, up there, and then we'll have a nice party, a real party, with more white chocolate cheesecake and less taunting…' Malavika rambled on.

'Yes…and may be then, I will not be eyeing your husband anymore…because I will be too old to,' Nethra smiled.

'Ah! You are too never old for love, Nethra…' Malavika pressed her hand tightly.

They laughed and cried.

Malavika slipped into comma two days later. Water had filled up her lungs completely. She died twenty-five hours later.

The Brussels Offer

Mussoorie, 2029

'Amit Bhargava is attending Phase IV…' Nethra said.

She was sitting in the living room, with Mrityunjay. It was late evening, birds were returning to their nests, feeding their young—Tibetan girls and boys were walking back to their homes, chatting excitedly—there was a lot of din outside, a lot of activity, but the inside of their home was quiet, and warm.

Mrityunjay's face showed no emotion. He had become far less predictable these days.

'And you are the Course Coordinator!' he spoke flatly.

'Yes….'

Silence.

'He was sitting in the OT lounge the other day, alone, for a change! I went up to him—asked him how he was doing and about his wife, his kids…. He seemed pretty taken. He had been avoiding me for the past week, looking for me from the corners of his eyes, avoiding me directly but still looking for me. This is what it does to people—hatred and jealousy—it fills them with disquiet. He still hasn't forgiven himself…' she said.

'Forgiven himself? He doesn't even think about it…. Don't you understand that? He is too mean to think about his actions, their impact on others' lives. He doesn't repent hurting others…. But it seems *you* have forgiven him…' he stared at her, frowning.

'To refrain from imitation is the best revenge, Mrityunjay,' she said, 'the misanthropic ought not to be treated as they treat mankind. And before you say it, that is Marcus Aurelius for you.'

Mrityunjay sighed.

'What did he say?'

'Nothing substantial, as usual. At first he was startled, probably confused. Then, the garb was back on. He grinned and muttered some gibberish. When I was leaving, he said "Let me know if you need anything!" in that overbearing, pompous tone of his,' she smiled wistfully.

'And you are so happy now, so satisfied…aren't you? Why did you have to do that?' he fumed.

'Because I wanted to plant that seed inside him…the seed of repentance, and I know I have.'

'I don't think so,' he sighed again.

'In any case, you met the kids after a long time today. Eleven months! You have never been away for more than a fortnight. They have been talking about your visit for the past week. The way they dote on you makes me jealous,' she said.

'I am proud of you, Nethra. You have raised them well. They are growing into very fine people….'

'This has been a joint effort. You know that. But is a typical thing, isn't it? Bringing up children…more so when they are growing into adults…I always felt it was my destiny to be a mother…and I have been very fortunate,' she looked at him.

'The kids have been more fortunate,' he smiled softly.

'I am learning a lot with them. I am reliving the anticipation, the confusion of youth and the joy of childhood, all over again… and I have learnt to love, without fear,' she smiled back.

'But you know that one day, very soon, Nethra, your birds will leave their nest….'

'And I am waiting to embrace that day, Mrityunjay, with my arms outstretched. I am waiting for my birds to leave the nest.'

'The day they will go, I will be a very satisfied person.... I have loved them and wanted them to grow and unfold for their own sake and in their own ways, and not for the purpose of serving me. My love must help them grow away from me, it must help them become fully functional human beings.'

'Seems you have been reading a lot of Eric Fromm these days,' he grinned.

'As hard as I might try, you will always be a step ahead,' she sighed.

'Well, consider this,' he bent towards her now, his body leaning out of his chair, his eyes looking into hers, his voice reduced to almost a whisper, 'I have got two placement offers right now—one is as Assistant Professor, Wharton School, Pennsylvania, the other with the UN in Brussels. It's a coordination role at the Office of the Director...good thing about the latter is that they were very keen to offer you an assignment too...a five year international deputation at UNDP's Representation Office in Brussels...you only have to apply...It will cruise through the clutter in between.'

Nethra smiled widely, then broke into a laughter.

'I am serious,' Mrityunjay said.

'I am serious too, Mrityunjay Ranjan, Professor, Wharton! If my memory doesn't fail me, someone was smoking his life away with a demented *sadhu* on the banks of River Shravani some thirteen years ago. He called himself Philosopher Warrior...and thought that he had screwed up his life completely.'

'Pain made me more sane, Nethra. It forced me to become more sane...and it was only when I allowed myself to go beyond the realm of pain, having experienced it full throttle, that I discovered that strange threshold of solace I had never known,' he spoke as if in a daze.

Nethra understood what he meant, and wondered how effortlessly he had expressed what she too had realized.

'Think about the second offer, Nethra,' he came back to the

subject again, 'Ananya will be leaving soon. You can bring Niramaya along. It will be a one of a kind experience and we all can travel the world then....'

'But it's the first one that's your true calling...isn't it?' she asked. 'The second one is a compromise which you have fished out because you are concerned about us and you want to be close to us...but trust me Mrityunjay, you need not worry. Both of them are doing well...and so am I. I have no desire to travel the world now. The more I have travelled, the more I have understood that all I am looking for is a quiet within. I want stillness...my only desire is for stillness now. I have found a home here and I am happy...happy teaching the young and the old.'

Mrityunjay fixed his eyes on the other end of the room. He could not think of anything more to say. This was his second proposal to her, the second after twenty years—and he had spent the past six months thinking about it, searching for a job in Europe, a place Nethra had always wanted to stay in, liasioning with the UN Office to find an opening that would suit Nethra's profile as an IAS officer—and here he was, rejected again, a dismissal as offhand as the first.

'I knew you wouldn't come. I knew you will again have some grand, philosophical nonsense which you will dish out to shoo me away, to shoo me out of your life,' he shook his head, his eyes fixed on the floor.

Nethra was silent, because Niramaya had barged into the living room with a huge book now. She wanted Mrityunjay to read out and explain the 'Dark Matter' section in a children's encyclopedia.

Nethra wrote him an e-mail instead.

'Even if I wish to Mrityunjay, I cannot shoo you away—because I depend on you, for the smallest of things—the smallest of things you wouldn't even know. You are my anchor, the scaffold that supports my life, and keeps it from falling apart. I wouldn't have survived these years Mrityunjay, never, had it not been for you.

Whenever I am faced with a question, a problem to which I do not have an answer, I think of you. If possible, I call you and the answers come to me automatically. They always do. I love you, Mrityunjay. I love you with all my heart. And it is only with you that I have realized what love is all about...that love is not about the longing or the indulgence, that it is about loving and giving. I have been a big fool all this while. You have taught me what love is and I am still learning from you, from every little thing you do, from the way you turn up every weekend, regardless of the several things that hold you back, from the way you shoulder my kids' hopes, their emotions, the way you respond to them. They make such a fuss about women and sensitivity. I am only beginning to know you, Mrityunjay, and the more I know you the more I wonder if there could be a purer soul, a more loving soul.'

She wrote this mail but did not send it. It was saved for some later time, saved as a draft, a draft that her relationship with Mrityunjay was.

The Bird & Her Muffler

Their house atop the hill across the Academy gate—the bunglow of the Joint Director, LBSNAA—was often referred to as *Wuthering Heights* by locals. It was a solitary house with a lovely garden and a tree orchard at its side. From the rear of the house, one could clearly see the Tibetan monastery at a distance, its red flags fluttering in incessant breeze.

The afternoon sky was grey and unusual. The winds blew with great intensity, making leaves rustle and sending trees in the orchard swaying from one side to the other. The birds had created quite a din today. Sparrows went about twittering, crows cackled excitedly and the pigeons were cooing with a rare conviviality. Nethra and Ananya sat in the garden, on the grass, listening to the sounds of silence. Niramaya was running all over, laughing and running, with her wild hair let lose. She loved this weather. She was happy.

In another three days, Ananya would leave to pursue her dreams. She had noticed that *Mai* had been very quiet lately.

'Is there something you would like to tell me before I leave?' Ananya turned to face *Mai*.

'Why do you ask that? You know everything already...' *Mai* said.

'You trust me too much, *Mai*...all my friends...they keep fretting about anxious mothers and pedantic fathers,' Ananya smiled.

'I love you too much, that's all,' *Mai* smiled back.

'Still?'

'If you really want advice, here is the one thing you should remember, always…learn to love, and to live for today, to live fully, completely in today.'

Ananya continued to look at her, waiting for an explanation.

'It will be difficult for you to understand this now, understand this emotionally I mean, you are too young. When we are young, capable and strong, we get blinded Ananya, and we fail to tune in to our life. We do not really understand the importance of love, of the people in our lives…till we face the prospect of losing them, or till we actually lose them.'

'Then one day, when they are gone, we ask ourselves if there was anything we could have changed…if we could just add a few more words we really wanted to tell them, words we never said because we were either too proud or too busy…or if we could wipe away some of the things we did or said…so it is important that while you reach for your dreams, you also learn to love fully, to give love and allow love to come to you—freely, unconditionally. And forgive people. People will disappoint. Forgive them. Forgive someone every day,' *Mai* said.

Ananya nodded. Nethra knew these words could not mean a lot at this time. But they had to be said.

'There is so much stress outside, *Mai*…in my friends' homes… their parents fret so much about success, and achievement. How is it that you never….'

'Because one remembers most clearly what one has missed, Ananya. One remembers it and repents it and spends the rest of his life cautioning others, overdoing on the caution front. I have missed the things I told you about. When I was young, I was so much like you, that I wonder if you would…but you are a very perceptive child, Ananya, a receptive soul, a rare child. You understand most of the other things, the obvious things. I should only tell you what isn't so obvious.'

Niramaya was running towards them now, circling round and round in between.

'You know what I want to be *Mai*, when I grow up?' she went about running and frolicking, not bothering to stop by for a moment.

'Yes…' Nethra whispered, 'a bird…a free bird.'

The mango trees and the guava trees swayed from side to side. Only the mountains, the snow-clad Himalayas on the horizon looked unperturbed, grave and distant—as if observing the levity with greater profundity than was necessary.

Ananya placed her head on *Mai's* shoulder.

'If you believe in what you just told me *Mai*, if you understand it emotionally…' she said, 'then why don't you go with *Dada*?'

Nethra looked at her daughter, surprised.

'I am sorry I read your draft mail. You hadn't logged out. I talked to *Dada* before he left. He told me about the Brussels offer.'

Nethra was looking at the mountains now.

'Why don't you let love come to you, *Mai*. Why don't you realize that one day, *Dada* might be gone too? Apply for that assignment in Brussels, *Mai*…it has been *twenty years*. I had read this somewhere—accept the things to which fate binds you, and love the people with whom fate brings you together, and do so with all your heart…let love come to you now, *Mai*.'

Ananya's eyes were brimming now,

'Don't turn away from true-blue love….'

Something heavy had filled up Nethra's chest and tears had swelled up in her eyes too. She closed them lightly, and unwrapped the brown muffler from across her neck, placing it in Ananya's hands.

'Here…' she told her daughter. 'Pack this in your luggage…it will keep you warm,' she smiled as she stroked Ananya's auburn blonde hair with her fingers. The winds were blowing softly against her face, and the distant sound of bells from the Happy Valley was filling up her head with a rare lightness. She was happy. Like Niramaya, she too wanted to fly.